RULE 34

CHARLES STROSS

orbit

www.orbitbooks.net

ORBIT

First published in Great Britain in 2011 by Orbit
This paperback edition published in 2012 by Orbit

A CIP catalogue record for this book
is available from the British Library.

ISBN 978-1-84149-774-7

Typeset in Sabon by M Rules
Printed and bound in Great Britain by
Clays Ltd, St Ives plc

Papers used by Orbit are from well-managed forests
and other responsible sources.

MIX
Paper from
responsible sources
FSC® C104740
www.fsc.org

Orbit
An imprint of
Little, Brown Book Group
100 Victoria Embankment
London EC4Y 0DY

An Hachette UK Company
www.hachette.co.uk

www.orbitbooks.net

RULE 34

BY CHARLES STROSS

For George and Leo

Acknowledgments

No author works in a vacuum, and this book in particular benefited from the critical input of dozens of people. First and foremost I'd like to thank my agent Caitlin Blasdell for her patience and perseverance. I'd also like to thank my test readers, notably Stew Wilson, Marcus Rowland, Vernor Vinge, Sean Eric Fagan, David Skogsberg, Jeffrey Wilson, David Goldfarb, Soon Lee, Skip Huffman, Ross Younger, Harry and Omega, Dave Brown, Milena Popova, Anthony Cunningham, and Roy Øvrebø.

(If I've forgotten to mention you, please accept my grovelling apologies.)

In Scotland, you can't believe how strong the homosexuals are.

—TELEVANGELIST PAT ROBERTSON,
ON *THE 700 CLUB*,1999 (ATTRIB: BBC NEWS)

PART 1

LIZ: RED PILL, BLUE PILL

It's a slow Tuesday afternoon, and you're coming to the end of your shift on the West End control desk when Sergeant McDougall IMs you: **INSPECTOR WANTED ON FATACC SCENE.**

"Jesus fucking Christ," you subvocalize, careful not to let it out aloud—the transcription software responds erratically to scatology, never mind eschatology—and wave two fingers at Mac's icon. You can't think of a reasonable excuse to dump it on D. I. Chu's shoulders when he comes on shift, so that's you on the spot: you with your shift-end paper-work looming, an evening's appointment with the hair salon, and your dodgy gastric reflux.

You push back your chair, stretch, and wait while Mac's icon pulses, then expands. "Jase. Talk to me."

"Aye, ma'am. I'm on Dean Park Mews, attendin' an accidental death, no witnesses. Constable Berman was first responder, an' she called me in." Jase pauses for a moment. There's something odd about his voice, and there's no video. "Victim's cleaner was first on the scene, she had a wee panic, then called 112. Berman's got her sittin' doon with a cuppa in the living room while I log the scene."

What he isn't saying is probably more important than what he is, but in these goldfish-bowl days, no cop in their right mind is going to say anything prejudicial over an evidence channel. "No ambulance?" You prod. "Have you opened an HSE ticket already?"

"Ye ken a goner when ye see wan." McDougall's Loanhead accent comes out to play when he's a tad stressed. "I didna want to spread this'un around, skipper, but it's a two-wetsuit job. I don' like to bug you, but I need a second opinion ... "

Wow, that's something out of the ordinary. A *two*-wetsuit job means *kinky beyond the call of duty*. You look at the map and see his push-pin. It's easy walking distance, but you might as well bag a ride if there's one in the shed. "I was about to go off shift. If you can hold it together for ten minutes, I'll be along."

"Aye, ma'am."

You glance sideways across the desk. Sergeant Elvis—not his name, but the duck's arse fits his hairstyle—is either grooving to his iPod or he's *really* customized his haptic interface. You wave at him, and he looks up. "I've got to head out, got a call," you say, poking the red-glowing hover-fly case number across the desktop in his direction. He nods, catches it, and drags it down to his dock. "I'm off duty in ten, so you're holding the fort. Ping me if anything comes up."

Elvis bobs his head, then does something complex with his hands. "Yessir, ma'am. I'll take care of things, you watch me." Then he drops back into his cocoon of augmented reality. You can see him muttering under his breath, crooning lyrics to a musically themed interface. You sigh, then reach up, tear down the control room, wad it up into a ball of imaginary paper, and shove it across to sit in his desk. There's a whole lot more to shift-end handover than that, but something tells you that McDougall's case is going to take priority. And it's down to the front desk to cadge a ride.

* * *

It's an accident of fate that put you on the spot when Mac's call came in; fate and personnel allocation policy, actually: all that, and politics beside.

You don't usually sit in on the West End control centre, directing constables to shoplifting scenes and chasing hit-and-run cyclists. Nominally you're in charge of the Rule 34 Squad: the booby-prize they gave you for backing the wrong side in a political bunfight five years ago.

But policing is just as prone to management fads as any other profession, and it's Policy this decade that all officers below the rank of chief inspector must put in a certain number of Core Community Policing hours on an annual basis, just to keep them in touch with Social Standards (whatever they are) and Mission-Oriented Focus Retention (whatever that is). Detective inspector is, as far as Policy is concerned, still a line rank rather than management.

And so you have to drag yourself away from your office for eight hours a month to supervise the kicking of litter-lout ass from the air-conditioned comfort of a control room on the third floor of Fettes Avenue Police HQ. It could be worse: At least they don't expect you to pound the pavement in person. Except Jason McDougall has called you out to do some rare on-site supervision on—

A two-wetsuit job.

Back in the naughty noughties a fifty-one-year-old Baptist minister was found dead in his Alabama home wearing not one but *two* wet suits and sundry bits of exotic rubber underwear, with a dildo up his arse. (The cover-up of the doubly-covered-up deceased finally fell before a Freedom of Information Act request.)

It's not as if its like isnae well-known in Edinburgh, city of grey stone propriety and ministers stern and saturnine (with the most *surprising* personal habits). But propriety—and the exigencies of service under the mob of puritanical arseholes currently in the ascendant in Holyrood—dictates discretion. If Jase is calling it openly, it's got to be pretty blatant. *Excessively* blatant. Tabloid grade, even.

Which means—

Enough of that. Let's see if we can blag a ride, shall we?

* * *

"Afternoon, Inspector. What can I do for ye?"

You smile stiffly at the auxiliary behind the transport desk: "I'm looking for a ride. What have you got?"

He thinks for a moment. "Two wheels, or four?"

"Two will do. Not a bike, though." You're wearing a charcoal grey skirt suit and the police bikes are all standard hybrids, no step-through frames. It's not dignified, and in these straitened times, your career needs all the dignity it can get. "Any segways?"

"Oh aye, ma'am, I can certainly do one of *those* for ye!" His face clears, and he beckons you round the counter and into the shed.

A couple of minutes later you're standing on top of a Lothian and Borders Police segway, the breeze blowing your hair back as you dodge the decaying speed pillows on the driveway leading past the stables to the main road. You'd prefer a car, but your team's carbon quota is low, and you'd rather save it for real emergencies. Meanwhile, you take the path at a walk, trying not to lean forward too far.

Police segways come with blues and twos, Taser racks and overdrive: But if you go above walking pace, they invariably lean forward until you resemble a character in an old Roadrunner cartoon. Looking like Wile E. Coyote is undignified, which is not a good way to impress the senior management whether or not you're angling for promotion, especially in the current political climate. (Not that you *are* angling for promotion, but ... *politics*.) So you ride sedately towards Comely Bank Road, and the twitching curtains and discreet perversions of Stockbridge.

Crime and architecture are intimately related. In the case of the red stone tenements and Victorian villas of Morningside, it's mostly theft from cars and burglary from the aforementioned posh digs. You're still logged in as you ride past the permanent log-jam of residents' Chelsea Tractors—those such as live here can afford to fill up their hybrid SUVs, despite the ongoing fuel crunch—and the eccentric and colourful boutique shops. You roll round a tight corner and up an avenue of big stone houses with tiny wee gardens fronting the road until you reach the address Sergeant McDougall gave you.

Here's your first surprise: It's not a tenement or a villa—it's a whole town house, three storeys high and not split for multiple occupancy. It's got to be worth something north of half a million, which in these deflationary times is more than you'll likely earn in the rest of your working life. And then there's your next surprise: When you glance at it in CopSpace, there's a big twirling red flag over it, and you recognize the name of the owner. *Shit*.

CopSpace—the augmented-reality interface to all the accumulated policing and intelligence databases around which your job revolves—rots the brain, corroding the ability to rote-memorize every villain's face and backstory. But you know this guy of old: He's one of the rare memorable cases.

You ride up to the front door-step and park. The door is standing ajar—Jase is clearly expecting company. "Police," you call inside, scanning the scene. High hall ceiling, solid oak doors to either side, traditional whitewashed walls and cornice-work and maroon ceiling. Someone's restored this town house to its early-nineteenth-century splendour, leaving only a handful of recessed

LED spots and covered mains sockets to remind you which century you're standing in.

A constable sticks her head around the door at the end of the hall. "Ma'am?" CopSpace overlays her with a name and number: BERMAN, MARGARET, PC 1022. Medium build, blonde highlights, and hazel-nut eyes behind her specs. "Sergeant McDougall's in the bathroom upstairs: I'm taking a statement from the witness. Are you here to take over?" She sounds anxious, which is never a good sign in Lothian and Borders' finest.

You do a three-sixty as Sergeant McDougall comes to the top of the stairs: "Aye, skipper?" He leans over the banister. "You'll be wanting to see what's up here . . . "

"Wait one," you tell Berman. Then you take the stairs as fast as you can.

Little details stick in your mind. The picture rails in the hall (from which hang boringly framed prints depicting the city as it might once have looked), the discreet motion detectors and camera nodes in the corners of the hall ceiling. The house smells clean, sterile, as if it's been mothballed and bubble-wrapped. Jase takes a step back and gestures across the landing at an open door through which enough afternoon daylight filters that you can see his expression. You whip your specs off, and after a momentary pause, he follows suit. "Give me just the executive summary," you tell him.

McDougall nods tiredly. Thirtyish, sandy-haired, and built like a rugby prop, he could be your classic recruiter's model for community policing. "Off the record," he says—*on* the record, in the event one of your head cams is still snooping, or the householder's ambient lifelogging, or a passing newsrag surveillance drone, or God: But at least it serves notice of intent to invoke the Privacy Act—"This'n's a stoater, boss. But it looks like 'e did it to 'isself, to a first approximation."

You take a deep breath and nod. "Okay, let's take a look." You clip your specs back on and follow Jase into the bathroom of the late Michael Blair, esq., also known as Prisoner 972284.

The first thing you clock is that the bathroom's about the size of an aircraft hangar. Slate tile floor, chrome fittings and fixtures, expensive curved-glass shower with a bar-stool and some kind of funky robot arm to scoosh the water-jet right up your fanny—like an expensive private surgery rather than a temple of hygiene. About the stainless steel manacles bolted to the wall and floor inside the shower cubicle we'll say no more. It is apparent that for every euro the late Michael Blair, esq., spent on his front hall, he spent ten on the bathroom. But that's just the beginning, because beyond the shower and the imported Japanese toilet seat with the control panel and heated bumrest, there stands a splendid ceramic pedestal of a sink—one could reasonably accuse the late Mr. Blair of mistaking overblown excess for good taste—and then a steep descent into lunacy.

Mikey, as you knew him before he became (the former) Prisoner 972284, is lying foetal on the floor in front of some kind of antique machine the size of a washer/dryer. It's clearly a plumbing appliance of some kind, enamelled in pale green trimmed with chrome, sprouting pipes capped with metal gauges and thumb-wheels that are tarnished down to their brass cores, the metal flowers of a modernist ecosystem. The letters *CCCP* and a red enamel star feature prominently on what passes for a control panel. Mikey is connected to the aforementioned plumbing appliance by a sinuous, braided-metal pipe leading to a chromed tube, which is plugged straight into his—

Jesus. It is *a two-wetsuit job.*

You glance at Jase. "Tell me you haven't touched anything?"

He nods, then adds, "I canna speak for the cleaner, ma'am."

"Okay, logged."

You walk around the corpse carefully, scanning with your specs and muttering a continuous commentary of voice tags for the scene stream. Michael Blair, esq.—age 49, weight 98 kilos, height 182 centimetres, brown hair (thinning on top, number two cut rather than comb-over)—has clearly been dead for a few hours, going by his body temperature. Middle-aged man, dead on bathroom floor: face bluish, eyes bulging like he's had an aortic aneurysm. That stuff's modal for Morningside. It's the other circumstances that are the issue.

Mikey is mostly naked. You suppose "mostly" is the most appropriate term, because he is wearing certain items that could pass for "clothed" in an SM club with a really strict dress code: black bondage tape around wrists and ankles, suspender belt and fishnets, and a ball gag. His veined cock is purple and engorged, as hard as a truncheon. That, and the hose up his arse and the puddle of ming he's leaking, tell you all you need to know. Which is this: You're going to miss your after-work hairdresser's appointment.

"Call SOC. I want a full scene work-up. I want that *thing*"—you gesture at the Cold-War-era bathroom nightmare—"taken in as evidence. The fluid, whatever, get it to forensics for a full report: Ten to one there's something dodgy in it." You look him in the eye. "Sorry, Jase, but we're gannae be working late on this."

"Aw shite, Liz."

Aw shite indeed: With a sinking feeling, you realize what's up. Jase was hoping you'd take it off his plate, eager-beaver ready to grab an opportunity to prove your chops in front of head office so he can go home to his end-of-shift paper-work and wind down. Well, it's not going to happen quite like that. You *are* going to take it off his plate—as duty DI, it's your job. But that's not the end of the game.

"You've got to ask where all this"—your gesture takes in the town house around you—"came from. And I find the circum-stances of his death highly suggestive. Until we can rule out foul play, I'm tagging this as probable culpable homicide, and until CID move in and take over, you're on the team. At least one other person was involved—unless you think he trussed himself up then slipped and fell on that gadget—and I want to ask them some questions."

"Reet, reet." He takes your point. Sighing lugubriously, he pulls out his phone and prepares to take notes. "You said he's got form?"

You nod. "The conviction's spent: You won't see it in CopSpace without criminal intelligence permissions. He did five years in Bar-L and forfeiture of proceeds of crime to the tune of 2 million euros, if I remember the facts correctly. Illegal online advertising and sale of unlicensed pharmaceuticals. That was about six years ago, and he went down for non-violent, and I don't think he's currently a person of interest." You pause. "The housekeeper found him, right? And the security contractors—"

"'E's with Group Four. I served 'em a disclosure notice, and they coughed to one visitor in the past two hours—the cleaner."

"Two hours?"

"Aye, they was swithering on aboot privacy and confidentiality an' swore blind they couldna give me oot more'n that." He looks at you hopefully. "Unless you want to escalate . . . ?"

"You bet I will." Getting data out of sources like home-monitoring services gets easier with seniority: The quid pro quo is that you need to show reasonable cause. Luckily cause doesn't get much more reasonable than a culpable homicide investigation. You glance at Mikey again. *Poor bastard.* Well, maybe not. He went down as a non-violent offender but did his time under Rule 45, like he was a kiddie-fiddler or a snitch or something similar. For good reason: *Something similar* is exactly what he was.

You walk towards the door, talking. "Let's seal the room. Jase, I want you to call Sergeant"—*Elvis*, your memory prompts—"Sorensen, and tell him we've got a probable culpable homicide I want to hand off to the X Division duty officer. Next, call SOC, and tell *them* we've got a job. I'm going downstairs to talk to Mags and the witness. If you get any serious pushback or queries from up the greasy pole, point them at me, but for the next fifteen minutes, I want you to run interference."

The next fifteen minutes is likely to be your entire quota of face time with the witness before a blizzard of virtual paper-work descends on your head—that's why you're leaning on Jase. And you really want a chance to get your head around what's going on here, before the regulars from X Division—the Criminal Investigation Department, as opposed to your own toytown fiefdom (which is laughably a subsidiary of theirs, hence the "D" in front of your "I")—take the stiff with the stiffy off your plate.

It's a dead certainty that when the shit hits the fan, this case is going to go political. You're going to have Press Relations and Health and Safety crawling all over you simply because it happened on your watch, and you were the up-and-coming officer who put Mikey in pokey back when you had a career ladder to climb. Not to mention the fact that something has twitched your non-legally-admissible sixth sense about this whole scene: You've got a nasty feeling that this might go beyond a mere manslaughter charge.

Mikey was a spammer with a specialty in off-licence medica-tion. And right now you'd bet your cold overdue dinner that, when Forensics return that work-up on the enema fluid from the colonic irrigation machine, it'll turn out to be laced with something like Viagra.

* * *

Shock, disgust, and depression.

You are indeed late home for your tea, as it happens—and never mind the other appointment. Michael Blair, esq., has shafted you from beyond the—well, not the grave, at least not yet: But you don't need to mix the metaphor to drink the cocktail, however bitter. So you're having a bad hair day at the office tomorrow, and never mind the overtime.

Doubtless Jase is going home to his wife and the bairns, muttering under his breath about yet another overtime claim thanks to the ball-breaking politically oriented inspector who disnae ken her career's over yet; or maybe not. (He's still young: born to a couple of ravers after the summer of love, come of age just in time to meet Depression 2.0 head-on. They're a very different breed from the old-timers.) And on second thoughts, maybe he's a wee bit smug as well—being first on scene at a job like this will probably keep him in free drinks for years to come.

But in the final analysis your hair-do and his dinner don't signify. They're unimportant compared to the business at hand, a suspicious death that's going to make newsfeeds all over the blogosphere. Your job right now is to nail down the scene ready for CID to take over. There's a lot to do, starting with initializing the various databases and expert systems that will track and guide the investigation—HOLMES for evidence and case management, BOOTS for personnel assignment, VICTOR for intelligence oversight—calling in the support units, preventing further contamination of the evidence, and acting as first-response supervisor. And so you do that.

You go down to the kitchen—sterile, ultra-modern, overflowing with gizmos from the very expensive bread-maker (beeping forlornly for attention) to the cultured meat extruder (currently manufacturing chicken *sans* egg)—where you listen to the housekeeper; Mrs. Sameena Begum, middle-aged and plump and very upset, wringing her hands in the well-appointed kitchen: *In all my years I have never seen* anything *like it.* You nod sympathetically and try to draw out useful observations, but alas, she isn't exactly CID material.

After ten minutes and fifty seconds, Jase can no longer draw off the incoming flak and begins forwarding incoming calls. You make your excuses, send PC Berman to sit with her, then go outside and start processing a seemingly endless series of sitrep requests from up and down the food-chain.

An eternity later, Detective Chief Inspector MacLeish from CID turns up. Dickie's followed by a vanload of blue-overalled SOCOs and a couple of freelance video bloggers. After another half-hour of debriefing, you finally get to dump your lifelog to the evidence servers, hand over the first-responder baton, finish your end-of-shift wiki updates and hand-offs, and head for home. (The segway, released from duty, will trundle back to the station on its own.)

The pavement smells of feral honeysuckle, grass, and illegal dog shit. You notice cracked concrete slabs underfoot, stone walls to either side. Traffic is light this evening, but you have to step aside a couple of times to dodge kamikaze Edinburgh cyclists on the pavement—no lights, helmets, or heed for pedestrians. It's almost enough to make you pull your specs on and tag them for Traffic— *almost*. But you're off duty, and there's a rule for that: a sanity clause they added to Best Practice guidelines some years ago that says you're encouraged to stop being a cop the moment you log out.

They brought that particular guide-line in to try and do something about the alarming rise in burn-out cases that came with CopSpace and the other reality-augmentation initiatives of the Revolution in Policing Affairs that they declared a decade ago. It doesn't always work—didn't save your civil partnership in the end—but you've seen what happens to your colleagues who fail to ring-fence their professional lives. That way lies madness.

(Besides, it's one of the ticky-boxes they grade you on in Learning and Development/Personal Welfare/Information Trauma Avoidance. How well you let go and connect back with what the folks writing the exams laughably call *the real world*. And if you fail, they'll downgrade you on Emotional Intelligence or some other bullshit non-performance metric, and make you jump through some more training hoops. The beatings will continue until morale improves.)

It hasn't always been thus. Back before the 1990s, policing used to be an art, not a science, floundering around in the opaque darkness of the pre-networked world. Police officers were a breed apart—the few, the proud, defenders of law and order fighting vainly to hold back a sea of filth lapping at the feet of a blind society. Or so the consensus ran in the cosy after-hours pub lock-in, as the old guard reinforced their paranoid outlook with a pie and a pint and stories of the good old days. As often as not a career on the beat was the postscript to a career in the army, numbing the old combat nerves ... *them and us* with a vengeance, and devil take the hindmost.

It all changed around the time you were in secondary school; a deluge of new legislation, public enquiries, overturned convictions, and ugly miscarriages of justice exposed the inadequacies of the old system. A new government and then a new culture of intelligence-driven policing, health and safety guide-lines, and process quality assurance arrived, promising to turn the police into a shiny new engine of social cohesion. That was the police force you'd studied for and then signed up to join—modern, rational, planned, there to provide benign oversight of an informed and enabled citizenry rather than a pasture for old war-horses.

And then the Internet happened: and the panopticon society, cameras everywhere and augmented-reality tools gobbling up your peripheral vision and greedily indexing your every spoken word on duty. Globalization and EU harmonization and Depression 2.0 and Policing 3.0 and another huge change of government; then semi-independence and *another* change of government, slogans like

Reality-Based Policing gaining traction, and then Standards-Based Autonomous Policing—back to the few, the proud, doing it their own way (with permanent surveillance to log their actions, just in case some jakey on the receiving end of an informal gubbing is *also* lifelogging on his mobie, and runs screeching about police brutality to the nearest ambulance chaser).

Sometime in the past few years you learned a dirty little secret about yourself: that the too-tight spring that powered your climb through the ranks has broken, and you just don't care anymore.

Let's have a look at you, shall we? Detective Inspector Liz Kavanaugh, age 38. Born in Newcastle, went to a decent state grammar school: university for a BSc in Crime and Criminology in Portsmouth, then graduate entry into Lothian and Borders Police on Accelerated Promotion Scheme for Graduates, aged 22. Passed your Diploma in Police Service Leadership and Management, aged 25. Passed sergeant's exam, aged 27. MSc in Policing, Policy, and Leadership, aged 29. Moved sideways into X Division, Criminal Investigations, as detective sergeant, aged 29. Aged 31: passed inspector's exam, promotion to Detective Inspector. Clearly a high-flyer! And then ...

If it had all gone according to your career plan—the Gantt chart you drew by hand and taped to your bedroom wall back when you were nineteen and burning to escape—you'd be a chief inspector by now, raising your game to aim for the heady heights of superintendent and the sunlit uplands of deputy chief constable beyond. But no plan of battle survives contact with the enemy, and time is the ultimate opponent. In the case of your career, two decades have conducted as efficient a demolition of your youthful goals as any artillery barrage.

It turns out you left something rather important off your career plan: for example, there's no ticky-box on the diagram for HAVING A LIFE—TASK COMPLETED. And so you kept putting it off, and de-prioritized it, and put it off again until the law of conservation of shit-stirring dragged it front and centre and lamped you upside yer heid, as your clients might put it.

Which is why you're walking to the main road where you will bid for a microbus to carry you to the wee flat in Clermiston which you and Babs bought on your Key Worker Mortgage ... where you can hole up for the evening, eat a microwave meal, and stare at the walls until you fall asleep. And tomorrow you'll do it all over again.

Keep taking the happy pills, Liz. It's better than the alternative.

ANWAR: JOB INTERVIEW

Four weeks earlier:

In the end, it all boils down to this: You'd do anything for your kids. *Anything.* So: Does this make you a bad da?

That's what Mr. Webber just pointed out to you—rubbed your nose in, more like—leaning forward in his squeaky office chair and wagging the crooked index finger of righteousness.

"I say this more in sorrow than in anger, Anwar"—that's how he eases himself into one of the little sermons he seems to get his jollies from. You're the odd one out in his regular client case-load, coming from what they laughably mistake for a stable family background. You're not exactly Normal for Neds. So he harbours high hopes of adding you to the twelve-month did-not-reoffend column on his departmental report, and consequently preaches at you during these regular scheduled self-criticism sessions. As if you didn't get enough of that shite from Aunt Sameena already. You've already got it off by heart. So you nod apologetically, duck your head, and remember to make eye contact just like the NLP book says, exuding apologetic contrition and remorse until your probation officer drowns in it.

But Mr. Webber—fat, fiftyish, with a framed row of sheepskins proclaiming his expertise in social work lined up on the wall behind him—might just have got your number down with a few digits more precision than you'd like to admit. And when he said, *I know you want to give Naseem and Farida the best start in life you can afford, but have you thought about the kind of example you're setting them?*—it was a palpable strike, although the target it struck wasn't perhaps quite the one Mr. Webber had in mind.

He must have seen something in your expression that made him think he'd got through to you, so rather than flogging the dead horse some more, he shovelled you out of his office, with a stern admonition to send out more job applications and email a progress report to him next Thursday. He didn't bother giving you the usual social-worker crap about seeking a stable life-style—he's already clocked that you've got one, if not that it's so stable you're asphyxiating under the weight of it. (See: Not Normal for Neds, above.)

And so you duck your head and tug your non-existent forelock and shuffle the hell out of the interview suite and away from the probation service's sticky clutches—until your next appointment.

* * *

It is three on a Thursday afternoon, and you're out of your weekly probation interview early. You've got no job to go to, unless you count the skooshy piecework you've been doing on your cousin Tariq's dating website—using his spare pad and paid for in cash, which you are careful to forget about when discussing income opportunities with Mr. Webber and his colleagues—and you've not got the guts to go home to Bibi and the weans in midafternoon and hang around while she cooks dinner in that eloquently expressive silence she's so good at, which translates as *When are you going to get a real job?* It's not like you've been out of Saughton long enough to get your legs back under the table anyway; and on top of that, you're not supposed to use a network device without filling out a bunch of forms and letting Mr. Webber's nice technical-support people bug it (which would tend to rule out your usual forms of employment, at least for the nonce).

Which can mean only one thing: *It's pub time.*

To be a Muslim living in Scotland is to be confronted by an existential paradox, insofar as Scotland has pubs the way Alabama has Baptist churches. Everyone worships at the house of the tall fount, and it's not *just* about drinking (although a lot of that goes on). Most of the best jobs you've ever had came from a late-night encounter at the pub—and paid work, too, for that matter. You're not a good Muslim—in fact you're a piss-poor one, as your criminal record can attest—but some residual sense of shame prompts you to try to keep the bad bits of your life well away from the family home. *Compartmentalization*, Mr. Webber would call it. Anyway, you figure that as long as you avoid the fermented fruit of the vine, you're not *entirely* doing it wrong: The Prophet said nothing against Deuchars IPA, did he?

The more devout and twitchy-curtained neighbours don't know anything about your private life, and you want to keep it that way: Our neighbour Anwar, he's a good family man, they say. And if you want the free baby-sitters and community bennies, you'd better keep it that way. So you are discreet: You avoid the local boozers and are at pains never to go home with beer or worse on your breath. Which is why you go about your business in a snug little pub that sits uphill from the top of Easter Road, close by the Royal Terrace Gardens, for a wee outing afterwards.

Of course, going to the pub is not wholly risk-free. For starters there's your phone, set to snitch on your location to the Polis—and if they call, you'd better be there to give them a voiceprint. (It's not like you can leave it at home: You've done the custodial part of your sentence, but you're still under a supervision order, and carrying a phone is part of the terms and conditions, just like wearing a leg tag used to be.)

Your phone copies them on everything you text or read online, and you heard rumours when you were inside—that the Polis spyware could recognize keywords like "hash" or "dosh." You figure that's just the kind of stupid shite paranoid jakies make up to explain why they got huckled for shoplifting on their second day out of prison—but you can't prove it isn't so, which is why you keep a dirty sock rolled over the phone's lower half. (And your *real* phone is a pay-as-you-go you got Bibi to buy you "for the job hunting.")

But anyway: *pub time.*

You're in the back room, surfing on a pad borrowed from the bar as you work your way down your second pint, when the Gnome materializes at your left elbow with a pot of wheat beer and a gleam in his eye. "Good afternoon to you, Master Hussein! Mind if I join you?" The Gnome is a vernacular chameleon: Going by his current assumed accent—plummy upper-class twit—you figure he's in an expansive mood.

You nod warily. The Gnome is not your friend—he's nobody's friend but his own—but you understand him well enough, and he's interesting company. You've even spent a couple of relaxing afternoons in his bed, although he's not really your type. "Bent as a seven-bob note," the Cardinal pronounced him when the subject of trust came up in conversation: "Yes, but *he disnae get caught,*" you pointed out. On paper, he's a fine, upstanding member of the community; despite looking like the personification of Uncle Fester cosplay fandom, he even managed to get himself elected as town councillor in some deity-forsaken hole in Galashiels. (Probably on the Hairy Twat vote. You can persuade the remaining students at

Herriot-Watt's out-of-town campus to vote for *anything* if you get them drunk enough, and there's precious little else to do out there but drink.) "Have a seat."

The Gnome sighs appreciatively and smacks his lips, then sits in contemplation of his beer for a minute or two. "What brings you to my office today?"

"The usual." You frown. The Gnome claims to work for the university computer-science department, on some big make-work scheme called ATHENA, but he seems to spend most of his time in the back rooms of pubs: You figure he's most likely working on his own side projects. (He maintains that nobody can earn a full-time living in academia anymore, and who's to say he's wrong?) "I've just had my weekly sermon, and I don't need a second serving right now."

The Gnome chuckles, a quiet hiccuping noise like a vomiting cat. "I take your point." He necks another mouthful of beer. "And is business good?"

"Don't be daft, Adam." You switch off the pad. "I've only been out two months; my mobie's running six different kinds of Polis spyware, and I can't even surf for porn without official permission. What do *you* think business is like?"

The Gnome looks duly thoughtful. "What you need is a line of work that is above reproach," he declares after a while. "A business that you can conduct from a cosy wee office, that is of such utter respectability that if they're getting on your tits, you can complain about how shocked, shocked! you are, and they'll back off."

"I couldna hack the law courseware you pointed me at," you remind him. "And besides, I've got a record now."

He's shaking his head. "No. No-no-no. I was thinking . . . " He cocks his head on one side, as he does when he's hatching one of his malicious little schemes. "I was thinking, how would you like to be *an honorary consul*?"

"A *what*?" Visions of a residence on Calton Road and a shiny black BMW hybrid with diplomatic plates clash confusingly with your gut-deep sense that such a scam is beyond even the admittedly impressive grifting capabilities of the Gnome. "Don't be silly, I was born over here, I don't even hold dual Pakistani citizenship—"

"You don't understand." He takes your wrist. His fingers are clammy from his beer glass: "Let me explain. You don't need to be a native. You just need to be a fine upstanding citizen with an office and enough time to attend to the needs of visiting nationals. The high heid yins all have proper embassies staffed by real diplomats, but there are plenty of small players ... play-states, just like Scotland's a play-state, hived off the old Union for the extra vote in the council of ministers in Brussels and some plausible deniability in the budget. The deal is, we find some nowhere country that can only afford a proper embassy in London or Brussels, if that. They issue you with a bunch of papers and an official phone, and you're on call to help out when one of their people gets into a spot of bother over here. If you're really lucky, they'll pay you an honorarium and the office rent." He *winks*; the effect is inexpressibly horrifying.

"Get away with you!" You take another mouthful of beer. "You're winding me up."

"No, lad, I'm serious."

"Serious?"

He chugs his pint and smacks his lips. You roll your eyes: You recognize a shakedown when you see one. "Mine's a Hoegaarden," he says, utterly unapologetic.

Five minutes later, you get back from the bar and plant his new pint in front of him. "Spill it."

"What, the beer"—he kens you're not amused and shrugs, then takes an exploratory sip. "All right, the job. I have a mutual acquaintance who happens to work for a, shall we say, *small player*'s diplomatic service as a freelance contractor. They're a very new small player, and they're hiring honorary consuls for the various Euro sub-states—"

You've had enough of this bullshit. "Do I look like I was born yesterday?"

"No." His brow wrinkles. "Here's the thing: Issyk-Kulistan is a *very new state*. It used to be part of Kyrgyzstan, but five months ago there was a vote on independence, and they seceded, with official recognition ... " You stare at him. The Gnome has a warped sense of humour, but he's not crazy. He's got dozens of fingers in scores of pies, some of them seasoned with very exotic spices. And right now he's got that intense brow-wrinkling expression he gets on his gizz when he's desperately serious, or trying to pinch a jobbie in the lav. He's droning on: "No budget to speak of, but they're soliciting recommendations. The angle is, they're dirt-poor—all they've got is a played-out gas field and a bunch of collective farms. Their capital city's smaller than Stirling; in fact, the whole country's got the same population as Edinburgh. I *believe* the real story is that Issyk-Kulistan was let go by Kyrgyzstan because unemployment's around 40 per cent and the big man in Bishkek wanted an excuse to cut their bennies. Think of it as national downsizing, Anwar—Kyrgyzstan's got a budget deficit, so what are they going to do? Cut overheads! Anyway, the Independent Republic of Issyk-Kulistan can't afford a real diplomatic corps. Indeed, there's probably nae cunt from Karakol in the whole of Scotland. Or Latvia, Iceland, or Moldova, for that matter. Which is the reason—"

You look the Gnome in the eye and utter three fateful words: "Adam: Why. Me?"

What follows is blether: masterful blether, erudite and learned blether, but blether nonetheless. You swallow his flannelling. It's all sound and fury, signifying naught; but you've got a scooby that there's more to this than reaches the eye. The Gnome *knows you*, and he wants someone he knows in that shiny black diplomatic limo with the IRIK plates, which means he's got some kind of caper in mind. And *you* know Adam, and you know this about him: He may be bent as a seven-euro note, but *he disnae get caught*. Ever.

Which is why . . .

* * *

Three days later, you are certain you're about to die.

You are twenty-eight years old and a miserable sinner who has been a bad husband to his long-suffering wife and a terrible father to his two children. (To say nothing of having failed to even *think* about making the hajj, liking beer and other alcoholic beverages altogether too much, and indulging in such unspeakable perversions with other men that Imam Hafiz would swallow his beard and die of shame if he heard about them). You *deserve* to die, possibly, probably—for God is Great and he knows *exactly* what you're thinking—which is probably why he has seen fit to inflict this destiny upon you, seeing you strapped into a business-class seat in an elderly Antonov that rattles and groans as it caroms between clouds like a pinball in the guts of the ultimate high-score game.

The Antonov's cabin is musty and smells of boiled cabbage despite the best efforts of the wheezing air-conditioning pack. Here, up front in business class, the seats are tidy and come with faded antimacassars bearing Aeroflot's livery: But behind your uneasy shoulders sways a curtain, and on the other side of the curtain you swear there is an old lady, headscarf knotted tightly under her chin, clutching a cage full of live chickens. The fowl, being beasts of the air, know exactly what's in store for them—they squawk and cackle like nuns at a wife-swapping party.

The plane drops sickeningly, then stabilizes. There's a crackle from the intercom, then something terse and glottal in Russian.

Your phone translates the word from the cockpit: "impact in ten minutes." You're almost certain you can hear the chink of vodka glasses from up front. (The stewardesses haven't shown themselves in hours; they're probably crashed out in the galley, anaesthetized on cheap Afghani heroin.) You yank your seat belt tight, adjust the knot of your tie, and begin to pray. *Save me,* you think: *Just let me walk away from this landing, and I'll give up alcohol for a year! I'll even give up cock, for, for ... As long as I can. Please don't let the pilots be drunk—*

There is a sudden downward lurch, a jolt that rattles the teeth in your head, a loud *bang,* and a screech of tyres. One of the overhead luggage bins has sprung open, and there is an outbreak of outraged clucking from the economy-class area behind the curtain as a small, terrified *pig* hurtles up the aisle towards the cockpit. Now you see one of the cabin crew, her beret askew as she makes a grab for the unclean animal—she wrinkles her nose, and a moment later a horrible stench informs you that the animal has voided its bowels right in front of the cabin door.

"Bzzzt." Your phone helpfully fails to translate the electronic throat-clearing noise. "Welcome to Issyk-Kul Airport, gateway to the capital of the Independent Republic of Issyk-Kulistan. This concludes today's Aeroflot flight from Manas International Airport, Bishkek. Adhere to your seats until she reaches the terminal building. Temperature on the ground is twenty-nine degrees, relative humidity is 80 per cent, and it is raining."

The Antonov grumbles and jolts across cracked ex-military tarmac, its turboprops snarling rhythmically at the sodden atmosphere. *At least it's Aeroflot.* You're not a total numpty: You did your leg work before you came here and you know that the local airlines are all banned from European airspace on grounds of safety (or rather, the lack of it). And you're up to date on your shots, thanks to Auntie Sam's abortive attempt to arrange a family reunion in Lahore last year. You also know that the unit of local currency is the som, that it is unsafe to wander round the capital at night, and that your hosts have booked you a room in the Amir Hotel.

The only important bit of local nous you've *not* got straight is what the capital's called—is it Karakol, or Przewalsk? They change the name whenever there's a coup d'état, as long as there's an "r" in the month. It *should* be Przewalsk—but how do you pronounce Przewalsk, anyway?

As the airliner taxis the short distance to the stand, you take enough shuddering breaths to get over your conviction that you are about to die—but now a new anxiety takes hold. You've been told you'll be met at the airport, but ... What do you *really* know? A dodgy Skype connection and the promise of a car ride: that and five euros will buy you a Mocha Frescato with shaved glacier ice and organic cream to go. For all you know, the Gnome's idea of an amusing jape is to ship your sorry ass to an ex-boy-friend of his who runs a leather bar in Almaty frequented by former US Marines, where they'll steal your passport and tie you face-down to a pommel horse—

You're walking through the humid rain-spattered air towards a terminal building, your shirt sticking to the small of your back. *I must have zoned out,* you realize nervously. You can't afford to do that: not here, not with the job interview that's coming up. Ahead of you the doors are flung open on a dusty arrivals hall. A porter shuffles past you, leading a motorized baggage trolley out towards the small Antonov. There's a bored-looking crowd just beyond a rope barrier at the far side of the hall, and among them you see a man with an upraised sign: ANWAR HUSSEIN.

"Mr. Hussein?" A broad grin and a bushy salt-and-pepper moustache: firm handshake pumping up and down. "I am Felix Datka." He speaks English with a heavy Russian accent. "Welcome to Przewalsk!" *So that's how you pronounce it.* "Have you had a good journey from Scotland? Please, let's fetch your suitcase, and I will drive you to your hotel."

You have arrived in the Independent Republic of Issyk-Kulistan. And you relax: Because now you know you are among friends.

* * *

"And that was the worst part of it," you tell him, wiping your moustache on the back of your wrist.

"It was?" The Gnome blinks rapidly, as if there's a mote in his eye.

"*Yes.* Once he told the porter to give my suitcase back and we escaped from the pickpockets, or the police—I'm not sure who were which—he had a black Mercedes SUV! Well, it was mostly a Mercedes and mostly black—bits of it were made locally in this car factory they've got that runs on chicken feathers and corn husks or something, and the paint didn't match"—just like the shite your supplier Jaxxie runs up on the DRM-hacked fab in his garage— "but from there it was an hour's drive into town, and then dinner in a traditional Kyrgyz restaurant"—actually a McDonald's, after Mr. Datka tipped you the wink that most of the posh restaurants in town were Russian-owned and not halal: But you don't want the Gnome's pity—"the next morning, he picked me up and drove me to the Ministry building. Big concrete slab full of bureaucrats with boxy old computers, sitting around smoking." Your nose wrinkles at the memory.

"The Ministry." The Gnome hums and strokes his chin. "Hmm. Indeed. And how did it go, then?"

"It was a job interview." You shrug. Back in your normal drag, jeans and a sweat-shirt and your favourite Miami Dolphins jacket, it's all mercifully fading into a blur: the stiflingly close air in the aircon-less conference room, you in the monkey suit your cousin

Tariq sourced for you from an Indonesian tailoring dotcom, sweating bullets as you tried to answer questions asked in broken English by the bored bureaucrats on the other side of the table. "They asked me lots of questions. How long I'd lived in Embra, what was my citizenship status, what I did, did I have a criminal record, that sort of thing."

"Did you tell them the truth?" The Gnome lays his hand on your knee, very solemnly.

"I lied like a rug." You weren't sweating bullets because of the questions (you realized it was a shoo-in when you clocked you were the only candidate they'd bothered to fly out for the interview): You were sweating bullets because it was *hot.* Even the criminal-background question was meaningless. If they didn't already know the answer to the question, they weren't networked well enough to spot a ringer.

You shrug again: "Who're they going to call, Europol?" You let his hand lie: This is safe space, as safe as it comes, and you're still wound up from the nervous tension of a flight into the unknown. "They flew me to Moscow, economy class! Look, you said they've got no money. So what's your angle?"

You don't bother with *what's in it for me?* because that much is clear. You have got: a bunch of blank passports and a toytown rubber stamp set; a steel-jacketed data key locked to your thumbprint and loaded with encryption certificates; documents telling the government of Scotland that you are hereby authorized to act as the legally responsible consul on behalf of the embassy of the Independent Republic of Issyk-Kulistan to the EU in Brussels; and a corporate credit card. Yes, you've come up in the world. But as you feel the warm weight of the Gnome's hand on your thigh, you can't shift the feeling that there's more to this than him doing one of his on/off boy-friends a favour. You try again. "What's your angle?"

The Gnome sighs. "I wish you wouldn't ask awkward questions," he says, a trifle querulously. "But if you must know, I'll tell you." He leans across the table, and you instinctively lean towards him, until his lips brush your ear. "The angle, dear boy, is *money*— and how you, and I, and a couple of friends, are going to make a great steaming pile of it. Legally come by, no more and no less— and there'll be nobody to say otherwise." You can feel the heat of his Cheshire-cat grin on your cheek: You can smell his yeasty breath. You lean a bit closer, tensing expectantly. "The pen-pushers in Przewalsk want you for a sparkly consular unicorn. I think that's a *grand* idea. And I think it would be especially grand if you'd keep me informed of developments, as and when they happen . . . "

TOYMAKER: The Leith Police Dismisseth Us

It's four o'clock on a Saturday afternoon: Have you got somewhere safe to hide?

You're in the shed, guts churning and palms sweating as you set up the run that Gav's put on you for tomorrow.

It's a' the fault of that fucking cunt down at the Cash-For-No-Questions shop on Leith Walk. He wouldn't offer you more than fifty euros for the telly even though you could show him a receipt all legal-like to prove it wisnae hot. And he wouldna even *look* at your mobie. Or your bike. And the thing is, unless you get your hands on three large by Tuesday, you're getting malkied.

You owe the Operation's tax farmer three hundred euros for Services Rendered: and the Operation disnae take "Noo, ye ken I got knocked back by thi' bastid wot bought it" for an answer. Nor does the Operation play well with "A big boy did it an' ran away," "The dug ate ma hamewurk," or "Pay you next Tuesday?" The Operation's approach to dealing with Intellectual Property

Violations is drastic and memorable—you've seen the vid of that yin from Birmingham what crossed them, even signed a fucking contract *on paper* to say ye kenn't what ye was getting intae. Fact is, you're their fabber franchisee for Pilrig, and if ye couldna keep a float to cover your credit, *you shouldna have fucking signed the piece of paper, ye ken?*

It's nae your fault you're hard up. There's a recession on, you're long on feedstock, and your car got crushed cos ye couldna afford the insurance after that eppy bastid Tony and his fucking jakey friend ripped off your stash reet after you paid the overdue council tax (it was that or they were gonnae send the sheriff's court officers round; that would *never* do if them cunts keeked whit you'd hid in the shed). And then fucking Big Malc gouged you for three days' fab time an' gave you a gubbing when you asked to be paid—

None of which matters, likesay? The Operation's gonnae have their half kilo of flesh.

The shed at the back of your mum's hoose is cramped, dark, and dingy, surrounded by thigh-high grass and weeds land-mined with cat shit from the feral tom what lives next door. You took it over after your old man died, chucked the rusting lawn-mower and ran a mains extension oot the kitchen window—that, an' drilled through the brickwork under the sink and plumbed in a water hose. The fab needs water and power and special feedstock, and lots of 'em; like an old-time cannabis farm, back before they decriminalized it. You tiled the shed roof with stolen polymer PV slates (not that they're good for much this far north of Moscow) and installed shelves to hold your feedstock supplies and spares. It took you a year to scrimp and cadge and steal the parts you needed to bootstrap the hingmy. You *could* have saved for half that long and bought a shiny wee one in John Lewis, with the DRM and the spyware to stop you making what you will; but if you'd gone down that road, no way would the Toymaker take you on.

Which leaves you needing three big in four days, and nowhere to turn but Gav.

Not that there's aught wrong with the colour of Gav's money, but he's of a kind with Big Malc; a local business man, higher up the food-chain than most of the neds round these parts. There's something of the night about him, and the way he fucking girns without showing his teeth creeps you out, like he's fucking Dracula, likesay? And what Gav wants you to make for him, you really didna wanna get dragged inter that stuff. You could get lifted for this shit, eat some serious prison time, and all for three big? The fucking fuck.

There's a dump down in Seafield with a side-line in homogeneous graded sinter process metal powders; a grocery store that sells interesting polymers disguised as bags of bread flour. Cheap no-name pay-as-you-go data sticks and VPN software that disguises the traffic as noise overlaid on fake voice channels ... This stuff isn't rocket science anymore, it's not hacking anymore, it's just illegal as hell because it pisses off the Money. The law disnae appreciate the likes of you *schemie scum*, like the nice security man called you between the second and third drive-tasing, that time they caught you shoplifting in the St. James Quarter. The law especially disnae like your kind owning 3D printers, fabbers capable of taking a design template off a pirate website somewhere and extruding it into the real world to an accuracy of a few microns. The good law-abiding folks—they're welcome to run off Rawlplugs and coffee coasters and plastic Nessie tat for their weans. But the Polis don't like unmonitored fabs. They could be making anything: plastic chibs that dinna show up on metal detectors, meth-lab-in-a-brick solid-state drug labs, home-brew handguns—or what Gav is buying.

"Here's the photies," Gav told you in his flat English accent. He seemed to savour the words: "Fifteen shots each of the subject." He slid an ancient memory stick across the table-top towards you, its surface rubbed down to anonymous white plastic by age. You made it disappear hastily. "Stitch 'em up and render the parts to scale— there's a model there. It needs to be ready by Sunday night. Mozzy will pick it up and pay you at six sharp."

"Eh, but ye ken it's a big load of work? It'll take twenty-four hours to fab 'em, likesay?"

"So? You'd better get started. *Likesay.*"

You bite your tongue. He's takin' the pish, but the way he smiles tells you he kens he's got your number. *Cunt.*

Gav's buying on behalf of someone who'll be *really embarrassed* if his habit comes out, that you can tell. The stick feels like it's burning a hole in your pocket as you walk home from the pub. The job's simple enough, but if they catch you with it . . .

Someone's been naughty with their phone. They've been taking pictures. Innocent enough, and they've been careful, no upskirt perv service shots that might tip the Polis off; but once they've got enough angles it's over to you (via Gav). There's software that'll stitch together a polygon map from a bunch of images, working out the perspectives and textures from all the angles. And once you've got the skin, you can drop it over a model of a doll and send it to the printer. Which will generate the pieces of a hard plastic skeleton surrounded by textured, colourized, soft plastic skin that the customer can squeeze and suck without any risk of screaming or telling, ready to clip together around servo motors to animate and sensors to react: and the beauty of it is that she'll never know, this four-year-old whose animatronic double is going to star in some paedo's sex life.

Well, it's no' like you can ask Gav: and anyway, you need his money. Otherwise, you won't be able to pay off the Operation.

The fab's still warm from that bampot Malc's job, so you start by stuffing fresh cans of feedstock up its arse—this job's a hybrid, multiple plastics in the same structure and a skeleton made using the special brew that's been doing the rounds these past couple of months. The work-space is clean, and there's no crap lying around from the last run, which is good, and it's big enough that if you twist the model just *so*, you can make it in one run.

So you cable your laptop up to the fab, stick your special dongle in its side, swipe your thumb print across it for access, and log in to Evil Santa's workshop to download the templates for a bad night out in toytown.

* * *

Early afternoon.

You blink yourself awake in gritty-eyed confusion, stirring from sleep on the living-room sofa. You're surrounded by the detritus of a chaotic Saturday night; greasy pizza box upside doon on the carpet, empty tinnies of Zywiek Super rolled under the TV console, game controller dumped in the ash-tray in a confusion of dowts—you swear under your breath: "Jesus Fuck."

Ye didna get to bed in the end; microwave pizza and cheap Polish beer fuelled you on an epic raid in *Axe Cop 14*. You and the Grief Street Gang tooled up on what's left of your stash of Provigil and chopped seven shades of shit out of the Baby Panda Squad in return for—

For—

Shite. It's three o'fucking clock in the *afternoon*! Yon cunt Mozzy's gonnae be round in a couple of hours. The fucking fab's gonna be chirping its heart out, *feed me, clean me*, the usual after job shoe-shaggy it insists on. You gotta get the cargo bagged up and the hell out of your hoose in case that fat twat Mozzy skelps you. You're gonnae plant them underneath an abandoned car in a back

alley somewhere, demand the money up front in return for directions, likesay? Not good to be caught out the same way twice.

You roll off the soiled sofa, gurning, and stagger out to the
lavvie. The keekin-glass shows you an orc with eyes like red-
rimmed piss-holes in a block of lard. *Jaxxie, this is your life!* Loser,
tosser, fabmonkey to the gentry of the night—it's a' there. You look
away hastily, stumble out and through the grimy kitchen to the
backdoor and the shed.

The shed. You open the door and step inside. First up, you ken
it smells *wrong*. Fabbers have their ain smell; not humming, like,
but a goosh of hot plastic and metal. When it's working hard plastic, there's a *lot* of hot metal, and steam from the chiller circuit.
This is like all soft placky. Which is wrong. So you hit the light
switch.

Something's gone very wrong with your fabber.

The red supply blinkenlights are pulsing manically across its
front, and the lid's come open. Not only that; it's rising on a fucking pillar of multicoloured hingmies pushing their way out of the
extrusion cell like a loaf of bread that's risen too far. *Fuck, the fucking fucker's fucked!* You grab the handle on the lid. A lime green
hingmy pops up at you and you clock what it is, and that's when
you realize that no, the fucking fucker isnae fucked, it's *you* what's
fucked.

The evidence is all over the screen of your lappie, which, fucking eejit that you are, *you left online when you went inside last
night*.

You grab the lime green plastic dildo. It's an anatomically correct cock, but it's the wrong colour, only about eight centimetres
long, and there's something embossed on it—a URL. As you squint
at it, another wee plastic cock—this one cherry red—topples off the
mound that's rising from the fabber's guts and bounces across the
floor. "Jesus fuck." You stare at the lappie in horror. About sixty

dozen overlapping windows are warning you that spyware has been detected, inviting you to download an antivirus package from the app store of a fly-by-night scamware vendor in Hainan. You ken it's the same site as the URL on the dildo. "Jesus fuck," you repeat.

It's ransomware, pure and simple.

"Tha' dug ate ma' hamewurk."

Never mind Gav and his minions. Tomorrow you're gonnae meet the Operation's tax farmer, who expects you to pay up for your key to the dark gates of toyland.

Twenty-seven hours to lay your hands on three large. You are *so* fucked.

* * *

Hello.

We interrupt your scheduled browsing to bring you news of an unfortunate incident.

Stuart Jackson, aged twenty-two, a resident of Hamilton Wynd, Leith, has just visited our local business-development executive, the Toymaker—that would be me—to plead for assistance in restructuring his debt.

Perhaps you are thinking that the Operation is unduly harsh in its treatment of defaulters. And it's possible you have some sneaking sympathy for Jaxxie, a secondary-school drop-out struggling to make his way in a cruel and bewildering world that has written him off as being of no conceivable value.

Well, you'd be wrong.

This vale of tears we live in holds a virtually unending supply of Jaxxies, eager neds ready and willing to sell crack to their grannies and jack their neighbours' laptops to pay for the next bottle of Bucky. Jaxxie is distinguished from the rest of them solely by a modicum of low cunning, a propensity for graft, and a minor eye for space-filling structure that—if he had applied himself to his Standards and Baccalaureate—might have found him a place on the rolls of a distance-learning institution and ultimately a ladder up to what passes for a respectable middle-class profession in this degraded age of out-sourcing.

But Jaxxie is lazy. Jaxxie *disnae enjoy the learnin'*. Jaxxie is a petty criminal who pays his way by acting as an outlet for the Toymaker's bottom-tier products. And Jaxxie slept through his Economics classes in school.

As you have doubtless realized by now, the Operation's products are all illegal; this imposes certain regrettable cost externalities on us—you can't buy insurance and police protection for your business if what you manufacture ranges from MDMA labs to clitoridectomy kits.

We have learned over the years that it is necessary to take a stern but honest line with junior franchisees who ask for business-development capital loans, then default on their line of credit. In our world of unregulated free-market enterprise there is no "society" to off-load business externalities like insurance onto, no courts to settle disputes equitably, and no presumption of goodwill.

We have given Jaxxie every opportunity to pay off his debt on time. We even steered business his way—when he was too lazy to get on his bike and look for work—by way of our local salesman, Gav. Despite having a suitable contract dropped in his lap, Jaxxie still managed to drag defeat from the jaws of victory. This is the point at which our patience would normally be exhausted: We are not a welfare scheme, and we cannot afford to continually make allowances for incompetence when it impacts the bottom-line.

But Jaxxie's debt is not substantial. Furthermore, we are aware that he is willing and eager to repay it, and would certainly have done so on time had not "the dug ate ma hamewurk." We are therefore pleased to announce that we are going to exercise the prerogative of mercy on this occasion.

Jaxxie: We hope you will take this punishment, which is intended to teach you a valuable lesson, in the spirit in which it is intended. It may strike you as unpleasant and draconian—but consider the alternatives! We have a franchise relationship model to defend. As it is, your punishment will not hurt much. You'll make a full recovery. And it won't even impair your ability to continue in your chosen profession.

Just don't fuck up and make us come for your *other* kidney.

LIZ: Morning After

Wednesday morning starts out moist and grey in that way Edinburgh gets in summer, when the haar comes boiling up from the Firth and fills the streets with a humid Whitechapel haze, misting your specs and clogging your lungs like a stifling blanket.

You find yourself thinking about work over breakfast (a couple of cereal bars and a half litre of apple juice). Work is both a relief and a distraction; it beats sitting and staring at the walls, aimlessly surfing the net, or grocery shopping (all activities that leave you twitchy and numb, vulnerable to the little existential doubts that nibble at your will-power when you don't have a focus). Besides, you've got a nice little bundle of puzzles on your desktop: your own investigation case-load plus trouble tickets escalated by your team because they're not amenable to a five-minute clean-up. If you lose yourself in the in-tray, time passes that bit more quickly.

So it is that after breakfast you pull on a clean suit, grab your bag, and head for the gym; and after a brisk half-hour work-out and a shower, you catch a microbus to the station. While you're waiting at the bus-stop (expect five minutes between vehicles, according to the flickering sign—more like ten if you account for traffic jams) you put on your specs and log in to the daily news flow. Surprise—Dodgy Dickie MacLeish has got an ops room up and running for last night's case, and he wants you to check in.

Kibitzing on a Charlie Hotel investigation (Culpable Homicide, CH to its friends) is not exactly going to contribute to your own team-performance metrics, but it's a higher-priority job than most, and it's a whiff of the unusual: So you hurry on down to briefing room D31, grabbing a coffee on the way.

Police briefing rooms haven't changed much over the years. They retain the same scuffed white paint, checkerboard-fading LED panel lighting, and cheap furniture: the spoor of an institution focused on results, not appearances. The centre of the room is dom-inated by a horseshoe of battered active surfaces for the collaborative push-pull noodling. CopSpace is crammed full of Post-its, work flows, time-line charts, and urgent-project waves. When you arrive, Dickie's chatting to a knot of suits, but he clocks your availability sharpish and breaks off. "DI Kavanaugh." He nods. "In bright and early, I see." You register his glower but cut him some slack: File it under *up all night with no sleep*. The first law of detection is *the longer you leave it, the harder it is to collar the culprit*; 80 per cent of cases are solved within forty-eight hours, after which the probability of a clear-up drops drastically—and Mac is well aware of this.

"I was already past shift end when the call came in," you reply automatically. "What's turned up?"

"I was hoping you could shed some light on the initial contact." His manner's abrupt. "The log here says first contact was Jase McDougall and PC Berman, sent to a priority 3 by Control responding to a call from a MOP, Mrs. Begum. The home help. You were in Control when the call came in—what did they tell you?"

That one's easy. "Nothing." You take a cautious sip of your coffee and wince: It's bogging. "That is, I didn't take the call—I think you'll find it was Sergeant"—*Elvis*—"Sorensen? When Jase called for supervision, I was coming to the end of my shift, so I decided to visit the site in person before heading home. When I got there, Jase told me that PC Berman took the initial contact and yanked his chain. When he got to the scene, he pulled me in. So I was the third on scene."

"And then you called me immediately." Dickie nods, his expression grim. "May I ask why you didn't file it as an accident?"

"Sure." Your cheek twitches: You take another mouthful of the bitter gunk from the bottom of the cafetière. "I've had dealings with Mr. Blair before—in fact, we go back a way. He's a fine upstanding pillar of the underworld. If he'd fallen downstairs and clouted his head, I probably wouldn't have rattled your cage, but the manner of his passing was such poetic justice, so to speak ... "

"You think it's a hit."

This is treading close to dangerous ground. *Change the subject.* "Let's just say, if this was my investigation, I'd want to rule that out. Did SOC do a work-up on the, er, fluid? Like I suggested?"

He glares at you. "How did you *know*?"

"Know what?" you ask. Then you cotton to the work flow he's fingering in CopSpace, and grab hold of it for yourself. It flips open in all its wikified hypertextual glory, full of long medical terms that fail to signify, beyond the words "Sildenafil" and "Ritonavir." "Um. Bear with me a moment while I come up to speed? I need to look this up—"

Dickie snorts. "Don't bother. Sildenafil's better known as Viagra. That's nae going to do for anyone on its lonesome, but Ritonavir—that's an old HIV anti-viral drug—apparently it messes up Viagra when you mix them, makes it ten times as strong or something. And enema fluid. Apparently it's *all the rage*."

You've run across the enema thing before, for alcohol and other drugs, but this is a new one on you. "Did he add the drugs himself, or is it a set-up?"

"He's HIV-positive, and had blood-pressure issues on top. He's on Ritonavir and a bunch of blood-pressure meds. There's a bunch of open packets of capsules in the bathroom cabinet; but they're none of them administered by enema. The patient information for the HIV drug is full of warnings about Viagra, not that most eejits bother reading the leaflet. And there's a bunch of empty capsule shells in the bathroom bin." And there, in a nutshell, is the veiled accusation: *murder most foul*. "We got a core temperature reading that suggests he was lying there since midnight the day before. I'm still waiting on the post-mortem report, but my money's on the first option—someone who knew about Laughing Boy's dangerous habit spiked the cocktail. That machine ... " He points at a 3D projection of the death scene, floating atop one of the surfaces. "It's a collector's piece."

You zoom on the thing, click through to its notes, and boggle slightly. "It belonged to *who*?" *Who* is apparently some VIP called Nicolae Ceauşescu, who was ... *Dictator of Romania prior to the revolution and his subsequent execution in 1989* ... "That's crazy!" The wiki goes on to say that the President for Life acquired a deathly fear of germs while in prison during the Second World War, and consequently never wore the same clothes twice. He started every day with an enema. Hence the Soviet spa equipment, which your friend Mikey subsequently acquired at auction and used for ... "Oh my. Talk about your hidden depths."

Dickie remains dour. "I ken this is new to you, but when ye've finished giggling, we have a job tae do?"

You wave it off. "No, it's all right. I'm done now." You take a deep breath. "Oh my. Yes, you've ... You've messaged Sally in Press Relations, haven't you?"

He nods lugubriously. "It's all in process, and as soon as the post-mortem's in, I'm escalating. Liz—ye kenn't the subject. Care to venture any speculation?"

What he's asking you for is strictly against the spirit of intelligence-led policing, but you're willing to cut him a lot of slack; he's thirty-six hours into a solid candidate for fucked-up homicide of the year, and he wouldn't be shooting the breeze with you if he had any leads. "Sorry; it's all ancient history. I haven't had anything to do with Mikey since we put him away, and I don't know who his current contacts are. Have you pinged Probation yet? Is—was—he under any supervision orders? Do we have a handle on his social networks?"

"Yes, no, and no, Liz. Well, it was worth the ask. I'll be thanking you for dropping by, and feel free to look in if you remember anything." He steers you doorwards, and you go gracefully. It wouldn't do to be cluttering up the ops room when he nails down the probable cause of death and officially escalates the investigation to Murder One. And so you proceed in the general direction of your team's office, almost regretting that this is the last you'll have to do with the case.

Famous last wishes ...

* * *

Welcome to exile.

You get to your team's office through a maze of twisty passageways and a short-cut across one corner of a car-park, then in through a wooden gate set in the stone wall of what used to be the police stables. Lothian and Borders maintained a mounted unit right up until independence—at which point, the drop in demand for royal escorts sent the nags to the knackers and the budget to the UAV squadron. At which point the old stables were refurbished as accommodation for whoever lost the toss-up, meaning you and yours.

The former stables are picturesque but not really fit for office work. There are no windows (except those in walls that face in on the grassy courtyard), they're cold in winter and stifling in summer, and the stone walls are a royal pain in the ass for wireless and cable ducting. On the other hand, you've got *esprit* up to here—everybody's got something in common to grumble about.

Rather than a big, open-plan briefing room with surfaces and signal strength up to five bars, you've got a confusing, pokey maze of thick-walled rooms lit by LED down-lighters hanging from the overhead beams. And you've got a confusing, pokey maze of misfits to work with. Your department, the Innovative Crime Investigation Unit, has four permanent staff and another eight part-time bodies. For your sins in a previous life you're the inspector in charge, reporting to Chief Inspector Dixon, who wears two hats—CID and U Division, IT. It's not your only job, but it occupies a good 80 per cent of your working hours. Working under you are Sergeants Cunningham and Patel, aka Moxie and Speedy, and Constable Squeaky: And they in turn train and supervise an indeterminate and ever-changing population of porn monkeys in uniform.

Welcome to the Rule 34 Squad.

"Morning, skipper." It's Moxie, squirrelled away in the centre of a nest of archaic flat-panel displays, nursing a blueberry-and-mint latte and a ring Danish as he twitches at the incoming feeds and waves rolling up his screens. "'Ad a good holiday?"

"Not really." It's your turn to suppress a twitch. "Seen Speedy today?"

"Rest break." A stream in one window freezes and zooms front and centre for his attention. "Uh." He forces his attention back to you, and you stifle your exasperation: "What was the question?"

The rest of the force uses ICIU as a dumping ground for the weird ones. It's always like this with your team of crack ADHD poster children and borderline aspies.

"Meeting. My office, ten thirty. I haven't scheduled it yet, so consider this your one-hour reminder."

"Okay!" He frowns slightly, eyes flickering as he saccades between your face and the conflicting priority interrupt on screen two. "Um. I think." Whatever he thinks, he thinks better of it and stops. You lean past his shoulder and glance at his screen.

"This is about the anomalous short-tandem repeat hits on the used cartridges in the Stockbridge recycling bins, right? You think you've found something?"

He makes up his mind. "Mebbe, skipper, but it's really fucking *out there*, know what I mean?"

Now you let out your exasperated sigh. "Meeting, ten thirty, remember? Have an informal report ready for me." You straighten up. "Be seeing you." And you beat a retreat to your office (for unlike the sergeants and constables in their cubes, you rate a solid wall of your own to bang your head against).

Rule 34: If you can imagine it, there's pornography about it on the Internet. "It" is the generic "it"—cars, mobile phones, two girls/one cup—grotesquery knows no limit. Originally a throwaway gag in a web comic, popularized by the denizens of 4chan, Rule 34 has come to dominate your life: Because if you turn it on its head and start looking at the net.porn, sooner or later you have to ask, *Is whatever is depicted here happening on my beat?*

ICIU isn't about porn (the war on porn is long since lost, though none dare admit it) so much as it's about Internet memes—random clumps of bad headmeat that have climbed out of their skulls to go walkabout on the web. Often they're harmless—a craze for silly captions on cute cat photographs—but sometimes they're horrendous: And fuckwits see this stuff and think it's cool, so they imitate it. It was bad enough back in the noughties when it was just happy slappers posting videos of muggings on YouTube; these days a meme can migrate from some cam-wearing pervert's head in the

Philippines and have local copy-cats slashing prostitutes in Leith and Detroit and Yokohama the same day.

And when you mix memes with maker culture, you have something even weirder: everything from counterfeit pharmaceuticals through to design patterns for nightmares. Things that escape from the darker reaches of cyberspace and show up in suburban dungeons, eldritch fads and niche cultures that have zero local history until they detonate suddenly, leaving a pile of traumatized and bleeding civilians on your door-step.

Your job is to police all this stuff, to chase it down from both ends—the online supply of designs and the meatspace supply of materials that turn those designs into physical artefacts. Because of resourcing constraints, you mostly focus on the former. But it's the latter that worries you most.

You log in to your surface, send out the short-notice meeting reminder to all concerned, and splat up the conference flows on all three walls around you. Then you lean back in your chair and speed-read as you try to catch up with a day out of the blogosphere.

A decade and a half ago, blogging—whether writing your own or reading them on the job—would pull you a formal disciplinary hearing. Now it's part of the work-load, and they grade you according to how many comments your postings get. You—and about three thousand senior ICIS professionals in other jurisdictions around the planet—share the work of monitoring the net and tracking the spread of disturbing new trends. You pool the stuff your tame porn monkeys throw up, and they do likewise. There are mailing lists and chat rooms and regular face-to-face international conferences for meme cops to attend. Every week—or more frequently, if necessary—you send out a bulletin for CID and U Division and everyone who needs to be aware of the latest nasty surprises. Several times a day you field puzzled enquiries from officers trying to get their heads around something that *just disnae make sense*; and you've got your own investigations to run, nosing into anything ICIS dredges up that looks like it originated in your town.

CopSpace is all-encompassing these days, with gateways into the sprawling Interpol and Europol franchises. And your occupation is very atemporal, very post-post-modern. So your first real job of the day is to set up a query agent to look for case files containing Viagra, spammers, homicide, and enemas in close proximity. Then you add a personal note to a co-ordination wave, asking if anyone else has seen anything relevant; tweedle a brief announcement of the facts of the case (suitably blinded) in case any of your colleagues in other jurisdictions have useful suggestions: and on your public blog, ask if any MOPs who were in the vicinity of Mikey Blair's demesne would like to drop by for tea and a chat. Only then do you get to start sifting through your regular inbox and prioritizing the day's routine work-load.

Item: There's a Person of Repeated Interest in Pilton who's just turned up at the Royal Infirmary with forty sutures in his lower back, a nasty case of MRSA, and a missing kidney. Question from CID, *Do we have an organlegging problem or is this just punishment surgery?*

Item: a Person of Repeated Interest in Cramond has been found unconscious in a gutter, sporting unusual leg injuries. Recovering in hospital, officers called to deal with the reported shooting incident took possession of the recovered projectiles—ultrahard plastic spheres about a centimetre in diameter that show signs of having been produced on an unregistered fabber, invisible on X-ray, which had been fired into the meniscal cartilage of each knee at point-blank range. PORI is being uncooperative: *Are there reports of kneecapping using this MO elsewhere on the net?*

Item: We recently lifted another PORI in Craigmillar on a

public-order charge. IT Forensics found his phone contained numerous videos which we are treating as Extreme Pornography as per CJ&L(S)(2009). A query with cause on the NPFIT database failed to identify where he downloaded this material—it certainly wasn't logged over the public Internet. *Query: What should we be looking for? Blacknet, sneakernet, or some other option?*

This is the problem with being on the Rule 34 Squad: You get to wade through everyone else's shit, but your own case resolution metric is in the tank. For example, if you could get the resources to track down where the feedstock for that metal-hard polymer the black hats are putting through their fabbers is coming into the city from, you could follow it to the customers and shut the bastards down for a very long time indeed (Firearms Act, 1968, as amended). If ICIU was classified as a support unit rather than a bastard offshoot of CID you'd be in the clover. But it isn't, so you're expected to spend your time running dumb-ass web searches on behalf of the real detectives—support unit stuff—while trying to meet utterly inappropriate performance metrics for arrests and convictions. No gold star for you.

On the other hand, CID can't do without the Rule 34 squad these days, doing the stuff nobody else wants to take on. So you get to keep this job so that they don't need to sit in ancient Aeron chairs all day, drinking bad coffee and staring up the Goatse-shaped ring-piece of the prolapsed, ulcerous arse-meat of the Internet until their eye-balls melt.

The members of your constantly rotating pool of Internet porn monkeys typically last three months on the team; then they flee screaming back to the blessed relief of patrolling the sinkhole estates and vomit-splattered pub doorways of the wrong side of town. Most of them are volunteers—officers who figure a few months off their feet in a nice warm office with a nanny-free net feed is a soft touch next to collaring neds in Craigmillar or public-order headcases off

Lothian Road. Oddly, they don't often come back for a second tour of duty in bad head park. A small subset are here reluctantly: You figure some of the more unscrupulous brass in E Division may be using ICIU as a punishment posting.

But for you, there's no escape. The Internet amplifies *everything*. You'd thought you'd seen the lot, you with your background in homicide and computer crime and years on the beat. You've seen rape and murder and the vileness that men and women do to one another. But the horror of their actions pales into insignificance compared to what they fantasize about. And on that note, it's just you, Moxie, Speedy, and Squeaky against the scum of the Internet: So it's a blessed relief when you get to spend a day on the control centre desk and an evening mopping up after a guy in a gimp suit who autodarwinates with extreme prejudice.

Keep taking the happy pills, Liz. It's better than the alternative.

(Didn't you have a meeting to be going to?)

* * *

Your meeting rolls round, and then a lengthy chat with Chief Inspector Dixon, your boss (who mostly seems to want to catch up with the latest scuttlebutt about Dickie's dastardly deviant's demise— prurient curiosity never goes out of fashion, even among those who ought to know better), then an hour-long mentoring session with Speedy (who is arsing around trying to make up his mind whether to go for his PIP entry exams with an eye to making inspector some year or other—not totally impossible, you will concede, but he'll have to get his shit together and *focus* if he's to have a hope).

You attempt to put in half an hour collating the paperwork on the DNA tests on those black-market feedstock canisters that have been turning up fly-tipped in residents' recycling bins, but there's nothing conclusive; it's one of those hundred per cent under-resourced investigations that's going to go nowhere until you find something concrete to justify the resourcing without which—

Lunch is a speedy bowl of microwave seitan bulgogi noodles slurped down at your desk with the door shut: Then it's on to the afternoon. First you have a dedicated off-the-hook hour for training courseware; then it's over to room D31 to give Dickie's DCs an off-the-cuff (and off-the-record) briefing on Michael Blair's colourful pre-mortem history. After which it's back to ICIU and a half-hour mentoring Constables Janie Jones and Baz MacIntyre on the banality of evil, the evil of banality, how to tell the difference between faked videos and the real thing, and the best way to keep a sense of perspective while watching vids of kittens being dropped into food processors in slomo (or whatever else the griefers are amusing themselves with today).

Sometime during the afternoon, your phone begins to shake, rattle, and roll for your attention, requesting a personality change. At least, you *think* it began during midafternoon—you tend to ignore it while you're busy. When you finally get annoyed at the desperate arm-waving, you swipe the screen: It does a Jekyll-and-Hyde swap from its officious duty VM to your home phone's personality.

You have face-mail. "Liz?" It's Dorothy. You startle and guiltily look over your shoulder, but the door's shut. "Long time no see. Uh . . . I'm in town again? And I was wondering if, if you'd like to meet up? I'm free tonight, if that's convenient, or we could talk?"

Well, that's a turn-up. But it also up-ends all your carefully controlled tranquillity. You and Dorothy have history. (Or herstory.) Your heart beats faster for a moment, the phone clammy in your palm. "I—" You stop. *Talking to voice mail: ungood.* You text her back, quickly, suggesting meeting up in a friendly wine bar in the new town. Then you take a deep breath and swipe your phone back to its on-duty persona. You take another deep breath as you try to gather your scattered thoughts. You're not sure how you feel about this; it's been months, hasn't it? But suddenly you feel almost hopeful. Which is *bad*, because you're meant to be on duty. So you turn back to the waves and streams of ICIS chatter, and see—

> KARL@Dresden, DE, 15:56 -1:00H: Hi guys we have a weird one here today! One of our local low-lifes tried to off himself in a really original way—we think. $PERP owns a fancy sun-tanning bed. (Don't ask.) Apparently there is a common software hack to override the 10-minute maximum exposure and tanning intensity limits, and he drank half a bottle of schnapps spiked with oxazepam before getting in. Not sure why ... Anyway, third-degree radiation burns to 95% of body! Man, those UVA LEDs are scary! There is rumour about tanning and street drugs producing endorphin high—are any similar reports?

You're not sure just what it is that makes the hair on the back of your neck stand up, but you sit there and stare at the transcript for a long moment, then air-type:

> QUERY: What is $PERP's background?

It's a minute or so before Karl spots your addition and replies, during which time you're perusing a report on trends in toxicant inhalation among youth in the seedier Parisian banlieues, then:

> $PERP is a scam artist—bulk-mailing fraud and tax evasion. Why?

Your fingers shaking, you reply:

> Maybe nothing, but we have a weird one here, too. Our $PERP had a record: pharmaceutical spam, illegal sale of medicinal products,

**counterfeit goods. We are investigating as murder due to
circumstances of death.**

More waiting:

What circumstances?

At this point you pause to authenticate Karl's identity
credentials. Karl Heyne is indeed an officer of some kind in the
Kriminalpolizei in Dresden, according to your departmental
authentication server. He is, in the loosest possible sense, one of
your colleagues. But on the other hand—you check the department newsfeed for confirmation—Dickie has indeed escalated the
case of the late Mr. Blair to Murder in the First Degree as of
lunch-time, and the ironclad rule of criminal intelligence is: *assim-
ilate everything, disclose nothing.* You think for another minute,
then:

**I am not principal investigator. Suggest you contact DCI MacLeish
(profile attached) for further information. Tell him I noted
circumstantial similarity.**
(Bye.)

At which point you could wash your hands of the whole affair
and consider your duty done—but that's not enough, is it? You
stare at Karl's note for a full minute, letting it all percolate together,
trying to quantify your sense of déjà vu.

Item: $PERP is a spammer.

Item: $PERP is found dead, in a weird and improbable accident,
at home.

Item: rogue domestic appliances are implicated.

Item: so are inappropriate intoxicating substances.

Naah, that never *happens, not in real life, outside of the movies. Does it?*

"Dickie will think I'm off my trolley," you mutter to yourself. Then you pick up your phone, shake it, and speed-dial.

"Chief Inspector? If I can have a moment ... ? Really? That's too bad ... Listen, I don't want to add to your work-load, but I have a possible lead from—it's a long shot—Germany. Yes, it's intelligence-led. They've got a circumstantially similar case on their hands in the past twenty-four hours. No ... Not *exactly* the same, but I spotted at least four points of similarity. So far, no, no, they're still treating it as accidental-but-weird. No, I know. I told him I'm not the lead, gave him your details. Yes, I—I'm sorry, but in my judgement there's something very fishy about it, and I think you need to talk to the man. No I—no. Look, you know what I do, don't you? I'm here to watch for—well *shit*."

You put the phone down carefully, in case it explodes. Or maybe in case *you* explode. Anger management is one of those compulsory people-skills hingmies they put you through on a regular basis; clearly Dickie's overdue for his next refresher.

You can fully appreciate how busy he is, and how he's got the brass breathing down his neck—Scotland as a nation gets about a hundred murders a year, but Edinburgh accounts for less than a tenth of that—and you know this is but a circumstantial *what-the-fuck?* indicator, most likely a coincidence. But there's no call to bite your head off. If Dickie disnae want to carry it, he can always fob you off on one of his minions. There is absolutely *no* fucking call to swear at a fellow officer like that, much less a sometime class-mate, and it is indicative of a distinct lack of respect and professionalism, and you have half a mind to—

No, scratch that. Leave the formal complaint for some other time, when he isn't being shat on from above and trying to juggle a murder investigation and his regular case-load. Now is not the time to go nuclear, whether or not Dickie deserves it. You've had years of practice at swallowing this shit. Often as not, they don't even realize they're dishing it out: coming from a macho subculture, gobbling pints and proton-pump inhibitors to keep their stomachs from exploding with all the bile and suppressed rage that goes with the job—no. Just *no*. Bottle it up for later.

And speaking of bottling it, you put in three and a half hours of overtime yesterday, it's forty minutes to end of shift right now, and if you don't claw back some personal space, HR will notice and send you on a mandatory work/rest chakra-rebalancing course again (because the new-age hippie counselling shit is cheaper than paying for stress-related sick-leave).

Anyway, haven't you got a date?

It's time to go home and shower, then off to the wine bar to see what Dorothy wants—whether it's you, or just a familiar face in a strange town. And to maybe bring down the wall and get comfortably numb for a few hours before you climb back into the broken hamster wheel of your career and scamper round again and again . . .

* * *

Maybe you didn't know it at the time, but you and Dorothy have been friends for, oh, ever so long. Since maybe back before you were in primary two and Miss Simpson started in on the utterly bowdlerized sexed coursework, which was all they were allowed to hand out back then. Back in the early nineties, in the dog days of Section 28—the part of the Local Government Act that banned local councils and education authorities from admitting that homosexuality even existed, much less allowing teachers to tell isolated kids that being destined for the Adam and Steve alternative didn't mean they were pariahs or perverts—back then, even aged eight, you'd figured out for yourself that this stuff was all wrong. *You'll never get me to do* that *with a boy*. Well, *maybe*—but why bother? It's an awful lot of hard work—and no little mess—for something that doesn't look much like anything you'd call fun.

On the other hand, that was before you hit your teens—and ran into crushes and BFFs and all the weirdly incomprehensible playground politics that never really made sense to you. Because your crushes were all wrong, and you were afraid to talk about them: *Is she a lesbo?* was about the second worst thing they could say about anyone, and you knew that if you gave them even a hint about what you dreamed about, about what made you wake flushed and sweating in the small hours, it'd be the absolute end, utter humiliation for the rest of your life.

So you giggled along with them, and learned to lie, didn't admit to watching and rewatching Xena on video until the tapes chewed themselves up, and made a point of going to church so that when you said you believed in no-sex-before-marriage, they believed you and forgot to ask the obvious follow-on question: *So who's the lucky boy, then?* You even did the Alpha course when you were eighteen, and lied enthusiastically right up until the speaking in tongues bit (which caught in your throat).

But then it was time for university. Where you met your inner Dorothy and got to know her ... quite well.

Learning who you are is something every teenager goes through: But if your identity isn't an identikit match for any of the role models on offer, it can take quite a while and take you up some strange paths on the way. You figured out you wanted to be a cop quite early—maybe it was Uncle Bert's fault (even though he never bothered taking the sergeant's exam), and maybe it was connected to the hard-shell uniformed image: self-sufficient, justified, not taking shit from ignorant assholes. You wanted that, you wanted it *badly*, and you believed in rules and telling the truth and punishing bullies. But maybe there was something else going on as well, something you didn't understand at the time.

When you got your A-level grades and that place at university and broke away from the home-town claustrophobia for the first time, you didn't bother joining any wishy-washy clubs and societies: You signed up for Archery and SCUBA Diving rather than the Feminists Society or LGBT Soc. You did your drinking in a pub on the wrong side of the tracks, where you unconsciously felt safe, not realizing that you were missing out on all the torrid flesh-pots of academia; and it was from the local bears that you learned about gay culture at second hand. Learned their jokes, learned their slang, learned "friends of Dorothy" as archaic code for the love that dared not speak its name (once upon a time).

You never realized that the Feminists Society was the bed-hopping club of your dreams; or that if you'd hung out in the Student's Union on campus, you could have had your pick from the conveyor-belt sushi buffet of dungaree-wearing baby dykes in LGBT Soc.

(At least, until they learned you were studying to be a cop.)

Mary was the turning point. Portsmouth, Pompey: a naval town, going back hundreds of years—and where you get warships, you get sailors. Some of whom—you can imagine Kylie in Lower Sixth hissing it in disbelief—were *lesbians*. Who did *not* hang out around the university campus but were certainly willing to take a gawky post-teen with aspirations towards a uniformed service under their wings and teach her stuff about herself that would be a source of nostalgia many years later. Mary was blonde and friendly and brisk, and for a while you'd been her girl in port: which was good while it lasted (Twelve months? Eighteen?) and left you on a tide of tears, clutching a much better understanding of who you were going to be when you grew up.

All of which is fifteen years and more in your past, but goes some way towards explaining how you got a bona grip on Polari before anybody told you that you were the *wrong kind of feminist*; why you sigh whenever you see a navy ship in the waters of the Firth; and how come you think it's hilarious that your on-again off-again will-she-or-won't-she nuisance lover is called Dorothy Straight.

ANWAR: Office Worker

You smell hot oil and cardamom as you walk through the front door: "Hi, Bibi, I'm home!"

She's in the kitchen. "Yes, dear," she calls distractedly. "Have you seen Naseem? I sent him round to Uncle Lal's for a bunch of methi, and he's not come back. I think he's playing with his English friends again"—in Bibi's world *English* is a wild-card ethnicity: It could equally mean Scottish or Lithuanian—"and he's forgotten, the little scamp ..."

"No, haven't seen him." You suppress the urge to grump at her (*What am I, his nursemaid?*) as you close the front door and hang your jacket up. The boy will be fine; you can locate him on GPS just as soon as you take the sock off your phone ... "I've been looking for an office. I think I've found one."

"Oh, good! Hey, come and be a dear and help peel these onions? You know they make me ..." *cry*, you mentally auto-complete, suppressing a snort and heading into the kitchen. It's one of Bibi's stranger foibles: Despite the day job, she insists on cooking, but she can't, absolutely *can't*, peel and chop onions.

(You said "no" and watched her try, just the once, years ago: The memory of what it did to her eyes is still enough to make you wince. Now she's got a German gadget to chop them up, but getting the outer skin off first is a man's job ... where *is* that boy?)

You join Bibi in the kitchen, where she's frying up spices, and take a knife to the offending onions. (It's probably her contact lenses. Why can't she just wear spectacles while she's cooking?) "Your auntie Sameena called round earlier, you know? She was wanting to know all about this mystery job of yours, but I told her it was none of her business until you are good and ready to tell everyone. *Trade secrets.* That hushed her up, I can tell you. She watches too many trashy spy soaps from Karachi; she thinks you're still secretly a black-hat hacker ... "

You wordlessly pass her the bowl of onions. She stuffs them into the German gadget, closes the lid, and stares at you significantly as she puts some serious arm action into the handle. It's a sign that she expects you to read her mind—she's a firm believer in male telepathy, and you've never quite had the nuts to break it to her that she'd do much better at silent communication if she simply stuck to jerking your dick in Morse code. You waggle your eyebrows at her. "What is it?"

She pauses, then looks up at you. "What *is* this mysterious job that you need to rent an office for, oh my husband?" She's using this oddly stilted excuse for a private language she picked up from fuck-knows-where—some Bollywood musical version of domestic married bliss perhaps—she's even *batting her eyelashes*. You may be telepathically deaf, but even you can figure out that this is the feminine equivalent of boldface and double-underlined capitals.

You lean close, put an arm around her shoulder, and ask her: "Can you keep a secret, oh my wife?"

She leans against you, seeking contact, which is nice (for once, there are no kids present). "If you ask me to, nicely ... "

You kiss the top of her head. "All right. But please don't tell your mother; she'll get too excited.

"It's all to do with that job interview I had last week. The one the Gnome sent my way—"

"I knew it!" She tenses angrily. "That rat!" She doesn't pull away, but you can feel her quiver with indignation, and something inside you locks up tight.

Bibi doesn't know your exact relationship with Adam, but he's been around occasionally, and she doesn't like or trust him: She knows he's a business associate, and that's bad enough for her—the kind of business associate whose company landed you in Saughton, she thinks. Nonsense: It was just a spot of bad luck. But needs must, and ruffled feathers need smoothing: "No, love, it's not something I'm doing for him; it's just something he was able to point my way. It's not big, but it's useful, and there's money in it, and more importantly, it'll convince the social workers that I'm getting my life straightened out."

"Is it legal?" she asks, pointedly.

"It's more than legal: It's for a government."

"Well then." That shuts her up for a moment, but not for two: She's not stupid. "What government? The Scottish—"

"Hsst, no." The current administration is a hive of snake-fondling Christians, in league with the Wee Frees; luckily it looks as if they're going to go down hard at the next election. "You see, the job interview wasn't in London, and I didn't get the sleeper train: I had to fly all the way to Przewalsk! And I got the job. I'm going to be"—you savour the moment as you prepare to tell her—"the honorary consul in Edinburgh for the Independent Republic of Issyk-*ouch!*"

You were about to say *Kulistan* when your loving, obedient wife dropped the German gadget on your foot. "Oh!" She ignores your injury and scrabbles around on the floor in pursuit of the onion compartment, which has taken on a life of its own and is rolling enthusiastically towards the table. You stifle a rude word—being German, the gadget is over-engineered and surprisingly heavy—and instead bend over and pick up the detachable handle. The plastic collar where it fits onto the onion eviscerator (or whatever it is called) has broken, and there is a smell of burning—worse, of hot metal—from the frying pan.

Bibi stands up, snorting deeply like an angry heifer as she clutches a clear plastic tub of finely chopped onions: Her chest rises and falls fetchingly under her blouse as she stares at you in disbelief. "Honorary *what*? You're making shit up again, you worthless sack of—" Then she blinks and lunges past you in the direction of the cooker: "Oh, my pan! Oh no! This is a disaster!"

Right at that moment the front door opens with a fanfare of brassy pre-teen boys' voices, and everything gets a little vague. You are not sure how the plastic-collared German onion-destroying gadget's handle ends up in the frying pan, or why the turmeric ends up in the bowl of gram flour and the whole mess ends up on the floor, or where the smell of burning plastic is coming from, because the smoke detector has gone off its little electronic trolley and is screeching loud enough to wake the dead: But you beat a hasty retreat from the self-deconstructing kitchen.

"Go and help your mother," you sternly tell your son, who is clutching a paper bag and chattering excitedly about something football-related that he and his friend Mo have done. Then you tiptoe away with a sinking heart. Bibi will blame you for setting the kitchen on fire, *and* she'll make you go chase after a template for the broken part of the German gadget and repair the thing. Why do your attempts to do good for her always seem to end up this way?

* * *

Your hard work has paid off. In the process of examining commercial properties you stumbled upon some most remarkably posh digs at a knock-down price for your consular mission. It's in one corner of a modernist glass cube that is embedded like a gestating alien larva within the bowels of the former post office headquarters on North Bridge. The Gothic architraves of Scottish Baronial limestone pulse with an eerie green radiance after dusk; passers-by who peer between the sandstone window casements can see the cleaning robots casting long shadows across the cube's windows as they skitter hither and yon. It's supposedly haunted by the ghost of a Microsoft sales rep who hanged herself in the central atrium a couple of decades ago. Some of the Ghost Tours from the Royal Mile have taken to stopping by late at night.

Admittedly, your stipend does not stretch to anything particularly plush: Your wee niche in the former Microsoft HQ is a three-metre-by-four room in a shared office suite. It's half-filled by a scratched-up pine desk and a pre-owned Aeron chair the management threw in as a sweetener. The rest of the suite is overrun by programmers from a local gaming corporation who rent two entire floors above you. They're working on some kind of Artificial Reality project—you made the fatal mistake of asking one of them, and your eyes glazed over before he reached the fourth paragraph of nerdspeak without stopping to draw breath. But at least you're not hot-desking, or hanging out your shingle above Rafi's phone-unlocking and discount-print shop on Easter Road. No, indeed. You've come up in the world, you have an office of your own, you wear a suit and tie to work, and people *respect* you.

(Well, we'll soon see about that.)

Mr. Webber was certainly taken aback at your last interview. "Representing a consortium of central Asian commercial interests in the Midlothian region?" He doodled a note on his tablet. "Well, Anwar, you never cease to surprise me. A family connection, I assume?" You grinned and refrained from blabbing, but produced the documentation when he asked to see it. The smug bastard *really* raised an eyebrow when you showed him the letterhead. He's going to check it out, but the beauty is that it *will* check out. Which means your future sessions with him will be reduced to thirty-second ticky-boxes rather than real probation interviews. Going straight doesn't get much straighter than wearing a suit and working for a foreign government.

Actually, there's fuck-all work in it. You've set up your office and your desk just so, and you've skimmed the helpful handbook they've prepared for honorary consuls. The first IBAN draft hits your bank account with a thud, and now you're sitting pretty. Cousin Shani's handling your tax—she's an accountant—and you're in credit and in employment. But after the first few days of scurrying around filling out online forms, it's a bit boring. As the Gnome surmised, few natives of Issyk-Kulistan pass through Scotland. In fact, it's a *lot* boring. There isn't even any email to answer.

Alas, you've got to be behind the desk during core hours, all twenty of them a week. After a bit, you ask Tariq if you can borrow a pad so you can work on his dating website while you're holding the fort: Nobody who walks in will know it from what you're supposed to be doing, and you can do with the cash.

So you're there one midafternoon, grinding your teeth over a broken style sheet, when the doorbell chimes. At first you mistake it for your IDE complaining about a syntax error, but then it rings again, and you see the desk set blinking its light at you. You've got company.

"Hello? Uh, consulate of the Independent Republic of Issyk-Kulistan?"

The desk set clears its throat. "Hello, the consulate? Please to be letting us in?"

You stare for a couple of seconds, then figure out which button to push on the antique console. You hear the front door open and hide Tariq's pad before you stand up and go to see who it is.

Two men are peering twitchily around the lobby area of the shared offices. One's in his late twenties, and the other is considerably older. They've both got close-cropped hair, bushy moustaches, and an indefinable air of perplexity that screams *foreigner* at you. The younger one is clutching the handle of a gigantic rolling case. "Hello? Can I help you?" you ask, politely enough, and the young guy nearly jumps out of his skin.

"Er, hello, this is consulate of ... Przewalsk?" The younger guy's English is clearly a second language—or third. "Hussein Anwar?"

"That's me," you say, nodding. "Can I ask what your business is, sir?" You really want to get back to fixing Tariq's botched style sheet, and you haven't snapped into the right head space, but it comes out sounding patronizing and officious.

The old guy turns to his young companion and rattles something off. The young guy replies, then turns to you. "He says we need to speak in your office. We are visiting trade delegation. Felix Datka sends us to you."

Oh. Well *that* puts a different face on things! "Certainly, if you'd like to follow me?"

Your office is equipped with two plastic visitors chairs and a regrettably non-plastic rubber plant, which has hideous yellow-rimmed holes in its leaves but refuses to die despite your daily libation of coffee grounds. You usher the trade delegation past the plant and wave them into the seats. "What brings you to Edinburgh?" you ask.

"Emails are you has read, the?" begins the old guy before his young companion takes over: "My friend here, he is being lead trade mission to sell produce of our factories to foreign markets. There should an email be. We bring here for you a consignment of trade samples, to be distributed to visitors."

The old guy nods emphatically. "You give we." He waves at the huge and villainous suitcase, which is already settling into the carpet. "Samples."

"Uh, yes. I see. What kind of samples?"

You watch, fascinated, as the young guy fiddles with the substantial locks on the case. He opens the lid with a flourish, not unlike a magician pulling a rabbit from a hat. "Look!" he announces.

The suitcase is full of white paper bags. He pulls one out and hands it to you. The label reads: INSECT-FREE FAIR TRADE ORGANIC BREAD MIX BARLEY-RYE. "For Western home bread-maker machine," says the young guy, as the old guy grins broadly and nods. "Is produced by People's Number Four Grain Products Factory of Issyk-Kulistan! Taste very good, no grit, batteries included, just add water."

"Batteries?" You shake your head.

"Yeast," he says hastily. "You give. Visitors."

You eye up the enormous suitcase. "You want me to give visitors bags of bread mix?" you ask him. "But I don't have room here—"

The old guy nods again. "Give he you visitors bread." He looks at you, and suddenly you recognize his expression and you just about shit yourself. "Is visitors, yes? Email, is."

"The instructions are for you in the email," the young guy adds helpfully. He stands up. "We go, now. Other consuls, more trade!" He grins alarmingly widely and reaches out to shake your hand. His skin is dry and hot, his grip tight as a handcuff. "Am thanking you. You are good man, says Colonel Datka."

* * *

After the "trade delegation" leaves, you sit behind your desk breathing heavily for a couple of minutes. The suitcase crouches behind the dying rubber plant, like a snooping secret policeman intent on exposing your guilt. *Who do they think I am? Does Datka think I'm stupid, or something?* You glare at the case. It's obviously drugs. That's what this is all about. They've figured out how to use diplomatic bags and "trade delegations" to smuggle heroin out of Abkhazia or Ruritania or somewhere, and now you're expected to play host to an endless revolving-door parade of dealers. Well, it won't do! You weren't born yesterday. If they think you're going to tamely take the fall, for a mere thousand euros a month—

You've got a wife and kids to look after. And you've *met* Datka. *Colonel Datka.* Spoken to him. He's not stupid, he's got to know this is shit.

Curiosity gets the better of you, and you reach for the white paper bag on the edge of your desk. It weighs about a kilogram. You close your eyes, hefting it. The suitcase has got to hold at least fifty more of them, from the way it's digging in the carpet. If this is heroin, it's got to be worth half a million on the street. *Datka's* met *you.* Would *you* leave yourself in possession of half a million in heroin, sight unseen?

Holy Moses, Jesus, and Mohammed, peace be unto him: No, you wouldn't. But Datka knows where you live, he knows where Bibi and Naseem and Farida and everything you hold precious can be found, and you've met plenty of cheerfully ruthless men who wouldn't hesitate to use—

Your hands are sweating, and you feel yourself shaking as you tear open the flap on the bag of INSECT-FREE FAIR TRADE ORGANIC BREAD MIX BARLEY-RYE, Produce of People's Number Four Grain Products Factory of Issyk-Kulistan, and jam your thumb inside, crush the coarse flour against the paper, raise it to your mouth, and suck.

It's just flour.

INGREDIENTS: *Malted Barley (40%), Rye (30%), Wheat (20%), Ascorbic acid, fructose-glucose concentrate, Sodium Metabisulfite, Sodium Chloride, Amylase, Protease, Vegetable fat (3%), Raising agent (yeast).*

Add water (320ml to 500g Bread Mix), place in bread-maker, and select "wholemeal rapid" program.

Your shuddering gasp of relief is that of a condemned man receiving his pardon on the steps of the gallows; it's no less heart-felt. You lean back in your chair, eyes screwed shut. You've never been much of one for your daily observations, but right now you make a mental note to lay in a prayer rug against the prospect of future roving visits by feral international trade delegations. God is indeed great: He's sent you organic stone-ground bread mix instead of heroin.

The only question is, why? And so at four o'clock you switch on call divert, lock the office behind you, and go in search of the Gnome.

This afternoon, Adam is holding court in the back of the Halfway House, a wee nook alongside Fleshmarket Close, an improbably stepped thoroughfare that runs up the arse crack from the City Art Gallery to Cockburn Street. (You know you're in the Old Town when the street's so steep they've been talking about fitting an escalator for the tourists.) You take a short-cut through the upper retail deck of Waverley Station, dodging the commuter crowds, and reach the front door with only a slight shortness of breath. "Ah, Anwar," calls the Gnome: "Mine's a pint of sixty bob."

Bloody typical. You sidle up to the bar and smile ingratiatingly until the wee lassie deigns to notice you and pours your pints—your IPA and the aforementioned sticky black treacle syrup for the Gnome. You carry it to the back. The Gnome smacks his lips and slides his pad away. "I didn't think there was any signal down here," you say.

"There isn't usually." The Gnome looks pleased with his pint of mild. "Mm, it's in fine form today. Chewy, with a fine malt after-taste and some interesting hops."

You open your messenger bag, extricate the (slightly leaky) sack of bread mix, and plop it on the table in front of him. "Would it go with this?"

The Gnome stares at it for a moment, then picks it up. "You scanned it," he says tersely. "Where did you get it?"

"No RFIDs," you tell him. "Only the best organic ingredients, said the visiting trade delegation. I'm to hand them out to visitors, according to *Colonel* Datka." You chug half your pint in a single panicky sharp-edged gulp. "What have you got me into?"

The Gnome, for once, is at a loss for words. "I dinna ken, sonny," he says, lapsing into a self-parody of his ancestral Ayrshire accent. "Sorry. It appears to be ... Bread mix." He peers at the label. "Lots of malted barley: I suppose you could use it for home brewing. Some hops, a couple of demijohns, the yeast's probably not ideal ... " He trails off thoughtfully. Then he looks up at you. "It's bread mix," he says crisply. "Tell yourself it's just bread mix. Give it to anyone who stops by. Tell *them* it's bread mix. If by some chance the police pay you a visit? It's just bread mix."

You've got that frozen feeling again. "Fucking *fuck*, are you telling me—"

The Gnome reaches out and grabs your wrist. "It's *just bread mix*," he hisses. He stabs at the bag with one index finger: "If you put that in your bread-maker—if you've got one—it will *make bread*. End of story. That's all you need to know."

You pull your hand back. "No it isn't."

"Believe me," he says slowly.

You cross your arms, mulish. "Tell me. Or it's all going down the shitter tonight."

He begins to smile. "I wouldn't do that. Dough tends to clog the pipes. Just think of the plumber's face . . . "

Despite yourself, you begin to relax. "What is it, really?"

The Gnome fidgets with his drink for a few seconds, then takes a mouthful and wipes his lips dry with the back of a grubby sleeve whose self-cleaning fabric he's long since overloaded. "It's bread mix. What you mean is, what *else* is it."

"What? What else *can* it be?"

"Keep thinking that thought." He smiles disquietingly. "Probably nothing, without Secret Ingredient X." He whistles between his teeth. "'*Once the rockets are up, who cares where they come down? That's not my department,' says Wernher von Braun.*"

"Secret Ingredient X?"

"You read about so much stuff in the science blogs these days." The Gnome holds up his pint. "Zymurgy: the oldest human science."

"Zy—"

"Fermentation. Brewing. *Saccharomyces cerevisiae*, brewer's yeast. It was one of the first organisms to have its genome sequenced, you know that? It's used in baking as well; it's what makes the bread rise." He picks up the packet. "This bread mix is interesting. You could brew with it. The beer would probably taste like shit—it doesn't have any hops—but it'll still be beer." And with that, he slides it into one capacious coat pocket.

You take another deep gulp from your pint glass. "So?"

"So think of *S. cerevisiae* as a handy little biological factory." The Gnome peers at the bag of bread mix. "Normally it'll produce bread. But suppose you want to send some interesting chemical feedstock to someone. All they need to know is that they chuck the bread mix in a sterile demijohn with five or ten litres of warm water.

And then ... It produces crap beer. Only before they put it in the demijohn, they add Secret Ingredient X, which is probably some dietary supplement you can buy over the counter in any health-food shop. And in the presence of Secret Ingredient X, some extra metabolic pathway gets switched on, because this is not your ordinary *S. cerevisiae*; this is mutant ninja genetically engineered superyeast."

"But what does it *make*?"

The Gnome finishes his pint and meets you with a bright-eyed smile. "I really have no idea. And you know what? I don't particularly want to know. *You* don't want to know. Colonel Datka doesn't want you to know; otherwise, he'd have told you. It's a lot simpler if all anybody knows is that you've been told to hand out free samples of organic bread mix by your employer's trade delegation. Oh, and we didn't have this conversation, and we weren't in the back of a pub where there's sod-all phone signal and no free net access and no CCTV because it's quarried out of the side of a granite cliff-face. Are we singing from the same hymn book?"

After a moment, you nod. "Is this what you were asking me to keep an eye out for?"

"Could be." The Gnome reaches into one pocket and pulls out a fat lump of dead cow-skin, as battered and shapeless as if it has been whacked with a hammer. He opens it and pulls out a stack of banknotes. "This is for you. Don't spend them all in the same place."

You reach out and snatch the money. There's the thick end of a thousand euros there, maybe more. Before the savage deflation of the past few years, you might have thought he was cheaping on you. But not now. It's enough to pay the mortgage arrears for three months. "I don't know if I should be doing this."

The Gnome's grin slips. "Neither do I, laddie, neither do I." He puts the wallet away, then pats you on the knee. "But just consider the alternatives."

TOYMAKER: Headhunter

Ants. I am surrounded by fucking ants. Can't they get *anything* right?

This is not rocket science. (Rocket science: fucking 1930s shit invented by Nazi übermensch engineers and so easy that by the 1990s even a bunch of camel-fucking towel-heads could master it.)

This is not AI. (Artificial intelligence: fucking 1950s shit invented by Jew-boy intellectuals at Stanford and MIT and so useless that by the 1990s its highest achievement was beating a vodka-swilling Russian commie dog-fucker at chess.)

This is not genetic engineering. (Genetic engineering: fucking 1970s shit invented by ... you get the picture.)

This is *logistics*!

It goes back to the fucking Stone Age!

They can put a genetically engineered AI on Mars, but they can't shift a fucking suitcase between two hotels without losing it.

I am surrounded by ants, and if this continues I am going to pull on my size-fourteen boots and go for a stomp. See if I don't.

This isn't a complex job. Truly, it isn't. I move hotels every day or two—in fact, I've been doing it every day or two for several years now. It's not as if my job's compatible with having a mortgage or living in a fucking suburban shoe-box with an avocado bathroom suite and a bored housewife and nosy neighbours peering over the picket fence, is it? Santa's got a lot of travelling to do if all good children are going to get their toys, and the jet lag's a motherfucker. (And so's my carbon footprint, but that's not *my* problem: The whiners'll figure out a way to fix global warming. Meanwhile, I fly business class.)

As I was saying, I travel a lot, and I travel light. 5.62 kilograms, to be precise. That's the maximum payload weight I allow myself to pack in my trolley case—that, and the clothes on my back and the contents of my briefcase. If it goes over 5.62 kilos, I have to throw something out. You can get a lot into 5.62 kilos: shaver, suit, change of shirt and underwear, commercial samples, computers. Hotels have same-day cleaning stores that sell toiletries and I'm on expenses and if something starts getting shabby I buy a replacement and it goes in the trash, *capisce*?

My needs are simple: I need a hotel room and my luggage and a desk to sit at with the pad at the end of the day (and no, I'm not stupid—I don't keep anything important on my pad, it's all waiting in the cloud—I am in a very virtual line of work, almost ethereal).

Anyway, this is what I am paying you for.

It inconveniences me mightily if I get to my new hotel room after a hard day's work and my rolling flight case with 5.62 kilograms of home is not there waiting for me.

I need a change of underwear, and I need a shave, and I need my luggage. Only somebody has *lost my shit*.

I hold you responsible.

I see you nodding like a parcel-shelf dog. No, don't look at me like that. This is about logistics, the necessary life-support infrastructure for the modern commercial traveller. If you can't get your logistics right, you don't deserve to be in the hotel business, and I will personally make it *my* business to see that your corporate customer-satisfaction officer learns that there is a day manager on the front desk at this hotel who is *fucking off the customers*. And it won't stop there. You will start to piss away corporate hospitality accounts like a junkie bleeding out into the urinal through his dick. Your staff will cross the road to avoid you, and you will see vultures circling overhead because your days in the hospitality trade will be numbered. You will lose your job and the government will foreclose on your mortgage and you will be cast out on the street to starve like an abandoned dog or be eaten alive by feral mutant children who will skull-fuck your rotting corpse through the eye-sockets with their huge gangrenous organs. This is all because you neglected to pay sufficient attention to your one most important customer today, namely *me*. No, don't you fucking look at me like that, you cunt! If it's not me, then it could be anybody else who walks up to your desk today, this month, this *year*.

It could be *anybody*, as long as they hate you with a fiery, all-consuming passion and decide to devote the next few months of their life to monstering you into an early grave for the sheer fun of pulling apart a quivering lump of feckless time-expired meat.

Get me my luggage, mister hospitality manager. It was due here two hours ago via interhotel transfer from the Marriott on Lothian Road—here's the receipt. I'll be generous: You've got a couple of hours to save your job, your career, and your life. I'm going to go hunt down some dinner. Make sure my luggage is in my room and waiting for me when I get back, and we'll say no more about this matter.

—What line of work am I in, you ask?

It's not really any of your fucking business.

I sell toys.

* * *

You're the acting Toymaker in Edinburgh this month, here to take care of a nasty little headache for the Operation (along the way to setting up a new subsidiary). Supply-chain logistics and order fulfilment in the Central Belt—the Edinburgh–Glasgow M8 conurbation, where two-thirds of the population of the gallus wee free time-share republic huddle together below the highlands—have taken a dive in the shitter of late. Unfulfilled demand remains high, but supply is patchy, and there is a risk of ad hoc competition emerging.

Competition would be bad. The Operation likes its subsidiaries to maintain a supply-side monopoly and goes to some lengths to keep it that way, even tolerating competition between local franchisee storefronts—it's a significant opportunity cost, but deterring interlopers from entering the market in the first place is cheaper than dislodging them once they're dug in.

Scotland is a mess. Word came down from the very top: Someone needs to go into the field and fix things. It's not just a matter of repairing the existing franchise, but of evaluating new market opportunities and if necessary taking the over-the-hill cash cow to the slaughterhouse, then bootstrapping a new clean-room start-up to replace it. Scotland is a small but significant market. As an entrepreneur backed by the Operation's training, guidance, and investor confidence, you can seize the opportunity to make your mark without pissing on the gate-posts of any of the big incumbents. So you raise your virtual hand, volunteer for the job, and pull on the green wellies to wade out into the sticks and take control.

Contrary to what you told the swithering fuckwad on the hotel front desk, it is not your habit to fly everywhere business class. In fact, you avoid flying wherever possible. You have gone to great lengths to maintain a clean identity, using all the tools the Operation has made available to you. Airports are surveillance choke points, and the ubiquitous camera networks have AI behavioural monitors these days. Your unfortunate medical condition has certain side-effects—nobody say "Voight-Kampff test" or you'll rip their fucking lungs out and shit down their windpipe—and if someone's told them to look for members of an organization that pursues an enlightened policy of positive discrimination with respect to people with certain neurological disabilities, you'd have nowhere to run. (It's outrageous—blatant discrimination—but it seems there's one rule for the neurotypical, and another for people like you.)

So you travel by train and ship. Freighter from Anchorage to Vladivostok, trans-Siberian express to Moscow, more tedious railway time-table shite until you arrived in the Schengen zone, then finally some blessed modernity. Two fucking *weeks*, and all because you're a persecuted minority.

The shiny new shinkansen blasted through the English countryside at over three hundred kilometres per hour, but you couldn't help noticing that not even Japan Rail could fix the English public-service disease. You reflected on the issue at length—perhaps if they made their train managers chop off a finger joint every time they were five minutes late or ran out of coffee in first class—but on reflection, you decided the health-and-safety busybodies would have a cow. And so you glared stonily at the refreshments manager before you went back to refactoring the structure of the regional business unit that the Operation sent you to kill or cure.

There are numerous obstacles to progress.

Your predecessor in Scotland, the man who established the Operation's subsidiary in that country, died unexpectedly two years ago—of high blood pressure, not low treachery. He was a knuckle-dragging gangster of the old school, a veteran of the underground wars that thrashed the siloviki revenants out of the EU a decade ago. A street warrior, not a theoretician, in other words—and his business philosophy reflected his background. But he understood the basics.

All the Operation's subsidiaries and start-ups operate on the principle of making dreams come true: recondite or frightening and illegal dreams, true, but dreams nonetheless. They require a marketing operation to bring the wares to the attention of the buying public, a fulfilment arm to get the goods to the punters, and a collection arm to pay for it all. So far, so good.

Violence is a regrettable but necessary overhead on the balance sheets of the Operation's start-ups. Like any enterprise that operates beyond the boundaries delineated by governments—with their self-proclaimed monopoly on the use of violence and their hypocritical attitude towards the legitimacy of certain markets—they must provide for their own defence. To the Operation's way of thinking, there is much to be said for the rule of fist and baseball bat: By keeping the beatings sub-lethal, costs are constrained—and the threat of escalation remains in reserve. Blood is a big expense, as the man said. Bodies are costly, warfare is capital-intensive, and if you have to dig out the machine-guns and start hiring soldiers, your profit margin is about to go into a power dive.

Your predecessor, despite resembling a rabid silverback gorilla in both physical appearance and personal hygiene, understood this instinctively: He ran a tight ship and maintained credit control in a drastically hands-on manner. He had a rep for tittering unnervingly as he stroked his baseball bat and stared at his debtors' knee-caps. Almost everybody paid up on the spot: Nobody wanted to find out just what he was laughing at.

Unfortunately you lack the physical presence and instinctive sense of the theatrical to make this strategy work. Moreover, since the Gorilla went to monkey heaven, the franchisees and street-level clients have become unduly frisky. Getting a handle on the major defaulters is proving tedious although there are plenty of small fry to make an example of and opportunities for profit along the way: Thanks to the Organization, you are in a position to outsource enforcement to contractors in the budget-medical-supplies business.

But you *don't* want to waste your time playing hands-on god-father to a slumful of nitwitted glue sniffers. It's a lousy business model, with no scope for exponential scaling and monetization of the sweat equity you're going to have to inject to make any head-way. The outputs from the Gorilla's franchise scale linearly with the human inputs, because criminal retailing is labour-intensive. And while the Gorilla was content to weed his patch in person, you have higher ambitions than a lifetime of stoop labour.

The first thing they teach you in VC school is to pick a business model with scope for non-linear growth. Consequently, you have concluded that it would be far better to trash the Gorilla's opera-tion completely and establish a new one of your own design ("leveraging best-practice agile methodologies to maximize return on stakeholder investment in accordance with the Operation's total start-up commitment protocols," as your funding pitch puts it) than to try to nurse the emphysemic mafia hold-over out of its intensive care bed and back into a wheelchair.

So you drew up your plans and pitched them at the Operation, talked through the cash flow and gained their grudging assent—and more importantly, the first round of stakeholder equity to bootstrap the new business, on condition you keep the old cash cow pump-ing for the time being. And now you need to recruit an executive team for the start-up.

You're about to go Gangster 2.0 ...

* * *

One of the disadvantages of the virtual corporate lifestyle is that it keeps you too busy for the local health clubs and dojos. In response, you've developed a number of ad hoc work-out substitutes. One of them is that you never catch a bus or a taxi if you can rent a bicycle or walk. Another—which also happens to be good COMSEC practice—is never to contact clients via the networks if you can visit them in person without being observed. So when you walk out of the Hilton, your first stop is the Lothian Bike railing outside.

You always plan to turn up on a client's doorstep spick and span, unexpected as a hangman. To this end you buy lightweight business suits that are impregnated with a magic nanotech fabric treatment that sheds sweat and body odours, not to mention dirt flung up from road surfaces. Before you start pedalling, you fire up a nifty (and highly illegal) applet that makes the jailbroken disposaphone you're carrying emulate a cluster of zombie GPS transmitters: You tell it to send your rented bicycle's tiny mind on a random tour of the Old Town. (It's all for the best if nobody can interrogate the bike about your movements later.)

Once you're on the bike lane, the lack of wireless access leaves you blind—but it's a welcome, familiar feeling, like having your own personal cloaking field. It's a good palliative against the anxiety you feel for your missing luggage. The police INDECT networks might still be able to track you if they were watching right now, but the rich data they depend on is so bandwidth-intensive that it isn't routinely archived: In another twenty-four hours, there'll be no trace that you ever came this way. Before you set off, you downloaded a map and memorized a series of left/right branches and waypoints—it's an archaic skill called "orienteering"—so you make good time, despite the lack of navaids.

You review Number One Client's background yet again as you pedal along beneath the trees that line Dean Park Crescent (all the crescents here are tree-lined these days, legacy of a government scheme to roll back urban warming), giving your thighs as thorough a work-out as any stationary cycling machine.

Number One Client has been of interest to the Operation for some time. He has a number of technical aptitudes that have brought him to prominence in the employment database, and to your personal attention as a candidate for head-hunting. In particular, he's been of use in the past for organizing medium-scale redistribution of grey-market fabber feedstock. He's proficient in highly scalable network-mediated marketing operations with high-yield outputs, and has a proven record of organizing wholesale-supply-chain ventures that include unmonitored cross-border trade, central multi-carrier dispatch of bespoke custom products, and VAT evasion. Which, all in all, is a pretty good match for what you're looking for in a chief operations officer.

The Gorilla didn't see any reason to employ someone with Number One Client's characteristics, but you've already established his operational shortcomings. The Gorilla's idea of how to sell this particular product was straight out of the nineteenth-century arts and crafts movement. Whereas Number One Client's business experience is a comfortably close approximation to the enterprise you intend to bootstrap; the only question remaining is, is Number One Client suitable management material? Especially at the level you're planning to grow the business to.

Number One Client is not, alas, a flawless ruby in the dust. He has a criminal conviction and has served a stretch in prison—that, on its own, is sufficient to disqualify him from executive progression within the Operation. But failure to obey the eleventh commandment is no obstacle to a management post, under suitable governance, and you need somebody with Number One Client's aptitudes and (equally importantly) local connections. A preliminary interview is indicated.

And so you turn into an avenue of big stone houses and dismount at the kerb beside Number One Client's town house, lock the bicycle, walk up to the front door, and (careful not to touch it with your bare skin) ring Michael Blair's doorbell.

LIZ: BLACK SWANS

You're out of the office early (flexitime is one of the perks of the back-office inspector's rank these days) and go home to get changed for your date with Dorothy. Not that you're flustered or anything: If your life was a house, she'd merely be the unexploded bomb ticking away in the wreckage of your cellar, capable of blowing you all the way to Oz at any moment.

You rush home and:

- dive into the kitchen for a glass of wine, only to stare in dismay at the dirty plates in the kitchen sink,

- dive into the bathroom for a quick shower, only to stare in dismay at your haystack hair in the mirror,

- dive into the bedroom for a fresh outfit, only to stare in dismay at the contents of the wardrobe (two stale party frocks, various jeans and tees, and at least eight neatly laundered business suits and accompanying blouses).

This is your life, and there's no rug big enough to sweep it all under—at least not in the half-hour you've allowed yourself for doing the Clark Kent/Superman phone-booth thing before you rush out again. So you compromise on:

- a glass of water,

- your hair savagely brushed and tied back to conceal the creeping anarchy and split ends,

- a different trouser suit,

- earrings and a necklace that'd get you sent home from the station in disgrace if you wore them on shift (just to remind you that you're off duty).

Before you go out, you stare at the bathroom unit uncertainly, reflecting. You've spent twenty minutes rushing around like a schoolgirl on a first date, and to what end? It's not like Dorothy doesn't know what you are—faking soft edges will cut no ice. The thought's meant to count, isn't it? Or the gesture. You're dressing up for her, or not dressing up for her—you're old enough that you ought to know your own mind. You've been kicked in the teeth by love often enough that you should have figured out who you are by now. But you've fallen into an existential trap with this vocation of yours, haven't you? It's easy to know how you're meant to function when you wear a uniform: You do the job and follow the procedures, and everyone knows what you're meant to be doing. What you wear dictates how you behave.

. . . But there's no uniform for a date with Dorothy.

You panic and get changed again, and in the end you make yourself late enough that you end up calling a taxi, sitting twitchily on the edge of the grey-and-orange seat as it grumbles uphill towards George Street. It bumps across the guided busway that bisects Queen Street and chugs up Dundas Street, wheezing to a halt at the corner: You pay up and climb out, and a trio of miniskirted girls nearly stab you to death with their stilettos as they stampede to get in. Just another night out on the tiles in Auld Reekie, nothing to see here but a single thirtysomething woman in sensible shoes walking towards a wine bar full of braying bankers.

Dorothy has found a stool at the bar and is sitting with her back to you, nursing a caipirinha and keeping a quiet watch on the huge mirror behind the bar. Stylish as ever, she makes you feel like a gawky schoolgirl just by existing. You make eye contact through the looking glass, and she gives a little wave of invitation as you walk towards her, a flick of the wrist. Then she's turning, smiling, and you embrace self-consciously. She smells of lavender water. "Hey, darling, you're looking gorgeous! How are you keeping?"

"I'm good. Yourself?" You step back, find there's a gap in the row of bar-stools—but the next one over is already occupied by a bloke who's the spitting image of a kiddie-fiddler you helped put away ten years ago. (Only ten years younger, of course.) You turn away from him hastily as Dorothy's smile opens up like the sun, and she waves past you, attracting the barman's hypnotized gaze.

"I'm in town for the next two weeks"—she runs a hand through her hair, which is a deeper chestnut red than it was last time you saw her, and about ten centimetres longer—"visiting the Cage out at Gogarburn for an ongoing evaluation at the bank: Then I've got a spot evaluation on some American company's local operation." The Cage is the secure zone within the National Bank of Scotland campus: Dorothy is an auditor, the kind who gets to travel a lot. Her little black dress is more boardroom than cocktail bar—doubtless her briefcase and jacket are waiting in the cloakroom—but with her string of pearls and porcelain complexion, she could make it work anywhere. "They've stuck me in a tedious hotel in the West End, Julian is in Moscow this month, so of course . . . " She raises a meticulously stencilled eyebrow at you.

"We can see about that." The barman pauses in front of you. "White wine spritzer, please," you tell him, and flash your ID badge before he can card you. You wait until he delivers before continuing: "Have you eaten yet?"

"No. But there's a place round the corner that's been getting good reviews." She looks at you speculatively.

"Do you have any plans? Outside of work?" You can't help yourself: You have to ask.

"I don't know yet." For a moment she looks uncertain. "This is an odd one." You catch the warning before she continues. "I may have to put in lots of overtime. I was hoping we could catch up if the job permits."

Dorothy's always like this. Babs accused you of being married to the job (and she wasn't wrong), but Dorothy makes you look like a slacker. That alone would be enough to make your relationship with her an on-again off-again thing: And that's before you get round to thinking about Julian, her primary.

So you nod, hesitantly. "I don't have a lot on in the evenings this week. And I'm free Saturday and Monday. Is there anything particular you want to do? Theatre, music—"

"I was hoping we could start by finding somewhere for dinner?" She bites her lip. "And then I'd like to pick your brains about a little problem I've got at work . . . "

* * *

Dorothy is indeed staying in a boring business hotel in the West End. You end up in the bar around midnight, by way of a sushi restaurant and a couple of rounds of margaritas. You're not sure whether you're meant to play predator or prey here—it's been months since the last time your paths intersected—but you've got a plushly padded booth to yourselves, and you catch her stealing sly glances at you in the mirror while she's at the bar ordering a round. "I can't stay too late—I'm on shift tomorrow," you tell her regretfully, as she sits down opposite and bends forward to peel off her pumps.

She curls her lower lip, pointedly not pouting. "That's a shame," she says. You freeze, outwardly expressionless as her unshod left foot comes into contact with the inside of your right calf. *Question answered.* "Didn't you say you're free Saturday?"

You catch your breath: "Yes, I am." Actually, clearing weekend leave usually takes advance notice, but you're on weekday office hours right now: You can swing Saturday and Monday if you need to. Maybe even swap Sunday for Monday . . . Her stockinged foot caresses your ankle. It's smooth, muscular (all those hours in hotel health clubs), reminding you, rubbing. "That's assuming I don't get roped into the latest mess."

She shows you her teeth. "What could possibly be more important than next Saturday?" (She's playing with you. If her own job demanded it, she'd stand you up in a split second.) "I thought nothing ever happened in Innovative Crime? Have they got you back on CID?" She pulls back her foot, leaving you tingling.

"The day before yesterday I was on a community team assignment and got called in on what turned out to be homicide—not your usual ned-on-ned stabby action: more like Tarantino meets Dali."

"Wow." Her eyes widen. "Why are you here, then?" She nudges your foot again: But this time it's an accident, not enemy action.

"Because after I corralled the witness and set up the incident room, CID turned up and took all my toys away." You shrug. "Not that I've got a problem with that. I don't need an extra helping of crap to top up my regular work-load. But Dickie—uh, we're on Chatham House rules here, aren't we?" She nods. "He's the big swinging dick on the investigation, and he's your classic narrow-focus, results-oriented, over-driven, alpha-male prick. He's treating it as a regular crime and he's looking for a suitable perp. Which is normally best practice and the right thing to do, except I happen to know that there was a death in, um, another jurisdiction around the same time, and it bears significant points of similarity. All of which scream *meme* at me. Internet meme, class one, virulent. Only Tricky Dickie doesn't want to know."

"Oy." Dorothy leans back and takes a deep breath, then raises her glass. "I didn't hear any of that, I take it."

"No, of course not." You nod at her. "What's *your* sob story?"

"Work." She pulls a face. "Another bloody ethics-compliance audit. You walk in the door, and everyone gets defensive, like they expect you to put them on a ducking stool and accuse them of witchcraft or something."

"Ethics: It's not just next door to Suffolk anymore." It's feeble and she's heard it a thousand times but it still raises a smile.

Dorothy's job is an odd one: catching corporate corruption before it metastasizes and infects society at large. After Enron collapsed—while you were still in secondary school—the Americans passed the Sarbanes-Oxley Act, accounting regulations for catching corporate malfeasance. But all they were looking for was accounting irregularities: symptoms of maladministration. The unspoken ideology of capitalism didn't admit, back then, of any corporate duty beyond making a return on investment for the shareholders while obeying the law.

Then the terrible teens hit, with a global recession followed by a stuttering shock wave of corporate scandals as rock-ribbed enterprises were exposed as hollow husks run by conscience-free predators who were even less community-minded and altruistic than gangsters. The ravenous supermarket chains had gutted the entire logistic and retail sector, replacing high-street banks and post offices as well as food stores and gas stations, recklessly destroying community infrastructure; manufacturers had outsourced production to the cheapest overseas bidders, hollowing out the middle-class incomes on which consumer capitalism depended: The prison-industrial complex, higher education, and private medical sectors were intent on milking a public purse that no longer had a solid tax base with which to pay. Maximizing short-term profit worked brilliantly for sociopathic executives looking to climb the promotion ladder—but as a long-term strategy for stability, a spiralling Gini coefficient left a lot to be desired.

The European Parliament responded by focusing on corporate governance. If corporations wanted to be legal citizens, the politicians riding the backlash declared, they could damned well shoulder the responsibilities of good citizenship as well as the benefits. Social as well as financial audits were the order of the day. Directives outlining standards for corporate citizenship were drafted, and a lucrative niche for a new generation of management consultants emerged—those who could look at an organization and sound a warning if its structure rewarded pathological behaviour. And as for the newly nationalized supermarket monopolies, a flourishing future as government-owned logistics hubs beckoned. After all, with no post offices, high-street banks, or independent general stores, who else could do the job?

"It's a bank." Dorothy shrugs. "We're running a three-year review for them, focusing on human resources, internal promotion practices, and how they monitor compliance with social-policy directives for dealing with customers in default." Defaults are a political hot potato in this deflationary age. The ground still hasn't stopped shaking from the collapse of the noughties investment bubble, and only government intervention has stopped Scotland—

and the other western EU members—following America down the road of mass repossessions, Greenspan favelas, and civil unrest. "Bankers aren't stupid this decade; they know what happened to their predecessors. What we're worrying about is getting to the *next* decade's managers before they unlearn the lesson. And there's some other stuff, but I can't talk about that."

Her mention of *other stuff* is uncharacteristically low-key. And you know Dorothy well enough to have a clue what makes her tick. "Usual rules?"

"Cross your heart and hope to spontaneously combust, more like."

"Well." You take a lick of salt from the rim of your glass, roll your tongue at her. "We can see about that."

"I'm serious." Her lips pale.

"So am I. What do you think would happen if I compromised a live intelligence-led investigation?" (Translation: *Why do you want to tell me this?*)

"Much the same." She looks at you for a moment. "Is your phone on? Remove the battery."

You stare at her. Then you reach into your handbag and take out your phone and pop the back of the case. "There's a camera behind the bar. It's overlooking the till, but it can see the mirror."

"I know. I checked earlier. It's hi-def, but we're far enough away that it won't record a good enough picture for lip-reading. And we're less likely to be overheard here." She pulls out her own phone and removes the battery. You suddenly feel as naked as you've ever been with her.

"You didn't look me up just for old time's sake," you accuse.

"Not—entirely." She doesn't try to look away. "I'm sorry. Yes, I have an ulterior motive. I need a sanity check, Liz."

"A sanity check? Banking ethics isn't my—"

"This isn't about banking. You're on my disclosure notice;

nobody's going to think twice about me hooking up with a girl-friend."

The indefinite article stings, a reminder of where you stand with Dorothy. "Disclosure notice. I'm not sure I like the sound of that."

She waves it off. "It's a sealed declaration of interests, for the enhanced background enquiry—so I can't be blackmailed. It's basically just an enhanced CRB check with extras, Liz." She pauses. "You're not in the closet. I mean, at work. Are you?"

"Not for years."

"Good. Look, what I'm concerned about is that nobody's likely to listen in on this, and anybody who notices us here is going to assume the obvious." She slides her leg against your knee again. "Oh yes, I'm looking forward to Saturday. Are you?" Her eyes are gleaming. You focus on her lips, glossy and plump with anticipation, and shiver.

"If I were a man, I'd call you a cock-tease." You manage to summon up something not unlike a coy smile.

"I'd like to take you upstairs after this drink, but I think my room's probably bugged." She says it so casually, it takes you a moment to understand her words. "I can understand if you don't want that. Listening in, I mean."

It's like a bucket of cold water in the face. "Who's bugging you?"

"I'm not entirely sure. It goes back about two months; I ran across some rather weird correlations when I was going over the transactions for—um, never mind. Anyway, my boss buried my email and reassigned me when I tried to raise it with him last month. Said it was circumstantial, and we didn't have the resources to go after random leads. Well, I've been doing some more digging, and when I got here, I found a concealed camera in my bedroom and one in the shower."

There is a famous optical illusion: a silhouette of a vase,

which—once you know what to look for—suddenly flips into a sil-houette of two faces looking at each other. (Or vice versa.) You're looking at Dorothy's face and one moment you could have sworn she's excited, turned on—and the next, she's frightened. *Context is everything*.

"What do you think's going on?" you ask her.

She shoves her glass to one side of the table and leans forward. "I can't tell you the details. But part of what we do is abstract social-network analysis on waves, IM, email, phone calls—looking for indicators of pathological communications patterns. If you can track who's talking to who, you can work out which parts of an organization work together, and see emergent patterns of behaviour. It goes back to the classic study on Enron's email corpus in the noughties, but there's been a lot of work since then on agent-assisted NLP and transitive clique identification ... There's also some promising work on determination of ethical or conspiratorial networks. There are other data sets we can trawl exhaustively—the banking crisis, the full corpus of internal communications left behind in the wake of the Goldman Sachs collapse. All the data sets from businesses we've audited since the corporate-responsibility cri-teria were introduced, suitably blinded and anonymized. We use them to spot warning signs. You get a different pattern of com-munication in groups who're colluding to instigate a cover-up, for instance."

At this point, you're working hard to keep your eyes open. Dorothy would have made a kick-ass accountant if she hadn't decided to go into corporate psychoanalysis: She could bore for Europe in the Olympics if she wanted to. But you ken where she's going with this. It's not so dissimilar to what you do in the Innovative Crime Investigation Unit—which, come to think of it, is how you met her in the first place, at a conference on pre-emp-tive gang-crime prevention. "What did you find?"

"What got my attention is the bank I'm here to audit—I got an anonymous tip to look into something and, well, there's a pattern of communication in their investment arm that looks worryingly similar to some of the crazier stuff that was going on in 2007. Subprime investments, dangerous quant stuff. Unethical, if not illegal. Only it's not real estate this time, Liz. I pulled the audit trail, and it turns out they're investing heavily in options trades based on government bonds from a breakaway republic in the back end of Asia.

"What's alarming me is … round about 2009, one of the things that happened during the great recession was that banks almost universally ran out of liquidity, all over the world, simultaneously. It got to the point where national regulators started turning a blind eye when their banks accepted deposits in cash from, uh, irregular sources. Money laundering. Some say up to a third of a trillion dollars in black money was laundered into the global banking system during the crash. It was the last hurrah of the great drugs cartels: Decriminalization and the dollar collapse effectively bankrupted them over the next decade. But ending the war on drugs didn't end organized crime, and there are still gangs out there with money to launder. Anyway, I got a tip-off. Began looking for signs of weirdness in the money supply in the, the Republic of Issyk-Kulistan. We've got far less data on them than on our own banks, but I didn't have to look hard. If they're so poor, and they've got a 40 per cent unemployment rate, how come their GDP rose 30 per cent on independence?

"Anyway? I took it to my line manager, and he told me to lay off. It's all inconclusive, and anyway, it's outside our purview. Drop it completely, in other words. Then I got sent up here to do a routine audit, and it turns out that my hotel room's bugged. Also—I think I spotted a man following me yesterday. On the tram, home from work. I never thought I'd say this, but I'm scared, Liz."

* * *

There's a time to stand on your work/life balance metric, and a time to throw the rule-book out the window. Dorothy is clearly frightened—so scared it took her three cocktails and a presumptively bug-free bar to open up to you. Unfortunately, a lot of what she told you is as confidential as the contents of your own ongoing investigations (i.e. it's a honking great disciplinary—or even criminal—offence to talk about it out of school), not to mention reeking of some kind of artificial reality game to anyone who doesn't know that she really *is* a chartered social-pathology analyst who works for the Department of Trade and Industry's Ethical Oversight Inspectorate. (A fancy way of saying she's a canary in the kind of coal mine where they call the Serious Fraud Office to deal with the cave-ins.)

So, despite being off duty, you put the battery back in your phone and file, in quick succession: an open case report ("female reports being trailed by unidentified male") with a note that this is subject to investigation under the Protection from Harassment Act; a note for the intelligence desk (subject reports threatening behaviour: Due to sensitive nature of employment they suspect a possible violation of Whistleblower Protection Act); and finally a memo to yourself ("look into organized crime/connection with Issyk-Kulistan"), which you will probably off-load onto Moxie's overflowing to-do heap on the morrow.

The latter might be treading dangerously close to misuse of police resources for personal gain, but your soft-shoe shuffle if anyone asks will revolve around a third-party tip-off about persons of interest to an ongoing organized-crime investigation in another force area: At worst, the skipper will yell at you and deliver his #3 Not Getting Distracted lecture again.

All of which adds up to this: If Dorothy needs to talk to a con-

trol-room officer in a hurry, they'll clock her CopSpace trail, realize that a detective inspector's taking her concerns seriously, and
listen. (Probably.) Which is the sort of thing that sometimes saves
lives, and certainly you'll sleep a wee bit more soundly for knowing she's safe under the watching eyes of your colleagues. "That's
filed," you tell her, and yawn. "Are you going to be okay for the
now?"

"I'll have to be." She smiles shakily as she stands up. "I'll not
be asking you to come up to my room." She rolls her eyes in the
direction of the camera dome behind the bar, and you don't have
the heart to remind her that for every one she can see, there'll be at
least two that she doesn't. "Saturday ... your place?"

You stand up, too. "It's yours. If you want to come back with
me tonight—"

She leans forward, and of an instant you're hugging each other.
Her breath is hot against your neck. "Better not," she murmurs. "If
I'm really being watched, I'm contagious. All the same, I'm going
to check into a different hotel tomorrow and hope it throws them,
whoever they are."

"Sounds like a good idea."

"I think so. So. Are we on for the weekend?"

"If you want—"

She turns her head and kisses you hard on the mouth. You swallow a gasp, suddenly acutely aware that you're in public—then she
pulls back, leaving your lips tingling. "Yes, I *want*. Good night, darling." Her smile is a fey thing. It fades as she walks towards the
lobby, leaving you standing by the table, your nipples tight, your
breath stolen, and your head full of harm.

ANWAR: Diplomat

Over the next four days you fall into a comfortable work-day pattern. Get out of bed, go to the bathroom and get dressed and go downstairs to the kitchen, where Bibi has just about finished getting the breakfast down the bairns before she heads out to sign into the pharmacy at the Leith Walk Tesco. You drink a glass of tea, eat your muesli, grab your phone, and kiss Bibi good-bye. From your front door, it's twenty minutes to the office on foot or, if it's pishing down, thirty minutes by way of a quick dash to a shelter and a long wait for the tram.

Not much happens at the office. A couple of times a day, some chancer rings your buzzer, wanting a bag of bread mix and a novelty tourist brochure. (You've got a stack of the things in a cardboard display by the door; they cycle tiredly through a grey-scale slide show of yaks, yurts, and tractor factories—the Ministry of Tourism's budget doesn't stretch to colour e-ink, let alone hiring a photographer to update their archive footage.) You sadistically abuse the rubber plant whenever you can be bothered and expense a couple of big colour picture frames for the wall, loaded with the least-kitsch corners of the Ministry's wallpaper archive—mostly mountains and mosques—to make it look more like an authentic consulate.

On day three, a certain existential anomie sets in. So you amuse yourself with your bootleg phone and specs: You pull down your favourite procedural wallpaper from the cloud and overlay the bare, beige office walls with a gigantic play-space hosting an improbable orgy-themed mashup from XXXMen and BackRoom-Boyz. It's machinima-generated real-time porn, and you don't want to look at their faces for too long or you'll get creeped out by the inbred uncanny valley features, but all that pumping and writhing and sucking is a good distraction from the fact that is slowly sneaking up on you: You're *bored*.

Here you are in your good business suit, sitting at a desk in the consulate, prim and proper as can be, like a maiden aunt haunted by fantasies of debauchery. *And there is nothing to fucking do.* Welcome to boredomspace. Since you hung out your shingle you have entertained one visiting trade delegation, six assorted shifty-eyed locals in search of a loaf, two adventurous backpackers, a yak-milk importer looking to make an end-run around EU animal-husbandry regulations, and seven confused visitors looking for the games company upstairs.

There are, of course, the language lessons: On your own initiative you've expensed a set of Rosetta Stone courseware on Kyrgyz, and you're trying to spend half an hour a day on it. But you've never had much of a knack for language study, you keep tripping over the Cyrillic alphabet, and the spoken tongue sounds like you're gargling rusty nails (and leaves your throat feeling like it, too). Google Translate doesn't handle Kyrgyz very well: Luckily the Ministry of Foreign Affairs conducts all their correspondence in mangled English. You really wouldn't bother except for a nagging sense that at the next interview, it might be good to know what they're saying behind your back.

In the end, you find yourself reading the small print on the back of a bag of bread mix and thinking about what the Gnome said about home brew. *Shite beer,* he'd said, *unless you add a cofactor.* Well, it's not like you know a lot about brewing to begin with, is it? So you hop on the web and, at considerable risk to your soul, begin searching for websites dedicated to the unclean pursuit.

When the buzzer goes off, you're queasily engrossed in an account of certain jail-cell antics involving buckets, sugar, yeast, and unspeakable contaminants. The things neds will do to get off their heids ... you jump, swear quietly, and hit the entryphone button. "Come in."

You're standing up when the door opens. Your visitor is probably white underneath the grime, walks with an odd shuffle, and could benefit from a shower and a session at a launderette. He's probably about twenty and painfully thin. You smile politely. "Welcome to the Issyk-Kulistan Consulate, sir. Would you mind stating your name and business?"

"Ahm Jaxxie. Icannaehingyurrrbagaffbreidmix, likesay?"

Oh, he's one of *them.* You nod sympathetically, walk over to the trunkful of INSECT-FREE FAIR TRADE ORGANIC BREAD MIX BARLEY-RYE, and pull out a bag. "One of these?" you ask, remembering to breathe through your mouth as you approach him.

"Gimmedat hingmie." He makes a lunge for the bag, and you pull it away from him. He wears no specs, which is probably a good thing: He doesn't look like the type to appreciate the panting contents of the leather sling he's standing in front of in pornspace.

"You know how to use it, right?" You stare at him. "You know about the cofactor. What is it?"

Jaxxie stares at you in confusion. "Whut?"

"The stuff you add to the bread mix when you're making beer. What is it?"

"Whut? Ayedinnaekenyeraxent, man. Whityurwantin?"

"What. Have. You. Been. Told. To. Add. To. This. When. You. Brew?" You hold the bag up. Jaxxie's eyes track the bag like a dog hoping for a treat, oblivious to the gamine sailor boy and the pair of huge leather bears making out lasciviously at his feet.

"Ung. Hingmy. Aw*that*." He produces a small glass bottle of tablets from somewhere in his Swiss Army jacket. You peer at the label: Selenium. "Gedditat Hollandunbarrut, likesay? Fuckin'ippies."

"Very good." You smile ingratiatingly and hand over the bread mix. "Don't do anything with it that *I* wouldn't do." You wink at the virtual Marine who's rubbing his crotch on Jaxxie's leg and show him the door. *Dietary supplements, right.* The virtual marine is strangling the one-eyed trouser python and making calf eyes at you: Annoyed, you kill the wallpaper and drop back into beige-walled boredomspace. "Fucking hippies." You sit back down at the desk and go back to reading up on home brewing. Maybe, you reflect, jailhouse recipes aren't the best way forward.

* * *

You are a lucky man in many respects. You have a house (a genuine, authentic house with its own roof! Not a tenement!), an adoring wife with a respectable and moderately lucrative profession, and two bouncing children who squeal with delight when they see you (although of late you could swear that Naseem is holding back a little, in a faint foreshadowing of adolescent male surliness).

You also have two aunts, an uncle, a mother-in-law, six assorted grandparents, a vast and inchoate clan of in-laws and first cousins and nieces and nephews, and other, more distant relations whose precise proximity to your blood line can only be expressed algebraically—

What you *don't* have is privacy.

Privacy is a luxury; to buy it you need to be able to buy space and fit locks, to switch off the phone and live without fear of dependency on others. Privacy is a peculiarly twentieth-century concept, an artefact of the Western urban middle classes: Before then, only the super rich could afford it, and since the invention of email and the mobile phone, it has largely slipped away.

Not that you normally need privacy. Your home life is happily lived in the presence of others: It's not as if you don't share a bed with your wife or put up with her mother popping round for a bag of rice and a sink-side chat every day. The other corners of your life you discreetly hide away in public houses and public toilets (although to be perfectly truthful, the latter make you increasingly nervous: You've begun to pick your partners for their bedroom décor as much as their looks). Still, once in a while, you want to bring something home with you without attracting Bibi's attention or the bairns' curiosity. And so, it's time to go up to the loft again.

When you bought (or, more accurately, inherited) the house, you knew it had a loft—but not much more. When you first got up there, you weren't impressed, but since then you've fitted DIY insulation and nailed it down with boards and carpet tiles so you can walk around. A loft ladder followed, and LED lighting tiles and mains outlets; you're hoping soon to have enough cash to pay for a dormer window to replace the Velux. Bibi doesn't come up here (she doesn't like ladders—gets dizzy), and you've told her it's a storeroom. Which is true up to a point, but you've got a chair and some bean bags and a projection TV and a small fridge for the beer. Before the filth collared you, you kept your water-pipe and a stash up here: But you don't want Mr. Webber to get the idea you're living a "disorganized lifestyle," so you've reluctantly laid off the skunk. There's also a tin-can aerial lined up on Cousin Tariq's roof, an interesting router running firmware he downloaded off the dark side of the net, and a clean pad he gave you to work on when you got out of nick. But you haven't spent much time up here since you got the new job.

That's about to change, isn't it?

There's a wee hole-in-the-wall shop just off Easter Road, run by a middle-aged white guy with a straggly beard—Cousin Itt would probably grunt *'ippie* on sight—that services the home-brew hobbyists. The shop smells of yeast and hot plastic from the fabber he's got in the back for running up obscure knobbly connectors; most of the stuff he sells is off-the-shelf, though. When you walk in, he's deep in conversation with a fat middle-aged woman with crimson hair, whose unseasonal shaggy black coat makes her look like a tank in the sheep army.

You spend a few minutes gawping at the gleaming stainless steel machine—it looks like a dissected automatic washer/dryer—that sits in pride of place on the shop counter. It's some sort of German vorsprung-durch-technik microprocessor-managed brewery in a box—put in raw materials, select program, leave for a month, drink the output—but you don't have a thousand euros to spare for it. Then you poke around the shelves for a bit, hunting for the items on your shopping list. The shopkeeper's still yacking to the woman, who seems to be some sort of local beer monster, and pays no attention to you until you get to the throat-clearing toe-tapping stage. "Aye, sir? What can I do you for?"

You ignore the slip of the tongue. "I need these. And, uh, a siphon. And an airlock, I think." You've been doing your homework, but you're not entirely sure what an airlock looks like until he steps out from behind the counter and produces a transparent plastic hingmy.

"Boiled water goes here," he says, showing you how. "Then you stick it in the bung like so. If you're just getting started, you might want one of our starter packs. What kind of beer were you after?"

"Um, I've already got one," you say: "a present."

"IPA or Lager?" asks the woman, chipping in. "Is it bottom-fermenting or top-fermenting?"

You look at her blankly. The shopkeeper clocks what's up and none-too-subtly eyeballs the nosy lass to butt out. "It's okay," he says quietly, "I've got a starter FAQ on the website. In five languages." He passes you a card. "If you want, I've got a friend who can rent you some cellar space—"

"No, no, that won't be necessary," you say hurriedly: "I just need the, uh, apparatus?" Obviously he kens the ethnic angle, thinks you're wanting the opportunity to quaff a wee bevvy at home with no betraying six-packs.

"Well that's okay, then. Twenty-four ninety-six, please."

You hand over the cash and flee, then realize once you're out of the door that you forgot to ask for a bag and you're going home clutching a huge plastic bucket labelled FERMENTATION BIN and decorated with pictures of overflowing beer glasses. And he forgot to offer you one! *Have these people no shame?*

Bibi, for a miracle, is not in the kitchen when you open the front door. You head upstairs at a dash and hurl the incriminating bucket up the loft steps before she has a chance to see it. You've still got to figure out how to get twenty litres of freshly boiled water up to it, and how to keep it warm afterwards, but at least she doesn't have to know about you conducting your filthy *haram* experiments under her roof.

There is, of course, the old electric kettle, if you can remember where it's lurking. It's corroded and leaks alarmingly around the water gauge, but you don't think Bibi threw it out. You clamber down the ladder and go into the kitchen to hunt around. Finally you think to look in the cellar, where the mains distribution board, the gas meter, and several piles of junk lurk villainously in wait for unshod feet. The kettle is resting under a layer of mouldy plaster dust in one of the slowly deliquescing cardboard boxes. The cellar smells of damp brickwork, and your sinuses clamp shut in protest before you can beat a retreat. Which is why Bibi finds you in the kitchen, clutching a dusty kettle and breathing heavily through your mouth, when she bustles in with a wheelie-bag full of groceries.

"Help me unpack this," she says breathlessly, then notices the kettle: "Oh good, are you taking it for recycling?"

"I need it for the office," you say, then the breath catches in your throat as a convulsive sneezing fit takes hold. "Aaagh! Choo!"

"Not over the saag, you naughty man!" She thrusts a wad of tissue at you. "This bag needs refrigerating. When you're feeling better?"

You blink red-rimmed eyes at her. "The cellar is *damp*."

"Oh dear, has the dehumidifier filled up again?"

"What dehumidifier?"

"The one we borrowed from Martin, silly. Don't you remember?"

She looks at you with a speculative expression that puts you in mind of a stableman sizing up an elderly mule for the glue factory. You sigh. Now that she mentions it, you remember her telling you something about dampness and a gadget the old guy next door had offered to loan her. "No, no I didn't," you admit. "You say it's filling up?"

"Yes," she says brightly: "It needs emptying once a week!"

"Damp. In the cellar." If Sameena's plans to try and hold a family reunion in Lahore to corral everyone into buying into some kind of extended family takeover of a half-completed hotel complex had worked, you wouldn't have a problem with rising damp in the cellar. (You might have to dodge the occasional lunatic in explosive corsetry, but it can't be any more risky than running the gauntlet of the random bampots down the Foot of the Walk on a Saturday night.) Alas, you were one of the idiots who balked at the idea of turning to the hospitality trade. "Besides, it rains too much there!" you moaned at your mother-in-law, regurgitating childhood memories of a June vacation. Oh, the irony.

"Yes. I think it's getting worse." Your wife tilts her head on one side as she looks at you. "What are you going to do about it?"

You sigh, deeply. "I'll see if I can round up someone who knows about such things."

She hands you a cardboard punnet full of mushrooms. "You'd better. Or we'll be growing these down there."

You help Bibi unpack the groceries that need refrigerating, then retreat upstairs to the bathroom, clutching the kettle. Not being entirely stupid, you wash the filthy thing out in the wash-basin, then take it up to the attic and return for a bucket of water (which you manhandle up the ladder precariously, with much sloshing and dripping).

Finally, you glance at the brew shop's website, where there is indeed a multilingual FAQ. It's in Arabic, Turkish, and Farsi among other languages, if you recognize the characters correctly: You'll have to settle for English.

"First boil 20 litres of water and allow to cool to 40 degrees ... "

You plug the kettle in, fill it up, throw the switch, and all the lights and electrics go out. A few seconds later, you hear Bibi cursing most immodestly downstairs.

You're really going to have to tackle the damp now, aren't you? Otherwise, you're never going to hear the end of it.

* * *

On day four of your new occupation, you receive an invitation to a diplomatic reception at the Georgian consulate.

Actually, you received it on day two, or rather your spam filter received it, whereupon it languished in MIME-encapsulated limbo until you could be bothered to skim the contents of the mailbox, swear, then freak out and run squawking in circles.

"You are invited to attend an informal cheese and wine reception at the Georgian Consulate on Brunswick Street on—" (*tonight*) "—

at 7:30 P.M., hosted by the Trans-Caucasian Inward Investment and Tourism Trust. RSVP, etc."

After about fifteen minutes you wise up and dash off a hasty query to Head Office: *Should I stay or should I go?* You haven't been keeping up with the daily bulletins from the Diplomatic Service—they are replete with information about yak wool exports, the lemon harvest, and the urgent need to redress the balance-of-trade deficit, but not so fascinatingly full of matters of statecraft—so you have not the veriest inkling of a clue as to whether the Independent Republic of Issyk-Kulistan is on kissing terms with Georgia, or at war, or something in between. All you really know about politics in the part of the world you represent is that it can be alarmingly personal at times, not to mention bloody-minded, brutal, Byzantine, and any number of other unpleasant adjectives beginning with "b."

There's no immediate reply, so you call the Gnome. "Help," you say succinctly.

There's a brief, pregnant pause. "Help what?"

"I've been invited to a diplomatic reception! Help!"

"You're beyond help, laddie." He sounds amused. "You'll just have to fend for yourself. Is it one of the Middle East missions?"

"No!" You swallow. "It's Georgia."

"Georgia next to Alabama or—oh, I see. Well you may be in luck, then: They drink alcohol. Just remember not to mention the South Ossetian question, the Transnistrian dispute, Azerbaijani shi'ite separatism, or the existence of Abkhazia. You've never heard of any of those places, so you should be able to quaff a free bevvy or six and leg it without giving mortal offence."

"How do you know all this?" you ask in something like awe.

"I looked it up on wikipedia. Oh, and try to remember, the Russians are *not* their friends. Have a fun party! Cunt." He hangs up.

(*Cunt* isn't an unusual expostulation from the Gnome; it's commonly directed at any lucky acquaintance who has gotten to stick their gristle missile in a particularly cute twink, and indicates envy rather than ire. Nevertheless, you feel acutely inadequate: It's a shame you can't send the man himself in your place, but he'd probably piss in the punchbowl and start a trade war or something. Just to drop you in it. The cunt.)

There is no reply from the Foreign Ministry, and with a sinking heart you realize it's Thursday afternoon over here and probably closing in on sundown—they'll be knocking off early for Friday. You're on your own. So you apply yourself to wiki-fiddling for a couple of hours of fascinated voyeuristic geopolitical prurience— you had *no idea* the IRIK had such *interesting* neighbours. Then it's knocking off time for you, too, with a few hours to fill until the party.

The shortest route to the Brunswick Street consulate is via Calton Hill, and your favourite pub; so you decide to fortify yourself with some water of life and a pitta wrap before you nip round and do the James Bond cocktail-circuit thing.

The Gnome is not in residence at this time. Neither is Olaf, the Norwegian barman you quite fancy. It's still quiet—the Friday night meat market hasn't opened yet—so you sit in a corner and quietly shovel back your ale and chicken tikka wrap. You've got time to borrow a pad, boot an anonymous guest VM, and spend half an hour poking around a somewhat dodgy chat room Tariq introduced you to—one that you're not supposed to go within a thousand kilometres of during your probation, maybe because it has something to do with the seamy underside of Internet affiliate-scheme marketing. (But they'd have to swab the screen for DNA to prove you were there: And anyway, you're just looking, aren't you?) Right now it's a big disappointment. Nobody seems to be posting there this week—it's like the usual denizens have all gone on holiday. *Or been lifted by the Polis, more like,* you think uneasily and log out of the anonymous guest account, which goes poofing up to bit-rot heaven.

With a sinking heart, you stand and make your way round the hill towards London Road, and thence towards the Georgian consulate, which is itself ensconced in a different-kind-of-Georgian town house opposite a row of imposingly colonnaded hotel frontages. Scotland, being one of those odd semi-autonomous states embedded within the EU post-independence and still only semi-devolved from their former parent nation, doesn't rate actual embassies. Nevertheless, the glowing affluence of a real consulate fills you with mild envy: There's a shiny black BMW hybrid in diplomatic plates plugged into the charge point outside the front door, and a flag on a pole sticking out of the second-floor window-casement. Not to mention bunting and coloured lights inside the wedged-open front door.

A Scottish woman in a trouser suit and expensive eyewear clocks you and smiles professionally. "Mr. Hussein. We've been looking forward to meeting you! Have you had your tea, then?"

Your ears perk up at this decidedly non-Edinburgh hospitality, but your stomach's been rumbled: You nod. "Alas, yes, Ms.—"

"Macintosh, Fi Macintosh." She beckons you in like an affable praying mantis—she's about ten centimetres taller than you, and looms alarmingly. "Notary and assistant to the first consul. That's Dr. Mazniashvili. Won't you come in? We have grape juice—or wine, if you're so inclined."

"There's more than one of you?" you ask, as she ushers you into a space not unlike a dentist's waiting room—except that the receptionist's counter has been stacked three bottles deep in refreshments, and there's a table stacked high with trays of canapés. Several patients sit in chairs around the room or stand in small clusters, talking quietly with pained expressions. You pounce on a tumbler, splash a generous shot of Talisker into it, and raise it: "Your health."

Fi half smiles, then picks up a tall glass full of orange juice. "Prosit," she replies. "The meat cocktail snacks are halal, by the way." She takes a sip. "Yes, there are four of us here, but only the first consul is a Georgian national. I understand you're not actually from Issyk-Kulistan yourself?"

"No." You glance from side to side. Here you are, trapped with a glass of single malt and a red-headed stick insect—what can you say? "That is to say, there aren't any natives of Issyk-Kulistan in Scotland, as far as the Foreign Ministry was able to determine, so they put the job out to tender and ended up hiring me."

"Ah." She nods slowly. "One of *those* jobs. I don't suppose it's terribly busy, is it?"

You suck in your lower lip and clutch your tumbler close. "No, not really."

She nods again. "You're the sixth, you know."

"The sixth? Sixth what?"

"Sixth pseudo." She peers at you over the rim of her glasses, which are recording everything and projecting a head-up display on her retinas. "They offered you a steady job in return for processing forms, notarizing documents, sorting out accommodation for distressed natives, and so on. Didn't they?"

"I don't see what business of yours my employment is," you say, perhaps a trifle more waspishly than is tactful.

She blinks. "I'm sorry, I didn't mean to intrude." She nods sidelong at a fellow with a face like the north end of a southbound freight locomotive. "That's Gerald Williams. He's the honorary consul for the Popular Democratic Republic of Saint Lucia. You might want to look up the, ah, constitutional crisis there seven years ago. They were the first pseudo—in their case, they used to be a real country, albeit a wee one. But after the big hurricane, a consortium of developers literally bought the place—made the population an offer they couldn't refuse, relocate somewhere with better weather and about ten thousand euros a head. Now it's a shell country, specializing in banking and carbon-credit exports—they're still signatory to the climate protocols."

She knocks back her OJ like she's trying to wash away the taste of a dead slug. "They're legit, if shady. I shouldn't really say this, but I hope you double-checked who you were doing business with. One of these days, we're going to see a really nasty pseudo, and the consequences are going to be unpleasant all round." She smiles tightly. "Georgia's celebrating it's thirtieth anniversary later this year, and we're throwing a party. Perhaps you'd like to come?"

"I'd—love to," you manage. "What did you do"—*to get this gig*, you're about to say: It comes out as—"before you worked for the Georgian consulate?"

"A doctorate in international relations, specializing in the history of the Transcaucasus in the latter half of the twentieth century. I did my field work in Tbilisi." She reaches for the mixers and tops up her OJ, then adds a splash of vodka. "It was this, or move to Brussels. I can do simultaneous translation between English and Kartuli, you know." Her smile broadens. "And yourself?"

Rumbled. You shrug. "I'm trying to learn Kyrgyz." *Badly*, you don't add. Nor do you mention that your highest degree is a lower second from the polytechnic of real life with a postgraduate diploma in Scallie Studies from Saughton. "And I've got a great line in bread-mix samples from the People's Number Four Grain Products Factory of Issyk-Kulistan. Guaranteed insect-free!"

"So your republic exists primarily to export bread mix to the EU?" She sniffs, evidently amused. "Wait here, Mr. Hussein, I'll be right back." And with that she disappears into the front parlour of the Georgian consulate.

You amble around the room for a while. The background chatter is getting louder, and more visitors are arriving—to your untrained eye it's impossible to tell whether they're diplomats or art-school drop-outs, but they seem to know what they're doing, and a high proportion of them look even less Scottish than you. You find yourself chatting to a poet who lives in Pilton—apparently an émigré from Tashkent, if you understand his rapid-fire Turkish-accented Scots dialect correctly. You smile and nod politely and work your way towards the bottom of your tumbler.

The world is taking on a rosy glow of bonhomie when Fi—or should that be Dr. Macintosh?—returns to the party. As it happens, you've just turned away from your poet to refill your glass, so she heads straight towards you. She's got a small, dog-eared paperback in one hand. "Sorry, ran into a spot of bother in the kitchen," she says unapologetically. "Listen, you're obviously new to all this, and I suddenly remembered I had a book that came in handy when I was getting started. An introductory text." She pushes it at you with a slightly furtive expression: The penny drops, and you slide it into your jacket pocket and thank her effusively. "No, really, it's the least I could do. Don't take it too seriously, but you'd be surprised how far it'll take you. It does what it says on the can." She smiles. "I'd better circulate now—we're beginning to fill up. See you around ... "

As she turns away, you risk a quick scooby at the book's cover. On the rebound from the double-take you glare at her receding back—then remember where you are and whose whisky you're drinking, and force yourself to calm down. *The Idiot's Pocket Guide to International Diplomacy* indeed!

What kind of amateur does she take you for?

TOYMAKER: Hostile
Takeover

It's like the punch-line to a knock-knock joke gone wrong:

(Knock-knock)

"Who's there?"

"I was looking for Mike? Is he in?"

"Please step inside, sir. Do you have some form of ID?"

You are not stupid: You aren't carrying anything illegal on your person—it's all in your head. Even your fall-guy phone is only guilty of behaving in a shifty manner. So you do not attempt to flee. Instead, you do as the uniformed gentleman requests and meekly step into the front hall to help him with his enquiries, whereupon you realize that something is very wrong indeed because the walls and ceiling and floor are covered in clear plastic anticontamination sheets, and there's a scene of crime officer in a bunny suit coming down the stairs. "Will a driving licence do?" you ask the cop.

You can see him giving you the quick up and down with his glasses, which is an oh-shit moment. "What's your name?" he asks.

"John, John Christie," you volunteer, reaching for your wallet. "Is Mike here? Is there some kind of problem?" You force an expression of worried concern, a little apprehension. Under the circumstances, it comes easily enough.

"A driving licence will do. Pass it here, please." You fumble the card and slide it towards him. Most of the John Christie ID is loaded in your phone, from microcredits to bank accounts—it's very solid. "Why are you here?"

"I was hoping to see ... Mike ... " You slow your spiel as if uncertain, even though any fool can tell that something has gone seriously non-linear here. You make an effort to memorize the dibble's name-plate: PC BROWN, presumably working for INSPECTOR SCARLET of Rainbow Division. Just your luck you aren't wearing a lifelogger, or you could stand on your rights a little harder—but no, that might not be a good idea. Every instinct is telling you to disengage. Mike's obviously in big trouble, which means you won't be hiring him—that's for sure. You need to get clear before the cops start focusing on you. A factoid pops out of the Mike Blair file and screams for your attention, and you instantly realize it's a good one. "He said to drop by if I was ever in Edinburgh."

PC Brown turns your driving licence over in his hand, and you can see some flickering in his glasses. He's got a contactless reader, online to the DVLA database and then back to CopSpace once they've authenticated it. The photograph matches, and the licence is genuine. He glances back at you and twitches his head, superimposing a head-up ghost image beside your face. Then he hands the card back. "Where did you meet Mr. ... ?"

"Mike? It was at the Admiral Duncan, in London, about six months ago. Or maybe eight? Or was it after Pride? Anyway, we, er ... got to know each other quite well." You clear your throat. "It's personal. He invited me to drop round if I was ever in Edinburgh, and I'm here for the next week on business, and I was hoping he didn't have anything else on for the weekend. Is something wrong?"

Brown's expression morphs through a whole sequence of emotions as you give him the Big Lie, backed up by some telegraphic wiggling of eyebrows and seasoned with just the tiniest bit of camp. You have not, in fact, ever met Mike (and you hope to hell he's lying dead in an autopsy room so he can't contradict you); even if you had, you wouldn't want to fuck him. On the other hand, the Operation's files went into quite a lot of detail on the subject of his personal life, and getting off with him after a Pride march in what has long been one of the biggest knocking shops in London is entirely plausible. The Scottish Polis get all red-faced and sweaty at the merest suggestion of locker-room homophobia: It's amusing to watch the cop switch from investigating-person-of-interest mode to dealing with bereaved significant other in the space of a sentence. (It works even better if there *is* some latent locker-room homophobia, so you're careful to lean just a little too close and hold the eye contact a second too long.)

"Is something wrong?" you ask, feigning worry, as he begins to open his mouth. And you know that, really, *nothing* is wrong. If you were neurotypical and going up against the speech stress analysis he's watching in his fancy-pants glasses, you'd be in deep doo-doo, getting flustered from all the falsehoods: But you're not, and the cops' sexy tech passes the handicap to *their* side when they get to deal with the likes of you. It's only if they get you in front of a psych with a PCL-R check-list that you've got to start worrying.

"Mr. Christie, John, I'm really sorry." He takes a deep breath. "Would you like to sit down?" He's all solicitude, waving you into the spotless kitchen (which is interestingly bereft of forensic turds). "I'm very sorry, but—"

"Oh God," you say, shoving the "distraught" slider all the way up to eleven. "He's been in an accident, hasn't he?"

There's another cop coming down the staircase, and they're going into full-on sit-down-and-have-a-cup-of-tea mode, as if they expect you to go into shock. "What makes you think there's been an accident?" asks Brown, but it's just a residual autonomic cop reflex—he's already bought your spiel on outline.

"Mike's big on water sports," you say off-hand, then make to look horrified. "Oh God. What's happened?"

"I'm really sorry." PC Brown looks sideways at the newcomer, DET SGT GREEN. (*Yeah, right,* you think.) "Um. There's been a, a fatality, sir. We're still trying to ascertain the precise nature of events." Which means it *wasn't* an accident. "I'm sorry to intrude on your grief, sir. But if you don't mind, I'd like to take a saliva sample." They've already got your fingerprint biometrics off the driving licence: This means they're serious about logging identities.

You nod shakily. "Sure. Oh God." You hunch up a little and do the weepy thing—not too much of it, you don't want to ham it up and tip them off. "I can't believe it." Which is *entirely* true. Mikey's dossier said he's never been involved in anything serious enough to warrant a hit—that was one of the reasons you were going to interview him. Walking in on a homicide investigation is classic dumb bad luck. Your immediate task is to stop it graduating into a classic fuck-up, which is best done by cooperating with the cops for the time being. There are forms you can serve later to get "John Christie's" DNA taken off the database once they figure out that he's an innocent bystander, then you can retire the ID with a "do not recycle" flag.

Brown produces a sample tube and a cotton swab, and invites you to say "Aaagh," which you do with alacrity. After which it's all tea and sympathy, minus the tea, and "we're terribly sorry, you're free to go, sir," after they get you to repeat in front of their specs that you haven't seen Mike for at least half a year. And why should you not be free to go? "John Christie" is simply a contact whose state-issued biometric ID checks out, who has donated a DNA sample for the investigation, and who is at best an embarrassing distraction from the job in hand.

You leave by the front door and pedal very slowly, being careful to wobble for the cameras until you're out of sight of the house. *There's been a fatality.* Hence all the plastic sheeting and the DNA swab dance routine. *We're still trying to ascertain the precise nature of events.* Which means it wasn't an accident: Accidents don't call for a detective sergeant to cover the site. Something has gone seriously fucking wrong here, and it looks like you may need to abort the operation, close up shop, and leave town on the schedule you just fed the Polis.

But first, you've got a fall-back option.

* * *

You bicycle away from the former abode of Michael Blair, your mood very dark. Somehow, all the fun has been sucked out of this venture before it even got started. Number One Client had the supreme bad taste to get himself whacked at a maximally inconvenient time. You've still got a job of work to do, but the hotel lost your luggage, and on top of that you've got the added vexation of falling within the penumbra of police sousveillance (which will take some work to get disentangled from when it's time to leave).

Luckily—ironically—you haven't done anything illegal yet. All you have to do is be John Christie for a week, then switch to another primary ID and stay clean while the paper-work to pull his DNA off the system chugs along. It's not like you're a serial killer or anything, is it? But it's still a nuisance.

So you decide to execute your fall-back plan and visit your Number Two Client.

While you were doing the weepy in front of PC Brown the sun came out and most of the clouds have fucked off to Glasgow. Alas, there's a brisk breeze blowing. You can die of sunburn and hypothermia during a Scottish summer—simultaneously, with added insomnia on top from the midnight sun. (It goes below the horizon, but it never really gets dark.) Swearing at the weather under your breath, you cycle uphill into the wind for half a kilometre, then pause at a cycle rack to ditch the wheels.

Once you're clear of the pedal-powered snitch, you can safely reboot the phone and hit the online maps for a route to Number Two Client. Actually, you're querying for a route to the boutique chocolate shop in Fountainbridge, above which they live and run their business—another way to avoid cropping up in a CopSpace crawl—but no matter. You haven't memorized this particular route because you expected to be holed up with Mikey-boy for the whole morning and a chunk of the afternoon, but again: no matter. Your candidate for chief operations officer may have drawn the ace of spades, but you're still holding a card for the CFO. And according to the dossier head office sent you, Vivian works from home.

The Polis know you're in town, so hiding your trail may actually be a bad idea at this point. Accordingly, you hoof it to the nearest bus-stop and call a micro. While you wait for it, you review what the Operation knows about her (and is willing to stick in a mangled bitmap image file on an off-shore cloud).

Vivian Crolla. Age forty-eight, single, chartered accountant by trade—not so much an adornment to her profession as a butt-nugget dangling from its arse-hairs. She has been investigated by the ACA disciplinary committee three times but escaped unscathed save for a reprimand on the first occasion (now timed-out). She's been investigated by the Revenue twice (inconclusively). She has come to the attention of the Serious Fraud Office and escaped without receiving as much as a police caution. She's so slippery, you could skin her and market the hide as a surface for frying pans. And that's just her public persona.

What the Operation knows about Vivian is enough that if you were with the Polis, you'd be smacking your chops and writing her up for the Procurator Fiscal while mentally drafting the press release. When she was the Gorilla's banker, she ran the most efficient money-laundering operation ever seen north of Hadrian's Wall, and if it wasn't for the ongoing deflationary spiral and a slightly embarrassing problem repatriating her overseas assets while under the nose of the Revenue, she'd be living in a castle in Fife with a helicopter and pilot for the weekly shopping trips to Jenners. As it is, you figure she's only marking time until she retires in style, at which point she'll leg it to Palermo, where they have retirement homes stacked to the ceiling with her type of merry widow.

The bus, when it comes, is empty. You hole up in what used to be the driver's seat, and it moves off silently. It's a great way to tour the Athens of the North, and you watch entranced as it rolls over the speed pillows and cobble-stones on its way south-east. You've bid a fiver for a route divert, and for a miracle there's no other money-bags aboard to up the ante: It's going to take you close to Vivian's front door.

Now, *this* scene is one you haven't rehearsed for, and so you're going to have to play it with a certain delicacy. But it's not rocket science. You've got a handle on Vivian and her history. She's even worked for the Operation before—unwittingly, at a lower level, but nonetheless. There are strings to pull, but she's an experienced player, predictable up to a point. That's why you were leaving her for the second interview.

The bus whines as it crawls up the slope, then totters anaemically along Lothian Road, stopping to pick up and put down the usual losers along the way. You keep yourself buttoned up, avoiding eye contact. (Back home? It'd be a stretch limo with tinted windows all the way. But a start-up job in Scotland calls for the People's Car and plenty of warm bodies to get lost among.) It rolls slowly past your hotel, then the row of pompous fin-de-siècle bank frontages thrown up a couple of decades since and now half-boarded-over: Then at the big five-way intersection, it hangs a right, and your phone pleeps a set-down alert at you.

One hundred and twenty metres to destination. Fucking bus company. You start walking.

This part of town has an uneasy relationship with affluence. Besides the obligatory state-owned Tesco Local, there's a weird mix of closed and barricaded shop-fronts, charity stores with windows stuffed full of last decade's brown leather sofas, and imaginative little boutiques selling up-market tchotchkes. You pass a kebab shop and an Asian jewellery store before you reach the chocolatier and the usual anonymous black door beside it.

There is a buzzer. You mash your thumb on the button for flat 1F2 and wait. And wait. After a minute, you push it again and hold. Just your luck if Vivian's chosen this lunch-time to go do her shopping. There's no reply, but the door opens in your face; a young guy slithers past you, earbuds screwed in as tight as his closed face. You catch the door with your toe and a moment later you're on your way upstairs.

The tenement stairwell is grey and dusty, worn flagstones and black-enamelled cast-iron handrails leading up into the gloom. On the first-floor landing you find three heavy-looking doorways. The tarnished brass name-plate saying CROLLA ASSOCIATES tells you all you need to know, and you push the doorbell beside it. There is, as you expected, no response. You stand, holding your breath.

Well, you've come all this way: Why stop here?

There's a multifunction pen in your pocket. It doesn't look like anything special, but there are five cartridges and a bunch of complicated springs inside that barrel. And there's a wallet in your other pocket, and along with the phone and driving licence, it contains a couple of other cards. One of which might have raised an eyebrow if the Polis had Dumpster-dived your pockets and thought to peel away the laminated stickers to reveal the intricately etched sheet of fullerene-reinforced plastic within. But even then, it's not obvious what the etching is, and you've got an explanation for how you came by it that would get you off the hook under most circumstances. Except these.

You take thirty seconds to twist and warp some springy bits of steel-tough plastic free from the card, another twenty seconds to swap them in place of the ball-point cartridge, and ten seconds to bump the lock. Then you step inside Vivian Crolla's apartment.

* * *

You let the door slip shut behind you, and in that very instant you realize that something is irrevocably awry.

It's never entirely quiet in a Scottish tenement flat. The floor-board-creaking footfalls of upstairs' unseen neighbours. The drone of a news channel on next door's PC. If the windows look out over the front, there's the interminable road noise of a major thoroughfare (muted, now, by last-century standards, but still present). The faint susurration of Arctic methane flowing through the pipe to the fuel cell: the whir of the refrigerator in the kitchen.

The windows face out back, the neighbours are at work, and you can't hear the fridge. Is that all? There's a faint hissing from somewhere.

You glance up. The illumination filtering into the rectangular central hall comes through open doorways, and it has the numinous tint of daylight. You take your picklock card and use its edge to delicately swipe the light switch, leaving no prints.

"Vivian?" you call quietly.

There's a strong floral stink in the flat, as from one of those fucking air fresheners women like to put in the bathroom to make out that they shit roses.

"Vivian?" you ask again, walking towards the living room. "I got your email. Vivian . . . "

There's a scrap of paper on the floor. You frown and bend to pick it up. It's white, overprinted in mostly green ink (with faint yellow and pink tints), approximately six centimetres by twelve in size. You remember its like from your childhood: It's a foreign bank-note. "The Royal Bank of Scotland plc PROMISE TO PAY THE BEARER ON DEMAND ONE POUND STERLING, At their head office here in Edinburgh, by order of the board, 30th March 1999."

Dead words. Dead currency. Dead bank. Broken promise.

Inside the austerely furnished living room, there lies a mattress. It has been cocooned in shrink-wrap plastic, sealed against the elements. The fragile husk of Vivian Crolla forms a mound under the polythene integument, like a pupa bonded to the surface of a leaf. She's barely one metre fifty in her stockinged feet, grey-haired and thin, as if all the juices of a life unlived have been sucked out of her. She's neatly dressed in a dark suit and pearl necklace, all present and correct but for a missing shoe and a premature death. There is a rip in the side of the shrink-wrap, a deep gash that plunges into the interior of the mattress, from which irredeemable green-ink promises bleed halfway across the carpet.

(*Damn her, why couldn't she have stuffed her mattress with fifty-euro notes instead of unrecyclable toilet paper?* a corner of you thinks irreverently.)

You bend close to her and touch her shoulder through the plastic. She's cold and stiff. Someone obviously shrink-wrapped her onto the mattress while she was unconscious or already dead. But who, and why? Rising, you stalk through the kitchen, her office, the bathroom. The stink in the bathroom is chokingly thick, almost unbreathable: The electronic air freshener is farting away like a cow with irritable-bowel syndrome.

You lick your dry lips. "This isn't funny anymore," you complain, an ironic metacommentary on your internal turmoil. Then the true state of jeopardy slams into you like a railway spike of purest distilled paranoia, and you see, with merciless clarity:

Someone has gotten inside your decision loop.

They're a rival or an enemy. They've identified and killed your chosen COO and CFO, hours or days before you were ready to make them employment offers. They're sending you a message: *Get out of town. Get out of town* now. *Run away, little business man, while there's still time.*

You *can't* get out of town, even if you want to. The Polis have got your DNA on file as belonging to John Christie, a contact of Mike Blair (deceased). You need to dance the John-Christie-is-an-innocent-bystander fandango until you can serve the paper-work to get your samples destroyed, or your usefulness to the Operation will be at an end: and with it, your career.

To make matters worse, you're here *now*. Vivian Crolla isn't going to vanish silently from Scottish society without anyone asking questions: Sooner or later, one of her business associates or relatives or nosy neighbours will crawl whimpering to the public servants, who will break down her door, pinch the bridge of their nose beneath suddenly watering eyes, and call for CID and forensics. And then it'll be déjà vu all over again, and you'd better hope you're not shedding flakes of dead skin because if they get a sequence match linking you to both scenes—

You begin to sidle back towards the front door, shuddering beneath the livid caul of rage that has settled over your shoulders, all the while thinking:

Once is happenstance, but twice is enemy action.

Someone's going to bleed for this. And it's not going to be you.

LIZ: SNOWBALLING HELL

Thursday morning dawns moist and miserable. You turn yourself out of bed, scramble two eggs, and remember to bag up the plastic waste for collection on your way out the door. Then—forty minutes before you're due on shift—your phone pulls on its work personality and rings for you. It's Moxie. This can only be trouble.

"Skipper?" He screws his face up like a hamster worried you're going to steal his peanut: "You decent?"

You take your thumb off the camera. "I was about to head in. What's come up?"

"I think you want to be here half an hour ago; it's about that wave you were tracking with ICIS? I got a call from a lieutenant in the Dresden KRIPO; he's trying to get in touch with you urgently about an investigation?" Moxie's bamboozled befuddlement is not unreasonable—death in Deutschland isn't a regular bullet point on your daily team briefings.

"I'll call him as soon as I'm in the office." You pause. "Anything else?"

"Yes. Uh, Chief Inspector MacLeish wants to see you. It's about the Blair case. He's raising a request for research and says it's priority one." Screamingly urgent, in other words.

"Well, ping him and tell him I'm in transit." You hang up and neck your coffee, burn your tongue, swear in an extremely unladylike manner as you grab for a glass of tap-water, then run through your check-list and are out the door in record time. You make it to the end of the road as a minibus trundles away from the stop, swear again, and drop the ghost of a tenner on its icon. For a miracle, it accepts the bid, whines to a halt, and kneels as you run to catch up. The other passengers glare irritably at you as you climb aboard, slightly breathless. You take a seat, then realize you left your hairbrush at home. So: another bad hair day is already underway.

There's no hurrying the bus as it meanders around the back streets, diverting to pick folks up and drop them off. Sooner or later, your work-subsidized travel pass will get you to the office, but unlike a taxi, there's no quality-of-service guarantee and no privacy. So you're left tapping your fingers in frustration, unwilling to log into CopSpace in public (because you're an inspector, and your work is a wee bit more confidential than J. Random Plod's notebook: There's a lot at stake if your desktop leaks). So much for telecommuting. Policing is one of those jobs that will always revolve around a meatspace hub, if only because you can't build a cellblock in cyberspace.

So it is that you arrive at work at 8:42 A.M., ahead of your start of shift and in a timely manner ... but disastrously out of touch with the events unfolding around you.

Your first inkling that this may be something worse than a regular bad-hair day comes as you step down off the bus and walk towards the front entrance in Fettes Avenue. They unwired the police HQ comprehensively back in the teens: Consequently, it senses your approach and it knows how to get your attention. The left arm of your spectacles vibrates for attention, and you instinctively touch your phone in acknowledgment. Blinking arrows glide urgently across the powder-blue furnishings in the waiting area, urging you inward: GOTO ROOM D31: BABYLON BRIEFING TO COMMENCE IN 15.

What on earth ...? You barely have time to wonder, before a blizzard of Post-its spring up, occluding nearly every hard surface in sight, and you see the grisly news: Dickie has added you to the team investigating the Mike Blair murder.

You whistle tunelessly through your front teeth and straighten up, then head towards the meatspace incident room: There's a list of fifty-odd officers on the case, from constables up to the DCI himself, and probably a super watching over *his* shoulder and demanding hourly updates for the PR flaks at the Ministry of Justice. As you expected, Mikey's double-wetsuit misadventure has gone political, on top of the usual three-ring circus that shows up for every murder case. (It's the one crime for which all the police forces of the former United Kingdom pull out *all* the stops—but the 95 per cent clean-up rate you take a justifiable pride in comes at a ruinous, multi-million-euro expense.)

Access to CopSpace—an augmented-reality overlay that maps a view of the criminal-intel knowledge base across the physical world in front of your eyes—doesn't make police stations with control centres and briefing rooms obsolete. Quite the contrary. It's not so long ago that you and your colleagues were plunged into the collective nightmare of a total breach of network security and had to fall back to prepaid supermarket mobies and passing around notes printed on *manual typewriters*. Maintaining a physical command centre is vital. Policing requires systematic teamwork, which means communication; and even when they're working, online conferencing systems just aren't quite good enough to make face-to-face meetings obsolete. Working teleconferencing is right around the corner, just like food pills, the flying car, and energy too cheap to meter.

There's a scrum in the corridor outside D31, so you hang back a bit and wait for it to disperse. Then Moxie shows up. "Skipper." He nods—sketchy acknowledgment—and you nod back.

"What's the story?" you ask him.

Moxie's gaze flickers sidelong, taking in the neighbours. He clears his throat. "Lieutenant Heyne from Dresden *really* wants to talk about his suspected homicide, skipper. So I—"

"Homicide?" you ask. "I thought the victim was in hospital."

"Died overnight." Moxie shrugs uncomfortably. "There's also a Sergeant Nobile from the Gruppo Anticrimine Tecnologico in Rome who wants to bend your ear. Urgently."

Oh Jesus. You rack your brains: "What force is he with?"

"Wait a sec." Moxie's looking it up in the directory. You could have done it yourself, you just thought he might have done the leg work already. "It's part of the Guardia di Finanza, the national financial, customs, and economic police?" He looks slightly boggled, eyes twitching as he saccades through the infodump. "They also do cybercrime, he's on the Europol R34 distribution, says it's about the homicide in Dresden and, uh . . . " He nods at the front of the queue, which is beginning to shuffle into Mac's briefing. "An associated murder in Trieste. There's more. That feedstock you were looking for—"

"It'll have to wait." There's the usual pre-caff mumbled meet and greet in the doorway, then you're in and looking for a free seat near the back. Not fast enough; MacLeish is waiting just inside and makes eye contact.

"Inspector." He nods. Subsequent words flow like grit through engine oil. "You were right; thanks for forwarding me that case."

You show him your best botox face: It's a moment to take home and treasure, but you're not going to waste your brownie points gloating in the middle of a murder investigation. "I gather a bunch more contacts have come in overnight."

"Aye, well ... this is really fucking abnormal, if you'll pardon my French. Never seen anything like it."

"Me neither," you concede. "What do you need from ICIU?"

"All your Bing and Google mojo, and a pipe into Europol. Oh, and anything you know about grey-market fabber feedstock. Why don't you sit in the front row?"

After that, there's no escape.

* * *

"Morning, peeps."

Dodgy Dickie stands before a plain white wall bearing the Lothian and Borders logo, and below it a new name: Operation Babylon. The atmosphere in the room is expectant, and just a little angry: one-third suits, one-third boots, and a mashup of civilian support specialists.

"We've got a murder. Not your normal ned-on-ned stabby, unfortunately: This one's got legs. We're out of the golden forty-eight"—he means the first two days of the investigation—"and to make matters worse, DI Kavanaugh, who first clocked it as a culpable homicide, has drawn some really disturbing parallels with at least two other killings and an ongoing investigation into contraband supplies."

What? you wonder, puzzled. Then an IM sidles into your specs. It's Moxie. **SORRY SKIPPER MAC ASKED ABOUT GREY FABS AND INCOMING CASES.** Well, *that* tears it: Dickie is ahead of you on your own portfolio. You'd turn and glare at your sergeant, only he's wisely decided that discretion is the better part of valour and staked out a corner at the back. *Great.*

"Here's the situation." The wall behind Dodgy Dickie does a wipe to reveal Mikey's bathroom death scene. "Note the victim is taped and gagged. It's set up to resemble an accidental autoerotic fatality: The thing he's plumbed into is a mid-1960s colonic irrigation machine, a collector's piece formerly owned by the late

Romanian dictator Nicolae Ceaușescu—apparently he insisted on daily enemas. Ahem. Note the evidence of sexual stimulation. The enema fluid contains a borderline-toxic concentration of a medicine usually prescribed for impotence, but that's not what killed him. Mr. Blair is HIV-positive and on multi-drug maintenance. He also has hypertension, and is on meds for that condition. Pathology tells us that one of the protease inhibitors he's on interacts very badly with Viagra. And the full work-up DI Kavanaugh ordered tells us that what he had in his system at the time was his prescription cocktail and a buttload of Viagra. But again, that's not what killed him."

Mac glances at you, his face unreadable. "The proximate cause of death was cardiac arrest. So we ordered a full work-up on the enema fluid, so pathology went trawling for known pharmaceuticals." They can do that, these days: They've got lab-on-a-chip analysers that can identify thousands of drugs in microgram quantities. Or so they told you on the last re-cert course you did on organic forensics.

"What they found was his prescription meds and the Viagra, and one last thing—the enema fluid was loaded with grapefruit juice." Grapefruit juice? You see winces going round the audience. Dickie continues: "I'm told that grapefruit juice is a catastrophe waiting to happen if you're on certain types of blood-pressure medicine—it interferes with them, just as badly as Viagra interferes with protease inhibitors. What we've got is a cocktail of drug interactions: Viagra and ritonavir, which massively increased the effect of the Viagra, which depresses the user's blood pressure, and grapefruit juice doing much the same to his ACE inhibitor."

He looks at his notes. "I'm told the grapefruit juice alone would have had the effect of causing a severe drop in blood pressure lasting a few hours. Add a cocktail of Viagra and ritonavir, and Professor Davies is of the opinion it'd be enough to push him over the edge." As chief pathologist, Professor Davies ought to know. "What's interesting is, who knew about Blair's prescription, and worked out precisely what to slip in his happy juice? And who helped Mr. Blair into his underwear. We'd *really* like to know the answer to that one ... but it's not the only lead I want us to follow up."

You're doing your best to keep your botox face in place. Otherwise, your eyebrows would be halfway to merging with your hair-line. Dodgy Dickie MacLeish is solid, unimaginative, and methodical: If he's haring off in search of a homicidal pharmacist, then either somebody's slipped him a Mickey Finn or all simpler explanations have already been ruled out. Which is very bad news.

"SOC did a complete sweep of the premises," Dickie continues. "In the process, they found these." He flicks up a picture of a wooden shelf bracketed to a whitewashed brick wall—a cellar, of course. There's a neat row of sealed black canisters along it. You swear under your breath: You've seen their like before, fly-tipped in on-street recycling bins all over town. "Fabber cartridges. Unchipped, cheap knockoffs of the official product. These ones are all full of high-temperature thermosetting granules, presumably bound for a contraband factory somewhere in Edinburgh. They're untraceable and illegal, and their presence suggests a connection to an ongoing investigation of DI Kavanaugh's."

You sit there, quietly fuming, as Dickie rolls unconcernedly away from his ambush of your unfunded project: If you'd actually been able to devote resources to following up the empties for the black-market fabber trade, you might have got to Mikey before someone killed him. "Anyway, this is where things get weird."

The wall scrolls sideways to reveal a different bathroom demise. This scene's helpfully labelled in German, as you recognize from the six syllable train-wreck attached to the tanning-salon sun bed.

"Dresden, Germany. This is the bathroom of Markus Hasler, a fine upstanding son of the city with a background in pharmaceut- ical spam, illegal sale of medicinal products, and counterfeit goods.

That is a sun bed. At the same time our Mr. Blair was being plumbed into his personal jet wash—give or take a couple of hours—Mr. Hasler apparently drank half a litre of schnapps spiked with tranquillizers and climbed inside his sun bed. The control circuitry of which had been modified to override the safety shut-offs. He died in hospital yesterday without regaining consciousness."

There is a low muttering and shuffling going on around you and you nod, unconsciously picking up on the vibe: the rest of the room realizing they're in an out-of-Kansas situation. MacLeish continues implacably. "Both Mike Blair and Markus Hasler had prior conviction records in much the same field of criminal expertise. They died in not-dissimilar manners as a result of incidents that commenced within three hours of each other." He shifts from foot to foot. "There are reports of other, similar deaths in different jurisdictions this morning—that is, of persons involved in illegal network marketing activities, dying in circumstances superficially resembling domestic incidents."

Dickie catches your eye. "I'd like to thank DI Kavanaugh for drawing the initial match to my attention, and Sergeant Cunningham for flagging the additional cases that came in while Liz was off shift." Well *that's* torn it. And so, yet again, Moxie escapes a well-deserved bollocking for playing fast and loose with the chain of command.

"As of this meeting, we're continuing the investigation into the Michael Blair homicide. However, we're going to have to recognize the need to integrate into a larger Europol investigation into the multiple parallel killings of at least two and possibly many more convicted criminals across member-state borders. And that's why I've invited DI Kavanaugh to run the international liaison side of the investigation and provide input on the possible bootleg fabber connection."

He's got you, willy-nilly: drafted back into a CID murder investigation—and fuck your existing case-load and understaffed department. And there's no way he can't know what he's doing to your performance metrics. Dickie is clearly out to get you: *Once is happenstance, but twice is enemy action.*

Someone's going to bleed for this. And it's not going to be you.

* * *

"—the bloody hell did you think you were—"

"—wisnae my fault, skipper! It's tagged *priority*—"

"—doing going around the—"

"—*one*, mandatory escalate, so I pushed it at the duty inspector, and he—"

"—chain of command—"

Moxie raises his hands in surrender right as your frustrated snarl runs down.

You glance around. Then you stare into his eyes, hard. "Run that past me again."

Moxie swallows. "Like I said, it was an urgent request for input on a homicide investigation. You were off shift, and there was a no-delay flag on it: golden forty-eight. So I pointed it at the duty desk. I havnae been telling tales out of school to Dodgy, skipper, please! What would *you* have done?"

"I'd have—*fuck*." You restrain the urge to punch the corridor wall and draw a deep breath instead. The trouble is, Moxie isn't wrong. "Who was on the duty desk?"

"It was Inspector Rodney, ma'am." Sheila Rodney. Who doesn't, as far as you know, carry a knife for your back. But who knows well enough to forward a lead to the Blair murder investigation.

"Fuck." You take another deep breath. "Grab yourself a coffee, then see me in my office in fifteen minutes. You heard what Dickie said? That means your work-load just doubled for the rest of the week, so let's go run through it before I have to go talk to the Europol investigators."

"Fifteen minutes?"

"If I'm being pulled off ICIU for the duration, I've got to brief Doc Green."

Moxie looks at you as if your dog just died, and you don't have the heart to stay angry. You give him a gentle shove on the shoulder. "Get going, Sergeant. There's more than enough shit to go round, this time."

And then you head upstairs, across the walkway, into the adjacent block, and around the corner to Chief Inspector Dixon's wee office.

George "Doc Green" Dixon is (a) your nominal superior, and (b) not interested in the day-to-day running of ICIU, outwith its potential to dump embarrassing shit in his lap without warning. George is old-school, trained up via computer forensics to occupy a trusted niche in CID (trawling paedophiles' phones for evidence of thoughtcrime) while keeping one foot in the stirrup of the runaway horse that is Infrastructure IT.

He doesn't have much time for ICIU—especially after the time he dropped round when you weren't in, and Moxie showed him the Goatsedance video followed by a brisk webtour of the shocksites of Lothian and Borders, culminating in the infamous penile degloving accident fansite (which apparently left him with PTSD and permanent scarring on the insides of his eyelids). Ever since, he's been more than happy to leave you alone to run your little fiefdom as you see fit.

George is a verra verra busy man, as he never tires of reminding you from behind the cover of his salt-and-pepper moustache. He probably thinks his manner is avuncular: You think it's patronizing, but it's not your job to pass comment. In any case, he's effective. Before Dodgy Dickie dissolved the morning briefing, you'd already emailed Doc to beg a minute of his time, so you have no compunction about going straight round to IIT and hammering on his battered office door.

"Enter." Doc looks up as you open the door. For a moment you think he's playing a Sims game on his desk: Then you recognize the new annexe over the road. Sims, yes, but it's some kind of architectural model—he's probably looking for a way to shoe-horn more bandwidth through the crumbling concrete walls. "Have a seat. What's come up this time, Liz?"

You can't help yourself: You pull a face. "Have you been following Dickie MacLeish's murder investigation, sir?"

"No." He raises an eyebrow that looks like it's got a sleeping caterpillar glued to it. "Should I have?"

"It's a crawling horror. First, it's gone political. Secondly, it looks like it's not a one off. We've had contacts from Europol about similar killings in Germany and possibly Italy. It's a three-sigma match or better—if they hadn't happened simultaneously, we'd be looking for a serial killer. Anyway, the initial lead-in came via ICIU, and there's an input angle from one of my current cases, so Dickie just upped and announced that he's drafting me to coordinate with the foreign investigators, without so much as a by-your-leave."

"Well, *that's* nice to know," George says heavily. "Did he ask you first?"

You shake your head. "I'm not happy, sir. But it's a murder case, and a high-profile one. It'd look bad if I kicked up a fuss."

"Huh." A long pause. "What do you want to do?"

You do not fail to spot the emphasis. "What I'd *like* to do is to get on with running my unit, sir. It's not as if we're short of work right now. Trouble is, he framed it as a fait accompli. If you want me to hold the fort, I'm going to need some backup."

"Huh." Another pause. "What are your alternative options?"

You hunch your shoulders uncomfortably. "I can shovel a bunch of routine stuff off onto Moxie and Speedy. If I hold back about eight hours a week for ICIU, shelve my skills-matrix update sessions indefinitely, and bail on as much paper-work as possible, then I can probably give Dickie and the investigation three and a half out of five shifts a week for the rest of the month. I *think* the unit can function without my hands on the tiller for that long, assuming nothing unusual pops out of the woodwork. But it's going to be touch and go: All it would take would be one of my sergeants being off sick for a week, or another case like the Morningside Cannibals coming out of left field ... "

(The Morningside Cannibals: a circle of polite middle-class people who dined out on each other, with the aid of a medical tissue incubator tank. Figuring out what on earth to charge them with—cannibalism not being illegal in Scotland—was the least of your worries when the blogs moved in. In the end, they were reported to the Procurator Fiscal for outraging public decency and corpse desecration: a flimsy case, as the defence barristers pointed out in court, given that the dinner parties in question were strictly private affairs, and the human flesh on the plates had been cloned from ladies who were not only still alive but willing to testify that their own cultured meat tasted *nothing* like chicken. In the end, the case had collapsed amidst recriminations and calls for a change in the law.)

Mention of the Morningside Cannibals has the desired effect: Doc winces visibly. "Aye well, Liz, that's as may be, but let's not pile up speculative obstacles before we get to them?" He leans forward. "It sounds to me like Dodgy Dickie has got your number: Best not fight him in public. Leave him to me. I'll have a wee chat with Jackie Somerville and shake some resources loose from her department in return for your loan." He fixes you with a gimlet stare. "Just promise me you didna fix this up to weasel your way back onto a CID case?"

You shake your head vigorously. "Boss, would I do a thing like that?" You catch his expression: "That's live-rail territory. With respect, sir, if I wanted to apply for a transfer back to CID, you'd hear about it before it happened, and I'd be doing it with your say-so or not at all. Anything else would be grossly unprofessional conduct detrimental to the smooth running of the chain of command. Not to mention a real own-goal, career-wise. Right?"

A long pause, then Doc nods. "Exactly so, Inspector. I'm glad we understand each other."

"So am I. Sir."

"Get out of my office." He waves genially to defuse the curt dismissal. "Leave Dickie to me; just be sure to set your house in order before you go haring off in all directions, and keep me fully informed. Dismissed."

You get the hell out of Doc's office, and you're halfway back to the ICIU before you pause to wonder whether you're being set up, or whether this really *is* your route back into CID after your long exile on the Rule 34 Squad.

* * *

Moxie is waiting for you in your office and, for a miracle, he's brought you a mug of latte just the way you like it. He's wearing an appropriately sheepish expression, which finally makes your mind up for you. "Chill, Moxie. I'm not happy, but it's not your fault. Next time try to give me some more warning, okay?"

He looks relieved. "I wanted to, skipper, but Chief Inspector MacLeish scheduled you for the briefing before I could get to you."

Before he could get to you through regular channels, he means, but you don't pursue the point. "I've just had a little chat with Chief Inspector Dixon. He's going to try and square things with the deputy superintendent to get some backup in here. But in the meantime, it looks like Dickie's little empire-building gambit is working. I'm going to be very scarce around here for the rest of the month, or until Dickie gets his man. So how about we go over what you've got on your desk, what *I've* got on *mine* that's going to be added to your case-load while I'm gone, and what extra resources you need to keep your head above water in the meantime. Yes?"

Dawning horror steals across Moxie's face. "Whu—you're leaving me in charge?"

"Up to a point. I'll still be around, but only for about an hour a day." (Rule #1: always budget 50 per cent more time for your people than you tell them you've got.) "Think hard before you escalate. Speedy's off today: I'll be repeating this chat with him when he's back in. You're going to have to co-ordinate with him directly, not through me. Meanwhile, your case-load: Show it to me."

For about the next hour, Moxie subjects you to his team's current case-load in all its mind-numbingly recondite, not to mention perverse, detail.

Publicity surrounding the Morningside Cannibals has led to a spate of copy-cat offences against sanity, some of them literally so (as in: There are folks dining on cloned haunch of pedigree Siamese tonight). There's an anonymous perp randomly posting upskirt videos on neighbourhood blogs, captured by a microcam strapped to one of the too-tame squirrels in the Botanic Gardens. Moxie's looking for the fabber source of some disturbingly simple meth-lab-in-a-brick chemistry kits that are circulating among the usual numpties in Lochend, and there's the regular slew of urban-legend queries from the more gullible elements of CID to field. There's the hentai fan base to keep an eye on, with their current interest in Hitler Yaoi and holocaust tentacle porn—still illegal in Germany, which is giving rise to cross-jurisdictional headaches—and their ongoing attempt to exhaustively explore the M girls N cups polynomial space in NP time, as a computer geek of your acquaintance once put it.

(You're not quite sure what the *NP time* bit means, but the combination of cheap machinima tools and lots of unemployed games programmers have turned Edinburgh into a hot-bed of photorealistic fetish video production even though it's technically illegal. The burden of evidence is higher under Scottish law, so despite having tougher porn laws than England, the smart shocksite developers have all moved north, while their development tools and websites have migrated into the Russian blacknet cloud. Fighting it is an unwinnable battle, so your job is merely to flag up anything involving real-live actors—especially minors—and try to avoid unwittingly popularizing the stuff via the Streisand Effect.)

At the end of the hour you're just about reeling from the deluge, but you've given Moxie a framework for prioritizing his jobs over the next week, not to mention your home and personal mobile numbers and strict instructions to call you immediately if anything really fucked comes up. You can see he's getting psyched up, ready and prepared to perform triage on Tubgirl should the need make itself known—right up until the moment your mobie rings.

You answer it. It's Dodgy Dickie. *Shit.* "Wait one," you mouth at Moxie. "Yes?"

MacLeish looks like his ulcer's playing up again. "Inspector? Are you up to speed on the international angle yet?"

You bite back your instant reaction: "I'm in the process of clearing my desk and handing off all current ICIU operations to a subordinate. It's going to take me another half-hour today, and a couple of hours tomorrow when my relief sergeant is in the shop. So your answer is a conditional 'no,' sir. Has something come up?"

"You bet it has, and it's touching down at Turnhouse in an hour. We've got an investigator from Europol flying in to poke his nose where it doesn't belong. I want you to meet him and keep him the hell off my back. Is that understood?"

Your instant impulse is to tell Dickie to fuck right off, but the prospect of subsequently explaining your language to a disciplinary tribunal is not attractive. "I understand you consider my management of a secure hand-off of my departmental responsibilities is less important than what is basically a baby-sitting job, sir. I'm going to comply with your request, but not at the cost of making a hash of a bunch of other, admittedly lower-priority, investigations that are already in progress. I'll take care of the busybodies, but you *don't* tell me how to run my unit. Am I clear?"

For a moment, Dickie looks as if he's about to blow a gasket, but then he nods, jerkily. "Perfectly."

"Good." You hang up, and check your desktop. Sure enough, there's a stack of busybody IMs that have come in while you were briefing Moxie, insistently asking for you and demanding that you do this, do that, hither and yon. Dickie's management style is to shoot at the monkey's feet, make the monkey dance. Especially when the monkey was, ten years ago, number one in his graduating class, and as recently as five years ago, the number-one candidate for the post he's currently occupying. You rub your eyes. "I'm too old for this shit," you hear yourself say.

"Skipper?" Moxie is looking at you. "Anything I can do to help?"

"No, just as long as you're clear on where we're going. I've got to go out to the airport to meet a flight in. Cover my back?"

He sketches a videogame rendition of a salute. "Yes, ma'am!"

"Cool." You finish reading the IM stack, then your tenuous control fractures like a sheet of toughened glass held for too long over a naked flame of rage as you see your contact details. *"Shit."*

"Skipper?"

"That's all I fucking need this morning. *All.*"

"What—"

"Nothing you can do, Moxie." You get a handle on it fast, but for a moment you're blurring with bloody-eyed rage. Because you recognize the name on the passenger manifest, the Eurocop who's coming to visit and who Dodgy Dickie has detailed you to organize the disposition of. It's the man who cost you your career, five years ago.

Kemal.

ANWAR: COUSIN TARIQ

Wednesday evening in the Hussein household.

You have retreated upstairs to your den because your mother-in-law has come round to visit Bibi (who is home early from work), and she's in a state—utterly inconsolable, in fact. Most of the time Sameena is okay for an old bat, unless you happen to be single: She is afflicted with Bridezilla-by-proxy syndrome and is always in search of a wedding to organize. But tonight she's wailing and pulling her hair, upset beyond all reason. She supplements Uncle Taleb's income by housekeeping—to keep it respectable, she only works for gay men. Anyway, she found one of her clients dead on the bathroom floor this Tuesday, and it gave her a funny turn, and every evening since she's come round to angst and wail like a one-woman banshee convention. You'd think she'd be getting over it by now, but no: If anything, it gets worse.

Right now, despite Bibi plying her with tea and sympathy, she's so far out of her tree that the squirrels are sending out search parties: After half an hour of her wailing, you finally crack, climb the loft ladder, and pull it up behind you. Maybe you should tell Bibi to bring home some Valium from work? Nobody would miss it, and it'd be a small mercy for the old woman. But right now, her sobbing is getting on your tits mightily, so you stick your music library on random play, bury your phone under a cushion, and haul out Tariq's spare pad from behind the slowly bubbling beer bucket with the vague idea of seeing if he's got any work for you.

As soon as you open it up and get online via the dodgy directional aerial he set you up with, he calls you. "Anwar, my man! How are you hanging?"

Tariq has this annoying habit of trying to talk slang like the hep rappers and gangsta cats of previous generations. It's annoying because he gets it badly wrong every time. He wears a two-sizes-too-small pork-pie hat and dyes his moustache orange because he thinks it's cool (plus, it annoys the fuck out of Imam Hafiz—not to mention his elder sister Bibi). He also takes the piss out of everybody. What's really galling is that you've got a sneaky feeling that he might be onto something. Certainly, Tariq's gone further and got more in twenty-four years than you have in nearly thirty; otherwise, why would you be working for him?

"I'm hanging fine, cuz, just fine. But your mother is another matter. She is down in the kitchen with Bibi, and I am up in the attic and close to jamming cotton wool in my ears, I can tell you. She's fucking lost it, she's lost the plot, cuz."

"Did you know the stiff she found was murdered? It's on the *Spurtle's* newscrawl, the filth are all over it. That's some heavy shit right there, my man—and that's *before* you get into the juicier rumours about how he was whacked. Fucking chancer if you ask me, fucker deserved it. But it's hard on Mom, walking in on him while she was about her scodgies ... Listen, I've got a job on. Do you have time to look over some templates for me? I'm customizing a chat room for Ali, and I need someone to whack the scripts and try to make them fall over."

"Which Ali are you working for—short, fat Ali, tall'n'bearded Ali, or psycho punk Ali?"

"You know fucking well I don't work with Shorty McFatso, and Skinny McBeardy's a fucking space cadet—got no money because he spends everything he can scrounge on maryjane."

"What, he's got a Scottish girl-friend now?"

Tariq rolls his eyes as if you've said something dumb, then changes the subject: "I'm putting this board together on behalf of our mutual friend Ali the Punk, *capisce*? I just need a unit tester to walk the scripts over it. *If* you can spare me a few hours from your critically important diplomatic duties—"

"If you've got the money, I've got the time." It's not as if you're busy in the office. "I can start as soon as you like." You don't know much about Punk Ali, but you're pretty sure you'd have heard if he was a waster.

Tariq tilts his head slightly, casting his eyes in shadow: You can see the organized firefly flicker of his oh-so-posh contact lenses, retinal-scanning displays for the plugged-in generation. "Can you get away for an hour or two?" he asks.

"Guess so." Anything to get away from the fearful caterwauling downstairs. "Where do you want to meet?"

"You know the Halfway House, on Fleshmarket Close?"

Of course you know it; it's one of the Gnome's favoured hangouts precisely because it's half-underground, in a microwave shadow, where mobiles work erratically and GPS doesn't reach. Stands to reason Tariq would know about it, too. "Sure. See you there in half an hour?"

Tariq cuts the connection. You switch off the pad and lay it aside, then peer at the beer bucket. The wee transparent plastic hingmy—*airlock*? But you thought only spaceships had them—farts at you. It smells of yeast and a faint tang of something metallic. You fight back the urge to lift the lid and sneak a look inside (the brewing FAQs were all very insistent that you shouldna do that). "Sleep tight," you admonish it, then you drop the trap-door and scramble down the ladder and out into the night.

* * *

It's evening, but you need sunglasses: That's Edinburgh in late spring/early summer. The sun's low, but staying up later and later, and the local pagans will be doing that infidel sex-festival thing that the local Christians get so hot and bothered about on Calton Hill in a couple of weeks. You pull your shoes and suit jacket on and trudge up to the high street, then down the steep and garish shop-frontage of Cockburn Street to the top of Fleshmarket Close. You walk down the steps carefully, clutching the handrail until you come to the landing with the Halfway House. Tariq's in the back booth, of course, nursing a pint of heavy. You nod at him, then turn to the bar and order a lager. A minute later, you're squeezing in knee to knee with Cousin Porkie McWideboy. He raises his glass to you cheerily.

"I didn't know you drank here," you tell him. Which is the truth.

"I don't drink alcohol." Tariq wipes suds from his moustache.

"Neither do I." You raise your glass to him. "Watch me prac-tise not drinking alcohol." He looks irritated but responds in kind.

"Here's the package." Tariq slides a wee memory card across the table at you. "There's a hi-def movie file on this card. Play it, it's a movie. Change its suffix to dot-exe and run it, and it'll do something else. Remember to change it back again after you're done with it of an evening, awright?"

You eye the card with a distinct lack of enthusiasm. Then you pull out your phone, elaborately remove the Argyle sock, and inspect it carefully. There is, as you anticipated, no signal, so you roll the sock back over it and stare at Tariq pointedly. "I'm still on probation," you remind him. "I thought you said this was about testing a chat room?"

"It could be." Tariq's noncommittal. "There's a VM in there, and it's hosting a web app with a chat room. Nothing else. But you don't want it to go anywhere near the net. You're going to stay one hundred per cent off-line while you're running it, and you keep it that way. Get the picture?"

You get it all right, and it gives you pause for thought. If Mr. Webber gets the idea that you're a webmonkey for your cousin, he'll yell at you because you're nae supposed to go near a web server while you're on probation—but as long as it's *legal* webmonkey shit, you're pretty sure you can plead wife-and-two-bairns-to-support and get off with a slap on the wrist and a talking-to. They're supposed to be trying to rehabilitate you, after all, and Tariq's not one of the dodgy playmates named in the injunction.

But only because he was too smart to get caught.

This doesn't sound like your regular webmonkey business. There's no need to take elaborate concealment measures if something's halal—this business with stegged VMs and sneakernet exchanges in wireless shadows has got to be something else. Just like Colonel Datka's bread mix.

"I'm not taking it unless you tell me what it is." You leave the chip on the table, stranded sober and central between two beer glasses. "Seriously, cuz. A man could go to prison."

"Not really. Not unless you fuck up." His moustache twitches upward at the corners. "The VM contains a web app with a chat-room application and some test data. I want you to unit test the chat room and its templates for browser accessibility, search semantics, the usual shit. That's all, *except* I want you to keep your yap shut and make sure you're off-line while you do it. Five hundred euros, take it or leave it."

That's good money for a webmonkey, and you're tempted. *But.* "What's the payload going to be?" you ask.

"I don't know yet. Fresh bluefin tuna sashimi by airmail, fix your speeding tickets, your bank balance is temporarily overdrawn, hello I am the widow of Barrister Nkomo, dearly beloved in Christ can you be sincere, we know what you did last Saturday night. Who the fuck cares? It's just money. They give me the site, I mess with the chat-room software, you get to test it all works. That's all. There's no payload there." *Not yet.*

You watch as your left hand reaches out to cover the memory card. It's like it's at the end of someone else's arm, someone a couple of years younger, someone without a wife and kids to protect, someone who's never done time in prison. It's like it belongs to someone stupid and short-sighted. *You're* not short-sighted and stupid; you know better than to take on a Joe job—a hijacked copy of a legit website, one that Tariq's upstream mate is going to turn into a shell for some kind of scam after he finishes busily installing backdoors in the community portal. Knowing Tariq, it's probably going to host some horrible malware that's going to recruit unwitting mules to visit the chat room, then infest their phones and empty their bank accounts. *But it's not a Joe job,* you hear yourself thinking, *if there's no payload. It might not happen.* If the word *yet* didn't keep appending itself to that thought, you'd be a happy camper.

"Relax, cuz."

"Five hundred euros," you remind him, and stand up, leaving your half-full pint: You don't want to risk your mother-in-law smelling it on your breath and recognizing it when you go home.

"Five hundred euros for the father of my niece and nephew. Trust me, I wouldn't be asking you to do this if I thought they might end up growing up without their dad." Tariq raises his glass. "Just remember to stay off-line while you run it, and nothing can possibly go wrong."

* * *

When you get home an hour later, you find, to your relief, that Sameena has gone home. Bibi's in the kitchen, perched on a stool at the breakfast bar, poring over a pad, clearly engrossed. "Hello," you say, then pause. "Where are the kids?"

It takes a moment for her to look up. "Naseem's at PlayPal's. They're doing five-a-side football tonight. Farida's staying with her grandparents for the evening." Which isn't so unusual, but then she drops the bomb. "Is there anything we should be talking about?"

You hate it when Bibi gets like this: nostrils slightly flared, brows drawn in, squinting at you like you're a bug in a test-tube. You call it her professional face. "What are you reading?" you ask. It looks to be illustrated, but you can't read English upside down.

"Oh, just community practice training material," she says dismissively. "We have to do these revision exercises regularly to stay up to date. Current best practice in identification and clinical management of at-risk groups, communicating infection-control information about STIs to MSMs, that sort of thing." She rests a hand on the screen. "Where've you been?"

"Out seeing Tariq," you say. There's no point concealing it from her. "He's got a little job for me."

"Oh *Anwar*." She smiles, eyes narrowing. Then the smile fades, leaving only the set stare. "Tell me he hasn't talked you into one of his schemes?"

"I have a perfectly good job!" you protest. "I'm the honorary consul for the Independent—"

Bibi sighs and taps one of her shoes against the table leg. It begins to dawn upon you that you may be in real trouble here.

"How much did he promise you?"

Surrender is inevitable. "Five hundred euros. It's just a—"

She interrupts: "I'm going to *kill* my little shit of a brother one of these days." Your stomach does a back-flip. Your wife is a nice, quiet, well-brought-up lady who does not interrupt people unless they're in so deep they need to pause for decompression on the way back up. Right now, she's exuding more quiet menace than Keanu Reeves in *The Godfather* remake. "He knows where you've been, he knows you're on probation, and he ought to know better." Her hands are balled up into fists like walnuts, small and hard as wooden clubs.

"It's nothing, he just wants me to test a website," you protest. "Listen, it's not malware and there's nothing shady about it, it's just that he wants me to test out a chat-room set-up he's configuring for a friend. He knows I need the work, and I can be discreet—"

"Really?" Fist on hip, she glares at you. "If you're so good at being discreet, perhaps you'd like to explain *this*?" She points, and now you really know you're in trouble, because the object of her ire is sitting on the countertop beside the sink, looking for all the world like a bag of Produce of People's Number Four Grain Products Factory of Issyk-Kulistan—

"It's, um, bread mix?" Your heart sinks. "Isn't it?"

"Quite possibly. Although I don't suppose it meets EU standards on food safety. Or labelling. Hygiene, for that matter. And I'm curious, oh my husband, as to why anyone would bother shipping pre-packaged bread mix from Kyrgyzstan instead of bulk grain, or maybe flour."

"Oh, that's easy enough!" you exclaim with relief. "Colonel Datka's got his finger in the flour factory and is using the shipments to—"

"I'm told the going price is sixty euros a bag," she hisses: "For *bread mix*. Do you really want Naseem and Farida to grow up fatherless, my husband? Motherless, too, because I swear if you get yourself arrested again, I shall die of shame. But no, you don't need to worry about me; you just carry on and thoughtlessly follow your own selfish urges without considering the consequences, *man*."

She pronounces that last with such lip-smacking contempt that you recoil instinctively, racking your brain for an explanation. It must be the women's studies group at the mosque; they've clearly got to her. Next thing you know, she'll be ditching her jeans for a niqab and angrily denouncing the oligo-hetero-patriarchy on marches. The spectre of no more sex on the home front hovers over you, and despite your desire for dick, the idea of losing your wife to a bunch of hairy-legged feminist separatist fundamentalists fills you with horror.

"Please, Bibi, it's not like that! I only want what's best for the bairns. If I don't work, what kind of role model am I going to be for them? But the idiots in the probation service don't want me to use my skills—"

"I think you mean they don't want you to get yourself slung back inside for *breaking the law*. And do you know something, oh my husband? Neither do I! If this was just about the dodgy bread mix, I could ignore it. Or maybe if it was just the odd job for Tariq. I can even ignore the other stuff. I'm not blind. I know what our marriage is to you." She leans towards you and sniffs. "But he's had you in that pub again, hasn't he? And you couldn't even be bothered to hide it! You *smell* of *beer*. Mouthwash *right now*, or you'll set them a bad example." Her nostrils flare. "My mother would have a fit."

"Sammy isn't here," you say defensively. "And anyway, I only had one pint—"

"Oh yes, *just one pint*. That's like being a little bit pregnant, or just one casual sex partner, or just one arrest and criminal conviction. Or just one scam at a time. What does it take to get through to you? You've got to learn to think ahead! You've got to be more discreet!"

You blink at her. The anger seems to have ebbed into wide-eyed confusion. *She's really worried,* you realize. It's not just a bad day in the dispensary, so let's yell at the house-husband (though that's happened in the past). *What's got into her?* Then another thought strikes you. "You said it's changing hands for sixty euros a bag. Do you know who's paying that much for it? I know where to get more; we could clean up—"

* * *

That night, you get to bed down on the attic floor, with the burping brew-kit airlock to keep you company as you try to work out exactly what you said wrong.

Women! Who knows why they do what they do? Certainly not you—and you even married one.

TOYMAKER: REALITY EXCURSION

You!

Yes, *you*. Who the fuck did you think I was talking to, the Tooth Fairy? (That's him on the left)—Jesus? No, I'm talking to *you*, fuckwit. Whoever or whatever you are, watching over me . . .

I'm an executive, you know. That's why there's a chip in my head. The Operation put it there so they could keep track of me. You've got to look at it from their point of view; it's cheap due diligence—couple of dozen terabytes of non-volatile storage, mikes and GPS for metadata—"to deter you from going behind our backs," they said. It's not just a recorder, either. They can make LTE chipsets really small, you know? Phone chipset in the head. Maybe it's transmitting all the time, and you're sitting in a darkened room listening to my subvocalized thoughts. Or maybe you're just an AI application, running pattern-matching code on the speech-to-text output, somewhere in the cloud. What if it's receiving, too, controlling the old meatpuppet? Maybe there's a bomb in my skull.

Learning too much about our employers is a firing expense—
they're said to favour nine-millimetre—but what if they wanted to
be sure? Multi-channel redundancy via cognitive radio. Push a
button, bounce a signal off the moon, hello, bomb, pleased to meet
you! Let's go out with a splash.

You only live in my imagination. (I die, you die.) But I can still
talk to you. And we have a problem, my invisible friend.

... No. Let me be more precise. *I* have a problem. Enemies.
They've iced my primary candidates for COO and CFO before I
could doorstep them for a pre-induction assessment. To make
matters worse, I became a person of interest in the police investigation—purely by coincidence—and they took a DNA sample. I'm
pinned down here until we can file a Privacy Redaction Order and
get the sample incinerated.

And for the icing on the shit-cake, my fucking *luggage* is still
missing. Missing!

... That was as of three hours ago. Maybe the cunt on the
Hilton hospitality desk has found it. That'd be a shame: I was
looking forward to taking it out of his hide, with compound
interest on top. (Five point six two kilograms.) Fuck it, my
sample was in there. And my meds. I've been giving myself a little
holiday from the pills recently, giving myself a holiday to
remember what it's like to have a mind of my own. *Neurodiverse.*
(Losing it from the front desk onwards ... maybe that wasn't such
a good idea?) Guess I just have to hold myself together until I can
get my luggage back or I'll skin Mr. Hospitality in a bathtub full
of brine.

But anyway: I have a phone. I always have a phone, short of
brain surgery to separate me from it. Phones are deadlier than guns.
I need to talk to the business-support desk. Arms-race death match
between the cognitive radio free Internet rebels and the lizards who
run the secret world government: We use the rebels' remixers. And

the phone in my head connects direct through the undernet, diving for a nameless server in central Asia—

"Hello?"

Look around, my invisible friend, see the park, the mud grey field, and the trees? We have bandwidth here. The council installed routers in all the lampposts, the better to handle the feed from the webcams in all the street-lamps. The lizards want to catch the rape machines, but they're too cunning. Bushes block the electromagnetic emissions from the lights.

"Hello?"

"Uh, this is, is Able November in Edinburgh."

You—that is to say, me—use Able November as a code-name when talking to the Operation's call centre. This is the twenty-first century, and even international crime syndicates and off-shore venture-capital trusts—the two are sometimes hard to tell apart—need offshore call centres. You can't do business without the right tools, after all.

(Is that a police reconnaissance drone cruising just below the eaves of the tenements on the other side of the field? Or is it just a *very large* bat?)

"Hello, Able November. What is your situation?"

"Mike Blair has been murdered. Vivian Crolla has been murdered. My"—*fuck shit piss cocksucking*—"luggage has gone missing with my meds and I haven't had any for seventy-two hours. I am"—*mother-fucking ANGRY*—"losing my objectivity somewhat. Can you help? The meds are the hard part."

"I'm putting you on hold. Please wait."

You find a wooden bench and sit down, touching it, feeling the dry crumbling grain of decomposing dead lignified hermaphrodite flesh between your fingers. You obey the order to hold on instinctively, clutching the surface with one hand. If you lose your grip, you might fall up into the sky: You're very light. This is a really fucking shitty time to have an attack, but it's not so surprising. Every so often you cut back on your meds for a couple of days, reestablish your baseline. Is it just bad luck that when you're ready to go back on the pills, they steal your luggage and murder your contacts? The police have eyes in the sky, watching and waiting. How can these not be connected?

"Able November," says the woman you're listening to—her voice distorted by the hearing implant in your skull, drain-pipe echo of an encrypted tunnel—"what's that about your meds? Are you taking them?"

"No," you want to shout, but the phone is in your head, and if you yell aloud, someone or something bad might hear. *Gently.* The mike in your throat hears all. "My meds are in my luggage. My luggage has been missing for two days." Little white lies shining like baby teeth in a shallow grave.

"Okay, we can take care of that for you," says your operator. "I'm going to send your prescription through to the nearest pharmacy for an emergency resupply. Uh, your identity. Is it still clean?"

"No," you say. "No, no." It's your fault. You told the police to steal my DNA, didn't you? Mother-fucking ghost-chip-skull-bomb invisible capitalist friends, can't trust 'em anywhere. "It's ... " You realize you're hyperventilating and force yourself to slow down. "I visited Mike Blair and found a murder investigation in progress." Cops in ceramic terylene overalls picking tiny fragments of your skull off the bathroom floor ... "They sampled me as a POI. This identity's dirty. I need a fall-back."

"Okay, don't worry. I'm putting you on hold again."

You hold, while the police RPV ghosts across the park on silent ducted fans, searching the bushes for rape machines—no, *rape machines don't exist.* Crazy childhood phantasms that lurk into adulthood: They're less real than this phone in your skull, the lifeline to the Operation's soothing dream of control. Once you get on your meds again, the bad stuff will all go away. The same cannot be said of all the other shit. *You say paranoia, I say surveillance state.* Worried about being tracked by hidden cameras, stealthy airborne remotely piloted vehicles, and chips implanted in your skull? You're merely a realist.

The twenty-first century so far has been a really fucking awful couple of decades for paranoid schizophrenics. Luckily, you're not paranoid—you just have these little breakdowns from time to time. A medication side-effect—a side-effect of coming off your meds, that is. Usually at the least convenient time—like now. Something is watching you from the trash can alongside the footpath. Then it moves. A starling. (They're making a come-back from the brink of extinction.)

"I'm going to text a route to a local pharmacy to your handset. I want you to go there *immediately*, they know you're a tourist, and it's urgent. Don't leave until you've got your pills. Do you understand?"

You nod happily, glad that someone is there to catch your fall. *Not* a lizard—lizards never catch. "Yes." They want to brainwash you and make a good little worker-robot-slave out of your flayed soul.

"Okay. You're to stop using your current identity immediately after you get your prescription. There's a new background waiting for you, and I'll send you the collection details in the next message. Clear?"

"Yes." You swallow. Your throat is unaccountably dry. This always happens when the firewall in your head springs a leak. "What else?"

"We can't help with your contacts," she says abruptly, sibilants buzzing like an angry hornet just behind your left ear. "You're not the only founder-executive with problems today. We're busy fighting off denial-of-service attacks on all fronts.

Marketing/Communications are experiencing severe functional ablation, and it's degrading our ability to comply with our service-level agreements. Basic medical and identity services are running normally, but unfortunately as a Tier Two executive, you may experience delays in fulfilment of your general support requests. If you can find out who exactly killed your contacts, you are to let us know *immediately*."

Is it the lizards—your loyal lips are frozen shut. The operator does not need to hear about the lizards. (She's not the only one. Most people don't believe in the lizards and react badly if you try to tell them: It's the brainwashing.) The operator sounds tense and tired. She doesn't need any more worries. If you make her worry that you are losing it, talking about shape-changing lizards, she may push that button and bounce that signal off the moon and hello, Mr. Brain-Bomb, good-bye Toymaker. So you do not say one word about the lizards. Like the rape machines, they're imaginary haunts—*except,* an edgy feeling tells you, *they're not*.

"I'll do that," you reassure the operator.

"Okay, go get your meds." And a moment later the phone in your wallet vibrates and a couple of numbered tags show up on its map of the city, along with a helpfully walkable route.

You have a mission. You're going to get your meds, pick up your new identity documents, then look into replacing your luggage and finding somewhere safe to stay. That's all you can do right now. Maybe when you're back in familiar headspace, you can make plans for whittling down the number of your enemies; but that's not a job for this afternoon.

* * *

The nearest pharmacy turns out to be inside a red-brick Tesco superstore, the shiny green glass cylinder of a government-run vertical farm rising from the former parking lot behind it. You sidle up to the counter and make yourself known to the government employee behind the counter. She bustles off into the back room, and the pharmacist comes out. She's a pretty, petite woman, thirtysomething Anglo-Indian. "Mr. Christie?" she asks. It's an alias—it's *your* alias, for the next hour at least. "May I see some proof of identity?"

You show her your entirely authentic driving licence and she reads it with dark, unreadable eyes then scans your thumbprint and verifies it. "Thank you," she says. Into the back, then back out again with a bag: "You've had this prescription before?"

You nod, eagerly. It's a selective metabotropic glutamate agonist, sturdy and well-understood, a neuroleptic firewall proof against the rape-machine fantasies and mind-control issues you've had ever since the disastrous clinical trial they put you through during your teens. "My luggage went missing. I, uh, I really need this." You reach out, watching the minute tremors in your hand as if from a great distance.

"I'll say you do." She hands the box over with a curious expression on her face. "There's no charge: You're in Scotland, we still have a National Health Service. That's you, then. Have a nice day." They have a working health-care system here, don't they? You nod jerkily, then back away.

Outside the shiny socialized factory farm, post office, pharmacy, and general-purpose omnistore, you gulp down two tablets—one of the doctors at the clinic told you how to do that, pump-priming, years ago—and stand there shaking for a minute. Grey streets, tall buildings looking down on you with eye-socket windows. Bats glide overhead, or pigeons, or RPVs with terahertz radar eyes, vigilant for the deviant. You shiver. You need to get under cover before they come for you ... give the meds time to cut in. You haven't had an attack this bad since ... since ...

Don't think about it.

You are the Toymaker's avatar in this nation-state. You're the executive: strong, and determined, and entrepreneurial, and skilled. You're not some kind of paranoid-schizophrenic personality-disorder case, stoned on his own brain chemistry. There really *is* a chip in your skull, monitoring and controlling and stabilizing on behalf of the conspiracy for which you work. There really *is* someone or something watching over you, controlling from afar. The hallucinations are going to go away, then you're going to take this reality by the throat and twist it until it crackles under your fingers like ... like ...

The replacement prescription sits heavy in your pocket, reassuring, a chemotaxic anchor pulling you closer to the harbour of high-functioning quasi-sanity. Just knowing it's in your system makes you feel better. So you walk back along the main road towards town, taking your time (and avoiding the nosy buses and their intrusive cameras). About half a mile later you pass a hole-in-the-wall diner, where you pause to order a mixed meze and a plate of falafels. The bored Middle Eastern guy behind the bar spends his time between serving you hunched over an elderly pad, handset glued to his ears, evidently talking an Alzheimer's patient through replying to an email: "No, look, at the top, it says get mail, write, address book, reply, tap reply—no, not the red dot, *below* the red dot, what do you see?" His despairing half-duplex monotone soothes your rattled nerves, reassuring you that he's not remotely likely to be spying on you.

When you leave the restaurant, the day has brightened considerably. There are no bushes for concealment, no sinister shapes flitting past overhead—an unmanned police segway rolls up the hill, cameras panning in all directions, but even the neurotypical can see *that*.

Another fifty minutes of walking sees you back in the West End, approaching the marble-fronted monolith of the Hilton. You are relatively calm, at peace with what it is you are about to do. It's true they have misplaced your luggage, and with it your sample merchandise. However—let us retain a sense of proportion—this is not the worst thing that has happened to you today, is it? Once you have unpacked your 5.62 kilograms of home and bolted the hotel-room door you'll be safe. It just depends on whether the fool on the hospitality desk has found—

Your march across the polished floor of the lobby comes to an abrupt halt. There's a well-dressed woman waiting beside the desk, but nobody behind it. You can feel your arousal level rising: You *need* your *bag*; your commercial sample is sleeping in it; are they playing with you? The woman is watching you with elaborate in-attentiveness, carefully avoiding eye contact. "Do you work here?" you demand.

"No." *Now* she looks at you. A wry twist of the lips. "They're trying to find my parcel. I had it sent poste restante—FedEx say they delivered it this morning, but the hotel know nothing."

The very idea! Suddenly it strikes you. You shipped your luggage via Yamato, a takuhaibin logistics company, and they simply don't lose things. But if this woman's package went missing, and she used FedEx—"My luggage is missing, too," you confess. "Think they've got a problem?"

"I'd say so." She nods. "Mr. MacAndrews says they've been having network trouble all day. That's usually a euphemism for malware, in my experience."

An upswing in cybernetic infestation isn't *your* problem, but it puts the hospitality manager's attitude in a different light. Maybe he's not actually *trying* to fuck with you—

And here he comes, scurrying back out from a locked door with a box in his hands. He sees you and does a double-take, but goes straight for your companion: "Ms. Straight? We found it! They've got the computers working again, and it was sitting in our loading area along with the other inbound consignments." He looks at you directly. "Mr. .... Christie? Your luggage was missing, too, wasn't it?" *Cheeky sod.* You nod. "I'll just go see if it's turned up as well, now we've got our logistics working again."

He turns and rushes off, leaving your companion looking at her box. "Humph. I thought he was supposed to get some proof of identity before handing items over," she says disapprovingly.

"Well, that's his problem, isn't it?" you say, and smile at her. You focus on her properly for the first time, taking in: red hair, carefully styled; lips and eyes emphasized, but not heavy on the slap; wearing a green dress with a low neckline that's kept on the business side of sexy by a black jacket. Mature but rootable, in other words, and if she isn't on the pull, you're a cactus.

You haven't had any action for a couple of weeks now. You don't know where the local cruising grounds are, and here in the dour puritan anglosphere the hotel front desk doesn't provide room service. You have certain needs—exacerbated now you're coming down from your little reality excursion. You posted an ad on a swinger aggregator a couple of days ago, but no joy yet. The idea of her plumped wasp-sting lips wrapped around your cock appeals: You take conscious control of your smile and widen it.

"I suppose so." She catches your eye and smiles back. "I'll just have to wait."

Interested but coy: You've met this attitude before, and it bugs the living fuck out of you. Why don't these sheeple admit that it's pointless and drop the pretence that they care? *Oh, but I'd feel guilty,* they say if you ask them why they tipped the waiter/returned the excess change they were given/didn't pad the insurance claim/turned down the zipless fuck—even though there's absolutely no chance that anyone would catch them. You smile back at her and nod.

"Are you staying here for long?" you ask.

"Oh, just checking in for a few nights." She raises an eyebrow. "Yourself?"

"The same," you say honestly. "Here on business, just checking in, gone tomorrow. At a loose end, really."

Her pupils dilate slightly, and there are some other cues: You've studied this shit, looked into NLP, and you focus on emitting the right signals, mirroring her subconscious arousal. "That's a shame," she says. "What line are you in?"

That's off-script, but not too far off-script. "I'm in toys," you say. It's even true. "Re-establishing a local supply-chain subsidiary that's been neglected for too long." The door is opening: The irritating Mr. McAndrews is on his way back. "Busy by day, totally at a loose end by night. I don't suppose you'd be interested in dinner?"

Two out of three times, they say *no* at this point: If she says *yes*, you've got about a 40 per cent chance of finding out if she swallows. McAndrews is busy with the telescoping handle of what out of the corner of one eye you recognize is your case. You keep your eye-balls pointed the right way (which is *not* at Ms. Straight's face or tits).

"Sure," she says, her smile medium-flirtatious. "Meet here, eight tonight?"

"Glad to," you say, mirroring her expression and carefully concealing your satisfaction. Then you break contact deliberately, slewing towards Mr. McAndrews, who is wrestling your suitcase to a halt in front of you. "Ah, excellent. By the way, Ms. Straight here—"

"—Dorothy—" You glance back at her, let your smile widen, nod slightly.

"—was expecting you to ask for some ID—"

"Ach, yes, but you see, we have a record." McAndrews twitches at the discreet camera dome overhead. "Nobody would steal from us."

Dorothy is raising an eyebrow at you. "John," you volunteer.
"Mr. John R. Christie. If you could just sign here?"
McAndrews thrusts a tablet at you. *Bastard.*
"I'll see you this evening, John." She turns and is gone.

* * *

You take your luggage up to your room and go through it with
shaking hands. Here's the sample merchandise, occupying half the
case: You plug it in to charge, just in case a demo is called for in the
next couple of days. Here's your "sterile" pad—still in the box it
came in from PC WORLD—and here are your spare clothes.
Toothbrush. Shaver. Meds. Bling case. You carefully arrange the
small items on the desk in their correct order. Then you put the pad
online and tell it to download its work personality from the cloud
while you have a scalding-hot shower and change your clothes.

Of course you can't stay here. But you *must* stay here. Or
rather: "John Christie" has to stay where the police expect to find
him during their investigation. *You* can be someone else, somewhere else. And your sample merchandise had better be somewhere
else, lest the police find it in your custody. That would totally suck.

Luckily, there's a magical mystery tour in your phone that'll take
you out of John Christie's panopticon-enforced sheep's clothing and
give you a new suit and a second shot at lift-off. But the sudden
shortage of candidate executives for your business plan is disturbing: Finding two of them dead is not a coincidence. You need
backup before you start digging for the killers. And you're going to
get very little of it until the Operation cleans up after that DoS
attack.

A plan begins to come together in your mind. You'll renew your
room for the rest of the week, but you won't be there: You're going
to set up shop elsewhere. You're going to go and buy new luggage
and pick up your new papers, like Operation support told you to.

Leave your old luggage with the sample merchandise parked with a useful idiot, just in case the police come snooping. Forward all calls, sanitize the room with a brisk spritz of sports stadium DNA, and all that's left is the legal wrap-up: "John Christie" will still be staying in your hotel room, but you'll be gone. Meanwhile, tonight there's dinner—and hopefully *baka sekusu* with the Straight bitch for dessert.

You've had better days, but this one is showing signs of improvement.

The pad finishes downloading. You rename some files, point the browser at a malware site, and allow it to infect the machine, scrambling certain files to provide you with deniability if anyone searches it. Then you shove it in the room safe, pick up your meds, bling, and key-ring, pull on a pair of glasses, pick up your case (with fully charged sample merchandise), and head out the door.

Once you pair them with your skullphone, the glasses steer you across the main road and down a picturesque path that meanders through Princes Street Gardens, out of sight of the trams, around the base of the huge granite butt-plug on which the castle squats. The skullphone's display is austere, basic: You can only cram so much intelligence into a gram of glucose fuel-cell-powered silicon leeching off your blood sugar and dissolved oxygen. A third of a mile later, you cross a bridge across the buried railway station, then through a slightly tatty subterranean shopping mall where you spend half an hour hunting for the necessities to replace your regular luggage. Half the storefronts are shuttered, victims of high-street flight. Climbing the Waverley Steps you pause, then turn right and cross the intersection with North Bridge. According to the messages queued in your chip, your new identity documents can be obtained from an office on the third floor of the huge pile of Gothic limestone within whose windows you can just see an eerily glowing glass cube.

You walk through the revolving door and cross the lobby of the old post-office building to the glass-walled lifts that slide silently up and down within the echoing atrium. There's a transparent airlock in front of the lift doors. "John Christie, for the honorary consul of the Independent Republic of Issyk-Kulistan," you say, as the outer door closes behind you. There's a puff of air from the explosive detectors below, a beep, and the lift door opens before you. Thirty seconds later, you're standing in a narrow corridor, outside a glass door and an entry-phone. You push the buzzer. "Mr. Christie? Please come in, it's the second office on the left," says a Scottish-accented voice.

You silently repeat your line as you walk along to the second door and arrive as a thirtyish British-Asian man in a cheap suit pulls it open and looks up at you with a peculiarly bovine expression. "What can I do for you?"

"Colonel Datka sent me." You can see the key turning in the lock behind his petrified eyes. "I'm here to collect some papers. And I have a little job for you."

INTERLUDE 1

KEMAL: SPAMCOP

Welcome to the postnational age.

Here you are, sitting in the window-seat of a creaky old Embraer as it makes its final approach into Edinburgh airport, banking over the tidal barrage and the wind farms in the Firth of Forth: It's been five years since your only previous visit, and not long enough by far.

Eggs and spam.

Back then, you had the glamour and the mojo, the whole Men in Black thing working for you: the Europol supercop from l'Organisation pour Nourrir et Consolider L'Europe, travelling with a tiger team of forensic analysts and a digitally signed email from the Judge d'Inquisition to hand in case you needed to steam-roller your way across the objections of a provincial police force who didn't realize what they were dealing with. Except things went terribly wrong—the national-security dinosaurs rising from their uneasy sleep, opening the closet doors to draw forth a conga line of dancing skeletons. It still gives you the cold shudders, thinking about the ease with which a couple of teams of coke-fuelled black-hat Shanghainese hackers rooted the network backbones of a pair of peripheral states: And the shit you stumbled into out here on the edge of the North Sea was as nothing compared to what your colleagues had to clean up in Gdansk and Warsaw. Not to mention the chewing out your boss François gave you during your performance eval the following spring. Black marks on the Man in Black's record. And the rudeness of the Scottish police—that really rankled. Professional respect: Have these people never heard of it?

Eggs, ham, and spam.

The plane's wings buzz angrily as flaps extend: The wave-crests are an endless tessellation of white triangles below, marred by the wake of a sailboat. Four years in career limbo, reassigned to Business Affairs and buried leech deep in the bowels of the Department of Internet Fraud. Four years spent in a pokey little office in a corner of Madou Plaza Tower, where flies buzz madly beneath the chilly glare of LED spotlights, patiently paging through reams of spam in search of the websites of the idiots who pay to rent botnets by the hour—

Eggs, ham, sausage, and spam.

Some say the Internet is for porn; but you know that in truth the Internet is for spam. As communication technologies got cheaper, the cost of grabbing a megaphone and jamming it up against the aching ear-drums of an advertising-jaded public collapsed: Meanwhile, the content-is-king mantra of the monetization mavens gridlocked the new media in an advertising-supported business model. The great and the good of the Academy have been fighting a losing battle against the Anglo-Saxon hucksterization model for the past thirty years: But the sad truth is that the battle's lost. The tide of war was turned in Beijing and New Delhi, when the rapidly industrializing new superpowers climbed on the MAKE MONEY FAST band-wagon and gave free rein to the free market, red in tooth and claw—just as long as the sharp bits were directed outwards. And today the entire world is *still* drowning in a sea of attention-grabbing unregulated unethical untruthful spamvertising.

Spam, ham, sausage, and spam.

The white-noise roar of the cabin air-conditioning is augmented by a new noise, the wind rush from around the open nose-wheel door as the landing gear drops.

Most of the public don't notice it, but the war on spam goes ever on, and it's a war on two fronts. One front, your own, is fought by battalions of law-enforcement officers and prosecutors. The most egregious junk sells hard goods—stuff with a physical shipping address—to the vulnerable; fake pharmaceuticals to die by, trashy Tanzanian machine-tool parts, unlicensed herbal supplements from Nigeria, counterfeit designer clothes and handbags and heart valves made of shoe-leather. They show up, you order the goods, backtrace through courier and logistics to the mother-lode, obtain a warrant, pop goes the weasel, round and round the merry-go-round.

Spam, eggs, spam, spam, ham, and spam.

The brigades of system administrators and programmers on the other front tackle the problem from the opposite end, with ever-more-elaborate AI filters that scan message traffic and tell ham from spam. Ninety-five per cent of all human-readable traffic over the net is spam, a figure virtually unchanged since the late noughties. There are dumb filters and smart filters. Dumb filters look for naughty words. Smart filters look for patterns of diction that are characteristic of automatically assembled text—for much spam is generated by drivel-speaking AI, designed purely to fool the smart filters by convincing them that it's the effusion of a real human being and of interest to the recipients. Slowly but surely the

Turing Test war proceeds, as the spammers are forced to invest in ever-more-elaborate AI engines to generate conversations that can temporarily convince the spamcops' AI engines that they are in fact human beings.

Spam, sausage, spam, spam, spam, ham, spam, potato, and spam.

And still you're losing.

There's a bump and rumble, and you're shoved forward against your lap-belt as the regional jet's thrust reversers cut in. Welcome to the Republic of Scotland, semi-privatized satrapy of the former United Kingdom and sock-puppet independent vote on the Council of Ministers—soon to acquire the extra clout of a pair of senators, once the tedious ratification treaty completes and the European Parliament upgrades to a fully bicameral legislature. You're back, and this time you don't have a posse of high-powered forensic analysts behind you, or diplomatic letters of marque and reprise, or much of anything in fact: just a dossier, a disturbing-to-terrifying trend analysis from a research team in the Sorbonne, and a suggestive pattern of murders smeared bloody-handed across the width and depth of the EU.

Spam, spam, spam, murder, and spam.

Seventy years of research and development into artificial intelligence failed to deliver HAL 9000, but they did provide a huge array of toolkits for tackling complex problems. Today, in the wake of the bursting of the worldwide higher-education bubble, the big funding sources in computational artificial-intelligence research are computer games and cognitive marketing services, from personalized message generation to automated spear phishing. Some say the spammers are pouring more money into Minsky's inheritors than the US Department of Defense ever imagined. The spamcops retaliate. There's an arms race in progress, and some experts mutter dark warnings of the Spamularity: the global chaos that will ensue once the first distributed spamming engine achieves human-equivalent sentience. Possibly the only thing holding it back is the multi-tiered nature of the darknet economy: Malware that supports spamware frequently carries virus-scanning payloads that immunize host computers and phones against rival strains of infection. After all, it's a free-market economy, red in tooth and claw: And if you can't count on a state to keep the opposition in check, you've got to see to your security yourself.

Spam, spam, spam, spam, spam, spam, baked memes, spam, spam, spam, and spam.

This week, for the first time in a couple of years, the machine-generated spew has faltered significantly. Most of the usual darknets are still vomiting forth the gibber fantastic, but their core semantic networks aren't updating: It's the same flavour of froth as last week's, and thereby easier to filter out. No new botnets have surfaced, switching from build-out to broadcast mode: There has been a curious absence of new malware strains. Spam has actually *fallen*. It would be glad tidings, indeed, if not for the puzzling question of *why*. And those unsolved killings. Which is what your superiors have sent you to look into in Edinburgh: They skimmed the bullet point in your résumé and mistakenly assumed you'd be at home here, able to work hand in glove with the locals. Truly the jaws of irony are agape!

The battle against spam had grown into a bitter trench war fought on two fronts—and now a new front has been opened. Someone—or more worryingly, some *thing*—seems to have adopted a draconian approach to the problem you and yours have failed to solve in nearly four decades. And the question that everyone is worrying about is: Whatever next?

Spam! Spam! Spam! Spam! Lovely Spam! Nothing but spam!

FELIX: First Citizen

When the First Citizen has a bad night's sleep, he likes to share.

You have been recalled to the capital on urgent business—certain currency-triangulation transactions require your personal biometric signature, as one of the trustees of the national bank—and so it is no major surprise when your morning starts with the plaintive tweedle of the satphone. It sits on one of the fake Louis Quatorze bedside tables in your hotel suite. You roll over, dislodging the blonde Ukrainian girl from her death grip on the bolster (Why is she still here? Doesn't she have a bed of her own to go to?), and pick up the handset.

"Colonel Datka, sir? This is Eagle's Nest."

"Yes, yes," you say irritably, trying to focus on the illuminated dial of the alarm clock. It's four thirty, but when the Eagle's Nest calls, it is rash to hang up. "What is it?"

"His Excellency is asking for you. Are you presentable? We have a car en route."

Shit, you think. *Is Bhaskar all right?* You recognize the voice at the other end of the line: It's one of the First Citizen's regular bodyguards, Dmitry something, an ethnic Russian. (Minor reassurance: A stranger's voice would be worrying.) "I will be ready in five minutes," you say, and stifle a fear-threaded yawn. "Is there anything I should be prepared for?"

"I don't think so." Dmitry sounds uncertain. "He had a very disturbed night. The usual, is all."

"I'll be ready," you reassure the man, and hang up. The brunette has noticed your usual morning stiffening and is rubbing her lips against your manhood, but you have other needs: You shove her face away and clamber across her, pad past the empty champagne bucket towards the *en suite* bathroom. The solid silver urinal in the shape of a gaping, open-mouthed cherub swallows your steaming piss-stream. "Make yourselves useful and find me some clean underwear," you grunt at the girls. "I have an appointment with the First Citizen."

"Yes, Colonel," they echo, with the precisely correct degree of respect tinged with awe. They're almost annoyingly well-trained. Say anything you like about the plumbing: The Erkindik Hotel front desk supplies the best whores in Bishkek, if not the whole of Kyrgyzstan.

Ten minutes later, you're presentable, in the uniform of a colonel in the Army Intelligence Directorate, gold braid and red shoulder tabs and three rows of brightly polished medals—no less than is your due—as you head downstairs to the hotel lobby. (Bhaskar offered to promote you to lieutenant general a couple of times, but only halfway down the vodka bottle: Tact—or prudence—has kept you from reminding him of this when he's sober. In any case, chief of military overseas intelligence is a colonel's position in these half-assed times: You don't want to give General Medvedev cause to think you're making a play for his job.)

Two black-suited fellows from the presidential security detachment are waiting for you in the lobby. Four more stand on the sidewalk by the beetle-shiny armoured Mercedes. They see you safely on board, and seconds later you're slamming through the deserted pre-dawn boulevards of the capital in the middle of a convoy of armed pick-up trucks, blue lights flickering off the concrete frontages to either side, your armed guards scanning for threats with gunsight eyes.

The American has weaselled his way into your entourage again. (Let him have his illusory privilege of access: It's so much easier to keep an eye on him when he thinks *he's* keeping an eye on *you*.) He's sitting in the middle jump-seat opposite, clutching his pad in both hands like a determined chipmunk who refuses to give up his nut. "What is it this time?" you ask, staring pointedly at him.

"It's the exchange rate." Blue fireflies flicker and gleam inside his rimless glasses. "All it takes is a two-point fluctuation, and we lose a hundred million on the exchanges." He doesn't smile. How long is it since you could always tell an American by their smile? Good dentistry is expensive: Flashing bright teeth in these straitened times is like wearing a jacket that says MUG ME. "Can you talk him out of it?"

You suppress a sigh. "You seem to think Bhaskar is a tame bullock, to be herded this way and that. He isn't, and if you persist in this mode of thinking, he will give you a nasty surprise."

The American's lips curl. "Who's running this, you or the Operation?" he asks. "Without our collateral, you'd be—"

You smile without showing your teeth. He stops chittering, gratifyingly fast. Chipmunk-American has seen a pit viper. "We are duly grateful to our *investors*. Nevertheless, you will refrain from discussing the First Citizen in language more appropriate to cattle. Without his continuing patronage, your operation is *nothing*. We are not stupid, Mr. White. If you didn't need our special expertise, you wouldn't be engaged in this joint venture with, ah, those 'crazy Kyrgyz.'"

It's hard to tell if Mr. White blanches in the strobing glow of the
street-lamps and the blue LEDs of the lead escort, but your choice
of words echoes his own language. Stupid little geek probably imag-
ines you've cracked the encryption on his secure VoIP link,
forgetting who owns all the bandwidth in and out of both countries—both Kyrgyzstan and the recession-hit sock puppet in the East
that he's using for his little logistics operation. "I'm sorry," he says.

"Leave Bhaskar to me," you reassure him. "And leave the cur-
rency-stabilization talks alone. Your concerns are noted, and I
agree—it would be absolutely deplorable to lose a hundred million
euros of your money through inattention. Nevertheless, attempting
to micromanage the First Citizen would be unwise. Trust me on
this: I've known him for more than forty years." Since you were
both in the Young Pioneers together, back in the dog days of the
Soviet Union.

You consider saying more to the creep, promising a little something to sweeten the deal and keep suckering him in, but at that
point the convoy slows, and the car turns sharply, nosing over a
recessed barrier and down a steep ramp into an underground security check-point and parking garage. It's under the back of the New
Wing, across the street from the White House—Bhaskar's office
and bachelor pad, a hideous lump of white marble that looks like
a tax office fucking an airport terminal.

You leave the Operation's representative sitting in the limo as
the guards salute and wave you forward across the crimson carpet
and into the elevator with the best Korean terahertz radar and
explosive sniffers hidden in its walnut-veneered walls. Then it's into
the corridor under the road, and another elevator that whisks you
upstairs—then down another corridor that serves as a security fire-
break for the guards on Bhaskar's private quarters to check you
out, and finally another elevator. Then the doors slide open, and
you're in Xanadu.

Xanadu is three storeys high, ten metres on a side, and occupies about an eighth of the presidential palace's floor-plan. It's mounted on shock-absorbers driven into bed-rock and hermetically sealed from the rest of the White House by steel plates embedded in the walls: an insulated bubble of purest lunacy, the personal quarters of the First Citizen of the Republic of Kyrgyzstan. Whoever designed it was clearly channelling Samuel Coleridge on dodgy pharmaceuticals by way of Norman Foster rather than the ghost of Kublai Khan, but beggars—and First Citizens—can't be choosers: It came to light after you'd finished kicking that bum Adskhan into exile in Prague. Personally, if it had been you, you'd have demolished the thing rather than sleep in it, but after the second assassination attempt, Bhaskar got the message and retreated inside his predecessor's hermetically sealed pleasure dome.

You find him sitting in the sunken circular seat with the fish-tank floor and pink leather cushions, wearing one of those Japanese dressing-gown things and looking morose. There are bags under his eyes, and he has neglected to shave. His big, bony feet splay across the glass, footprints for the rainbow carp to gape and mouth at from beneath. "Is it morning?" he asks hopefully.

"It will be, soon." You carefully descend the steps—you've never trusted that glass floor not to dump you in the water—and embrace, cheek to cheek. "Are you well, brother? What's troubling you?"

"I can't sleep." The First Citizen—you remember playing "tag" in the woods out behind the apartment block you both lived in—looks despondent. "The pills aren't helping. I feel like I'm going mad at times, let me tell you. It's this artificial light: I never see the sun these days. Bad dreams, whenever I manage to get to sleep." He rubs his index finger alongside his crooked, slightly splayed nose.

"We should get you a woman—" You stop when you see the look in his eyes. He hasn't been the same since Yelena died. Some men need all the women they can get, but for others, one is all they want for a lifetime. "Or a bottle of vodka? And some dirty videos. When did we last kick back with a good movie?"

Now his shoulders relax. "I'm supposed to tutor a meeting of the All-Republic Commission on Finance this afternoon," he says quietly. "Most of those fucking peasants wouldn't know a credit default swap if it bit them on the bell-end. And listen, they aren't paying me to teach macro-economics at the state academy anymore. Those bastards, if they were my students, they'd be heading for a 'fail.' All they can think of is lining their own pockets. What the fuck do they care about the future?"

"The committee will still be there tomorrow, and the day after," you point out. "Send a reliable deputy ... " *Now* you understand the expression. "What is it?"

"What indeed?" He raises an eyebrow. "It's the future. I've been thinking about it a lot lately."

"What?"

"Listen." The First Citizen glances away. "Suppose I ordered you to arrest the American, the investment agent. No reason given, just shut his little crime syndicate down *right now* and bugger the big picture. Would you do it?"

"For you, boss? Of course, in a split instant." You shrug. "Of course, it would make a real mess," you add, conspiratorially: Subtext, *you'd completely fuck over our past two years' work*.

"Right, right." Bhaskar limply punches the open palm of his left hand, winces slightly from the carpal tunnel syndrome that's plagued him for decades. "You'd do it, but first you make sure I am fully informed as to the consequences." (Little does he truly appreciate the real risks involved: It's your job to protect your unworldly genius of a childhood friend from the real-world consequences of such a whim. To ensure that when it's time for you to bring the hammer down and Bhaskar to fix the deficit, there are no overlooked survivors with enough money to pay for assassins.) "I'm not asking you to do that. But the point is, at least I know where you stand. You're not afraid to tell me. But those fuckers on the all-state council? That rat-bag Kurmanbek smiles like a vulture and makes nicey-nicey noises, but do you think he'd lend me a horse if my pony was lamed—"

Kurmanbek is the vice-president—or rather, the ethnic Uzbek counterweight in the ruling coalition Bhaskar presides over: in other words, Nuisance Central. And, of course, Bhaskar's right: If he asked Kurmanbek the time, the answer would be whatever was most convenient for the veep. "Is the committee's immediate agenda critical?" you ask. "Because if not—why *not* send Kurmanbek to deputize? I'll have someone listen in"—you're talking about bugging a state committee—"and compare the minutes to what actually gets said. Worst case, you skip class. Best case, Kurmanbek hands you some live ammunition. But either way, you need a couple of days off, boss. Kick back with a couple of bottles and some decadent Iranian musicals. Maybe a game—when did you last go on an epic quest?"

The First Citizen brightens. "You're right, Felix. I should skip school more often!" You nod, encouraging.

It's got to be a horrible life, trapped here in a hermetically sealed bubble inside a presidential palace, unable to go out in daylight without a platoon of soldiers with fixed bayonets on all sides, children grown up and wife dead of a stroke these past three years. Not to mention that fucking annoying Georgian extradition warrant floating around Interpol like an unexploded bomb—you *know* Bhaskar didn't order the guards to fire on that crowd; it was a horrible fuck-up by an idiot second lieutenant—but the upshot is he's stuck here in the middle of Bishkek, not even able to go to the casinos in St. Petersburg for an evening at the roulette table. (Or whatever it is that he enjoys: Knowing Bhaskar, given the choice he'd probably disguise himself as a professor, sneak into the university campus, and teach a seminar on the history of monetarism. If all the Republic's previous presidents' vices were as recondite as his, *Moscow* would be coming to *you* for loans.)

You've had a ringside seat, seen what it's doing to your childhood friend, watched him reduced to fishing for assurances that he's still loved, shuffling around his carpeted pleasure-prison in the dark. If any smiling bastard tried to convince you to front a coup, you'd shoot him yourself, you think, just to stay out of the presidential padded cell.

Then the First Citizen puts a friendly arm around your shoulder and drops you in it head first:

"But tell me now, how is the Przewalsk business coming along? I've been fielding questions from the EU ambassador's office, but they're becoming more insistent, and that whining louse Borisovitch in State is starting to give me back-chat ... "

THE OPERATION: Blofeld
Blues

There is no sabre-scarred monocle-wearing bullet-headed bad guy stroking a white cat at the centre of this conspiracy.

Nor are there any tropical-island bases patrolled by Komodo dragons, assault-rifle-toting boiler-suited henchmen, or stolen nuclear weapons.

The wildest conspiracies are the quietest.

This one started out as a venture-capital partnership that has opted for mutual unlimited liability in lieu of filing certain important papers that the Internal Revenue Service would be very interested in seeing.

In this decade, the United States faces a cumulative gross budget deficit of around 30 trillion dollars—or about 16 trillion euros, or 20 trillion renminbi. It's the hangover from a century of imperial overstretch, the flip side of the butcher's bill from trying to force the world to play by the conqueror's rule-book for too long. The IRS is grabbing every bent cent they can find these days, trying to outrun the law of compound interest. However, their intrusive banking compliance regime doesn't reach as far as it did a decade or more ago because foreigners aren't terribly scared of Uncle Sam anymore. For the rising powers of the BRIC, helping the US government balance its books is not exactly high on the agenda of *realpolitik*. So while most Americans get to tighten their belts and swallow a painful prescription from the IMF, the few, the lucky— those who invested their assets overseas, before the money supply exploded in the wake of one banking crisis too many—are stranded, facing a 90 per cent marginal tax rate if they try to repatriate their wealth.

Hence, the Operation. Invest overseas, invest efficiently, invest for maximum growth, and who gives a fuck about collateral damage? They're foreigners. They got us into this mess, and now they're holding our heads underwater by debasing our currency. Fuck 'em if they can't take a joke!

The Operation is nominally headquartered in California.

To the IRS—and anyone else who enquires—it appears to be a small, somewhat lackadaisical investment partnership, with a software subsidiary who maintain the expert systems its strategic planning runs on. A couple of successful companies huddle close to the parent organization's feet: a small ISP, a private management college (not that anyone's paying for MBAs this decade, when they could be training as plumbers or auto mechanics instead), and an off-shore secretarial bureau. As VC firms go, the only thing distinguishing the Operation from its peers is how *un*distinguished it looks. Its managers seem to have poor judgement, funding too many second-rate entrepreneurs who drop out of sight after a couple of months. It's almost as if they don't want to make a profit, don't feel the visionary's urge to set the world ablaze.

Komodo dragons, nuclear missiles, and island bases are all high-maintenance overheads. They're *inefficient*. And the Operation values efficiency above all else.

The Operation proactively recruits executive-calibre material from among the unfairly-discriminated-against neurodiverse. It provides a supportive and caring environment in which these battered souls can grow and be all that they want to be. The hate-word "psychopath" conjures up visions of knife-wielding maniacs, but that's a far cry from the reality of the Operation's entrepreneurial spirit. In reality, it's an unacknowledged truth that amidst the cut and thrust of boardroom politics, a touch of antisocial personality disorder is an asset—the Operation merely makes the best of its human resources, polishes and trains them to keep their natural impulsive drives harnessed to the wagon of success. Their classes in corporate and managerial ethics really are first-rate: By the time they graduate and leave the nest, the new entrepreneurs know exactly what they must do to succeed.

One of the dirty little truths of organized crime is that for the most part its management is incompetent. No business exists in a vacuum, and no enterprise—criminal or otherwise—can succeed unless its clients and suppliers trust each other. Unreliable, incompetent, greedy, grasping, poor impulse control—these traits drag down and dismember the management of 'Ndrangheta, cripple the profitability of the Yakuza, and hamstring the Russian Mafiya. They're slow learners. Even as late as the early noughties, organized crime had barely begun to absorb the lessons of modern management; as for innovation, Al Capone would have recognized most of their business models on sight.

The Operation knows one thing, and knows it well—how to set up and manage a business for maximum growth until it's time to negotiate a successful sale and cash out. They have single-handedly dragged the management of vice into the late twentieth century, if not the twenty-first: a monumental, if questionable, achievement.

But now they're under attack.

The Operation's business is at its most effective when it can tap new audiences, gain new customers, expand markets—reach out to new sources of profit. Lack of brand awareness is the biggest obstacle to establishing any new sales channel (legal or otherwise), and you can't advertise counterfeit goods or illegal services through regulated media. Consequently, the Operation is highly dependent on all kinds of spam, from shoutcasting on in-game voice channels to the old search engine optimization racket.

Over the past three days, more than fifty individuals have died in unlikely and frequently messy manners—electrocuted by miswired domestic robots, hearts stopped by improbable prescribing errors, driven off the edge of multi-storey car-parks by malfunctioning car autopilots, shot by police in raids on the wrong address. Most of these people are not actual affiliates or employees of the Operation. They are, however, all involved at one level or another in the unregulated network-marketing sector.

Something must be done.

PART 2

LIZ: MOTE, EYE, REDUX

There is one good thing about being seconded to run interference for Dodgy Dickie's murder investigation, and it is this: CID always get allocated the best cars, right after Traffic. They get the same priority as the regular community patrols, and that's a hell of a long way up the pecking order from ICIU.

When you show up at the transport desk this time, you don't have to grovel for a segway: Instead there's an unmarked Chinese Volvo waiting for you, silver-grey luxury on wheels. As you slide behind the wheel and orient yourself with the controls, you see it's got a console full of extras on the passenger side—traffic data terminal, ANPR cameras, external laser projector, the works. *So this is how the other half drive,* you think enviously as you thumb the airport short-stay car-park into the autopilot and hit the GO button. A moment later, the car reverses out into the station yard and turns towards Queensferry Road in eerie silence: You're halfway to Turnhouse before it fires up the diesel generator under the bonnet.

Self-driving cars are a mixed blessing. Right now, you miss the bad old days when you needed to keep your hands on the wheel and your eyes on the road: It'd be a welcome distraction. But current health and safety regulations say that only officers assigned to ongoing pursuit and patrol driving duties—and the training that goes with them—are allowed to actually operate vehicles. It's something to do with the force being liable for damages if you run over any civilians. So you use the spare quarter hour to dig into the CopSpace image of Dickie's incident room and try to familiarize yourself with who's doing what (and how far they've got so far).

The car parks itself in a police-only bay near domestic/EU arrivals, at Terminal One. You head for the meeting point adjacent to Customs with a sinking heart. CopSpace at the airport is congested, full of security warnings and immigration tags as well as the usual detritus: criminals on probation, minicab drivers with unpaid licences, and the like. But after a minute, your specs lock onto someone and flicker for attention. You see a vaguely familiar face in the crowd, towing a neat carry-on bag as he stands in front of the exit, scanning—

Yes, that's him. You start forward. Medium height, dark eyes, Middle Eastern skin, sharp suit. He's looking around, but he hasn't clocked you yet. He's alone this time, no mob of super-cop extras in tow. His head turns. "Kemal Aslan, I presume," you say, preempting him. "Welcome back to Scotland."

His expression of annoyance is so quickly masked you can't be sure it even exists—is it your imagination?—and he extends a hand. "Ah, Inspector Kavanaugh." You take it and shake. His palm is cool and dry. "I hope you're well." He ducks his head. It's a long way from the arrogant confidence he exuded the first time you saw him, five years ago.

"Well enough." You gesture towards the exit: "I've got a car. How long are you here for?"

"As long as it takes." You head for the doors; he follows. "If you wouldn't mind stopping en route, I need to check in at my hotel? Then we should talk."

You stop. "I'm not entirely clear on what you think there is to talk *about*," you snap, and he recoils as if you've just bared your teeth at him. "We've got a sensitive time-critical investigation to run, and unless you've got some insight to contribute, something that we should know, you're just not that high a priority."

To your surprise he nods. "I appreciate that," he says softly. "But it is not the only investigation in progress. I am here to help— all of them. On my previous visit, we started out badly. I will apologize, if that is what you desire. But afterwards, we must work together. It is very important."

You manage not to gape at him, but you're momentarily at a loss: He delivers his spiel with a dead-pan sincerity that leaves you scrabbling for a handle to hang your anger on. Finally, you manage to say: "In the car. We can discuss this later." Then you start walking again, so wound-up that you're as jerky as a marionette.

The car is halfway to his hotel—a boutique establishment in Haymarket—before he speaks again. "Has there been any progress in your investigation?"

"I need to get you signed on and authorized before I can disclose intelligence material." You're already working out a shortest path in your head, a circuit of the necessary offices: You need to drag Kemal past the super's office door for pro forma approval, then your own desk to verify that authentication of his credentials is already in the channel via Europol, then up to Doc, who can tell one of his sergeants to give him external consulting access to the virtual incident room. His eagerness to get started ahead of the formalities is grating and borderline-toxic. (But then, you ask yourself, *What would you do in his shoes?*) "Can you tell me what's going on from *your* end of things?"

"It is a massacre," he says simply.

For a moment you think you misheard. "A what?"

"A massacre." He stares out through the ghost of the head-up display as the tidy shop-fronts of Corstorphine slide past. "We have linked eight deaths to the, the atrocity, already. They all occurred within a six-hour period. But the incident is ongoing: I expect more to come to light."

It's a really good thing the car's driving itself; otherwise, the force would probably be looking at an out-of-court settlement, and you'd be looking at the inside of an ambulance. "*What?* Where's this coming from?"

"The victims all died within the same period. They died at home, in circumstances superficially resembling domestic accidents. They were all—*all*—involved in online marketing activities of questionable legality. Some of them were found immediately, others took time to be discovered. We are currently examining a number of other deaths over the same period. I expect the number to rise, sharply."

Eight murders? You find the figure implausible, comically ludicrous. That's more murders than Edinburgh gets in a year—a really bad year at that. It puts you in mind of stories you heard at Uncle Bert's knee, from his time in the RUC during the Troubles. A faint inkling begins to dawn on you. "Tell me this isn't political? More of that shit, like five years ago—"

Kemal is shaking his head emphatically. "It's not political." That's hard to argue with. What kind of regular terrorist would target spammers?

The car cruises past a gaggle of uniformed school-children on the pavement: That's an extra half million in damages in the parallel universe where you're supposed to have your hands on the wheel. "So who do you think it is?" you ask him.

"Not *who* but *what*." He clams up, jaw shut.

"Uh-huh." *Does not compute.* "In my experience, crimes usually have perpetrators."

"But this is not a normal crime," asserts Kemal. "It is a cluster of anomalous deaths, distributed geographically but sharing a common *je ne sais quoi*, and occurring nearly simultaneously. This is not the, the symptom of normal criminal activity, no?"

"Oh, bullshit. Next thing you'll be telling me, it's aliens or artificial intelligence or some other science-fictional nonsense."

He's looking at you intently. "It all depends on what you mean by artificial intelligence."

You blink rapidly. "How many kinds could there be?" The ocular tic sets CopSpace in a tizzy, flashing through stacks of overlays that flicker across the staid stone-fronted houses: prevalence of porn downloads, undischarged ASBOs, unclosed burglary tickets. "Has someone been building HAL 9000 in their basement, then?"

The car slows, then turns into a side-street. "Not to the best of my knowledge." Kemal looks unhappy. "But I have been spending too much time tracking fraudsters on the Internet," he adds elliptically. "The spammers, they are ingenious. The programmers have a saying, you know? 'If we understand how we do it, it isn't artificial intelligence anymore.' Playing chess, driving cars, generating conversational text that can convince humans it's an old friend and please to click on this download link." He clears his throat. "You use Internet search engines, don't you?"

"What, like Google?"

"The programmers have another saying: 'The question of whether a machine can think is no more interesting than the question of whether a submarine can swim.' The search engines, they are not artificial intelligences, synthetic consciousnesses. They don't *need* to be. Perhaps we overestimate consciousness? After all, the spam filters everyone uses—you may not think you're using one, but your service providers handle the job on your behalf—are very good at telling human beings from bots. And the bots are good, too: They get better and better at emulating human communication, insinuating themselves into our conversations, all the time. For the past three years, they have been able to pass a noniterative Turing Test administered by human beings more often than real human controls. *We* can't distinguish spam from ham— not as reliably as our filters. And the filters are still fallible even though they are learning all the time."

You've had enough of this bullshit. "With respect, Inspector Aslan, I don't see what this has to do with our culpable homicide investigation. Spam fil—software didn't reach out of the net and spike Mr. Blair's enema fluid: There's a human agency involved at some level, and that's what we're going to find. Now I will grant you"—you catch yourself on the edge of finger-wagging, and issue yourself a cease and desist (just like the persuasion counsellor warned you to)—"someone may be using spam filters to track and to trace criminals involved in the bulk advertising industry, but you're not going to convince me that there's some, some murderous piece of software that's out to kill—" You're almost spluttering, and that's even more of a C&D situation when it comes to influencing people: So you make yourself stop.

Kemal is looking at you with a heavy-lidded expression that gives you a weird shiver of déjà vu.

"You are correct: Spam filters do not kill," he says calmly. "But people using spam filters to backtrace and select their targets are another matter."

"But *why*?" You shake your head. "It doesn't make sense!"

"I agree with you," he says with exaggerated, acidic dignity. "But somebody is killing them. Our task is to discover who, is it not?"

The car slows, then noses into a hotel car-park, while you're trying to come up with a sufficiently scathing rejoinder. Then you suddenly remember where you've seen his expression before: in the

bathroom mirror, this very morning, while you were choking on the
sure knowledge that you knew something important about the
Blair investigation, but that Dodgy Dickie was certain not to give
you the time of day.

Mote, eye, redux.

* * *

Kemal doesn't say another word as the car parks itself, but his
expression says it all for him. "I need ten minutes to drop my bag,"
he says, opening the car door.

"Of course." You climb out of the Volvo and collect his
wheelie-bag from the boot. The car beeps and shuts down behind
you as you take the escalator up to the lobby. You install yourself
in an understuffed leather sofa at one side as Kemal does his business with the self-service check-in, picks up a keycard, and is
whisked upstairs to salaryman limbo.

Kemal gives you just enough time to do the necessary one-eighty
reorientation and get your shit squared away. You're just finishing
up a memo to Doc—necessary clearances for Kemal—when he
reappears. "That was fast."

"I said I only needed time to drop my bag." You could swear he
looks wounded, but those big brown eyes of his make it his default
state. "Are we going now?"

"In a moment." You fold your desktop away into a corner of
your left eye and lever yourself ungracefully out of the sofa. Then
you dust yourself down. "There's a passable coffee shop round the
corner," you tell him. "I think you and I ought to go there and discuss the, the spam thing over a latte. Before I take you round the
shop and get you into the system."

He gives you the hairy eye-ball. "What is there to discuss." It's
not inflected as a question.

"We started out on the wrong foot." You take a deep breath. "I apologize, for what it's worth. I'll give you a fair hearing. But you need to know what you're walking into before you stick your nose round the incident-room door."

Kemal exhales. "Politics?"

"You could say that."

"I think a small espresso would be a good idea," he concedes. "In that case . . ."

You're not *entirely* sure why the sudden turnaround with respect to Kemal, but there are several factors feeding in to it. It's hard to stay furious at an abstract, and meeting him face-to-face you recognize only too clearly the stink of failure to launch. You may have been treading water for five years, but Kemal's spent them sliding down the greasy pole. Stripped of the Eurocop arrogance and the entourage of Men in Black, he's just a sad-faced little cop with a briefcase full of nightmares. And then there's the matter in hand: *Eight deaths.*

You don't owe Kemal the time of day, but it'd be grossly, unforgivably unprofessional to let your personal dislike get in the way of his investigation.

Sitting in the fake-eighties bachelor-pad bistro-hell coffee shop, you lay it all out for him. "You're walking in on a high-profile murder investigation. Lead investigator is Detective Chief Inspector Dickie MacLeish; he and I have a history, and it's not a good one. To be fair, he has a headache because firstly, Edinburgh usually gets maybe one murder a month, and secondly, the victim in this investigation had money and connections. He's under the spotlight already, and adding a foreign connection is—"

CopSpace clears its throat discreetly. You hold up a cautioning hand to Kemal and glance at the incoming. It takes a second or two to make sense of it, then you swear under your breath. It's a FLASH broadcast from the virtual situation room, which is exceptional in its own right—they'd usually only do that to alert everyone to an arrest warrant for a dangerous fugitive. This one is even more unusual. "Nine," you tell Kemal.

His face, glimpsed through a slew of rapidly accreting wikinotes, doesn't look remotely surprised. "Who?" he asks.

"One Vivian Crolla, accountant by trade." You read swiftly, then take in the preliminary crime-scene scans. "Jesus." You can't help yourself: "Somebody shrink-wrapped her to a mattress full of banknotes—"

"They *what*?" Now he raises an eyebrow.

You blink the overlay aside. "We should go and get you signed in," you suggest. *How should I know who* they *are*? you wonder defensively. *What kind of lunatic goes around shrink-wrapping people to bales of bank-notes*? "Michael Blair was one of her customers."

"Ah." Kemal raises his tiny cup, pulls a face, and knocks back his ristretto in one. You eye your own cup: It's half-full. Regretfully, you stand and turn your back on it. "Lead on," he says.

Back at HQ, it's as if a giant virtual boot has kicked over the anthill. You normally get plenty of passing trade at the station, but it's mostly beat cops checking in petty shoplifters and such-like at this time of day. Two Bizarro-world murders in rapid succession—with rumours of a Eurotrash gangland connection—have got folks nervous. They remember the hideous mess five years ago when everything fell over, back to manual typewriters and anonymous prepay mobiles while the spooks ran around upgrading the security keys on all the nation's key routers and praying that the hackers responsible weren't fucking with the air traffic control system or the reactor complex at Torness. The atmosphere today's a lot like that: Word has got around the canteen grape-vine that something really out of order is going on. And you're getting the hairy eye-ball from all sides as soon as you walk up to the desk in reception and sign a visitor's badge for Kemal.

You run him straight upstairs to CI Dixon's office, where Doc's secretary casually signs his ID onto the system—logging his biometrics solely on your say-so (talk about being granted a sufficiency of rope for a career asphyxiation!)—then you herd him along the corridor to IT Support, where a pathologically detached civilian contractor registers his phone and gets him logged into CopSpace. You've just short-circuited about two days of procedures specifically designed to prevent J. Random Unauthorized Person from getting into IT Support's hair, but you're in no mood to take shit right now. If Kemal's right about the scale of what's going on, Dickie needs to know the shape of the tiger he's got by the tail. And so, less than two hours after you picked him up, you're back in front of the door to briefing room D31.

* * *

"Inspector Kavanaugh." Dickie looks up from the surface in the middle of the room. It's displaying a 3D cutaway of a typical Edinburgh tenement, one-sixth of life-size, with SOCO annotations hazing the air above it as thickly as the cigarette smoke of an earlier generation. "This would be ... "

"Inspector Kemal Aslan, on assignment to Europol Business Affairs in Brussels from Emniyet Genel Müdürlüğü in Ankara."

Kemal clears his throat. "We have been monitoring an upswing in violent deaths of individuals engaged in the Internet fraud sector." He meets Dickie MacLeish's fiercely sceptical gaze: "Eight so far, across Europe, all within forty-eight hours. Nine, now."

You tag-team with him, piling it up on MacLeish: "Inspector Aslan is ready to give you an overview of the larger picture whenever you're ready. I checked him in with IT, he's on the system. His auths from Europol check out." (Which is an important point, as it's not so long ago that a nutter with a cop fetish managed to fast-talk his way onto a prostitution sweep in Portobello.)

Kemal doesn't switch target. "We believe there is a common mechanism behind the killings, although proving a culpable human perpetrator may be—"

He's about to get stuck into his spiel when a uniform from CID shoulders his way into your circle and clears his throat apologetically. "Inspectors." He nods at Dickie. "Skipper? Got a moment?"

"Aye?" Dickie cuts you dead of an instant. Kemal's neck muscles tense at that, but he bites his tongue like he's had lots of practice lately. You peer closer at the crime scene on the virtual dissecting table. It's one of those upper stairwell flats with a windowless hall and rooms branching off it on all sides. There's something in the living room, like a discarded square-cut sandwich—

"—The Blair scene yesterday, his ID was in the name of John, uh, Christie. It's just that it rang a bell with Mary as she was compiling the daily for Oversight. She's got a true-crime reading habit, and she looked him up online, and he's a ringer, sir."

"What kind of ringer?" Dickie's diction is clipped. He looks like he's going to blow a gasket: not unusual for him, but even so . . .

"John Reginald Halliday Christie—just like we logged on this guy's driving licence—was a serial killer, sir, the Notting Hill Strangler. Hanged for murder in 1953." He pronounces that last with relish. (There are quite a few in this building who'd like to see those days of rope-burn closure back again.) "After he'd set up his neighbour, Timothy Evans, to take the drop for him."

Dickie's left eyelid is twitching: Your cheek is threatening to come out in sympathy. "You're telling me that the civilian capture and release contact on the Blair house was using false ID in the name of a *serial killer*, and nobody clocked it?"

Constable Ballantyne shakes his head. "Constable Brown logged his ID and took a swab, sir—the driving licence checked out with DVLA and the mug shot matched. It wasn't false at that level—"

Now your cheek *does* twitch because this is the kind of shit that isn't supposed to happen. The Driver and Vehicle Licensing Agency database backs onto the Identity and Passport Service's database, and you can't get a driving licence without authenticating. Which means the joker who just horned in on your crime scene is walking around with a *genuine* identity record on the national system in the name of a long-ago-executed serial killer.

"—The birth date on his driving licence, uh, Constable Brown didn't clock it at the time: He was just checking that the name and face were valid. But in the database, it's given as 15 July 1953—the day the real Christie was executed. I reviewed Ed's helmet video, and the fly bastard sure doesn't look seventy."

He's been rattling on into a growing circle of silence for almost thirty seconds, oblivious to the gigantic loaf he's pitched in the middle of the investigation. It is becoming glaringly obvious that someone is deliberately fucking with the brains of Edinburgh's finest, and wants you to know it. Dickie, no cool cucumber at the best of times, is giving you serious concern for his ticker. Half the uniforms in the room are desperately trying not to boggle (and failing). The other half aren't even trying. A vein pulses weirdly in MacLeish's forehead: Then a curious ripple in the hairy salt-and-pepper caterpillar that passes for his moustache presages six urgently grunted words, pulled from so deep in his abdomen that you'd think DC Ballantyne had just kneed him in the nuts:

"Whoever this fucker is, *pull him.*"

Then, as an aside, Dickie adds: "Find that swab and run it on the—no." He nods formally at Kemal. "Put it on the wire to Europol and flag it as a suspect implicated in Inspector Aslan's investigation. *And* run it on NDNAD. Then backtrace the driving licence, find out who issued it, and open a new investigation: how this ringer got onto the IPS database. There'll be a counterfeiting offence in there, probably more than one." He knuckles his forehead as if squeezing out more charges, then glances at you and Kemal. "If you'll excuse me, I've got to update the super now." His banked anger is still there: But it's not pointed your way anymore. "What a pile of"—he claws at an invisible target—"shit."

The silence dissolves in a buzz of crosstalk. Kicked anthills, indeed. This might be a breakthrough in the long run, but in the short term, it's every case manager's nightmare: to have a suspect walk right into the middle of the crime scene, bare their arse at the officers on the spot, and waltz out again. The prurient eyes of Edinburgh are upon you, and this is juicy enough that it's not going to stay under wraps for long—it's going to be top of every newscrawl within hours, and Dickie's the one who'll bear the brunt of the jokes and finger-pointing.

Deprived of responsibility for the moment, you take the opportunity to walk around the table, showing Kemal how the investigation is set up—every police force does things differently. He nods appreciatively and asks sensible questions as you discreetly bring yourself up to speed. The Crolla scene is just as bizarre as the Blair bathroom. Here: a mattress stuffed with long-withdrawn one-pound notes that were cancelled more than a decade ago, even before the Euro switch-over. There: a woman's body, still wearing a business suit, shrink-wrapped onto the mattress with industrial-strength plastic sheeting. Preliminary pathology report: cause of death, anaphylactic shock—victim unconscious prior to death. The occlusive layer alone wasn't fatal, and there's no bruising or signs suggestive of forcible immobilization.

"There is something wrong about this," Kemal tells you, just as one of the uniforms walks over. "It's more recent, and besides, there is violent human agency—"

"Inspector?"

You squint at the constable. It's Mary Maguire, with the real-life-crime hobby: She's looking worried about something. "Yes?"

"I've got a call from the West End control desk: Someone wants an inspector on scene, and for some reason they put it through here and, uh, Inspector Mac's up to his eye-balls, can you take it?"

Several thoughts come to mind, the first of which is *You have got to be kidding*, but it would never do to say that. It would put you firmly in not-a-team-player territory, which is not what you want to do if you aspire to ever go back to CID work. *And precisely who do you think you are kidding about that?* So you bite everything back and nod. "Transfer it."

A moment later, you hear a still, small voice (with a pronounced Ayrshire accent) in your right ear. "Inspector? Control room here. We have a call from Sergeant MacBride for a DI to provide oversight on a scene in Polwarth, and the house is flagged in CopSpace with a prior you were involved with. BOOTS pulled your name out of the hat with a flag for another suspicious death that might bear on Operation Babylon."

Your eye-balls track to the translucent sign hovering above the investigation wiki: *Oh Jesus, not again.* "I'll be right over, send me the case work flow," you say. Then you catch Kemal's eye. "Come along. Apparently we've got another one."

ANWAR: RUNNING SCARED

It's going to be all right; it is not the time for you to meet your Maker yet.

The dead-eyed man with the American accent has gone away, leaving you shaking and throwing up in the toilet. *You should have expected this,* you tell yourself, as your stomach clenches with the aftershocks of icy terror: *It was too good to be true.* He has placed his mark on you. You have an inkling that no amount of soap and water will wash this stain from your soul, the knowledge that you are taking Colonel Datka's money on behalf of men like this.

Hard men you can deal with. You met plenty of them in Saughton and learned to hide your contempt. Underneath it all they were pitiable, as Imam Hafiz would put it: stupid, ignorant, and prejudiced, unable to use the brains that Allah, the merciful, the compassionate, gave them. Prone to fits of rage and frustration at the cards fate had dealt them, rather than holding them close and working out how best to play their hand. There were the violent cases, and the idiot drug users, and the ones who sat in their cells all day rocking from side to side as they listened to invisible voices—and while you hated and feared them for what they might do to you, you could also bring yourself to look down on them. *You* were only inside because of a spot of bad luck, and once you got out again, you'd be able to pick yourself up and get back on your feet. *They* had no legs to stand on, no foundation of support in society—

Colonel Datka's man is not one of their kind.

After his departure, after you finish throwing up, you go back to your cosy little office niche. But it's not so cosy now that the outside world has smashed the window and climbed in, ransacked the drawers and stirred everything around like a burglar. So you step outside for a few minutes, hands shaking, and look at the clouds scudding past overhead like the ghostly shadows of highland sheep. The sunlight on your hands and face is warming, but it doesn't melt the frost coating your heart. What is the tariff for aiding and abetting, anyway? Ownership of material likely to be of use in the commission of certain offences ...

It could be worse. Could be fucking Al-Muhajiroun, revenant Talib headcases or something. (No, that would be easy—pick up the phone, you know exactly who to call, all the wise heads at the mosque would say you did the right thing.) This is different, but—

Pull yourself together; it's only a fucking suitcase.

(*Yes, but there could be anything in it! You saw his eyes!* Body parts, heroin ... it's locked, of course. And it's not one of those dual-key jobs. There's no undetectable way of looking inside short of running it through the left-luggage X-ray machine at Waverley, and you're not about to do *that*.)

You drag the suitcase behind you like a guilty conscience. Slouch along Princes Street, keeping to the garden side, oblivious to the rumble and skirr of the trams. Trudge past the Waverley Steps, past the shopping mall and the stony classical frontage of the art gallery, across the road, past the sunken gardens and the big

Christian temple with the mossy graveyard below street level. Up Lothian Road towards the bus-stop. A police car whines past, and for a moment you are dizzy with terror. But it doesn't stop, and your heartbeat slows in time with your steps. The clammy cold sweat in the small of your back slowly dries as you repeat to yourself, *It's only a fucking suitcase.*

You should have let the Gnome pick it up for you; he is entirely to blame for your being in this invidious position, after all. The injustice claws at your stomach. "The angle, dear boy, is *money*— and how you, and I, and a couple of friends, are going to make a great steaming pile of it." May Allah, the compassionate, the merciful, have a special inferno set aside for the scheming bald arse-bandit and his great glistening pile of dosh. It's not *him* who has to—

The bus kneels and the glass doors slide apart like a mouth to swallow you down into hell.

You've tried to avoid this ever happening, and for the most part you've been successful. You have rubbed shoulders with hard men, violent men, thugs: But you've always got a place to go where you can be free of them. You have indulged your base urges in public toilets and other men's bedrooms, but never where you might be recognized and shamed by people who know you. You have done your absolute best to obey this single iron rule: Men's laws mean less to you than those of Allah, but this solitary unwritten one you cleave to like a drowning sailor to his life-belt. Until now.

You ride in a haze of misery, barely noticing your surroundings until it's time to get off. The suitcase is a drag on your wrist, as intolerable as a screw's handcuff, growing heavier with every step. You turn the corner, take the slope with ever-sinking heart, fumble in your pocket for the key, and carry the nightmare across the threshold and up the stairs to your den in the attic.

For the first time ever, you have broken the one unbreakable rule: Never let work follow you home.

* * *

Colonel Datka's man didn't give you a choice in the matter.

"You have an envelope waiting for me. I believe you live at"—the bastard has your home address on the tip of his tongue—"is that correct? You will take my suitcase home with you and store it. I may need to stay in your spare room, from tomorrow, for a few days. I trust you will have a spare key waiting for me here."

His smile was insectile, twitching mouth parts flexing around immobile mandibles, coldly inhuman eyes watching you through the wraparound display screens of his eyeware.

"If anybody enquires, you will tell them I am Peter Manuel, and I am a business representative."

"What kind . . . of . . . ?"

The mandibles clattered and chomped like those of an angry hornet: "I am here to *sell toys*."

"But my wife and children—"

"They will not be inconvenienced." His gaze was as unseeing as a corpse. "It is a fall-back position. Hopefully it will not be needed."

"But I—"

"Do you want more money?" He cocked his head to one side, scanning, sensing, focusing but not feeling. "Are we not paying you enough?"

You hastened to reassure him that indeed you were being paid an adequate sufficiency.

"Then what's the problem?" His stare went through you, bullet-blunt and tearing as it tumbled. "Remember the key. Tomorrow."

And he was gone like that: vanished, oblivious, leaving behind him the shattered and splintered wreckage of the invisible plate-glass window you had placed between your home life and your hustling.

You're going to have to tell Bibi *something*.

But what?

* * *

"You'll tell her what you always tell her, lad." The Gnome's familiar tones, the rolling R's and cut-glass sibilants of his currently adopted accent (upper-crust Morningside, posher than the King of England's) pronounce his diagnosis with utter certainty. You hate him for it, briefly: for his self-assured confidence, his smugly dispassionate claim on your future. He's like a spider, observing the world through the tiny tugs on the periphery of his web. "She expects the worst of you already; inviting some dodgy toy salesman to stay is nothing."

Actually it's *everything*, but you can't tell the Gnome this; there is no rupture in his world, no gap between the sacred and the profane. He lives his life entirely in the foreground, sly as a fox and just as shameful, and he wouldn't understand what's wrong even if you had the words and the will to tell him. Which you don't. So you burrow your arse deeper into the decaying armchair and squint at the pint of beer before you on the table. "He's a nut-case, though. Why me?"

"Because you're in the right place at the right time. Drink your beer, there's a good chap."

"It's not the right place. It's a fucking dangerous place." You obey his injunction and swallow another mouthful of sour fizz. "What's the angle? Come on. Tell me."

"The angle is, we make lots of money—"

You cross your arms. "Not fucking good enough, Adam." *Not lad,* you notice absently. You don't get to call him by any other kind of diminutive or belittling nickname. *Professor*, maybe. Come to think of it, that sort of sums up your relationship, doesn't it? "What's my angle? Why am I hanging my ass out here while foreigners use me as a distribution hub for bread mix and psychos invite themselves to stay with my wife and kids? What do I get from this?"

You stop and stare at the Gnome, giving him your best crack at Cousin Tariq's hard-sell hairy eye-ball.

"Diplomatic immunity—"

"That's nonsense, and you know it. Honorary consuls don't get immunity from parking tickets, let alone anything else. Especially not consuls working for a sock-puppet state that wouldn't even exist if its parent government wasn't so anxious to get rid of it that they rigged the independence referendum."

"Ah, that."

"Yes, *that*—I can read wikipedia, too! Seventy-two per cent voted against independence according to the UN exit polls, did you know that? Unemployment is running at 40 per cent. And Issyk-Kulistan, with about 20 per cent of Kyrgyzstan's population, inherited 80 per cent of its national debt. What the fuck is *that* about?"

The Gnome sits there listening to you rant, staring into the turbid depths of his half-drunk pint of 80/- and all the while swirling it gently, so that the suds form a slimy slick up the sides of the conic. He glances up at you with eyes as old as the hills. "So?"

"I've been doing some thinking," you tell him, and wait.

"A dangerous habit to get into, Master Hussein." His tone is light. "What *precisely* have you been thinking?"

"I've been thinking that ... this is a set-up, right? Some kind of scam to do with their national debt? And while they've got their hands off IRIK for a few years, organized crime moves in."

"Not exactly, but close." The Gnome takes a long suck on his bevvy. "What it's about is, a country like Kyrgyzstan can't afford to fuck with its credit rating, can it? They ran up some big debts over the last twenty years, building gigantic presidential palaces and new airports and so on. The usual prestige shit, presided over by a series of authoritarian ass-hats, would-be dictators-for-life who only averaged eight years in the saddle between revolutions. The gas-fields are played-out, now, so they're trying to restructure their debts, and finding it hard.

"But they're not fools.

"Corporations can't downsize and outsource the work overseas anymore—not like they could in the noughties—not without a hostile social-responsibility audit and crippling fines. But governments *can*. And they can get rid of the national debt by parcelling it up as, what's the term, debt securities. They hand the debt securities over to some fictional entity like, oh, a breakaway republic, in return for buying its independence. Don't look at me like that, there's a long history of countries buying themselves out; Haiti did it with the French empire. Issyk-Kulistan is buying its independence by taking on most of the national debt of Kyrgyzstan. The current Kyrgyz president is a very interesting fellow, lad. A compromise candidate, one who didn't offend any of the major power brokers—more importantly, before he was shoved into the hot seat, he was a professor of economics."

He holds up a hand. "Yes, I know what you're going to say: They don't *want* to be independent. Tough. Anyway, I suspect the angle they're playing in Bishkek is that IRIK has been set up to fail, declare bankruptcy, and Bishkek is expected to 'send in the army to re-establish order' or some such bullshit. Meanwhile, they've sold—through cut-outs—a ton of credit default swaps hedged against ARIK's national debt. In the short term, it looks like they're selling insurance. What everyone is supposed to think is that they're stupid-greedy, and when the IRIK collapses, the debt bomb will empty the Kyrgyz coffers."

"But that's stupid—" You swallow. "They can't do that! Can they? Isn't that what made the banks collapse?"

"Well spotted." The Gnome grins humourlessly. "It's not the only thing they might be doing, though. IRIK's credit rating has got to be in the shitter, so betting they'll collapse is a sucker bet. What I think Kyrgyzstan is doing is, they're selling CDSs to foreigners who *expect* IRIK to collapse under the debt. And they're over-selling, selling multiple CDSs leveraged against the same asset. Meanwhile they're using the income from the CDSs to *reduce* the debt load— until they arrange for reunification, which, with 72 per cent in favour, isn't going to be hard. The idiots who bet on IRIK collapsing will miss out on the fat payout they were expecting: Serves them right. What interests me is why the IMF and the credit-ratings agencies aren't yelling about it. The Kyrgyz government must have figured out a way to buy off the regulators and oversight agencies. So what's the angle? There's one obvious one: inward investment."

"Inward—who'd want to invest in Issyk-Kulist . . ." You trail off. The answer stood staring you in the eye a few short hours ago. "Oh."

"Yes, indeed. Picking the pockets of honest bankers is frowned upon in polite company, but the same people would tend to turn a blind eye to a lawful government's attempt to sting crime syndicates in the wallet by selling them junk credit default swaps leveraged on a sock-puppet's debt. Think of it as an anti-money-laundering operation on an epic scale—the cops have laid a trap for the gangs using an entire country as bait. The real problem is avoiding being assassinated afterwards: The RBN and the cartels take a dim view of overly successful confiscatory policies, and they're bigger than some governments."

The Gnome drains his glass then waggles it at you. "Will you stay for a refill? I think it's about time we had a heart-to-heart talk about how to buy and sell derivatives . . ."

* * *

When you finally go back to the house, you fail to work up the nerve to tell Bibi about your house guest. She's home late from work, tired and silent from too many hours in the pharmacy, and lavishes all her warmth on Naseem and Farida, who've been staying round at Mrs. Uni's house after school. The cone of silence she traps you in is poisonous and chilly; you know from bitter past experience that she will make you wait on the threshold for three days and nights before she relents.

Three days is her usual sentence for drunkenness and foolery: not one minute more and not a second less. She has the measure of a judge and the restraint of a probation officer. You've been on the receiving end of this sanction before. Bibi can be a harsh woman, when she wishes to teach you a lesson. And so you take the spare key wordlessly when you leave for work the following morning. Let John Christie—no, Peter Manuel—explain himself to her when he arrives, *if* he arrives. After all, it might never happen.

You sit behind your desk in a haze of mild dread for a couple of hours, a cup of tea cooling by your hand as you try to distract yourself by chasing naughty pictures on the Internet. But your heart isn't in it, and in the end you give up and stand, meaning to go in search of water to pour on the endlessly dying rubber plant, when your mobile rings.

Your heart sinks as you recognize Bibi's face: It's most unlike her to phone you from work. "Hello? What is it?"

"Anwar? Praise Allah, it's you! Please, can you go at once and look after my mother? She just called. I think she's having another of her funny turns—"

Sameena lives with her husband Taleb and Cousin Tariq and assorted grown-up children, their spouses and descendants in a

still-slightly-ramshackle town house Ali bought back in the
nineties. You weigh Bibi's plea momentarily. It's an imposition, and
it means closing the office, but on the other hand, it means early
release from the cone of silence. "All right, my love. Just for you
I'll close the office early and—"

"Please, Anwar! Just go, right now. You might need to call in
help—I can't leave the shop, but—"

Five minutes later, you're on your way, heart singing and feet
light. Bibi has not only forgiven but, in the urgency of her call, has
forgotten to be angry at you.

It doesn't last. The hairs on the back of your neck begin to rise
as you turn the corner on their cobbled side-street on the wrong
side of Bruntsfield Place and see two—no, three—police cars
sprawled across the parking bays. *Coincidence,* you tell yourself,
and anyway, even if Tariq's got himself into trouble, you're here
with the best of intentions, to give aid and comfort to his mother,
who is doubtless—

Their front door is ajar. As you approach it a fourth police car
turns the corner, lights flashing, and double-parks a couple of doors
along from you, and as you reach up and ring the doorbell, you
hear sobbing from inside, the sound of your mother-in-law losing
it wholesale in the kitchen.

The cop who opens the door is instantly suspicious. "Who are
you and what are you doing here?" he demands, scanning you with
a small forest of cameras. His free hand twitches in the direction of
a beltful of handcuffs. "You can't come in."

Your shoulders slump. "My wife got a call from my mother-in-
law," you say. "Is she all right? Has there been an accident?"

"What's your name? What's your mother-in-law's name?" He
looms over you, overbearing.

"I, uh, I'm Anwar Hussein. My wife's mother, Sameena Begum,
is she all right?" You blink at him, trying not to cringe away. Your

stomach is churning again. The rozzer's eyes twitch behind his head-up shades, fingers twitching on some kind of air keyboard, then his shoulders relax slightly.

"Who else lives here?" he demands. "Do you know them?"

You blink rapidly. "My mother-in-law. And my wife's brother and sisters. My father-in-law, Uncle Taleb—"

He shakes his head. "Are you next of kin?"

Ah. "Yes. What's happened—"

"I'm sorry, sir." Now that he's pigeon-holed you he switches to the next-of-kin script; unfortunately it's not the good-tidings one. He's got that *oh shit do I have to tell the family* look on his face. Your knees go weak. "I'll have to ask you to wait here for a few minutes while we finish securing the, the scene. Your mother-in-law is unhurt, but I'm sure she'll be happy to see you." *So who . . .* "My colleagues may need to ask you some questions."

Footsteps behind you. You look round and see a man and a woman, both in suits, with something about them that screams "cop." And now it takes all your will-power to keep your knees from collapsing completely because you recognize the woman; you last saw her face over a video link to the sheriff's court, laying a comprehensive smack-down on your sins in front of the beak.

"Good morning, Mr. Hussein. What brings you here?"

Her smile is bloodlessly professional.

You have to fight your own tongue to avoid blurting out *It wasn't me, I didn't do nothing.* "My mother-in-law—is she okay? What's happening?"

She loses the smile, looks past you at the bastard in black who opened the door. He obviously kens she's with the filth: funny handshake, raised eyebrows, that kind of thing. "Mr. Hussein." It's the cop. "Please come in, no, into the living room, my friend." It's all *my friend* and *come in* now. He backs up a step to give you room. Looking past you: "Confirmed next of kin."

"Oh sh—dear. Where's Sergeant MacBride? I'm here for his sign-off, this is Inspector Aslan, on secondment from Europol—"

You back into the cluttered living room, managing not to knock over a precariously positioned occasional table, and drop into the overstuffed sofa. You can hear muffled sobbing from the kitchen. The cop is swithering—head twitching from side to side like a hungry pigeon—between you, the bitch in the corridor, and the greetin' from the kitchen, which is now rising into a high, keening noise not unlike a broken smoke alarm but maybe two or three times as annoying. After a minute, he gives up and stands in the doorway like a human roadblock, relying on his shouldercam to keep an eye on you while he burps heavily acronymic police-speak back and forth with Inspector Butthurt. The other cop, the Easterner from Europol, is clearly kibitzing. You pull out your mobie, discreetly rolling its protective sock back into your jacket pocket, and IM Bibi. **AT TALEB'S. COPS HERE. WON'T LET ME SEE SAM. WHAT'S UP?**

The plod pile-up in the hall disintegrates: Inspector Butthurt and her trailer head for the kitchen, while Constable Bouncer stays on door duty. He glances in at you as the doorbell rings. "I'll explain in a minute, sir. If you don't mind staying right where you are."

The door opens. The pair of snowmen on the front step—that's your first impression—resolve into cops in white crime-scene overalls, humping battered flight cases full of gear. You've seen this shit on telly enough times to know what it means, but seeing it in Uncle Taleb's house lends it an air of unreality. The wailing continues until you're digging your fingernails into the frayed fabric of the armrests. You can barely hold yourself down in the seat. It's as bad as the other day, when she had that funny turn, finding that customer—

Sweat like ice trickles down your back. "Who's dead?" you demand, standing up.

"Sit down, my friend. Take it easy." PC Bouncer lays a meaty hand on your shoulder. You tense, but you know better than to struggle. They're trained like guard dogs, to react instinctively to challenges.

"I want to help," you say. "That's my wife's mother in there."

He shoves you back towards the armchair, gently but forcefully. "Who else might be here?" he asks, glancing over his shoulder to confirm that the bods in the bunny suits haven't left the front door open.

"Her husband Taleb, Tariq, Parveen, and Fara—they're my cousins—grandma, and if they're visiting, there's Uncle Akbar and his family—"

PC Bouncer is beginning to go as glassy-eyed as his portable panopticon of cameras and data specs. (White, Scottish: He probably counts his relatives on the fingers of one hand.) "Who would be at home during the day, my friend?"

He's getting on your nerves. "You're not my friend," you say before you can stop yourself. "I'm sorry," you add sullenly. "She needs help, listen to her ... "

He began winding up when you snapped at him but makes a visible effort to keep his lid on. "Let's try and keep this polite, shall we, sir. Deep breath, now. I'm going to ask you again: Who should we expect to find here during the daytime?"

Your mobie vibrates. It's Bibi's signature waggle. You keep a tight grip on it as you answer: "Sameena, sure. Taleb if it's a Friday." (Today is not a Friday.) "Tariq, he works from his lappie, so he's home a lot—"

What emotional defences you managed to reassemble in the wake of the Toymaker's visit collapse around you.

No point hiding: He saw your face. "Is it Tariq?" you ask, your voice going all wobbly. "Is he all right?"

You see at once from his face that your brother-in-law isn't all right.

Nor will he be all right ever again.

Nor can all the king's horses and all the king's men put Tariq together again.

* * *

It's very strange to be sitting side by side with Inspector Butthurt in your father-in-law's chintz-infested living room, chatting over cups of knee-cap-balanced tea (brought for you, incongruously, by a crime-scene cop dressed from head to foot in white plastic).

"I'm sorry we keep running into each other under such unfortunate circumstances, Mr. Hussein. By the way, is that your official registered phone?"

"Yes—" You watch nervelessly as she touches it, blinks a virtual fly away from the corner of her eye, and nods confirmation of some arcane suspicion to herself. Her movements are swift and precise. She's a tall woman; if she were a man, built to proportion, she'd be about the same height as Constable Bouncer (who is waiting outside)—a terrifying tower of muscular poise. Far scarier than the weedy Eurocop she came with, who is presumably in the kitchen right now, trying to get some sense out of Auntie.

"Well, that's a relief. You came here directly from the East End, I see. I'm going to have to image your phone and follow up your cell-proximity record to confirm what it says, but unless you've turned into some kind of criminal hacker master-mind in the last year it looks like you've got a watertight alibi." The dryness of her tone gets your hackles halfway up before you manage to remind yourself what she is.

"Alibi for *what*?"

"For—" For the first time she looks discommoded. Blinks again, evidently looking something up. "Sorry. Nobody told you?"

"Told me—"

"It's your cousin, Tariq Shaikh Mohammed. He's dead, I'm

afraid." She's watching you. You nod, still not quite believing it. "We received a call from Sameena Begum—"

"My mother-in-law. His mother."

"Oh dear." She glances away. The wailing has gone, replaced by occasional sobbing. And tea, probably. *They'll have her in another room,* you realize. *To get her story, and mine. Before we talk.*

"What happened? Was it an accident? Did somebody kill him?"

"Why do you suppose someone might have killed him?" She leans forward, and for a moment Inspector Butthurt is on your case, mercilessly digging. Your blood runs cold.

"I don't *suppose*," you tell her. "I have *no fucking idea*, sorry, I don't know. Young healthy man though, what's going to happen to him? Tariq's a—" You stop. "*Did* someone kill him?"

Inspector Kavanaugh looks at you for a while. "It's too early to say," she says reluctantly. "Investigations are proceeding."

And what the fuck does *that* mean? She's talking in cop-speak, the mysterious language the filth use to smear their own version of events over the true story. Familiar from a thousand blog bulletins. You shake your head. "What does that mean? Is he dead, or not?"

She makes a small noise at the back of her throat. Muted impatience or the beginning of a chest infection. "A couple of questions if you don't mind. By the way, did your cousin do any house-work? Cleaning, for instance?"

You stare at her in mute incomprehension. "House-work?"

"Dusting, washing up, vacuuming? That sort of thing?"

"Vacuuming?" You shake your head. "No, he's not the kind. Well, he gets stuff fixed when it's broken—I was going to ask him to sort out my wife's onion chopper, she dropped it the other day—" You realize you're rambling. So does Inspector Butthurt. She makes some kind of notation in her head-up memo, then changes the subject.

"Mr. Hussein, *can* you think of anyone who might have wanted your cousin dead?"

"I'm not sure," you say numbly. "It's not impossible. But Tariq was involved in stuff I don't know about." You take a deep breath, then hold up your mobie: "On probation, me. Keeping my nose clean. He knows it. Knew it. If he's doing anything dodgy, he doesn't want my snitchware anywhere near it."

Which is one hundred per cent true and will show up as such when the police evidence room speech-stress analysers comb over this part of Inspector Butthurt's on-duty lifelog.

That's the thing about talking to the police: You've *got* to tell them the truth, and nothing but the truth—just don't tell them *all* of it. They've got speech-to-text software and natural language analysers, proximity- and probability-matching tools controlled by teleworkers in off-shore networks—a mechanical turk—to make tag clouds out of everything you say within earshot of one of their mikes. It may not be true AI, but it can flag up inconsistencies if you're lying. They don't need that shit for 90 per cent of the job, the routine public-order offences, drunk and disorderly, but you can bet your shirt that everything said within a hundred metres of a suspicious death gets chewed up by the mechanical turk ...

"Go on," she prompts.

"Tariq's a smart boy. Runs a dating website: The spin for the old folks is that it's a virtual dhallal, a marriage brokerage, with chat rooms so the boys and girls can get to talk to each other safely—but I'd be lying if I didn't say that it's a knocking shop as well. The parents can register user IDs and track their kids' conversations, but there are some areas of the site that, well, they're age-filtered: It's the twenty-first century, innit? Oh, by 'kids' I mean it's strictly over-eighteens only. Because it's supposed to be about finding suitable partners for marriage, not one-night stands."

You run down. Not that you're giving her more than the most

superficial gloss on how Tariq set up the tagging system and real-time chat to show the old farts a very skewed view of the system; or the block-booked hotel rooms that users can sublet by the hour (at a 500 per cent mark-up for Tariq), or the proximity-matching service for halal doggers—pay your money, enter your preferences, go to *this* hotel room at *that* time and a suitable partner will be waiting for you—but Inspector Butthurt isn't an idiot.

She nods thoughtfully. "Nobody gets killed because of a dating website. What do you *suspect*, my friend?"

She's pushing your buttons but letting some morsels slip. The deadening fear is back: The man with the empty eyes, his luggage in your attic. The Gnome's outrageous proposition. Tariq's memory stick. "I *suspect*—I don't know anything for a fact—Tariq was into other stuff, too."

"Other stuff? Like what you were arrested for last time?"

Your mouth is dry. You nod. "I'm out of that, I swear. I've got a wife and kids to look after. And this." You twitch your phone, which chooses that moment to vibrate again. It's less intrusive than the old leg-tags, but no less an imposition. "And a respectable job."

"A job?" She raises an eyebrow.

"Yes." You need to rub her nose in it, make her recognize that you're a man of consequence these days. "I handle the consular affairs in Scotland of the Independent Republic of Issyk-Kulistan. I have diplomatic connections now, you know! I am required to be a man of utmost respect. And so Tariq knows he must leave me out of his madcap schemes."

"Wow." It's the nearest thing to an admission of surprise you've ever heard from Inspector Butthurt. So worldly cynical is she (from dealing with the scum of the earth on a shift-work basis) that it is clearly a test of her self-control. A lesser inspector would be shouting their disbelief in your ear. "Does your probation officer know about this?"

"Of course he does!" you splutter. She shakes her head, and a very curious expression steals across her face. *Respect or what?* "You can confirm my credentials with the Foreign Office," you add haughtily.

"Ah, that won't be necessary." It's glassy-eyed disbelief, you decide, twitching your security blanket of smugness closer. At last you've broken through her shell of assumed white English privilege. But she doesn't let the moment last. "Back to Tariq. What else can you tell me about him?"

"He was always too smart for his own good." You realize abruptly that you're never going to see him again, never engage in his line of crazy banter, never have to shrug off his sly importuning to get you on board one of his scams. The icy lid on your bottomless well of grief shatters, and you sniff, blinking back tears. You're unsure whether you cry for Tariq or yourself.

Kavanaugh touches your shoulder: You flinch. "Better answer your call," she says, rising. "I'll be back in a minute. Don't go away." And she leaves you alone to face Bibi, who is making urgent demands for reassurance you can't deliver.

TOYMAKER: Fucktoy

Snug as a sphex wasp larva in the belly of a paralysed katydid, you bed down in the Peter Manuel identity. You rent a room in a West End hotel to shower and change your clothes. One brief online session later, you've ordered a couple of shirts, a week's supply of socks and underwear, and a new shaver. Delivery post restante. Over in the Hilton, John Christie's room lies hollow and empty as a condemned cell. It may already be under active monitoring by the police, but you doubt they'll put a human-surveillance team on the case—human eye-balls are expensive—and if you don't interact with the hotel's digital nervous system they'll have no way of telling you're around. But they're not yet looking for Peter Manuel, and the cost of ambient DNA sequencers is high enough that they're not yet deployed outside of airports and other class-one security hot spots, and reliable automatic face recognition is right around the corner next week, next year, next decade, just like it's always been.

Standing under the monsoon shower, you review the afternoon's work. Parking your luggage with the dithering Indian guy was a by-the-book move, but maybe not such a bright one. It's always good practice to have a secondary safe house prepped and ready when things turn to shit, and you needed to get your commercial sample out of your immediate proximity lest the police decide to pull in "John Christie" for a grilling, but you can't count on him for more than documents and a mattress, and even that may be pushing a bit too far. He's a classic mark, easy to dominate but too fragile for heavy-duty work.

Something about his face brought out the long-forgotten old school bully in you: You wonder what it would be like to punch him until he pleads for mercy, then keep going. *Battered, blood dripping down her nose...* You're sprouting wood, you realize, but you've got a date for the evening and judging by this morning's chat-up, she's aiming for the same goal, so instead of reaching for the soap, you step out of the cubicle and towel yourself dry, then pad through into the bedroom and inspect your clothing options.

Building the new start-up can wait—anything you arrange in the current circumstances will just give the enemy a target. (You pick up a clean pair of boxers, hold them at arm's length.) On second thoughts, wouldn't it be a good idea? Draw out the bad guys by giving them a target? (The Straight woman's a hot dresser. You want to be clubbable, smart casual at least. Flash a bit of class along with the cash.)

Maybe you should set up a front, let the adversaries home in on it, then capture their assassin and pump them for information. (Suit and tee shirt? Or jeans and a jacket? The former. Armani tee. The Fabrice Gonet watch and the Edwardian silver snuff-box.) *Set up a target, to draw their fire.* (Hit the drug store for some meow-meow. Or better make that premium coke: She looks old-school.) Who could possibly fill those scapegoat shoes for you?

Hmm. Maybe you *will* move in with Mr. Hussein and his family tomorrow. See if he makes a suitable target: If not, that can be fixed.

(But first, you're going to make friends with Dorothy.)

DOROTHY: Safeword

As you spot him from across the bar, you've got to admit John Christie cleans up well.

One good thing about these on-site assignments with the bank is that nobody's ever sorry to see you leave on the dot. Nobody likes the inquisition. So as soon as it hits five, you make your brief apologies—little white lies, special pleading about having a life, they love these signs of human frailty—and catch the rush-hour tram back into town. There's still no word on the other, mystery job—the no-knock ethics audit you're meant to do on some NDA'd client's local management sometime next week—but that's no bad thing. You've got enough on your plate right now.

There's safety in numbers, up to a point. Liz has got your name on some kind of watch list, bless her, but that's a fat lot of use if your mystery stalker decides to jump you in the bushes while you're stranded between half-hour buses on a deserted industrial estate due to working late. Or if they decide to have a little tête-à-tête in your hotel room, just them and you and Mister Rubber Hose. But you're damned if you're going to turn up on her

door-step, shivering and small. Liz is desperately, blatantly monog-
amous, and if she clocks that Julian isn't your primary anymore ...
let's just say you need a wife like a fish needs a bicycle.

Speaking of bicycles, since you and he decided to plough your
different respective fields, you've not dated a man. Much less
ridden one. It's turning into a still, small irritant at the back of
your head: *Am I losing it? Turning into a hairy-legged man-
hater* ... Well no: But there's been a distinct shortage of cock-meat
on the buffet lately, and it's leaving you feeling a bit unbalanced.
If nothing else, dinner with John should beat room service for
amusement value. And if he's thinking along the lines you think
he's thinking along, maybe he's good for dessert, too. Subject to
certain reservations—

"Hi."

"Hi yourself. Can I buy you a drink?"

He offers you a chair.

"Sure. White wine spritzer. How about you?"

"I've already ordered. I wasn't sure you were going to show,"
he says disarmingly, tapping on the menu. "Agree on impulse,
regret at leisure."

"Oh really?" You raise an eyebrow. "You're absolutely right: I
nearly didn't. On the other hand, mysterious strangers have a draw
of their own. How does it work for you?"

He's stealthed, and you're letting him know you know. He
doesn't have a Facebook page. He's not on LinkedIn, or
Netwerked, or any of the others. The only match your agents could
find was a local listing on DoggerBank, but it didn't come with a
headshot. On the other hand, he's not in the public sex-offenders
register either.

"Sometimes well, sometimes badly," he admits. "I value my privacy, but sometimes it gets a bit lonely." He looks at you, and you
think, *My, what big eyes you have, Mister Wolf.*

"So tell me, Mr. Christie, where do I go to find out more about you?" you ask teasingly. "Besides the personals on DoggerBank? Wikipedia?"

He flushes slightly but doesn't deny anything. "I got a lot of shit about my name in high school. When they found out about him." He means the other John Christie, the one they hanged seventy years ago.

"No relative, I assume."

"None whatsoever." He waves a hand dismissively. One of the waiters is coming, starched apron and silver tray loaded with a tulip-shaped glass and a whisky tumbler. You wait for them to depart.

You lick your lips from behind the cover of your glass. "So, do you post to DoggerBank often?"

"I wouldn't know. Do you often read personals on DoggerBank?" He's echoing your posture, you think. To test it you rub one finger on the side of your nose. Sure enough, five seconds later he raises a hand. "I might," he says coyly. "If you want me to."

Well, it wasn't an off-puttingly *bad* ad. (*SWM seeks SWF for edge-play, penetration-OK, RF, safeword-OK.*) You sip your spritzer and breathe in, pushing your breasts up a little. "Do you want to fuck me, Mr. Christie?" His pupils dilate. Clearly, the answer is yes. But he's well-trained enough to say nothing, waiting: like a wolf, intent but distant. You feel a wave of heat, nipples tightening. "The safeword is fish, Mr. Christie. Can you live with that?"

"Fish." He nods. "Yeah." His close-cropped scalp shines slightly under the overhead spotlights. There's a moment of glassy-eyed focus, then he blinks, breaking the slightly creepy stare. "Sorry." He smiles shyly, losing ten years of age, suddenly cute. "I wasn't—I really *was* inviting you to dinner. The invitation stands, by the way. Do you always do a background check on dates?"

You smile and nod, let him see your teeth, let him know who's in control here. It took you a long time to train yourself to be this assertive, but it pays dividends. "Goes with the job."

"Really? What do you do?"

"I'm an auditor. Ethics compliance. It's not just a country next door to Sussex." You pull a self-deprecating face, but it's okay, he's nodding sympathetically. "I'm in town to check a bank—" You natter for a while, reassuring him you're a normal person when you're not answering DoggerBank personals, then he natters for a bit, ditto. He's in intellectual property, 3D extrusions, rapid man-ufacturing franchisees, and neighbourhood workshops making bespoke toys. It sounds pretty tedious, a needle-stick puncture to your fantasy of a dangerous but controllable stranger—

—You're sharing a bowl of organic-farmed oysters with him, he's laughing as you pour one down your throat, lip-smacking sug-gestively, then he's—

You're rubbing your ankle against him under the table. His breath catches, and you've got him in sharp focus. Your mouths are flapping, but the words are unimportant. Half-eaten salad in front of you, unappealing. You don't want to overfill yourself. His gaze has caught you: You're the focus of his world right now. Totally centered in his gunsights. Funny, the idea of a toy salesman who reeks of danger and makes your heart pound is ridiculous on the face of it. But it's not going to stop you playing footsie with the devil.

"Your room," you tell him, mindful of the listeners in your own.

You know what you want for dessert, and you're not going to find it on the hotel menu. So you lead him to the lifts and let him show you the way to the buffet, and then he feeds it to you hard and fast. Total abandon, clothes everywhere, barely time to roll on a condom before he pushes you down on the real bed. He's very dominant, not trying to hurt you but not asking for a lead, either. No ropes or toys, but he's somehow managed to immobilize you— not painfully, but. But. (*SWM seeks SWF for edge-play* ...) He's frighteningly focused when he enters you: For a moment you have second thoughts, wonder if he'd hear you if you said anything, but he's using his mouth and working a finger up your ass with a skill that is so *exactly* what you need that you grind back against him and begin to let go and flail around wildly as he pins you down and fucks you hard enough you're going to have bruises. You're close to coming when he stops: pulls out, rolls you face-down on the bed, and shoves himself up your anus. It's shocking, and you're trying to muster a protest—having difficulty getting enough air—then you feel him tense and shoot his load. And a few seconds later he rolls off you.

You're lying there in frustrated confusion. Your left wrist aches where he gripped it with fingers like handcuffs, and your backside is sore. He's in the *en suite*, you can hear by the splashing. *What the fuck?* He didn't even stay around to use his fingers. So much for the evening—it's not yet ten, and it's a fucking disaster. One star review: *Could screw better.*

You lever yourself up on your elbows. "You going to be long?" you ask.

The toilet flushes in reply. Christie comes out, wearing a hotel bath-robe. "You can go now," he says.

That wasn't what you were asking about, but you could do with the loo, so you nod gratefully and dash for the bathroom. Your make-up is mostly beyond repair, but you can manage a hasty wipe-down, then back on with panties, bra, leggings, and top. You flush the toilet. You're still trying to figure out what happens next when he calls again, "You can go now."

What the fuck? You step back out into the bedroom. He's sitting at the desk, back to you, focusing on a pad with the exact same degree of obsessive focus he was deploying on your tits an hour ago.

"Excuse me?" you ask, picking up your shoes and handbag.

"You can go now," he says for a third time, his voice empty of expression. "I have work to do."

The words sting you into anger: What does he think you are? But the lack of affect behind them suddenly chills you. It's as if there's something missing, something that was missing all along but you made yourself ignore.

"Was that all you wanted?" you ask him, trying to keep your voice from wobbling.

"I have to work now." He turns to look at you irritably. "Don't you have a room to go to?"

"Fish," you say. Then, uncertainly: "Safeword."

"Go away." He turns back to the screen.

Next.

You're standing with your back to the closing door, in the corridor. You slide your feet into your heels and shudder with an emotion you can't name: Then you turn and walk with exaggerated self-control towards the lifts. *Bastard.* Try not to think about him. What might have happened in there. The afterglow is shredded and faded to rancid rags that smear a greasy patina across the memory of pleasure. You have a nauseating awareness that you've been used: But you went in there meaning to use him for your own ends in turn. It's not as if you're a stranger to ass-play. So why do you feel so *wrong*? As you go back to your room and deadbolt the door behind you and run a long, hot bath, you're haunted by a simple question.

If you'd used the safeword on him, would he have stopped?

TOYMAKER: Abused

After you get rid of the bitch, you take half an hour to catch up on some admin work. You left the pad in here just in case: You pull your VM down from the cloud and write up a brief summary of your thoughts about what's going on and your revised business plan, and send it back to the Operation's servers. Doubtless next time you check in, there'll be some helpful notes from Control.

Factory-wiping the pad, you shove it back in the hotel safe and pull your clothes on again. You weren't planning to stay the night here anyway, and the Straight woman's presence makes it all the more important to move out. So you leave the room, walk to the fire stairs, and descend to the ground floor.

It's still daylight outside—the sun never seems to set on this fucking city—but you feel drained. It's some combination of the dour stone architecture, the weird Scottish people, a smidgen of your own paranoia, and the fact that a fucking murderer is stalking your start-up: It's getting you down. Perhaps you should've hit the meow-meow and taken the bitch clubbing first, taken the time to relax: But you're not planning on hanging around, and anyway, she was tedious. You've met her type before, needy thirtysomething singles: Thinks she's a swinger, but if you take the effort to keep her hot, the next thing you know she'll be making cow eyes at you and expecting an engagement ring. They get desperately serious when all you want is a fuck (and why are all these Anglo hotels so uptight about room service?). The hell with that.

You walk across the plaza in front of the hotel—a barren flag-stoned plinth—towards the round theatre on the other side of the road. There are some bars clustered behind it: In your Rough Guide overlay, they're helpfully tagged as "the pubic triangle." Maybe you should have gone there instead of scouring the hotel for desperate would-be housewives.

Five minutes' walking brings you to a corner where yet more of the desperately grey stone shit looms over you—they have houses with fucking *battlements* here, stone cannons carved into the eaves—haven't these people heard of earthquakes? You're still a bit nervy-scratchy from the day's events, so rather than piss around outside, you nod amiably at the bouncer and duck through a brass-trimmed door into a venue that promises two hundred kinds of whisky and beer besides.

You order an Irish and Coke, then look around for the darkest corner you can see and go hide in it. There's a secure note-pad app on your skullphone, works with your shades. You fingertwitch under the table, working out your priorities:

- Get your DNA off the police incident database. It's not vital, but if you can't manage it, you're going to have to go to extremes—find someone who's died and get the records corrupted—do-able, but very costly.

- Find out who's after your people and where they're getting their information from.

The latter ... you'd bet good money that there's a leak inside the Operation. Otherwise, how else do they know who you're targeting? So you're going to set up a target. Mister family man diplomat seems like a suitable option; fat, happy, and dumb. (Move in with him, put word up the line that he's your new COO, wait for someone to try to whack him, grab the killer, and extract names.) You do not commit this latter plan to your notepad. You've got to assume that anything in your skullphone is being monitored by Control, and that Control is leaking information to the—no, *they don't exist*. There are no killer lizards bleeding through from the other side of reality, the side that's all washed-out and grainy gray and suicidal. That's just a delusional fantasy, a side-effect of bad headmeat. And you're not delusional, are you?

Halfway down your drink, you notice a couple of low-lifes giving you the eye-ball from across the bar. You don't move your head, but you study them back from behind your glasses. Skinny, short hair, bad skin, track-suit-and-hoodie stereotypes: One of them's staring and muttering to his mate, who's nodding and *not* looking at you. You're acutely aware, of an instant, that you're wearing the Gonet on your wrist. Conspicuous consumption indeed. *Shit,* part of you registers, the part of you that remembers your time at school and the special education your uncle Al gave you: The rest of you feels a pulse or squeeze of momentary happy anticipation of release, not unlike what you felt with the woman. Sex and violence are all cross-wired at a low level in the brain, anyway. That's what they say.

You finish your glass, stand, and walk out of the bar with your back straight, not looking back. You slide the glasses into their case and pocket them. There's some movement behind you. You turn a corner and cut uphill through a grey stone canyon between windowless buildings. It's twilight now, and there's movement behind you, a scuffing noise like a rat in a hurry and a breath of air as you spin round.

There's only one of them and it's Sweaty McTracksuit, and the back of your head is no longer in front of his fist when he tries to deck you. Instead, your left heel is stamping on his right instep, you've got a lock on his arm, and you're twisting as he drops the home-fabbed knuckle-duster that probably came off one of your clients' machines and claws at your eyes with his left hand.

A second later, you've faceplanted him on a paving stone. Quick scan: *Two's company*. For a moment, you wonder if the enemy sent him, but no—he's just a fucking low-life mugger who's taken you for a tourist, gone after your watch and your wallet. You can't be having that. So you kick him sharply in the ribs, pick up the ultra-hard plastic knuckles while he's struggling to draw breath, hold down his right hand against the concrete, and use them to ensure he'll never play Guitar Hero again.

Ants. I am surrounded by fucking ants. Can't they get anything right? Even a fucking mugging?

Evidently not. It looks like Peter Manuel will have to teach the burghers of Edinburgh a lesson.

A lesson they won't soon forget.

LIZ: BEREAVEMENT
COUNSELLING

Mr. Hussein is pretty much right at the bottom of the list of all the people you ever expected to be doing the Victim Response Officer tap-dance for. It is, in fact, typical of how fucked-up this week has become that you find yourself sitting knee to knee with him over a cup of tea, commiserating (for tenuous values of commiseration).

Anwar is as bent as a three-euro note: just bright enough to think he's smarter than everyone around him, just stupid enough not to realize that they've got his number. He's a walking poster-boy for the Dunning-Kruger Effect: If he says he's going straight, it probably means one of his idiot friends told him shoplifting is legal. However, his lack of insight is a two-edged sword; it's glaringly obvious that he's worried sick about his cousin, who is lying dead in an upstairs bedroom while the SOCO team pin down the scene, but he's too dumb to actually *help* you. So you're supposed to treat him like any other victim ... or potential source of material evidence in what is rapidly shaping up to be the mass-murder enquiry of the century. Hence the house-work questions.

It only takes you five minutes to figure out that he is not, in fact, a killer. You don't even need the speech-stress analyser; he's not dissembling, his story lines up, and his probationware-riddled phone places him on the far side of town at the time. Everything so far checks out, and if the public CCTV confirms his movements, he's definitely off the hook. Anyway, he's not smart enough to have done something like this.

Right now he's a bit of a mess: not quite a blubbery mass, but obviously very upset. And he's beginning to push you for details. "I don't understand. What has happened to my cousin? Why are you here? Who did it? *What* did they do? Have you arrested anyone?"

"I don't know," you tell him, honestly enough. It's not as if you can give him information that might compromise an ongoing investigation, but even if that was not the case, the scene upstairs is more than slightly mad. "Listen, I'm going to check with my colleagues. I don't want to say anything until I know what I'm allowed to say, but I'll be right back. Drink your tea—I won't be five minutes."

You rise and step out into the hall, pull the door closed, and nod at the PC on duty, who steps sideways to cover the door.

You go upstairs. Kemal is standing on the landing outside the bathroom—*why* is it the fucking bathroom again?—airboarding notes. He shakes his head when he sees you. "You've seen it. What do you think?" you ask him.

Behind his Eurocop-standard specs, Kemal's eyes are tired. "Was the Blair murder scene like this?" he asks.

"I don't know. Haven't examined this one yet." But you've got a good idea what to expect. Otherwise, why the IM asking you to ask Mr. Hussein about domestic appliances?

You knock on the bathroom door, ignoring the yellow warning icons buzzing around it like angry hornets. "Hello inside?"

The door doesn't open, but a chat window drops front and centre. **SGT MADDOX, SOC: WHATSUP?**

"Sitrep," you call.

You hear a muffled voice: "Just a mo." Then a huge and grisly multi-media dump with about six gigabytes of metadata hanging off it drops across your view like a luminous crime-fighting jellyfish. In the middle there's a doorway-framed view of the bathroom. You zoom on it: It's live; someone's had the good taste to hang a webcam from the hook on the back of the door, so you've got the equivalent of X-ray specs.

Your view is partially obstructed by Maddox and her co-workers, who are dancing the dance of the forensic bunnymen within a much smaller stage than that afforded by the bad-taste palace of the late Michael Blair—but the focus of their attention is broadly similar. No dead Warsaw Pact dictator's colonic irrigation machine here, just a vacant-eyed skinny guy slumped half-out of the bath ... but what in James Dyson's name is the vacuum bot doing?

You don't have one of the things—your wee flat's too small to need it—but you get the picture: It's supposed to bumble around the house sucking on the rugs and scaring the cat, periodically retreating to its wall wart to recharge and hork up a cricket-ball-sized sphere of compacted fluff and household dirt. This is an upmarket jobbie, with two sets of wheels so it can walk up stairs and a couple of extension hoses so it can stick its knobbly nose into crevices where the sun don't shine. It features an especially big battery—which is currently one hundred per cent discharged, having shorted out through the bathwater in which the very dead Tariq is marinating.

There's a big evidence bag laid out beside the robot. And you don't need to be a technical genius to figure that cracking this case hinges on fingering whoever fitted a live wire down its snout and programmed it to go drinkies while Tariq was in the tub.

If someone's tampering with domestic appliances with murder in mind, the blogosphere is going to have a cow and a half. But that's the least of your worries right now.

You turn to Kemal. "You got that?" you ask redundantly.

"Was the other case like this?" he repeats.

"A bit." Shit, who are you trying to kid? You surrender to the inevitable and place the call. "Chief Inspector?"

Dodgy Dickie grunts. "What's up?"

"I'm afraid we've definitely got another one." You're registered on scene here, so you can add him to the access list. "Moderately bent business man in Bruntsfield, dead in the bathtub where his vacuum cleaner decided to electrocute him. I've got his cousin downstairs— former client of mine, not currently under suspicion—sweating bullets and trying not to incriminate the deceased. The MO is a dead ringer for Babylon." That the deceased was in the loop on repairing broken appliances—see also: back-street fabbers—you leave for later. It's certainly a suggestive avenue for enquiries.

Mac's initial response is unprintable. Then, "Hold the fort, I'll be reet round. This client of yours—dinna let him leave." He hangs up immediately, and his contact status, hanging in the corner of your vision, changes to mobile.

Dickie is showing worrying signs of succumbing to hands-on mode, the besetting cognitive error of any senior officer confronted by too much data—the illusion that if they just take hands-on control in the field, they can make everything come up roses. It leads to brigadiers focusing on a single infantry squad, and chief inspectors interviewing suspects instead of concentrating on running the hundred-headed murder team. (And, of course, if you try to point this out to him ... just don't go there.)

You hot-shoe it downstairs and back to the living room, which is becoming hard to get to—the hall is filling up with uniforms, stomping on each other's German-Army-surplus paratroop boots and trying to make themselves useful. You really want an opportunity to get Kemal alone and pump him, or failing that, to get Mr. Hussein to spill the beans on his cousin (assuming there are any beans to spill). But once Dickie arrives ...

"Anwar."

He's sitting in the armchair, shoulders slumped beneath the weight of an invisible storm-cloud. And he looks *guilty*, which will never do.

"In a few minutes, my boss on this investigation is going to arrive. He'll want to ask you a few questions."

Dickie is very old-school, inclined to go off like a shaped charge in the direction of the first plausible suspect who comes to his attention. This is not unreasonable: 90 per cent of the time, it's the right thing to do in an investigation, because 90 per cent of the time, the first plausible suspect is the right one. But you will eat your warrant card if Anwar is smart enough to arrange a scene like the one in the bathroom upstairs—much less to have orchestrated Mikey Blair's demise.

In the absence of a better target, Dickie's nostrils will start twitching in exactly the wrong direction, and he'll get all distracted and focused on the nearest Saughton graduate because it's easier than acknowledging how non-linear this investigation is going. And you don't want him to do that because, despite the ongoing bad blood between you, you are horribly aware that there's a repeat killer at large, and it would really suck if Dickie got hung up on Anwar, leaving the killer free to strike again.

"I am not officially cautioning you, and you are not under arrest, my friend. But it would be *really helpful* if you could tell me anything you know about any criminal activities your cousin was engaged in."

The slumped shoulders rise infinitesimally, then fall again. *Oh, it's like that, is it?*

You take your glasses off and, very deliberately, slide them into your pocket. "Anwar." You pause. (What you're about to say *might* break your career, if it comes out in the wash. If you've got any career left to break, that is.) "This is a murder investigation. Intelligence goes *in*, it doesn't come *out*. As long as you don't cough to any arrestable offences, we have no reason to lay a finger on you. And I can guarantee that anything you say that isn't a confession about an arrestable offence won't reach your probation officer's ears if that's what you're worried about. Maintaining security on a murder investigation is much more important to us than telling your social worker whether you've been saying your prayers before bed. So I'm going to ask you again: Do you know anything that *we* should know, to help us find your cousin's killer?"

You put your glasses back on. And while your head's bowed, and you're looking elsewhere, Anwar opens up.

*   *   *

Two hours later you're missing your lunch break for the sake of clogging up the meatspace incident room, laying it on the line for the peanut gallery.

"Here's our Anwar Hussein. On probation, done time for identity theft and fraud—not very smart. He's a foot-soldier, not a general: retired foot-soldier at that, or so he says. He gets a call from his wife, who got it from the first bystander, Mrs. Begum, to go visit Mrs. Begum and her son, the victim. He arrived on the scene after our first responder and Sergeant MacBride. Because he's on release, we have his probationware record, and I can confirm that he's been nowhere near the scene of crime for two days. Subject to confirmation by municipal CCTV, but it really doesn't look like he did it.

"*However*. Our Anwar is a bit of a wide boy, and his first reaction was to clam up. I was eventually able to determine that he's got a guilty conscience over some work the victim had asked him to do. There might be an issue of possible violation of probation terms here, but Mr. Hussein is eager to assure us that he hadn't actually got round to doing anything illegal as yet."

There is much rolling of eyes from the peanut gallery at this point, which you deliver with ironic lack of emphasis—*I didn'a* mean *to put me hand through tha winda an' take tha wallet, it just sort of* happened—so you feel the need to clear your throat. "He coughed to it voluntarily, and more to the point, he handed over the material which he claims his cousin Tariq gave him to work on, along with the device. It's downstairs in Forensics being imaged right now. If he hasn't touched it, then it may give us some insight into the murderer's motivation." *Assuming there* is *a murderer,* something in the back of your mind nudges. Because if you were wrong about there being no such thing as an artificial intelligence, things could get *really* embarrassing, couldn't they?

DCI MacLeish—for he is back from the Hussein residence— gives you the hairy eye-ball. "What sort of business was Mr. Hussein involved in, do you know?"

You stare right back at him: "I arrested him three years ago in the course of an ongoing investigation into an identity-fraud ring. He coughed to a variety of charges, including spear phishing, ownership of stolen authentication credentials, unauthorized access to personal account details, and Internet-banking fraud. Came to court, entered a guilty plea, two years in Saughton, cut on appeal to one plus one. *Interestingly*, Anwar was the only body we bagged on that case; I'm certain he wasn't working alone, but you know how these Internet cases are." You tap your forehead.

Dickie's eyebrows waggle, then he nods deeply, satisfied. (There is stuff you can say and stuff you can't say on the record—and *everything* that's said anywhere in a police station is recorded under rules of evidence these days—but waggling eyebrows and forehead tapping don't show up in the automatic speech-to-text transcripts. What you just sent via monkeyspace, bypassing CopSpace entirely, is that you know stuff but you don't want to contaminate the investigation by introducing hearsay or out-of-band intelligence. And Dickie, for once, agrees with you: He doesn't want you screwing up his investigation either.)

"Three victims so far," he rumbles. "Inspector Aslan, you have some input?"

Kemal is fidgeting with his glasses. "We have two more," he says diffidently. "One in Sofia, one in Trieste. That's all in the past hour. Bringing the running total to eleven."

Dickie looks simultaneously aghast and almost, in an odd way, hopeful: It's a clusterfuck, but it's not *his* clusterfuck, he's merely holding up a small corner, a few fragments of fatal fuckuppery. "Evidence."

A uniform at the back sticks up her hand. "Got one on the Crolla case," she offers.

"Go ahead."

"The warrant trawl of the national network monitoring database flagged up some chat-room transcripts. They match input from an avatar associated with an IP address allocated to Vivian Crolla's broadband connection. Assuming it's her, she had an, um, vivid fantasy life."

Ears prick up all round: Nothing gets your attention in a briefing like a drop of special sauce on the great and the good. (Hot sauce, even.)

"A number of enquiries about, uh, bondage practices involving plastic wrap and mattresses full of bank-notes." Bless her, the fresh-faced constable is looking even more rosy-cheeked than usual. "The aforementioned user posted a number of scenarios and, uh, there are some downloads, too. Stories centred on being immobilized and restrained while fully clothed, in proximity to large amounts of money. We're currently trying to track down some chat-room contacts . . . "

It's too much. *You* hear whackier stories from the twinks at CC's every Saturday night you go clubbing, but a fair proportion of the assembled officers are of a, shall we say, small-c conservative upbringing. As for the rest, some of them aren't as hard-boiled as they'd like to think. Muttered disbelief and the odd titter sweep the room.

"Silence!" roars Dodgy Dickie, the veins on the side of his neck standing out. "Ahem." He sounds surprised at himself. "Sarah, if you'd like to continue?"

"Uh, that's all I've really got right now, sir, until we question her known contacts. Details in the case file . . . " She flips a reference into the investigation space hovering above the big conference-table.

"The Crolla post-mortem examination report won't be available until tomorrow," Dickie announces, "but we have a preliminary. According to the pathologist, it looks like a massive allergic reaction while the subject was restrained. Anaphylactic shock. They're still looking for the cause—whatever she was allergic to—but suggest it's something that was introduced into her apartment's atmosphere while she was immobilized: I gather Iain's sent the empty air-freshener cartridge in the bathroom for analysis . . . "

You tap Kemal on the shoulder and jerk your head in the direction of the door. He blinks at you, then nods.

Outside, you march directly—or rather, via a bunch of scuffed and flicker-lit corridors and stairs that resemble a giant hamster maze that's gone to seed—to your own office in the ICIU. Kemal tags along like your guilty shadow.

"I seem to recall there was a book about it, years ago," you tell him as you take the fire door into the car-park, then the back corridor past the Air Farce control room—where the pilots sit in their twilit virtual cockpits, alert and ready to dive their stealthed carbon-fibre drones on the heads of any hapless dog-walker who forgets to scoop up the poop their mutt's just dropped on the Meadows—down past the flammables store, and along the side of the old stables. "About a guy who was into wrapping Roy Orbison in cling-film, uh, Saran Wrap. My mum used it to show me why I should never go with strangers. I had nightmares about kitchenware for years."

"You think ... the accountant ... "

You pause on the threshold of the ICIU suite. "I refuse to speculate: It's unprofessional, and besides, she might have had a *perfectly innocent* reason for owning a metric shitload of cancelled bank-notes in an obsolete currency. Not that you'd catch *me* shrink-wrapping myself to a pile of used bank-notes: The stuff's lousy with germs. People sneeze on it."

You take a tiny pleasure from Kemal's expression of cumulatively deepening distaste.

"This is my office, the ICIU. And here's Detective Sergeant Cunningham. Moxie, this is DI Aslan from Europol. He's here to *help* us." Kemal probably won't spot the slight emphasis on the penultimate word, but you can be sure Moxie will—and the warning eye-flicker. Your attitude to Kemal has changed somewhat since you departed to collect him this morning (was it only five hours ago?), but Moxie isn't Mr. Sensitive McNewage and can't be guaranteed to pick that up. You can quite easily live without him unintentionally reopening hostilities.

"Great, skipper, I could use some help. It's been one damn thing after another this morning. I've got six pending RFIs from some big intelligence investigation CID are running—"

Your heart sinks. "Is it Operation Babylon?" you ask.

"How did you know?" Moxie does his best hamster nose-rubbing imitation at you.

"Meet Operation Babylon's Europol liaison." You point at Kemal, who is looking around with an expression that speaks volumes in monosyllables. His gizz turns especially glassy as he spots Moxie's animated Goatsedance digiframe. (For which you make a mental note to bollock him later: Visiting brass could get *entirely* the wrong idea.) "It's a black hole, Moxie, coming to swallow us. What have you got in your queue?"

You settle Kemal down with a seat and a pad, then spend the next ten minutes with Moxie dissecting: a request for information about shrink-wrap fetish clubs in Midlothian; demands that someone in IT Support decode the charge sheet you filed against one Mr. Hussein, A., back in the day ("Conspiracy to Bamboozle the Police," suggests Moxie, identity-theft charges being confusing to officers more normally accustomed to breach-of-the-peace and public-order offences); an urgent enquiry for a backgrounder on spam filters (you boost *that* one to Priority A and sling it at your own job queue); a query from the desk sergeant at Gayfield Square as to whether he can arrest someone for running a home-brew fabricator (that'll be a "no," then—not without probable cause, and fuck knows how that one slipped into the Babylon queue); and a query about identity theft and a person of interest claiming to be Mikey Blair's boy-friend who left a DNA sample and a junk identity trail.

(Which is just *peachy*, because if *you* dig anything up on the random Mr. Christie and present it to Dickie, he really *will* have a coronary on the briefing-room floor.)

Kemal clears his throat.

"Yes?"

"I have an update from the office. They have a causal chain for one of our fatalities."

You would expect the man to look smug at this point, but he doesn't: haunted, more like. "What?"

Kemal shakes his head. "Vito Morricone. Dead in Palermo. A yahoo-yahoo boy. He died in a kitchen accident."

Moxie shakes his head. "A *kitchen* accident?"

"Yes. He was electrocuted by a deliberately miswired food processor." (You wince: You've had cooking incidents like that.) Kemal continues: "It was a high-end machine, able to heat or chill as well as mincing and mixing. Programmable, networked, you can leave cold ingredients in it and switch it on before you leave work, even change recipes remotely. His partner says that it broke eight months ago, and Morricone took it to a back-street repair shop, where they fixed it for him. The case is stainless steel. A replacement part—" He shakes his head.

"What kind of replacement?"

"The report does not explain this thing. But the local investigators report that the fixer bought the replacement-part design online from a cheap pirate shop, not from the manufacturer's website. It came with installation instructions, which he followed. Once installed, the machine could be remotely induced to short its input power supply through the case."

You give a low whistle of appreciation: Moxie claps, slowly. "Murder. Smoking gun."

"Yes, but." Kemal looks troubled. "The fixer does not appear to know anything. *Who* supplied the sabotaged component design? And why? The investigating magistrate connected to the same pirate design site and bought the same part: It is apparently harmless. And who sent the signal to activate it? We don't know yet."

"But it's an assassination? A well-planned one." You snap your fingers. "Tariq Hussein. The vacuum robot." The IM you got while you were talking to Anwar rises to the top of your mind. "Tariq got things *fixed*. Anwar said something about a kitchen appliance that'd broken. Huh." You pull up a memo window. "I want to know who fixed Tariq's vacuum cleaner and when. Ask Mrs.

Hussein about it. And"—the penny drops—"Mr. Blair's enema machine. Who repaired it last?"

"Minute those to BABYLON," you tell Moxie. He nods and keyboards it into the intelligence wiki, where some poor grunt will funnel it into Mac's inbound workstream and Mac (or one of his assistant managers) will assign it a priority level and add it to some other detective's to-do list. Policing, as with all procedural jobs, expands to fill all the time and consume all the resources available for it. And a job like this one is too big to handle in a half-assed manner.

It's a point of pride among the former nations of the United Kingdom that the murder clear-up rate is in three sigmas territory, somewhere over 92 per cent; but it takes bucketloads of manpower to get there, and process-oriented management and intelligence-supported work flow and human-resources tracking to keep the minimum investigative team of fifty-plus detectives properly coordinated. Most of the public still believe in Sherlock Holmes or Inspector Rebus, the lone genius with an eye for clues: And it suits the brass to maintain the illusion of inscrutable detective insight for political reasons.

But the reality is that behind the magic curtain, there's a bunch of uniformed desk pilots frantically shuffling terabytes of information, forensic reports and mobile-phone-traffic metadata and public-webcam streams and directed interviews, looking for patterns in the data deluge spewing from the fire-hose. Indeed, a murder investigation is a lot like a mechanical turk: a machine that resembles a marvellous piece of artificial-intelligence software, oracular in its acuity, but that under the hood turns out to be the work of huge numbers of human piece-workers coordinating via network. Crowdsourcing by cop, in other words.

* * *

(If you're one of the piece-workers in a mechanical turk—or one of the rewrite rules inside Searle's Chinese room—the overall pattern of the job may be indiscernible, lost in an opaque blur of seemingly random subtasks. And if you're one of the detectives on a murder case, your immediate job—determining who last repaired a defective vacuum cleaner—may seem equally inexplicable. But there's method in my motion, as you'll learn for yourself.)

* * *

You spend the next two hours with Moxie, churning through queries from Operation Babylon. Part-way through, Kemal disappears (to the toilet, you think at first: then to the briefing room, you decide), returning towards the end. You do lunch in the on-site canteen, communicating in defensive monosyllables: After his contribution from Palermo, he has nothing more to offer you. After lunch, you both attend the afternoon briefing in D31; then you sort Kemal out with a tablet, and he turns out to be surprisingly useful at handling those low-level queries you delegate to him. You update the ICIU shift roster for the next week and attend to another heap of inbound administrivia, before finally clocking off your shift and going home via the hair salon.

Home in your wee flat, you kick your shoes off and hang your jacket, visit the bathroom, and take a good close look at your new hair-do.

It's always hard to tell for sure at the hairdresser's, but here you can take your time and not worry about being unduly critical in front of the perfectly coiffured girl with the scissors and the long memory for casual insults from clients. You tilt your head and narrow your eyes and after a minute, you decide that, yes, you can live with it. It's shorter, but more importantly, it's *regular*. As business-like as your choice of footwear. Rest easy: Nobody's going to be passing sly remarks about your hair-do or your sensible shoes in the canteen behind your back. (Locker-room culture will never die: It just goes underground, as you know to your cost.)

You have plenty of time for a long comfortable lie in the bath followed by a TV dinner. You plant yourself on the sofa under your tablet, surfing the web while the vacuum sniffs and nudges around the corners of the living-room carpet, as the evening grows old along with your thoughts. Which, as usual, are increasingly bored and lonely. *Burn-out* is such an ugly turn of phrase, and in any case, it doesn't quite fit; it's more like you ran out of fuel halfway across the ocean, and you're gliding now, the site of your crash landing approaching implacably but still hidden from you by the horizon of your retirement. That's you in a nutshell, drifting slowly down towards lonely old age, the fires of ambition having flamed out years ago.

There was a time when, after working hours, you'd be off to the gym or auditing a distance-learning course or some other worthy pursuit. But these days, it's hard to see the point anymore.

The sad truth, which only dawned on you after you were fifteen years down this path, is that it doesn't *mean* anything. Your job, your vocation, your life's calling—you're like a priest who awakens one day and realizes that his god has been replaced by a cardboard cut-out, and he's no longer able to ignore his own disbelief. And, like the priest, you've sacrificed all hope of a normal life on the altar of something you no longer believe in.

Heaven knows, it's not as if the job doesn't need doing. Fifteen years in the force has taught you more about the stupid, petty, vicious idiocy of your fellow humans than you ever wanted to know. (It's also startled you—very occasionally—with their generosity, intelligence, and altruism. *Very* occasionally.)

But policing, crime prevention and detection, is a Red Queen's race: You have to run as fast as you possibly can just to stand still. You can collar criminals until the cows come home, and there'll still be a never-ending supply of greedy fuckwits and chancers. It's like there's a law of nature: Not only is the job never done, the job can *never* be done.

And then you hit your career derailment, passed over for promotion and sidelined into running the ICIU. And that's even *worse*. The movies playing inside people's heads every day are a million times nastier than what's out on the streets. Your colleagues have got no fucking *idea* what people day-dream and fantasize about: It's some kind of miracle you're not dealing with a thousand Hungerford massacres a day, going by what ICIU shows you. The sad fact is, the actual crimes that are committed are a pale shadow of the things people fantasize about. Even the poor-impulse-control cases who clog up the holding cells at the sheriff's court mostly have some rudimentary inhibitions that hold chaos at bay, most of the time.

But for the past couple of years, it's been sapping your will to live, never mind your ability to believe in the job.

You're just about thinking about retreating to the bedroom—a lonely end to a boring evening—when you get a text. It's from Dorothy. *How old-school,* you think.

YOU HOME? she asks.

YES.

CAN I COME ROUND? She capitalizes and uses correct written grammar, as formal as the way she dresses. **NEED COMPANY.**

Your heart flip-flops at the promise of company. **SURE**, you send, trying not to sound over-excitable, and tag it with your address and directions. Check the time: *It's ten thirty, for heaven's sake.* Doesn't she have to go to work tomorrow? Don't *you* have to go to work tomorrow? Your heart flip-flops again, and suddenly you feel hot and bothered; but a cool, collected part of you asks, *Didn't you have a date for Saturday?* Dorothy's the planning kind. *Why so sudden?*

BE RIGHT ROUND, she texts again. **NEED TO TALK.**

You shove your tablet away hurriedly, start to run fingers through your hair, then stop. You're a mess, and there's no time to do anything about it. "Shit."

Precisely eight minutes and forty-two seconds later, the doorbell rings. It's her, as you knew it would be. Swearing quietly, you buzz her up. The bed's made, the sofa cushions are plumped, there's coffee waiting in the cafetière in the kitchen if you need it, fuck knows what this is about but ...

You open the door. It's Dorothy. She looks at you with red-rimmed eyes, steps forward into your open arms—and begins to weep.

ANWAR: Sleep-walk

The cops don't so much let you go as politely direct you to the door with a stern admonition to keep out of their hair. There's a crossed wire somewhere; they don't seem to know whether to treat you as a victim of crime (Subtype: next of kin) or person of interest in ongoing investigation (Subtype: old lag).

You're numb inside by the time Inspector Butthurt finishes dragging the sorry story of Tariq's business out of you. You ken you probably didn't incriminate yourself overmuch, and as she pointed out, it's a *murder* investigation—they don't care about your probation as long as you're not plotting any bank robberies—but after you finished spilling in her lap, she wheeled in her colleague, Chief Inspector McHaggis, who is an entirely different species of arsehole, with his radge attitude and aggressively bristling moustache. He glared at you like he'd found you stuck to the bottom of his size-twelve para boots and curtly told you that he'd be in touch and in the meantime please do something about your mother-in-law (who is still wailing up a storm in the kitchen whenever she remembers).

Speaking of remembering, you remember phoning Bibi, who tells you to phone Imam Hafiz, so you phone the imam, who agrees to call your father-in-law, then come right round, and you wait on the street-corner for him to show up as, meanwhile, everyone in the local community wanders by, casually checking out the scene with their phonecams and occasionally pausing to tut-tut and share furtive condolences with you, all the time wondering if you are in fact some kind of serial killer and waiting for the police to come and arrest you. It is truly mortifying. And so, some hours later—when Bibi has efficiently squirrelled numb-faced Taleb and his grieving bride away in one of the hotels on Lothian Road and organized a rota of hot-and-cold-running daughters-in-law and nieces to sit and keep them company through the long night—you tiptoe away to a certain pub on the far side of Calton Hill, where the Gnome is waiting for you with a warm pint and a quizzical stare.

He glances at your face and shoves the beer in front of you. You take it wordlessly and chug most of it straight back. The Gnome looks concerned. "What kind of way is that to treat a pint?" he asks, then pauses, laboriously taking note of your face. "Ah, I see. Would you be in need of another?"

You nod. He makes himself scarce in the direction of the bar (despite those stumpy legs, he can shift when he needs to) and you put the remains of your first pint down on the table and try to shove away the enormous hollowness behind your breastbone. It won't budge. You glare at the pint. There's maybe an answer of sorts to your dilemma hidden in the glass, but you're not sure how to frame the question. To get blootered, or not to get blootered? (Bibi'll scream at you if you come to bed legless and stinking of alcohol, but *right now* you don't really care about that: plenty of time to shrug it off as an aberration later.) The real question is— *why?*

A new glass, clone of the old one, appears under your nose. You nod. "Thank you."

"What's the story?" the Gnome asks, not ungently.

"My cousin Tariq's dead," you tell him, wanting the words to sting.

Instead, the Gnome perks up. "Was it you who killed him?" he asks with pseudoprofessional cheer.

"The Polis think it was murder." You finish the first pint. The Gnome deflates, humour hissing away.

"Oh, lad ..."

"I had a visit from one of Colonel Datka's people this afternoon. I don't think it's a coincidence."

"Shite." The brass-necked gears are turning behind his eyes. "What makes you say that?"

"Tariq gave me a little job yesterday." You take a first mouthful of the second pint. Your lips feel comfortably numb. "Testing a chunk of a web app, off-line."

"That's no kind of connection, lad." He pauses. "Coincidences happen."

You feel like punching him for a moment: "Coincidences like *someone murdered him*? Right after he gave me a wee job? *While I have the attention of our friends from Bishkek?*"

You have the distinct sensation that Adam is giving you the hairy eye-ball. Wondering if you're reliable. "What do you think the web app's part of?"

"Honey trap, front end for a botnet, something like that." You take another sip. "Grow your penis, cheap off-licence gene therapies for that annoying melanoma, holidays in the sun with added drive-thru liver transplants, the usual." In other words, it's the same *the usual* that put you inside Saughton for a year.

"And now Tariq's dead? What happened?"

"I *don't know*. Got a call from Bibi, who heard it from Aunt

Sammy, who found him. When I went round, I walked into a cop convention. They figured out soon enough it wasna me what did it." You ken where this is going. "Don't worry, I didn't breathe your name. I had to cough to working on the side for Tariq, but I figure what he gave me isn't majorly incriminating, and anyway, it's a murder investigation. They won't be blabbing to Mr. Webber."

The Gnome turns an even whiter shade of fish-belly pink than is his wont. "I'll thank you for doing that much." He raises his glass and drinks deeply. "Do you know how Tariq died?"

"No." The ignorance burns your throat. "They wouldn't tell me anything, except that—except—" You can't bring yourself to finish it.

He leans forward. "Tell me about Colonel Datka's man."

Adam is treating the shrapnel of your life like some kind of puzzle game, you realize, just like Inspector Butthurt. The momentary flash and sizzle of resentment nearly throws what's left of your beer in his face. But what stills your hand is knowing that he's trying to help, in his slightly askew borderline aspie way. Help: You need it. So you tell him.

"He scared the shit out of me—even though he was polite. Eyes like a detective, you know? Only with a drum of unset concrete instead of handcuffs if you fucked him off."

"I do believe fear reveals your hitherto-unplumbed poetic depths." The Gnome is scrutinizing you like he's got you under a microscope. "What did he want?"

"A padded envelope from the office safe. And a bag of bread mix." You shiver. "He opened the envelope—there was a baggie in it, with a passport. Other papers. And he gave me a suitcase to take home. It's got a combination lock. Said he may need to stay with me for a couple of days from tomorrow." You shudder again. Those eyes.

"Well, you're in it now," the Gnome observes calmly.

"In *what*?"

"That remains to be seen." He leans forward. "But I've got a fair idea it means the end game is in train. Listen, can you lay your hands on five grand? Put it on credit if you have to, but you won't be able to pay it back for a month."

"What has that got—"

"It's time to cash out."

"Eh?" You think fast. There's the two grand you staked Uncle Hassan a couple of years ago, back before everything caught up with you—he's probably good for at least one. Maybe more. You've still got your credit card, but in these deflationary times, you can only draw five hundred in cash against it. You could pawn some of Bibi's jewellery to cover the rest, but she's bound to notice, and she'll want to know what you're doing with the money. And hurrying right behind the hamster wheel spin of your financial calculations is your native suspicion of anyone asking you to cough up cash on the barrel for something too good to be true. "Why now, Adam? What's the sudden hurry?"

"The sudden hurry, dear boy, is that your employers didn't go out looking to hire honorary consuls at not-inconsiderable cost on a *whim*; they obviously had a purpose in mind, and with a purpose goes a plan, and with a plan goes a time-table. I've been waiting for a sign that they were getting ready to go to the end game, and the arrival of your colonel's man means things are about to get too hot for you to stay in the bathtub—you'll be wanting out while the water's still clean enough that the Polis aren't taking an interest. So it's time to cash out."

"And how precisely am I going to do that?"

Adam bares his teeth at you. "You're going to do as I tell you and short a particular national bank's bonds. Trust me, you'll make a killing . . . "

* * *

There is no solace to be had in getting stinking drunk with the Gnome. So you take your less usual route home, up the hill and through the graveyard in search of a casual shag.

There is a younger man up there, short-haired and heavily accented: a small-town incomer, escaping from the usual, but with his feet under him enough to know the places to haunt. You make brief small-talk before he leads you round the back of an overgrown crypt, then it's hard up against the lichen-encrusted stone, tongues grappling hungrily and his hand down your trousers, squeezing your cock. He tastes of stale roll-ups and sweat, and when you go down on him, he washes away the memory of the day's horror with furtive joy.

After he sucks you off in turn, you stumble away in disarray, drained and feeling curiously vacant. You're late, and you feel like a complete fraud. Some family man you are, with the touch of another's lips on your bell-end. But at least Bibi isn't there to stare at you in silent irritation or chide you for drinking again.

When you get home, it's quiet and empty. Your wife is off auntsitting and has taken the kids to run errands or something. There's an uneaten portion of rice sitting in her fancy rice-cooker, and she's left some daal in the karai, to go cold for you in silent reproach. You fumble through the kitchen drawers until you find what you're looking for—a pair of plastic chopsticks (Bibi likes a Cantonese take-away once in a while)—then climb the stairs with heavy tread, pull down the attic hatch, and ascend, wondering what you're going to find.

Adam's slid a dagger of curiosity between the slats of your misery and paranoia. Investment opportunities aside, it's time to find out what the little fuck's playing with.

Your den is suffocatingly over-warm from the summer evening

sun, and you feel ill at ease, as if your personal space is under siege. The stranger's suitcase squats in the corner like an enemy garrison, a forbidding reminder of ill-advised treaties. Tariq's old pad sprawls out from behind the fridge. You stretch the metaphor until you see the fallen tombstone of a forgotten soldier and shiver despite the heat. The brewing bucket lies where you left it, under the beam of early-evening sunlight sluicing through the Velux: There's a yeasty smell in the air like rising bread dough, and the wee airlock thingy sticking up from the lid burps an alien curse as you stare at it.

It's a fab of sorts, the Gnome told you. A new kind of fab, or a really old one, depending on your perspective. Transmutation, liquid bread, water of life, *al-kuhl*. Not like the desktop fabs Tariq and his mates are using to run off air-guns and sex toys these days.

This is about using yeast cells as a platform for synthetic biology. As the Gnome explained it to you at great length—*there will be an exam later, Anwar*—in normal cells there's DNA, which is transcribed into RNA, which in turn is used as a punched-card template by protein-manufacturing machines called ribosomes. Each three words of DNA data—codons—correspond to a single amino acid out of a palette of twenty-one; the ribosomes read the codons, grab amino acids bound to carrier molecules out of the soupy intracellular medium, and glue them together to form new proteins or enzymes.

But in these cells there's a whole new biology. It uses *four* codons to represent a much wider range of amino acids, many of which are entirely artificial. Some of them code for the protein components of the molecular assembly line that replaces the boring Nature 1.0 ribosomes in the mechanosystem; others code for enzymes that synthesize the exotic new amino acids the synthetic biochemistry runs on. There's bootstrap code written for old-style ribosomes to get the new system up and running: That's what the health-food supplement switched on. Once it's running, the yeast cells are redundant, just a convenient platform for servicing the nanosystem.

Not that this is about shiny *Star Trek* nanites. Oh no, we're not *that* advanced. Nanotechnology is the shiny new magic dessert topping/floor wax/pixie dust of tomorrow, and always will be. This stuff is just synthetic biochemistry, with some funky new tools for handling buckytubes and exotic amino acids. Nothing strange about it at all, except that it's bubbling away in the bucket in the corner of your den and it smells like *money*, which is always enough to secure your exclusive attention.

What's in the bucket, Anwar?

Adam gave you some helpful pointers. If it's full of yellow crystalline sediment, back away slowly—but no, that's not so likely. You glance over your shoulder at the intruder's suitcase, but it just sits there, eyeless and unspeaking. Too many ideas are jostling in your head, seeking attention. *Bread Mix. Colonel Datka's man. Tariq's chat room.* The stuff you *didn't* tell Inspector Butthurt about: Tariq's unhealthy interest in making sure his chat-room environment wasn't as well guarded against malware as it looked, his secret VPN access to the webcrime bulletin boards, plausible deniability. And then there are the dark suspicions you don't dare voice even to yourself as yet: How accidental is all this? Where did Adam hear about the Issyk-Kulistan gig?

Thoughts fermenting in your head, you lever up the rim of the bucket lid and look inside.

The bucket smells of old socks and the broken promises of a hostile future, musty and somehow warm. You peer in and see only dirty grey-brown water, a scum adhering to its surface, bubbles forming at the edges: It's slightly iridescent, as if you'd spilled a drop of diesel oil on top. *Is that all?* you think, disappointed, and dip the chopsticks in it.

The kitchen utensils don't spontaneously catch fire, or dissolve, or morph into brightly coloured machine parts. You stir the scum on the surface around a bit, and it crinkles and crumples against them; then you pull them out again. A rope of congealed filmy scum sticks to the chopsticks, dribbling water back into the bucket.

"Yuck." You raise the chopsticks, and the floating sheet dangles from them, mucilaginous, like an elephant-sized snotter. You cast them aside, and they curl together, landing on the carpet in a stringy mass under the window. You clamp the lid down on the bucket of spoiled whatever-it-is and shake your head. Probably you'll have to take it downstairs, pour it down the toilet—hope the Environmental Health wardens don't have surveillance robots lurking in the sewers. It'd be just your luck to be busted for possession of an illegal chemical factory. Assuming the thing hasn't died or been infected by sixty kinds of bacteria.

You climb downstairs wearily and head for the bedroom. It's been a long day, what with the visit from Colonel Datka's man and the unspeakable event at Taleb's. *At least Bibi's taking care of the kids,* you think.

INTERLUDE 2

TOYMAKER: Happy Families

When you were eight, your dad taught you the correct way to peel a live frog.

You seem to recall him teaching you *lots* of things, but mostly he succeeded in annoying the hell out of you. It wasn't his fault: He was in therapy for most of your childhood, and it damaged him. Then *you* were in therapy, and it gets vague real fast.

One of the things he taught you early is that ants can recognize an intruder from another colony; they smell the strangeness and respond by chewing its legs off, immobilizing it until the soldiers come with jaws the size of legs and bite through its neck.

Humans are not dissimilar.

Dad was diagnosed, but never let it get in his way. He learned to cover up by copying, passing for another worker ant. But he wasn't very good at it.

"Look," said Dad, holding down the slimy, frantically gulping bull-frog, "it's simple. Just one cut *here* and—" He demonstrated. A flip of the fingers and inside out it goes. You laughed excitedly as the skinless amphibian flailed away at the bleeding air. "Looks real funny, doesn't he? Just like a little man. Now *you* try." And he handed you a frog and a knife.

In retrospect, you know exactly what Dad was doing: He was testing you to see if you were like him. Mom or Alice would puke their guts up if he did something like this in front of them, but Dad was curious. Did you share his unusual quirk, or were you doomed to go through life as just another soft-headed mark? So you got to peel frogs one happy summer afternoon with Dad, and it was true: They looked just like little skinned-alive men.

Father-son bonding experiences among the neurotypically diverse: putting the "fun" into "dysfunctional." You didn't realize it at the time, but Dad was teaching you stuff you weren't going to learn anywhere else: stuff like what you were, how to look "normal," how to pass among the ants, how not to get found out. All Mom gave you was your looks and good manners. (She had a great ass, though: Dad had good taste.)

You cling to the memory of that afternoon: Unlike most of your history, it remains vivid and fresh, not fading into the cloud-banks of the imagination. You didn't have many afternoons like that: Dad was always busy at work, buying and selling shit. He did it from an office suite just off Wall Street, and you and he and Mom and Sis lived in a fancy uptown condo overlooking Ninth Avenue when you were in Manhattan. Or maybe he had a room above a shop on Threadneedle Street and the maisonette was in Docklands? It's hard to be sure. You *do* remember there being a nice beachfront when you were vacationing on the West Coast, and a house on Long Island for weekends, and lots of plane trips. Mom did the stay-at-home thing and looked after you and Alice; and there was an old woman who kept the condo clean when you weren't there, and an

ever-changing supply of kindergarten friends to torment experimentally. And Bozo the Cat (until he went away).

But that was before the car crash turned everything to shit.

You were nine. One day a year earlier, Dad came home early
and pulled your mom into the kitchen and shut the door. There
were words, loud words. Later, your mom came out to talk to you.
Her eyes were red-rimmed, and her make-up was smeary. "Your
daddy and I have *agreed*," she said, with a funny little twitch.
"We're moving to California, to Palo Alto. He needs to be nearer
where the money comes from."

This was cool with you, as long as there was beachfront and sun
and other kids to score off. Mom didn't seem too happy when you
said so. She got a bit too excited and shouted at you and cried
because she liked the big city, Singapore or Hong Kong or wherever
it was. Well, silly her.

What you only figured out much later was that it was February,
Y2K+1. Dad's dotcom portfolio had vaped, and he had to steal
some more money. And this being Y2K+1, there wasn't a lot of
money in circulation to steal—at least, not from Dad's friendly
circle of day traders and stock-jobbers. So he'd been forced to
diversify and got fucked over when someone's Customs agency
intercepted one of the consignments. They didn't know it was him,
but someone in town knew his face, and he wanted some distance.
And there may have been something to do with the phone calls at
odd times of day and night, and the threatening letters, but that
didn't really signify at the time.

(Or maybe it was the old enemy, even then, plotting their takeover. Spying and hounding your father because they knew they had
to yank him out of the picture if they were going to get to you.)

Dad wasn't stupid: He had a plan. He figured there'd be a lot of
infrastructure left over from the dotcom crash, and all he needed to
do was stake out some vacant office suite and sooner or later a

team of double-domed nerds would show up to refill it (and, by and by, his wallet).

Well, Mom and Alice did the weak-sister thing and cried all the way to the beachfront house, but you were happy enough. School in the big town was boring, and anyway, a bunch of the other kids refused to play with you. The losers said you cheated. So you got to live in the sun-drenched sprawl off El Camino Reale and meet a whole new supply of interesting playmates, and Dad had a bit more time to play ball or take you hiking and do other dad things.

(But then there was the car crash.)

You were away at summer camp at the time. The camp counsellors came and took you aside and watched anxiously as you bawled your eyes out—not that stupid grief shit, but frustration: Who was going to come pick you up from camp now? Camp was getting tiresome. They were big on cooperative activities, nothing where you could score points off the other kids without being too obvious. The threat of being stuck there forever was very real in your going-on-nine mind.

But that didn't happen. Instead, the next day, a battered SUV pulled up outside the camp office. Half an hour later, the youngest counsellor came for you. "Your uncle Albert's offered to take you in while your father's in the hospital," she explained.

Albert? You'd never met him, although Dad had mentioned his elder brother's name once. And besides, you were bored with the camp. "Great!" you piped up.

If only you'd known . . .

* * *

You walk home to your snug wee hotel room, whistling happily to yourself. You lock the door, sniff, step out of your clothes and shower vigorously: yawn and crawl naked between the crisp cotton sheets to sleep the sleep of the righteously zoned out.

You wake early and amuse yourself for a while surfing on the hotel's in-room cable service. News streams bombard you with trivia; unemployment's up again, projects to retrain service-industry workers aren't delivering: Sow's ear into silk-purse futures are tanking. Another large vertical farm is under construction in Livingstone: The planning enquiry into the Torness "E" reactor unexpectedly drags on into a second month. The Scottish Parliament is discussing a bill banning factory farming of pigs on hygienic grounds and cattle on emissions: Farmers are protesting that they can repopulate bovine gut flora with kangaroo-derived acetogen cultures, dealing with the methane menace at source, and that the bill is pandering to vegetarian green voters in the run-up to the election next year ...

You make a note. *Research current steak consumption and supply-chain issues for black-market meat imports in event of ban.* (Prohibition is always good for business, and vat-grown tissue won't satisfy the more ruthless palate: Stress hormones are excellent tenderizers.) Then you channel-hop while you wait for room service to deliver your continental, surfing past the talking-head Jeezebot prayer breakfast and the traffic accident channel, pausing briefly at the Hitler network before you get to the baroque humiliations of the "So You Think You Want a Job" reality shows.

Job scams: Those are a perennial favourite, just like work-from-home and you-can-be-rich-too. But they're not only unoriginal, they're so old they can vote. Some of the scams are so well-known that the cops have bots looking for them—the half-life to detection is measured in double-digit hours.

Fuck. It was looking so easy when you came here. Commission the illegal breweries to manufacture the feedstock, the back-street fabbers to make the goods, the sweat-shop kids in the Middle Eastern call centres to operate them, the clerks to count the cash, and the foot-soldiers to keep the sales flowing—maintain tight communications discipline so that none of them can run the business without you, then find a franchisee and cash out. That's the basic iMob value proposition, isn't it? Gangster 2.0 is as much about searching for an IPO and an exit strategy as any other tech start-up business.

But this is semi-independent Scotland (a country with its own parliament, flag, tax law, and passports, but a military and foreign policy wing outsourced to Westminster). On the basis of your experience so far, it's also the land of the deep-fried battered Mars bar, remotely piloted airborne dogshit patrols, and accountants shrink-wrapped to mattresses. The latter is particularly disturbing insofar as it blows a honking great hole in your original business plan. But needs must. And Scotland has other assets, like Mr. Placeholder Hussein, who you intend to drop into the hot seat and stick in front of a fake organization to attract the attention of the adversaries.

You whip out your disposable pad, haul down your desktop from the botnet-hosted cloud once again, fire up the amusing little VoIP gateway app disguised as a board-game, work your jaw to wake your skullphone, and subvocalize. "Hello, Able November here."

"Just a second." (Pause.) "Oh, hello again. Sorry about the delay, sir. Are your medicines helping today?"

What is this, fucking Kaiser? "Yes, I'm much better now, thanks. And I'm using the new identity." *Beast of Birkenshaw my ass: another psychopathic serial killer? Mother-fuckers! What the fuck do they think they're doing, giving me these names?* "I'm calling because I need another minion; the first two broke. Is the denial-of-service situation any better today?"

"I can't discuss the situation at head office." She sounds a bit snippy. Then you realize; it's about two o'clock in the morning back in California. (Assuming that's where the Operation runs its call centre from.) And she's the same operator you spoke to yesterday daytime (assuming they're not using real-time speech filtering). "What do you want, Able November?"

"Like I said, I need a new gofer." Briefly you outline what you've got in mind. "And a new handle—some clever fucker thinks it's funny to keep giving me serial-killer names. I want that to stop."

"Please hold. This could take some time."

You're on hold for nearly fifteen minutes, as it happens: You amuse yourself with the pad, playing a couple of levels of Jack Ketch while you wait for the callback. Finally, your left ear vibrates. "Hi, Able November. What have you got for me?"

The operator is different this time, male with a Midwestern drawl. "Lemme see if I've got this right? Your last two recruits are dead? And you're still in the field? Why?"

It's time to poke the bear and see if it snarls, so you extemporize. "The cops got a DNA sample when I looked in on the first investigation. So the John Christie identity is pinned. And, incidentally, that name belongs to a dead serial killer, and so does Peter Manuel—someone's sticking ringers in your identity portfolio, and it's not fucking funny. I have to wait while Legal serve an injunction to get my sample destroyed when the investigation winds down—you know and I know that I didn't kill Blair. The original plan won't fly, but I figure I can salvage something from the wreckage. It was your Issyk-Kulistan scam that gave me the idea."

One of the annoying things about VoIP codecs is that they filter out nonvoice traffic. You can't hear the pursed lips of a huff of annoyance; the tells of a tense boiler-room background are silenced by digital audio filtering. So you have to wait three or four seconds, half of which is spent by the signal path as your words go wandering up to geosynchronous orbit and wobble back down to a ground station in the Sierra Nevada, out along a fat pipe, into vibrations in the air hitting the operator's ear-drum, and the return path therefrom. And then:

"The BZZT *fuck*?" (Cheap piece-of-shit throat mikes max out easily and start to clip when a pissed-off operator shouts into them.) "Wendy got me out of bed so—this—" (Ooh, lots of big tells! You hang on his loss of control, fascinated by the unintentional data leak dripping from the glass ceiling high above.) "—The fuck told you about IRIK?"

"Control sent me to the consulate here for new papers yesterday. They were probably panicking, or didn't get the memo about how secret it is. Don't worry, it's all under wraps. Nobody else knows. It's probably just a side-effect of the chaos caused by the, the attacks." *So the Issyk-Kulistan connection is another stove-pipe they're running? Juicy!* You allow a little wavery plaint to creep into your voice. "Is there anything I can do to help out . . . ?"

"You goddamn bet there is!" There's a heart-felt emphasis on the words. "Stupid dumb fucks are misusing the diplomatic channel for fucking stupid dumb-ass *smuggling*, would you believe it? Penny-ante shit. But that's neither here nor there. Son, you're in the field. You've seen what those mother-fuckers are doing to our proxies."

"The"—*rape machine lizard shapeshifters*—"adversaries, yes."

"Yeah, them. It's a network attack, we know that much. We even know what tools they're using. Anyway, I want you to go meet a man down at the university there in Edin-burg. A double-domed doctor of artificial intelligence. He knows about this stuff."

Huh? "What has artificial intelligence got to do with the adversaries?"

"Target acquisition, son. *Do* try and follow the plot: The victims are all involved in customer-relationship management. That, and the attack vector relies on combinatorial enhancement of precursor situations to domestic accidents. There's some network analysis voodoo as well, but I never got my head properly around that neo-Bayesian queuing-theory shit."

"But this academic"—you wince—"how's he going to help m— us take down the adversaries?"

"He's not. What he did was, he worked on the project that developed the tools our adversaries are using. Not deliberately—we don't think he's responsible; we're kind of in bed with him on another deal. What you're going to do is impress upon him the importance of sticking with his business partners. And just in case he doesn't get the message, you're going to persuade him to give you his source code, and you're going to upload it for us to do a walk-through. Fingerprinting. Just in case."

"Their source code? What, you're saying we're being attacked by some kind of *bot*?"

"Yep. Although the folks who designed it—along with MacDonald—may not even know what it's doing: Best if you don't know too much, either. We'll get you an appointment with Dr. MacDonald: When you go in, just tell him we want ATHENA."

"What about these dumb-shit identity packages?" you demand.

"We buy them from a reliable source, son." There's a pause. "I'll look into it. We'll get you a new face just as soon as we figure out what's going on. Don't you worry about that. In fact"—there's a longer pause—"you're a serial killer right now? I like that, son. Let's see if we can find you a job to go with it . . . "

* * *

You take after your dad, a high-functioning sociopath with an incurable organic personality disorder. It's one of the special-sauce variety, the kind with a known genetic cause.

Your uncle Albert was something different, and worse: He was a man of faith.

Albert and Eileen and the three girls lived in a paint-peeling house beside a dry creek in the ass-end of nowhere, about eight miles outside Lovelock, Nevada. Or maybe it was a croft in the Highlands, ten miles from the nearest wee free kirk. When you arrived, there were five books in the house: a Bible, a copy of *To Train Up a Child* from the No Greater Joy ministry, and three text-books borrowed, on a rotating basis, from the county library.

The Bible in question was not the King James edition; nor did it include testaments ancient or modern, commandments (other than "keep your gun clean and loaded and your ammunition dry"), or advice about not wearing mixed-fibre fabric and eating shell-fish. It was, nevertheless, adhered to as rigorously as any religious text, within the homeschooled homesteaded ranch of Albert and Eileen: And so you learned to live by the rules of *The End of America: How the Federal Government, the IRS and the Insurance Industry plan to use the UN to Destroy America, and how you can resist.*

You remember your first night at the ranch vividly—lying on the lumpy mattress on your stomach and trying not to cry with pain, terrified that if you made a noise, he'd come back—lying in the darkness and the stifling heat, listening to the crickets through the rotten, dry slats of the shuttered window, your entire back a mass of welts and bruises from your first real beating. You remember the taste of tears and blood, the sound of Uncle Al's rasping, tobacco-roughened breath as he raised the hose again—"Discipline, boy! Lack of discipline gets soldiers *killed*!"—and the stunning *thud* it made as it drove the breath from your body.

Albert and Eileen lived in a bunker at the wrong end of a very strange reality tunnel, in a world dominated by the spectre of the CIA-funded Jew-banker spooks who faked crashing the airliners into the Pentagon and the WTC to cover up how they'd bankrupted the nation by stealing all the gold from the Federal Reserve and used it to fund their evil scheme for vaccinating the children of dissidents with an autism-causing virus. (Lyndon LaRouche, in their recondite eschatology, was a Communist Sleeper Agent from North Korea.) Weirdly, they didn't seem to know about the lizards or the British royal family; an inexplicable omission in hindsight.

Less reclusive than some, Al and Eileen sent the kids to school, dealt with the devil under duress—Al did gun shows, trading and fixing partially deactivated weapons: He even filed tax returns now and then—meanwhile they hunkered down, waiting for the storm. There was no Internet and no television in the bunker. There was always plenty of work to fill idle hands, and a beating as final punctuation for insolent questions.

You learned what was expected of you very quickly after the first day. No back-chat, a "yessir" or "yes, ma'am" to Uncle Al or Aunt Eileen's orders, and keep your thoughts to yourself. The beatings fell off, became a random threat, a necessary dominance ritual. Al and Eileen treated their girls no less harshly, and Sara for one was always in trouble, unable to keep her yap shut: You remember the time Al broke her arm, and went on whacking her while she hollered with pain until Eileen realized what was wrong and scolded him into splinting it. Elizabeth, older and sneakier, was the snitch: You learned *that* fast.

And then there was Kitty, the youngest, aged six. You figured out how to use little Kitty to get what you wanted: Al and Eileen seemed to approve of their girls helping you out, helping you fit in, never quite realizing that their training cut both ways—they'd taught the girls to obey, out of fear, anyone stronger than they were. Including you.

You learned other things. Learned how to darn socks, shoot and strip an AR-15, identify a helicopter, plant a trip-wire. After a year, they enrolled you in school, ferried you to the bus-stop daily with the girls. It was impressed upon you that book larnin' was a privilege which could be withdrawn for any perceived deficiency: And what happened in the compound stayed in the compound, on pain of ... pain.

Uncle Albert probably thought he was doing a good job, beating the devilish inheritance of his jail-bird brother out of you. He had no idea how close to death's jagged edge he stood, how you'd memorized every step between your room and the kitchen, which floorboards squeaked when you stood on them: committed to memory exactly where the hurricane lantern and the kerosene were stored, the matches, the doorway, and the peg to lock their bedroom window shutters from the outside.

The rest is largely a blur: Even this much is reconstructed laboriously and painstakingly from the wreckage piled inside your skull.

What stopped you from doing the deed, even then, was a rudimentary cost/benefit analysis. You couldn't drive, and even if you could, you'd have had nowhere obvious to go—not with Mom dead and Dad in the big house for the foreseeable future for cutting the brake pipes. (The significant absence of Grandma and Grandpa on your paternal side did not escape you: Perforce, the family that preys together stays together.) And so you decided to bide your time until a suitable exit strategy presented itself.

As it turned out, you didn't have to wait all that long. Three years after you arrived, Uncle Al finally succumbed to The Lure of the Internet and traded an elderly shotgun and a gallon of white lightning for a hot (in more senses than one) laptop with a modem. He'd been hearing about these BBS things for years from his pals on the militia circuit, and figured he ought to take a look-see. You and the girls didn't get anywhere near Al's PC—for Internet access you were restricted to the school's rickety roomful of 486s, forced to expend tedious amounts of energy circumventing the district's brain-dead net nanny—but from afar you watched as Al made quite a stink, talking somewhat more freely than he should have. Scratch that: With online friends like Jim Bell and his assassination politics shtick, Al clearly didn't realize that he was breaking cover in a big way. But he lost interest rapidly and gave up dialling into AOL after a few months. And he probably thought that was that.

You were in school the day the Men in Black finally descended on the fuhrerbunker with a search warrant and the county sheriff's deputy in tow. (Surprise: The county wasn't on Al's side against the perfidious feds—perhaps if he'd paid his property taxes a little more promptly, things could have turned out differently.)

They called you into the principal's office while it was happening, and you sat there obediently, just like a serious and sober kid—the kind who would never dream of figuring out his guardian's password, logging in, and emailing ranting threats of physical mayhem to the IRS agents who were threatening Al with an audit because he'd declared an income of under five hundred bucks for the third year running.

The raid was inevitably followed by a brisk exchange of opinions—9mm for .357—followed by the arrival of a disappointingly non-black helicopter to evacuate Uncle Albert to the nearest trauma unit, where he was declared dead three hours later. But even in dying, Uncle Al tried to fuck you up. The coroner's verdict wasn't even suicide by cop: The last, most unforgivable insult Uncle Al heaped on you was to shoot off the top of his own brain-pan, thus neatly side-stepping the embarrassment of actually leaving Eileen, you, and the girls anything by way of his cheap life-insurance policy. (Even if Eileen hadn't been on her way to jail on her own behalf for greeting the sheriff's man with a .22 rifle.)

Anyway, you ended up in the children's home for a while, and that's when they discovered the bruises. You put on a good show, wailed the walls down describing precisely how you'd been beaten, and they listened to you. Then they decided to put you on anti-psychotic medication and anti-depressants, because obviously what you were describing made no sense, and you were disturbed and clearly at risk of self-harm. Between the cuts to the children's home budget and the second-rate quacks at the hospital, there was no budget for proper neurological screening or consultation. So there was no oversight when Dr. Hobbes signed you up for a clinical trial of a new high-specificity D2 blocker being pushed by his favourite supplier of gold-plated fountain pens. And you learned to keep taking the pills, because after a month on AL93560, if you *stopped* taking them the rape machines hiding in the bushes outside your window would whisper unspeakable propositions to you by dead of night.

But then your luck changed, in an unbelievable and positive direction.

Who knew people had two sets of grandparents? Not you, that was for sure!

Dad's parents were safely dead, and Mom had never mentioned whose crotchfruit she was in your presence—leaving you with a blind spot so fundamental that you'd never even noticed it until they turned up at the supervisor's office one morning and asked for you.

"He poisoned your ma against us," Grandma Jane said sadly, when you asked her about it—much later, of course. "I knew from the first that he wasn't right in the head, and I tried to tell her, but she wouldn't listen. And he *frightened* her! He wouldn't even let her email. God knows what he did to make her put up with him— brainwashing, probably. But we found you in the end. Found you in time to rescue you. Praise the Lord."

Jane and Frank were retirees, but only just (still in their sixties) when they found you, much as they'd found Jesus in the traumatic aftermath of losing their daughter to Satan's godson two decades ago. They weren't rich enough to travel widely, but they'd planned their retirement with care, and they had a decent home and two big cars to park outside it. Too bad that in the gaps between her church activities and his golfing afternoons, they were looking for something to patch the hole in their hearts—a hole just exactly the right size for a cuckoo.

Having just had your second family disintegrate under you, you weren't about to let this particular gift horse get away. Jane and Frank had driven cross-country to rescue you from the paint-peeling orphanage in Lovelock, planning to whisk you away to suburban Phoenix. It was the least you could do to be their duly grateful grandson. No need to mention Elizabeth, Sara, and Kitty, all in similar straits: You couldn't possibly impose on Jane and Frank's generosity on their behalf.

And so you arrived in Phoenix in the company of grandparents 2.0. And you were duly appreciative of this third chance at a stable family life that fate had handed you, and you resolved not to break it by accident.

* * *

It is now late morning, the day after. You're still waiting for the fucktards at head office to get you an appointment with the mad professor, and there's no point bugging the Hussein mark while he's at work. So it looks like you have a few hours off. Might as well go tour the city centre, hit a cafe, have a latte, sketch out your plan for world domination. Stalking-horse, of course, but if it suckers the enemy in, who cares?

The weather's good as you walk along Princes Street; shame about all the shuttered shop-fronts and the builders everywhere, stripping away the mother-of-pearl accretions of architectural history to reveal the Georgian skeleton of the road. With most of the surviving shop chains moving to out-of-city retail parks—those that haven't succumbed to online stores and custom fabrications—the once-vibrant commercial high street is being flensed of commerce and turned back into an aspic-preserved tourist draw, a false-colour reconstruction of its late-eighteenth-century youth.

That's all it's good for, of course: If it was up to you, you'd bulldoze the lot of it, stick in a link road between the M8 and the A1(M), and a shopping mall featuring a thirty-metre-high pink marble statue of yours truly buggering a lizard. But these effete pseudo-Brits have never been too clear on the importance of thinking big, or the grand gesture for that matter. There's that bloody stone-spike memorial to a *writer*, of all things—and the statues of philosophers! What the fuck is all *that* about?

You people-watch as you walk, ever alert for the alien menace. A police drone buzzes dismally above the high-speed rail terminal below the castle; closer to home, an arsehole in a kilt makes cat-strangling noises with the aid of a sack of pipes, squawking every time he changes note. These are street performers, constructing the dialectic of urban civilization—the watcher and the self-consciously watched. Here's a human robot in silver spray paint and make-up, twitching to archaic German synthrock. There's a white-faced girl in a pouffed-up wedding dress standing on a plinth, pretending to be a statue because if you can't dance and can't sing, what fucking use are you? If they had any kind of audience, you'd be tempted to practise the lightfinger tricks you taught yourself at high school, but alas, the crowd's not thick enough—and anyway, you've got bigger targets in mind than a careless tourist's wallet.

You stick to the shuttered shops on the built-up side of the street, keeping to the far side of the tram tracks from the gardens—too many bushes, hiding-places for the enemy abduction machines. The battlements of the castle loom blindly above the seething insec-tile urban hive, the sash-windows and solar-powered street-lamps, the slippery slate roofs and the sandstone bricks of the eighteenth-century town houses creeping back into view as the ants scurry and chop away at the retail-age encrustation.

You've come a long way from Phoenix, from the dying suburbs and the empty houses, gouged-out windows staring like eye-sockets across the Astroturf lawns the despairing Realtors laid before them: well-dressed corpses awaiting resurrection, secure in their faith in cheap gas and a Horatio Alger-esque resurgence in global competitiveness.

You didn't realize at first that Jane and Frank were rescuing you for a castaway adolescence in a city where the price of housing had crashed 70 per cent in ten years. Phoenix wasn't dead like Detroit; the climate made it a natural for snowbirds, put a floor under the ailing economy. Geography made it a natural for immigrants from the south. But white-middle-class flight driven by the soaring price of gas and power left the schools half-shuttered and decaying, the malls semi-empty and desolate. Your pallid skin marked you out as alien, so after a few unfortunate early incidents, Jane and Frank plugged you into the homeschooling network. It was safer than entrusting your lily-white ass to the razor wire and watch-towers, metal detectors and Taser-armed guards on all the schoolrooms; the school board were determined to train the children of the future majority appropriately for a lifetime of providing gainful employment for jail guards. So you spent half your life in hikikomori retreat with your computer and distance-learning coursework, and the other half running wild. Jane and Frank didn't much mind. As long as you kept your room clean and called them *sir* and *ma'am*, they thought the world of you.

At night you flensed lizards and pinned the twitching bodies out on posts to warn the rape machines off. Some afternoons, you'd take off on your bike, pedalling out past the empty suburbs into the graves of aborted communities, where the dirt was gridded out for houses that never came. Beneath the summer sun, you'd shoot imaginary schoolmates with your BB gun, and later with Frank's old .22 rifle. You had to be careful with the latter: Once or twice the noise attracted cops, like a swarm of flashing blue and red hornets converging on a dropped sandwich. But they never caught you: You were wary, and Uncle Al's training stood you in good stead.

You made up for the lack of schoolyard socialization in other, darker ways. There were squatters in some of the half-abandoned suburbs, embryonic favelas and hippy communes growing like mushrooms on the corpse of the middle-class dream. The ones that survived more than a few weeks or a single visit from the Border Patrol were on the net and wired to the future: There were business opportunities here, an informal economy to raise money for bribes. Invisibility was expensive. And that in turn meant business opportunities for kids like you. Your peers were mostly dumb, ignorant fucks who didn't understand the risks and couldn't imagine what could go wrong. You? Not so dumb, alarmingly precocious in your ability to take on responsible tasks—and utterly conscienceless. It was a combination that appealed to Riccardo, with his regular consignments of cocaine: And later on it appealed to Ortiz, with his far-more-valuable incubators full of unregulated A-life cultures, and Jerome, with the botnet and the fast-switching domains and the kidsnuff websites starring dumb, ignorant drifters whose luck had run out.

Over the course of another three years you came to the attention of the Operation, who offered you a scholarship and a signing bonus and, best of all, co-founder equity if you'd let them guide your talents and find you a suitable start-up to run.

Which brings you back to Edinburgh, and a sunlit morning in the New Town, and the phone in your head buzzing for attention.

"Yo." You lick your lips as your eyes drift past a couple of cotton-tops to strip-search a MILF: "Able November." It's about 4:00 A.M. in California. This ought to be good.

"Afternoon, son. This is Control. Listen, I got the memo. I like the way you think, and if things were different, I'd say go for it. But right now our top priority is this MacDonald dude. We thought we had an arrangement, but we have some fresh intel this morning about what else he's doing with his ATHENA project, and it is disturbing. We think he is shorting us. So I'm going to IM you his address, and I want you to go there right now. I've got a list of questions we want answers to and, and then you need to, uh, downsize him."

You nearly trip over a loose paving slab. "I'm already on a police investigation's radar! Are you trying to burn me?"

"Uh, no—" Control, Wendy's boss, splutters for a moment. "We're gonna hang the frame on the bad guys who are attacking us. After downsizing, I want you to go to your fall-back position— you got one, aintcha?—go to that mattress. They're spreading so much shit that nobody's going to notice another body when this goes down. We'll get you out of Scotland in the back of a truck or a boat if we have to. Your DNA sample—there are ways of getting it cross-linked to another record, muddy the waters. Listen, I appreciate this sucks. It's your operation, the business reboot, and it's fucked before it got started, but, listen to this, if you do what we need here with MacDonald, we'll make it worth your while. We gotta hold off ATHENA while the Issyk-Kulistan op winds down and you, you're inside I.K. now, like it or not. We want you to tie up the loose ends in Edin-burg. Which means talking to Dr. MacDonald, then paying off that consul guy."

"The honorary consul?" You inadvertently make eye contact with a small child: It cringes away, grabbing onto its oblivious mother's hand for dear life. You hadn't mentioned the mark in your report: It's always best to keep your bolt-holes private. "What does he have to do with it?"

"Mid-tier distribution hub, son. He's seen too much—the foot-soldiers and the general both. He may not know what he's seen, but if he spills his guts, someone else might put it all together. Plus, MacDonald recruited him."

"MacDonald—" You stop yourself. Bits of the jigsaw are slotting together, and you don't like the pattern they're making. The earlier plan, to stick Hussein's head above the parapet to attract enemy fire—sounds like he *is* the enemy. Or part of it. *Working for the enemy.* Who have infiltrated the Operation more deeply than you had imagined. "Okay, you want me to give MacDonald an exit interview, then downsize the consul." Anwar, isn't it?

"Exactly, son." Control sounds warmly approving. "You can do that? Afterwards, the world is your oyster. Just saying."

"I can do that," you assure him. *It'll be a pleasure.* It's been a long time since you last peeled a frog.

FELIX: E-COMMERCE

Bhaskar may have his high-rise presidential pleasure dome to squat and gibber in, but it is beholden to you—both in your capacity as chief of overseas military intelligence, *and* the other hat that you wear—to run your operations from a hole in the ground.

This particular hole in the ground is operated by the head-quarters of the Twenty-second Guards Cyberwar Shock Battalion, who inherited it by way of a long and convoluted history of turf warfare and empire building from the former Soviet RSVN, who built it as part of their strategic nuclear dead man's handle system. It's buried two hundred metres under a mountain, in a series of rusting, dank, metal-lined tunnels that have long since outlived their original function. Ten years ago, funded by the last gasp of the oil money, your last-but-one predecessor had the nuclear command centre gutted and flood-filled with the latest high-bandwidth laser networking: Today its cheap-ass Malaysian Cisco knockoffs pack a trillion times the bandwidth of the entire Soviet Union at its height, which is to say about as much as a single MIT freshman's dorm room. Getting that bandwidth hooked up to the public networks on the surface was a herculean task, and has permanently rendered the nuclear bunker unfit for its original purpose—but, as Kyrgyzstan had shipped all its warheads back to Russia three decades ago, you're not too concerned. You've got a nuclear-war command bunker with Herman Miller conference chairs, Mountain Dew vending machines for your tame geeks, armed guards on the airlocks up top, and secure Internet access. A fair definition of heaven, to some.

(Although describing what you've got here as "Internet access" is a bit like calling a Bosnian War rape camp a "dating agency.")

Here is your office: heart of a spider-web, wrapped around a hard-used Eames recliner, keyboard sitting on an articulated arm to one side, headset to the other. All the walls are covered in 3D screens except for one, a bare metal surface studded with radiation sensors, air vents, and crossed by exposed pipes and cable trays. There's a tatty epaper poster gummed across it, sagging in the middle: It shows a constantly updated viewgraph schematic of global bandwidth consumption, fat pipes sprawling multi-hued across a dymaxion projection of the planet, pulsing and rippling with the systolic ebb and flow of data. The screens on the other walls all contain heads, perspectives shockingly preserved as if they are actually there in the flesh, freshly severed.

Teleconferencing, actually.

"How much longer do you propose to keep on stringing them along?" asks the delegate from Maryland. (She's blonde and thin as a rake and clearly addicted to amphetamines or emetics or both: You wouldn't fuck her at gun-point.)

"They already realize what is going on!" The delegate from Brussels is clearly irritated by her naïveté. The lip-sync in the teleconference loop is borked: The real-time interpreter net is clearly not keeping up with his waspish tirade. "It is inconceivable that they don't. Perhaps they use this as an opportunity to diminish their headcount. Or perhaps the short-term financial gain really *is* worth it to them—"

"Twenty-four hours." You cut in before his Belgian counterpart manages to crash the software. "That's all we need for the wrap."

"Twenty-four hours is too long!" insists the Europol delegate. "We are already have trouble securing for the operation. And these 'accidents,' they attract attention. I am hearing reports that are mortifying. What are you *doing*? We did not agree to this!"

"What precisely didn't you consent to?" You raise one bushy eyebrow. "I seem to recall the negotiations over the concordat were exhaustive."

"This!" A wild hand gesture sweeps into view briefly, providing insight. (The American or Japanese programmers who designed the auto-track for this conference system clearly weren't thinking in terms of cultures that are big on semaphore.) "The agents your associates have deployed are killing people! That was not part of our agreement. This arrangement was to suck in the assets of organized netcrime for civil confiscation, leaving an audit trail to facilitate prosecution of the perpetrators. Extralegal assassination is, is unacceptable! What are you *doing*?"

It's clearly running out of control, and you try not to sigh. "I am not *doing* anything: I'm not responsible for these deaths." You shrug, then lean back in your well-upholstered command chair. "I assure you, they are nothing to do with me." You look at Maryland. "Is your government . . . ?"

Maryland looks as if she's swallowed a live toad. "We're not in the remote-kill business these days. This isn't the noughties: Congress would never stand for it." Ever since Filipino Jemaah Islamiyah hackers pwned an MQ-9 Reaper and zapped the governor of Palawan with USAF-owned Hellfire missiles, the Americans have gone back to keeping a human finger on the trigger: not because a state governor from a foreign country was killed, but because of who was in the armoured limousine right behind him. (The prospect of having to utter the term *collateral damage* in the same sentence as *President of the United States* before a congressional enquiry had focused a few minds.) "Where's the attack coming from?"

"It's not part of the original picture." It's uncomfortable to talk about. "To make IRIK look plausible, it was necessary to provide a haven for certain undesirable elements. They run botnets, of course, but *their* customers are ... unclear. We had assumed the traditional, of course: spammers, malware vendors, child-labour sweat-shops providing teleoperator control of animatronic sex toys for paedophiles." You clear your throat. "What we *weren't* expecting: cheap grid computing for pharmaceutical companies solving protein-folding problems. A Chinese automobile company using a botnet to evolve the design of their latest car using genetic algorithms fed with data from consumer surveys. Artificial-intelligence researchers renting the same botnets that spammers rely on to train their spam filters. Who knew? It is a, a *soup* of virtual machines boiling out on the darknet, coordinated through channels that our targets operate from corrupted routers in the State Telephone Company hosting centres in Karakol. I don't have the resources to trace them, in any event. We will shut them down when we spring the trap and snap their worthless necks, but until we are ready to close the honeypot, I cannot stop the attacks."

"*Twenty-four hours.*" This from the delegate from Beijing, whose screen is an opaque black cube. "That is unacceptable."

"I fail to see why. The operation is proceeding nominally."

"The operation is out of control, Colonel. Sequestrating the assets of organized crime is acceptable. Creating a honeypot for international cybercrime in order to shut them down is acceptable. But sheltering murderers is not. There have been regrettable excesses. The younger brother of the chairman of a state party branch that I shall not trouble you with. The aunt of a Central Committee member. You must shut it down now—or *we* will."

You grit your teeth. Your stomach churns: "It continues for twenty-four hours, and no more. The operation will conclude tomorrow, at twelve hundred hours, universal time, and not a second earlier." Maryland and Brussels are opening their mouths: "We've got to let it run its course! If we don't, the CDOs won't be fully vested—the targets will not be bankrupted, but they *will* be annoyed with us."

"They'll be annoyed with *you*." Brussels looks smug.

"Ah, no, I can see you misunderstand me. They'll certainly be annoyed with me, but also with *you*, François, and *you*, Lorna, and you Li"—you stab a finger at Beijing—"because if any of you pull out of your side of the agreement prematurely, I will see to it that full details of this operation are published on the Internet, with all identifying names attached." Your smile tightens. "Thank you for your help." You stab a finger hard on the CALL TERMINATE icon before any of them have time to frame a reply, then curse them all for a donkey's illegitimate get. "Fuck me, when will they *learn*?" You roll your eyes. "Fucking amateurs." Jumped-up crime-control bureaucrats with delusions of special-operations grandeur.

You glance at your clock. It's almost four in the afternoon, and the latest auction of national-debt futures leveraged against Issyk-Kulistan are due to close in an hour. The inflow is tapering off, as expected, but as long as the gangsters keep paying, there's no reason to weld your wallet shut and go to the end game.

Eagle's Nest had fucking better be pleased with this day's work. You're not sure how much more bullshit you can take.

ADAM: LOLSPAMMERS

You should have known it was too good to be true.

With twenty/twenty hindsight, the alarm bells should have started ringing three years ago, when Larry gave his presentation during that BOF breakout session on Network Assisted Crime Prevention at the Fourth International Conference on Emergent Metacognition. You can see him now if you put on your specs and tell your lifelog to retrieve him: enthusiastic, lanky, Midwestern.

"Realistically, we're trapped between a rock and a hard place," he explained to the room, hands moving incessantly as he spoke: "The trouble is, there are *too many crimes*. Three and a half thousand new offences were created in just ten years under one British government. The US Code is even worse—something like a third of a million distinct activities can lead to felony charges by some estimates. Nobody can be expected to keep track of that; it's inhuman. But with the kind of filtering we're having to apply to keep the communication channels open and relatively spam-free, it's more than possible to envisage agent-based monitoring for signs of criminal intent."

They've been keyword-filtering email for decades, looking for terrorist needles in a haystack. But what Larry proposed was different: trawling for patterns of suspicious behaviour online. Take, say, a disgruntled employee bitching about how they hate their boss online. That's one thing. But if they start hunting the blacknets for templates for machine pistols and downloading VR training materials, that's another.

"But what if we go a step further?" asked Larry. "Subjects who exhibit signature behaviours online pointing to potentially violent outbursts may not provide law enforcement with sufficient evidence to justify an arrest. But that's no reason not to provide an agent-based intervention in the online space. Once ATHENA has a sufficiently large corpus of interaction patterns, we can use it to do behavioural targeting and apply inputs weighted to divert high-risk subjects towards less damaging outcomes. Or to indirectly flag them for police attention."

Your typical disgruntled employee is a fizzing human bomb for some time before they go postal. Their social contacts are fraying, inhibitions against violence decaying: They're muttering to strangers in bars, reading about serial killers and fantasizing bloody revenge by night. The police will never know until they explode with murderous intent. But the spam filters monitoring their communication channels will have everything they need to diagnose the downward spiral: From their increasingly disjointed mutterings to the logs of their incoming web surfing, the pattern's all there. And with enough data, all correlations become obvious. But what Larry was proposing . . .

"We've had behavioural targeting ever since the nineties: 'If you like product X, you'll love product Y,' because that's what everyone else with tastes like you bought. We can configure ATHENA to apply the same sort of recommendation nudge to behaviour to bring the subject's outputs back towards baseline.

ATHENA's already pretty good at discriminating human-content communications from non-metacognitive signals; can we take the discrimination further, reliably, and derive objective data about internal emotional states?"

You lean back in your office chair—it squeaks angrily under your weight—and stare at the dusty display case on the opposite wall.

"Say that again," you say.

"I'm sorry, Dr. MacDonald; it's been a big shock to all of us here ... can't quite believe it. The funeral's going to be held next Thursday morning. I'm sure everyone will understand if you can't make it—it's a long way to come—"

Your fingers move, eyes unseeing, to open the log of your last discussion.

ADAM@Edinburgh GMT +01:00: I didn't adjust the preferential weightings in the naive morality table. Did you?

LARRY@Cambridge MA GMT +05:00: Not me.

VERA@Frankfurt GMT -01:00: Do we have hysteresis here? There is feedback from the second-order outcomes-triggering network.

SALLY@Edinburgh GMT +01:00: I've been trying to get my head around the second-order table dependencies, and I really don't understand them. I think there's some redundancy, but the weighting obscures it. You need to iterate to figure out what's going on in there.

LARRY@Cambridge MA GMT +05:00: Could be there's feedback. ATHENA keeps reweighting its own tables to comply with the changing parameter space. That's the problem with self-modifying code: It doesn't sign itself.

CHEN@Cambridge GMT +01:00: the bias in tit-for-tat activation is 0.04. Yesterday it was 0.032. I checked. There's nothing in the commit log, so it must be internal.

ADAM@Edinburgh GMT +01:00: Maybe ATHENA is just getting annoyed at the spammers for taking all her CPU cycles.
LARRY@Cambridge MA GMT +05:00: LOLspammers. Caught between a rock and a hard AI.

He's dead now, and it's not fucking funny anymore. "How did it happen, do you know?" you ask aloud.

"The police are still crawling all over us, and the FBI are involved, too. They won't say much, but rumour is, the package was misdirected. It was meant for someone in the applied proteomics group— looks like some animal-liberationist crazy sent it in and it ended up in Larry's office. It's all a horrible mistake—"

There is a chill in your blood and ice in your bladder as you make yourself reply carefully, lying: "I agree: Of course it's a horrible mistake. I hope the FBI catch whoever did it quickly before they"—are duped by ATHENA into sending more packages by whatever stimulus/response tuple the weighted network has identified as most efficient in returning Larry's communication outputs back towards baseline—"kill or hurt anyone else."

Sally stays on the call a while longer, seeking reassurance: When you end the connection, you sit and stare at the pulsing green icon with the silhouette of an old-style rotary-dial telephone for several minutes, shaken and unsure whether you trust your own instincts.

Poor fucking Larry. You don't know for sure, but you don't *need* to know for an absolute fact when inference is enough: Three days ago he was getting alarmed at the rate of creep in ATHENA's morality tables, and now he's dead, courtesy of a misdelivered letter bomb.

Poor fucking Anwar. It begins to make a bit more sense, and you don't like it one little bit. His dodgy cousin—now deceased— and his phishing sideline: He'd have been planning on hosting his phishing website on a bunch of rented zombie smartphones, wouldn't he? Leaving exactly the kind of spoor in his communications that ATHENA would be looking for, with drastically re-weighted tit-for-tat metrics in the morality code . . .

You're on Larry's contact list, and Anwar's. From Anwar to what's-his-name, the dead cousin, is another hop. Three degrees of separation. From ATHENA's perspective, $DEAD_COUSIN might as well be a research affiliate. Or worse: Larry—and you—might be suspected of affiliation to the botnet herders $DEAD_COUSIN was paying.

You stand up, unsteadily, and go through to Reception. "I'm going out for a walk," you hear yourself telling Laura, as you pass her desk: "I may not be back for some time."

Then you go downstairs, out into the bright cold daylight, to try and convince yourself that you're jumping at shadows and the panopticon singularity does not exist.

PART 3

DOROTHY: Breakdown

Earlier:

You're scalding yourself under the hotel shower, trying to wash the feel of his fingers off you, when you hear the telltale chirp of an incoming text from your phone.

The finger-feel is everything: You tense as you massage your abrasions, trying to brush off your own awareness of how little you meant to him—not even the joyful sharing of sex with a near stranger—but the real world is outside the curtain, buzzing on the sink side like a lonely vibrator. It's someone on your priority list: It won't shut up. So after another minute or so, you turn off the shower and clamber out of the tub. You towel off briefly, then when your hands are dry, you carry the phone through into the bedroom, caressing it until it calms down.

BORED. It's from Liz. Your throat swells: You sit down on the end of the bed and give in to the sniffles for a couple of minutes.

My life is shit. That's a given. For a well-adjusted bi poly femme, you're having remarkably bad luck. Stranded up here in Edinburgh, dumped by Julian—your primary—you let Liz's insecurity drive you into ... into ... nothing good. But being a victim is a state of mind, isn't it? (*Isn't it?*) You shiver and glance at the door, dead-bolted and with the additional security of a barbed carpet wedge you bought on eBay. He's out there, in Room 502, two floors up and one corridor over. You can feel him—or maybe it's just the weight of your own queasy awareness pressing down on you. *Pull yourself together.* It's not like he's going to break in and rape you, is it? He's just a nasty wee shite, as they say hereabouts, a miso-gynistic pick-up artist who's too cheap to use a tissue.

Keep telling yourself that, Dorothy.

There's another muted buzz from your phone, in a cadence that tells you it's a work message. But you really aren't in the mood for the office on-call tap-dance: you're disturbed, lonely, and very pissed-off—partly at yourself for not spotting the sleazebag in advance, but mostly at him for being ... what? (You don't blame a scorpion for stinging: It's in his nature. Instead, you deal—with bug spray and boot-heel and extreme prejudice.) You feel like an idiot because—admit it—you wanted a bit of excitement rather than a nice hot cup of cocoa and Liz. Liz isn't *exciting*. She's a bit clingy, and what's left over from her compartmentalized cop-life is boringly normal: civil partnership, not swingers' club. So you went looking for excitement, nearly overran your safeword, and now you're projecting all over the other. Way to behave like a grown-up ...

The phone buzzes again. Work is calling. It's the backside of ten o'clock, according to the hotel clock radio. Responsible grown-ups who get work calls at that time of night check to see if it's important. The hotel comps guests a yukata, so you drop the towel and wrap the robe around yourself, then wipe your eyes and grab a hair-band before you answer: With customers all the way out to the Pacific North-west, there's always the risk of an incoming teleconference. But when you put your specs on and glance at the log, it's just a priority-tagged wave. URGENT CASE REVIEW REQUESTED.

Oh for fuck's sake—you follow the link, which leads into the agency's human-resources back-office cloud. There's an employee profile; they're asking you to fill out an anonymized interpersonal ethics evaluation. *Snitcheriffic,* you think, and open it, expecting to be asked to crit one of the eager-beaver banking IT managers you were meeting with this afternoon.

Instead, it opens on a mug shot of John Christie, and a quiz that, after a second of dumb-struck confusion you recognize as the PCL-R psychopathy check-list.

Hot and cold chills mesh with nauseated recognition. You cancel out of the form frantically, racking your brain for a connection. Head office booked you into this hotel, didn't they? What did Christie say—*here on business?* Did someone *put* him here? *But how would they know*—the front desk. Your luggage problem. *His* luggage problem. They put the frighteners on you to drive you out of your comfort zone, then banged you together with him. Emphasis on *bang.*

They? Who?

It stinks. You worked for McClusky-Williams for three years before they were taken over by Accenture, and three years since—as an independent division—and there's *no way* anyone at head office would pull a stunt like that. It'd be a Section Four Fail for starters, with five or six other ethical violations on top, and the consequences for an ethics-compliance group of failing a moral-standards audit start with drastic and go rapidly downhill—

Reluctantly, you open up the wave and follow the link back to the snitch wizard. Yes, it's him all right. You try to cross-reference to find his employer, but there's nothing in the system. Digging diligently, you get nowhere except that bloody wikipedia true-crime article about his long-since-hanged namesake. There's no job number or contract associated with this job, *it just came up in the system*. Your skin crawls as you think about what it means. You prod your way through the snitch wizard, following the script: glibness/superficial charm, *check*. Cunning/manipulative, *check*. Promiscuous sexual behaviour—*now hang on a minute*: The psych text betrays an implicit polyphobic bias—reluctantly: *check*. Your stomach clenches as you work down the list. You should have seen this coming for yourself—it was all there in front of you, wasn't it? Christie is a poster child for narcissistic personality disorder, and you walked straight into it.

The quiz vanishes, to be replaced by another inventory questionnaire, this one more mundane: It's an appraisal that evaluates key personality traits in an executive-founder. Private-equity outfits and VCs use it to filter their trained start-up monkeys. The target is—your heart sinks—John Christie.

"What the fuck?" you mumble to yourself, just as your phone vibrates again. It's your private personality module. You glance at the touch screen, leaving the quiz floating open in your specs. It's Liz again: **ARE WE STILL ON FOR SATURDAY?**

You flip the phone out of work personality.

YOU HOME? you text.

YES.

CAN I COME ROUND? After a moment, you reluctantly add: **NEED COMPANY.**

There's nothing for a minute. Then a tag pops up, showing an address book entry and a handy route map. Your heart flip-flops. All of a sudden a cup of emotional cocoa with Ms. Clingy is looking—well, you'll get restless eventually, but right now you're halfway to totally creeped-out and in need of hugs and reassurance.

BE RIGHT ROUND. NEED TO TALK. Then you go hunting for clean underwear.

* * *

Embarrassingly, excruciatingly, the panic attack you've been bottling up washes over you like a drenching cold ocean breaker just as you reach the end of Liz's leafy alley-way. You catch yourself and lean against a mossy stone wall, shuddering with fear, eyes clenched shut, twitching at the sound of every passing vehicle. It's dusk, and there are no other pedestrians around, which is a small mercy. The lane's cobble-stoned, with century-old trees lining the pavements and lending the air a damp, greenish odour—there's a faint sound of running water from the stream beyond the dead end of the alley. It's mortifying. *What if,* your subconscious nudges you, *what if Liz can see through you? What if she doesn't take you seriously—*

You force yourself to stand up, afraid of smearing lichen on your jacket. Something flitter-buzzes overhead: a bat, perhaps, or a Council drone checking for broken paving-stones. *What if she thinks you fucked Christie to get at her*—everything's bubbling up from the depths of your subconscious, like methane clathrates bursting from an overheated ocean floor. You freeze, unable to make your traitor feet move towards her door. But then you remember what lies behind you in the dusk-haunted corridors of the hotel. Can't go forward, can't go back: It's the existential dilemma in a nutshell, isn't it? You're scared of what Liz will think of you, that's a given, but the flip side of the coin is that you're scared of what Christie could do to you. That makes things a lot clearer, for which you are duly grateful. "Hi, dear, do you mind if I borrow your futon for the night? I just fucked a psychopath, and I'm afraid he's stalking me via my employers." It's not much of a script, but at least it's there. Your left foot slides forward, almost against your will, then your right. *It's going to be all right,* you think.

Until you climb the six stone steps to the wee front door of the colony flat and ring the doorbell, at which point you lose it again.

LIZ: It's Complicated

Later:

It's morning, and you're on the beat: High pay grade, brightly polished boots—but boots, nonetheless. That's what it always comes back down to, boots directed by BOOTS, the Bayesian Objective Officer Tracking System, an expert system by any other name, to tell you which street to walk down.

You can't do policing without boots (whether physical lumps of leather or virtual chunks of software). It takes boots to track down and interview the witnesses, boots to comb the incident scene for debris and clues, boots to define a territory and remind the trolls who the streets belong to, boots to do the necessary social-work clean-up duty after hours on a Saturday night, BOOTS to do the personnel task assignments and match capabilities to needs, BOOTS to take a series of jobs and parcel them out as efficiently as possible. Boots are an integral part of the process.

It's not like the brass don't *know* this, even though they're always looking for an alternative: surveillance drones in the sky, peepers on segways rolling alongside the gutters, social-networking Crimestoppers and anti-alcoholism initiatives. Boots are labour-intensive, they take training and command and control resources, and they don't—can't—give you scalable efficiency improvements. So they're unpopular with the buzzword-wielding consultants who keep coming back to shape your political masters' outlook an election or two after they got booted the last time for costing too much.

This morning you started by going straight to the shift-change Babylon briefing, your head still a-churn from the late-night encounter with Dorothy. And lo, Dickie's got a job for you. "Liz, we've got one that's right up your street." The moustache twitches in something between a smile and a snarl: "a possible expert witness for you to interview here—a Dr. Adam MacDonald, of the university informatics department." He flicks a tightly knotted bundle of mind-mapped notes at you. "He's an expert on the emergent behaviour of distributed oracular systems—whatever they are—and I want you to go pick his brains." A sniff. "One of your Europol contacts raised it this morning, and BOOTS fingered you to talk to him. Some pish about research into using social networks to distribute subtasks contributing to a fatal outcome. Ye ken it bears on that line about sabotaged dish-washers and back-street fabs ye've been pushing."

You're too tired to raise an eyebrow at the fact that Dickie's actually been paying attention to anything you minuted. "Wouldn't that be a Common Cause charge if we find them ... ?"

"Aye, it might be. Or it might not, if the participants dinna *understand* what they've been set to doing." Dickie twitches. "Well?"

"I'll get right onto it. Anything else?"

Dickie shakes his head. "Next agenda item ... "

There has been little progress overnight. The promised lead on

Mikey Blair's wild ride came forward voluntarily but turns out to be a rent boy who knows nothing about anything. They're still looking for Vivian Crolla's embalming expert, but much digging reveals that she has something of a reputation on the local fetish scene. Half an hour in the right pubs, and you could probably have figured that much out for yourself.

So it is that you and Kemal (who you pick up in the ICIU annexe, where he's talking to Moxie about something—fitting in too well by half, you think) end up visiting Appleton Tower.

It's not quite that fast, of course. You're still somewhat freaked by yesterday's late-night developments (Dorothy being an emotional wreck in need of support is unexpected: And the rest is just plain disturbing), so you're not paying one hundred per cent attention to the job. Which is why Kemal brings you up short as you're scurrying in circles trying to do three things at once. "What *exactly* are we being sent to do?" he demands.

"I—" You stop dead, caught in the act of rifling through Speedy's in-tray to see what Moxie left unfinished at shift change. "That's a good question." You pull up the stack of notes Dickie passed you and sign Kemal onto it. "Let me finish here, then we can go grab a coffee and read this stuff."

And so you go find the nearest Costa's in a wee shop unit on Raeburn Place, and get your heads into the backgrounder that turns out to be a committee report from Karl in Dresden, Andrea in New York, Felix in Bishkek, and a bunch of other ICIU cops around the world.

You read fast. "This is amazing." While you were off shift, the intelligence team working behind the scenes on Babylon have been busy. It looks like they traced the repaired vacuum cleaner, and then some: For a miracle, they've been sharing their research with their overseas counterparts, and they've been pooling results. "All the parts come from cheap generic-design storefronts."

"Who set them up?" asks Kemal.

"Good question." The storefronts all take PayPal, and investigation traces them to a variety of servers in the Far East. Most of which, upon further examination—where possible—turn out to be part of one of three botnets.

"People are dying in domestic accidents," you tell him, still skimming ahead through the notes. "A vacuum cleaner shorts its battery out into a bath, or a non-standard cartridge in a spa machine contains contaminated fluid, or a sun bed's safety interlock is disabled. In each case, the machine has been repaired in the past year. Whoever carried out the repair saved money by using an OEM part template bought over the net and printed on a local machine. The part is physically a correct fit, but compromised: The vacuum's hose contains an electrical connection and links to the power supply, the sun-bed latch . . . "

Kemal shakes his head. "Very strange."

"It's completely crazy, isn't it?" You skim another summary. "I don't see how it's possible—we're up to fourteen murders now? Then they'd need a lot of different sabotaged appliances, at least fourteen, probably more—"

Kemal nods grimly. "Many more. More than two per target, perhaps more than five. You should search the homes of your local victims, tear *everything* apart and see what else comes to light. There may be many more. I think we may be mistaking the elephant's tail for a bell-pull."

"But who's *designing* the things?"

"Ask this academic?" Kemal sounds disturbed.

"Got any ideas what to ask about?"

He pulls his specs on and points. "How about task distribution? And where the designs come from?"

"Huh. That side of it—I've been looking into this. The Chinese government began prioritizing design twenty years ago in their universities. India, more recently. The recycling initiative"—Make Do And Mend is big this decade—"and the Internet combine to give them ready access to markets, and the spread of cheap fabbers allows them to export bespoke design patterns. WIPO are trying to do something about the generics, but design and trade-secret laws are not universally harmonized. Not like copyright and patent regulations."

It's part of what you've been tugging on from the other end, the supply of feedstock to the grey-market fabs—you've been looking at demand for counterfeit or contraband goods, and the supply of raw materials and designs feeding them. This is clearly related, but not in a way you can put your finger on just yet.

Kemal picks up his coffee cup. "The problem is not to, to design replacement parts that have lethal flaws. The problem is not even to insert them in the victims' households—true, some will live large, not repair or recycle domestic appliances, but most will be vulnerable somewhere: an exercise machine at their gym, a brake assembly in their car. No, the problem is how to coordinate the operation." He looks you in the eye. "It is scary, yes?"

It's not so much scary as incomprehensible: This murder's MO stands in relation to a normal homicide as a super-jumbo to a Cessna. "Murder I can get, but why do it this way? It's positively baroque! Who would do such a thing? It's inhuman!"

"You're absolutely right," Kemal says, pushing his cup aside. "It *is* inhuman."

"You're not going on that AI trip again," you say wearily.

Kemal shakes his head. "Precisely who is sending us to interview this academic?"

"Tricky—" You stop. *BOOTS fingered you to talk to him.* "BOOTS," you say. An expert system for matching personnel assignments to tasks. "Huh." You finish your coffee. "But it's just human-resources software."

"If we know how it works, it isn't Artificial Intelligence," snarks Kemal. He stands up. "Shall we go?"

* * *

Edinburgh University isn't built around a campus: Its buildings are scattered through the south side of the city centre, sandwiched between the Old Town and the Meadows, rubbing shoulders with charity shops and cheap apartments and fast-food joints. Its reputation for academic excellence, combined with geographical dispersion, has stood it in good stead in these harsh times—unlike many rival institutions, it's still in business, although two-thirds of its students this decade have never set foot in Scotland in their lives.

You went to university and did the whole halls-of-residence, living-off-student-loans thing, back in the day. You did your Master's in Policing, Policy, and Leadership on day release with distance learning—no faculty within a couple of hundred kilometres offered it as a part-time residential—and you got a taste of the chill wind that was even then beginning to blow through the halls of academia: a wind that's since then risen to a howling tornado blowing shards of razor-sharp glass, stripping staff and student bodies to the bone as the whole structure of higher education changes. And you're paying for that sheepskin to this day. Was it worth it? Who knows?

One thing's for sure: University isn't what it used to be.

Some things remain. The old buildings, for example. Appleton Tower is every bit as much a crass brutalist statement on the edge of the Old Town as it ever was, if a bit more crumbly about the edges than when it was last refurbished nearly twenty years ago. It's a listed building: the concrete bones of a different era, tempered in the white heat of Wilsonian techno-optimism and remodelled in the late teens. But there's no desk-bound receptionist waiting to greet you behind the grime-streaked glass lobby doors that once handled a stream of students; nor will the door open when you push it.

Perplexed, you pull up a voice call. "Hello? Is that Dr., uh, MacDonald? I'm Inspector Kavanaugh. We have an appointment? I'm downstairs right now—how do I—okay, thanks, bye." You hang up and glance at Kemal, who is looking around with wrinkled brow, as if he's just smelled something bad. "Dr. MacDonald will come down and let us in," you tell him. "There's an access-control system." Now you know to look for it, the discreet box by the door tells you all you need to know. Receptionists are too expensive for universities in these straitened times.

In fact, it's not just the Appleton Tower lobby that's showing signs of wear and tear; half the buildings on Bristo Square are closed or boarded, one or two blinking LEASE AVAILABLE flags in your specs. For a couple of decades tuition fees rose faster than inflation, until the inevitable happened and the bubble burst. The collapse catalysed by the first of the top-tier universities rolling out their distance-learning products in the middle of a recession sent the higher-education industry into a tailspin. Ed Uni has always been one of the top double-handful, and is still viable: But times are harsh and full-time undergraduate students are an endangered species.

You're beginning to get impatient by the time you spot a sign of life through the window. At first, you think it's a homeless vagrant who's managed to sneak inside, but as he approaches the front door with a determined shuffle you realize that he's looking for you. He's bald on top, with a round head, stubby nose, and tiny, angryish eyes. With his tattered denim overalls and grubby coat, he looks like a member of the chorus from *Deliverance: The Musical*. You wonder: *Is there some mistake?* despite a nagging sense that you've seen him somewhere before. Then he opens the door, and speaks with an ultraposh Morningside accent: "Inspector Kavanaugh? I'm Dr. MacDonald. You'll be following me, please."

You wave Kemal inside hastily. "Certainly. Do you know why we're here?"

MacDonald sniffs, then gestures towards a darkened tunnel between lift doors. "I'm sure you'll tell me in your own good time," he says unctuously. "We can talk in my office."

The lift is battered and has clearly seen better days: It squeaks between floors, bumping and jolting to a stop on the ninth. "We don't use the bottom two floors at present," MacDonald tells you, punching buttons on an access-control keypad. "This way ... "

Here, at least, there's fresh paint on the walls, and the thin carpet isn't worn through. And there *is* a receptionist at a desk in an open area of corridor, her head bent over a pad. Fading print-outs pinned to corkboards on the walls and the gawky-looking student staring blankly at them tell you that you are, in fact, stuck in a time warp from the noughties, or maybe on the set of a documentary video about the rise and fall of higher education.

MacDonald pushes open a beige door and ushers you into a cramped office. There's a huge, old-fashioned-looking monitor on his desk, and a glass-fronted bookcase holding a small, dog-eared collection of journals and books. Judging from the dust and the yellowing corners, they haven't been read in a while. Trophy copies of his papers, you assume. He flops down into a cheap swivel chair, and gestures at the two fabric-padded bucket seats in front of his desk. "Make yourselves at home. I'm sorry I can't offer you any hospitality—our coffee machine's broken again, and the corporate hospitality budget is somewhat lacking this decade."

"Thanks," you manage. The sense of déjà vu resolves itself: You *have* seen him before. In a pub, somewhere in town? Brain cells grind into action, and you recite a memorized script. "We're here to gather information which may be of use to us in an ongoing investigation into a crime. I'm required to tell you that you are not under suspicion of any criminal wrong-doing—we're here to consult you as an expert witness—but we have to record this interview for use in our ongoing investigation, and if you incriminate yourself, the resulting transcript may be used in evidence." You tap the right arm of your specs, then clear your throat. "Are you all right with that? Any questions?"

"I shall remember not to confess to any murders I didn't commit." MacDonald seems to find your caution inappropriately amusing. You're about to repeat and rephrase when he adds, "I understand you're in need of domain-specific knowledge." He leans forward, smirk vanishing. "Why me?"

"Your name came out of the hat." You decide to press on. Probably he got the message: In any case, having an inappropriate sense of humour isn't an arrestable offence. "We're investigating a crime involving some rather strange coincidences that appear to involve some kind of social network." The half smile vanishes from Dr. MacDonald's face instantly. "You're a permanent lecturer in informatics with a research interest in automated social engineering and, ah, something called ATHENA. Our colleagues recommended you on the basis of a review of the available literature on, uh, morality prosthetics and network agents."

Kemal, sitting beside you with crossed arms, nods very seriously. MacDonald looks nonplussed.

"Really? Coincidences?" He pauses. "Coincidences. A social network. Can you tell me what *kinds* of coincidences we're talking about here?"

"Fatal ones," says Kemal.

Damn. MacDonald's expression is frozen. You spare Kemal a warning glance, then say: "We're here for a backgrounder, nothing more—to see if your research area can give us any insights into what's going on. I'm afraid I've got to admit that I'm not up on your field—tell me, Professor, what *is* automated social engineering?"

You sit back, mimic his posture, and smile at him. It's all basic body-language bullshit, but if it puts him more at ease ... *yes*. MacDonald visibly relaxes.

"How much do you know about choice architecture?"

He's got you. You glance sidelong at Kemal, who shrugs minutely. "Not a lot." The phrase rings a very vague bell, but no more than that. "Suppose you tell me?"

"If only my students were so honest ... let's review some basic concepts. In a nutshell: When you or I are confronted with some choice—say, whether to buy a season bus pass or to pay daily—we make our decision about what to do by using a *frame*, a bunch of anecdotes and experiences that help us evaluate the choice. You can control how people make their choices, even to the point of making them choose differently, if you can modify the frame. There's a whole body of research on this field in cognitive psychology. Anyway: Choice architecture is the science of designing situations to nudge people towards a desired preference. You might want to do this because you're marketing products to the public—or for public policy purposes: There's a whole political discourse around this area called libertarian paternalism, how to steer people towards choosing to do the right thing of their own free will."

Now it clicks, where you've heard this stuff before: There was a fad for it about ten years ago, trials on reducing binge drinking by giving pub-goers incentives to switch off the hard stuff after a couple of pints, free soft drinks and so on. (Which failed to accomplish anything much, because the *real* problem drinkers weren't in the pubs in the first place, much less drinking to socialize, but the Pimm's-quaffing policy wonks didn't get that.)

You nod, suppressing disappointment: *Is that all?* But

MacDonald reads your gesture as a cue to continue in lecture mode.

"It's another approach to social engineering. Take policing, for example." He nods at you. "There's the law, which we're all expected to be cognizant of and to obey, and there's the big stick to convince us that it's a lot cheaper to play along than to go against it—yourselves, and the courts and prison and probation services and all the rest of the panoply of justice. However, it should be obvious that the existence of law enforcement doesn't prevent crime. In fact, no offence to your good selves, it *can't*.

"For starters, in modern societies, the law is incredibly complex: There are at least eight thousand offences on the books in England and about the same in this country, enough that you people have to use decision-support software to figure out what to charge people with, and perhaps an order of magnitude more regulations for which violations can be prosecuted—ignorance may not be a defence in law, but it's a fact on the ground. To make matters worse, while some offences are strict-liability—possession of child porn or firearms being an absolute offence, regardless of context—others hinge on the state of mind of the accused. Is it murder or manslaughter? Well, it depends on whether you *meant* to kill the victim, doesn't it?"

He pauses. "Are you following this?"

"Just a sec." You flick your fingers at the virtual controls, roll your specs back in time a minute to follow MacDonald, who is on a professorial roll. "Yes, I'm logging you loud and clear. If you'll pardon me for asking, though, I asked about automated social engineering? Not for a lecture on the impossibility of policing." Perhaps you let a little too much irritation into your voice, as he shuffles defensively.

"I was getting there. There's a lot of background..." MacDonald shakes his head. "I'm not having a go at you, honestly, I'm just trying to explain the background to our research group's activity."

Kemal leans forward. "In your own time, Doctor." He doesn't look at you, doesn't make eye contact, but he's clearly decided to nominate you for the bad-cop role. Which is irritating, because *you'd* pegged *him* for that niche.

"All right. Well, moving swiftly sideways into cognitive neuroscience ... in the past twenty years we've made huge strides, using imaging tools, direct brain interfaces, and software simulations. We've pretty much disproved the existence of free will, at least as philosophers thought they understood it. A lot of our decision-making mechanics are subconscious; we only become aware of our choices once we've begun to act on them. And a whole lot of other things that were once thought to correlate with free will turn out also to be mechanical. If we use transcranial magnetic stimulation to disrupt the right temporoparietal junction, we can suppress subjects' ability to make moral judgements; we can induce mystical religious experiences: We can suppress voluntary movements, and the patients will report that they didn't move because they didn't *want to* move. The TMPJ finding is deeply significant in the philosophy of law, by the way: It strongly supports the theory that we are not actually free moral agents who make decisions—such as whether or not to break the law—of our own free will.

"In a nutshell, then, what I'm getting at is that the project of law, ever since the Code of Hammurabi—the entire idea that we can maintain social order by obtaining voluntary adherence to a code of permissible behaviour, under threat of retribution—is *fundamentally misguided*." His eyes are alight; you can see him in the Cartesian lecture-theatre of your mind, pacing door-to-door as he addresses his audience. "If people don't have free will or criminal intent in any meaningful sense, then how can they be held responsible for their actions? And if the requirements of managing a complex society mean the number of laws have exploded until nobody can keep track of them without an expert system, how can people be expected to comply with them?

"Which is where we come to the ATHENA research group—actually, it's a joint European initiative funded by the European Research Council—currently piloting studies in social-network-augmented choice architecture for Prosthetic Morality Enforcement."

You look at Kemal, silently: Kemal looks at you. And for a split second you can read his mind. Kemal is thinking exactly the same thought as you, or any other cop in your situation. Which is this: *What drug is he* on?

"Would you run that by me again?" you ask.

"Certainly." He nods. "Prosthetic Morality Enforcement. The idea is that by analogy, if a part of your body is deficient or missing, you can use a prosthetic limb or artificial organ. Well, our ability to make moral judgements is hard-wired, but it's been so far outrun by the demands of complex civilization that it can't keep up. For example ... have you ever wondered why discussions in chat rooms or instant messaging turn nasty so easily? Or wander off topic? It's because the behavioural cues we use to trigger socially acceptable responses aren't there in a non-face-to-face environment. If you can't see the other primate, your ethical reasoning is impaired because you can't build a complete mental image of them—a cognitive frame. It's why identity theft and online fraud are such a problem: There's no inhibition against robbery if the victim is faceless. So we need some kind of prosthetic framework to restore our ability to interact with people on the net as if they're human beings we're dealing with in person. And that's what ATHENA is about. Society has become so complicated that people can't reliably make moral choices; but ATHENA will nudge them into doing the right thing anyway."

His eyes glitter maliciously in their saggy pouches. "If it works properly, you'll be needing a new job by and by ... "

ANWAR: GETTING ANSWERS

Sleep comes hard, and after tossing and turning uneasily in the cold wide bed—Bibi is still away—you rise early and head for the office. You're running on autopilot, going through the motions in yesterday's soiled clothes because your mind is elsewhere, scampering and spinning the spiked hamster wheel of your fears.

Tariq is dead. That hurts, even before the stabbing fear that you might be responsible. *Answers.* There must be an answer somewhere. *Kicked the bucket.* The dead-eyed man and the not-beer bubbling away in the attic and the too-good-to-be-true job and Adam's sly suggestion that you've been trolled, and suggestion for cashing in on it—

You want answers.

Because if Adam's right, and the Independent Republic of Issyk-Kulistan isn't just a sock-puppet but a flat-out fiction, a Potemkin Republic set up to snare the siloviki, you're *in violation of the terms of the licence they made you sign when they released you.* And that's you, back inside that cell in Saughton for another six months. *At least.* If they don't find something new to charge you with.

(And your hamster-mind is skittering ahead in blind panic, trying to figure out ways around the onrushing wall of steel spikes. Maybe if you can prove you've been acting in good faith—or perhaps if it *is* a fake you can resign and dob them in to Mr. Webber or Inspector Butthurt, demonstrate you're a good and responsible citizen—assuming the madman with the suitcase doesn't come after you . . .)

The office is as you left it when you received Bibi's panicky call yesterday afternoon. It feels like an infinity ago. You sit down, open up your laptop, and check for email. Nothing from head office, just a handful of spam. Actually, there hasn't been anything from head office—the Foreign Ministry—this week. No updates, no memos, no bulletins and reminders about policy on export licences, charges for visas, cancelled passports, office supplies.

You frown and check your settings. They *look* all right, but how can you be sure? Maybe the Ministry's mail server is sulking. Or perhaps there's a public holiday that lasts all week, and nobody thought to tell you. Or a general strike or a meteor strike. Whatever the cause, it's disturbing. So you turn to your handy quick reference guide to running a consular mission, and bounce around the hyperlinks until you come to a list of voice contacts. *Ah, technical support.* Issyk-Kulistan is four hours ahead of Edinburgh; you paste the contact into your phone app and wait patiently as it tries to connect. And tries to connect. And clicks over to dump you in voicemail hell. An interminable announcement in the sonorous Turkic dialect rolls over you, before switching to English and informing you that: "You have reached the mailbox of senior consular support engineer Kenebek Bakiyev. Direct customer support is available on Mondays and Wednesdays between the hours of 8 A.M. and 1 P.M. For outside hours support, please leave a message after the tone. *BEEP.* I'm sorry, this mailbox is now full."

You stare at the screen. "What the fuck? What the fucking fuck?" The calendar on your desktop is telling you that today is Wednesday and the time is ten past nine, local time—ten past one in Bishkek.

You are not an idiot; you were not born yesterday. You know exactly what's going on here. You're supposed to buy the story and sit tight until next Monday, aren't you? It's a delaying tactic. What kind of technical-support line is available for ten hours a week, carefully timed for when most of its customers are still asleep in their beds? They're gaslighting you. Or maybe not. A sudden moment of doubt: Issyk-Kulistan is very poor. What if they can't afford to run a proper support desk or help-line? If this is the best they can do—how secure is your pay?

You check the phone wiki again and again. Digging deeper, looking for clues. Then a thought strikes you, and thirty seconds later you've got another number. You feed another contact to the phone app, and ten seconds later a voice answers you in the flattened vowels of London's East End: "'Ello, you've reached the consulate of the Independent Republic of Issyk-Kulistan. How can I help you?"

I not *we*, you notice. "Hi," you say, "this is Anwar, at the Scottish consulate. Listen, can you tell me, have you had any email through from the Ministry since Monday afternoon?"

It takes a minute or two for you to get Mr. East-Ender to grudgingly acknowledge your identity, and another minute for him to get the picture, but by the time you put the phone down, you know two new facts: that IRIK have only bothered to establish a one-man consular presence in *England*, and no, he hasn't heard anything from head office either.

Your moustache twitches at the half-imagined odour of dead *Rattus norvegicus*, and you turn to your browser. There are news aggregators and search engines and attention proxies, and you are a master of the web, a veritable expert. Even though you're having to pipe everything through a mess of translation agents, it is but the work of half an hour for you to churn through a hundred searches, refining and reducing and recycling your terms until you've got a pretty good idea of what's *not* going on. There's no public holiday today. There are no football matches, riots, or debates going on in the chamber of deputies. More significantly, a bit more digging reveals that there are no bandits, bank robberies, or bombings. In fact, Issyk-Kulistan is a bit of a news black hole. It's as if a cone of Internet silence has descended across the entire country, and nobody outside has noticed.

Your skin crawls; you're running low on excuses. *If Adam's right*—then the sock-puppet nation is about to be wadded up and thrown away. And you know too damned much. You know about empty-eyed men with suitcases they want you to look after, and trade delegations with bags of not-bread mix. You don't have to be Inspector Rebus to know what happens to bagmen who aren't sitting tight when the music stops.

You try a different strategy and waste a few minutes hunting for notifications of service outages afflicting the major trunks in and out of the country. Then you have a moment of blinding realization.

Voice mail.

You flip through the Ministry's online directory until you come to a different section. With a shaky finger, you drag the address card into your phone and prod the connect button, already rehearsing your abject apologies. It rings twice, then a man answers it, speaking an unfamiliar language. There's music in the background, tinny voices singing. "Hello?" you say tentatively: "Is Colonel Datka there?"

"One moment." The speaker's English is very good, almost unaccented. There's a scraping sound, as of a hand covering a mobile phone, some muffled conversation. "Felix is tied up right now, but he'll be along in a minute. Who should I say is calling?"

Your tongue swells abruptly, and you cough. "To whom am I speaking?"

"This is Bhaskar." Whoever Bhaskar is, he sounds amused. "And you are?"

"This is the Scottish consulate," you say, your voice barely above a dry-mouthed whisper. "I need to talk to the colonel."

"The—you say the *Scottish* consulate?"

"Yes." You swallow, hoping the phone app they gave you is adequately encrypted. "There's a problem."

"A *problem*. And for this problem you need to talk to Felix Datka." His tone sharpens.

"Yes." You realize you're clutching the edge of your desk as if it's a life-belt. "I know what you're doing, what you're using me for, and I don't, I can't ... "

"Wait, please. Ah, Felix—you, you had better explain this to the colonel himself. He will speak to you now." There's a muffled noise, as of a phone being passed between hands, and then a new speaker.

"This is Felix Datka. Identify yourself."

The background music has stopped. "It's Anwar, Anwar Hussein. From Edinburgh, your honorary consul."

The colonel snorts superciliously. "And you are calling because ... ?"

All your indignation comes boiling up at once.

"My cousin's dead, *Colonel*. Since your man arrived in my city, with his curious demands. Surely this is not a coincidence? And it is not bad enough being held up to ridicule by the other diplomats of this city, oh no! Everybody knows that Issyk-Kulistan is a front for some strange diplomatic game. And the trade delegations with the *bread mix* that is a culture medium for illegal nanosystems, you have me handing this stuff out openly as if on the street-corner! Where the police can find me, red-handed! And this week, this week even the news stops. There is no news, as if you cannot even be bothered to maintain the pretence! Have you no *decency*, sir?"

There is no sound from the other end of the phone, but a glance at the screen tells you the connection is still there.

"Sir?"

There is a pause. Then Datka asks, softly, meditatively, terrifyingly: "What do you mean, 'bread mix'?"

* * *

Light-headed and nauseous, you collect your possessions and walk out of the consulate. You leave behind: the safe and its contents, the travelling trunk with its commercial samples of bread mix, the laptop, the furnishings, the stale posturing and lies. You are going home, home to your family and your future and the things that matter to you. Fuck Adam and his stupid get-rich-quick scheme, scamming scammers. Fuck Colonel Datka and his secret policeman's eyes. Fuck the colonel's man Christie, whoever he is. You don't need any of them. They can't give you back Tariq's annoying jokes, his sly word-play. They can't give you an extra minute to say good-bye to your cousin. And if they can't do that, how heavily should your children's futures weigh on your shoulders?

If it comes to it, you'll turn yourself in to Mr. Webber and shop the lot of them. Go back inside Saughton, if that's what it takes to keep them away from Bibi and the bairns.

You are hungry—you forgot to make yourself breakfast this morning—and you are sick at heart as you march determinedly towards the tram stop. You're walking away from a good solid job that was paying you—well, it wasn't paying you well in purely monetary terms, but it got you respect. And after what you threw in Colonel Datka's face (or more accurately, his ear) you have zero expectation of keeping the job. Bibi will be livid. She'll also be exhausted from sitting up all night with Aunt Sameena and Uncle Taleb and the kids, and she's probably back at work by now—

Yes, you can see all this. *Nevertheless.*

You check your phone for the tram schedule, and it flashes a red warning at you: delays expected due to an accident on Leith Walk, get the bus instead. You can see at least one tram with your own eyes, but who knows how the network works? So you stop by the foot of the Mound, outside the big art gallery, and poke at the time-table. You've hit the morning lull after rush hour, it seems, when half the buses return to their depots. Irritated, you put your phone away and start walking. It's only a couple of kilometres, and the weather's fine. You'll even chance a short-cut over the Mound, normally a steep climb best left to the buses' fuel cell.

Halfway up the first flight of worn stone steps behind the gallery, your phone shivers. You glance at it, startled. It's an invite to join a new start-up group on some business network, one of the half-assed by-blows of LinkedIn and Facebook that offer virtual corporate hosting to folks too cheap to rent an office. Somehow it's dodged your spam stack. You're about to flag it when you see the sender's name. JOHN CHRISTIE. You mash your thumb on the delete icon with a shudder, like you're crushing a sleepy autumn wasp. A minute later, the phone buzzes again: It's a different invite, this time for some kind of file repository. Same sender. The menacing buzz of the hornet circling your head, looking to sting: He's relying on your natural curiosity to make you break cover, nose inquisitively into his new business scheme. It's a trap, of course. You've had enough. You flip the phone to flight mode and pocket it. It's not like you need a map to find your way home, and when you get there, you'll—

What will you do?

You're breathing harder as you climb faster, but you know

exactly what you're going to do. You're going to take his luggage and dump it out the back yard. You're going to call Inspector Butthurt and cough everything you suspect, the weird coincidences, the job that's too good to be true. Give them the bucket, the bread mix, and Colonel Datka's phone number, much good may it do them. You're going clean, the cleanest you've been: an end to the tears and the in-between ... yes. Get your priorities right: Naseem, Farida, Bibi, your parents and uncles and aunts and cousins and nephews and nieces and family—

There's a buzzing as of an angry swarm of bees from your pocket, then your phone rings.

You pull it out and stare at it. It's in flight mode: How can this be? It's ringing, though. The screen says INTERNATIONAL CALL.

You answer the phone. "Hello."

The voice at the other end of the connection is heavily accented, male. "Presidential palace," it says. "Please wait."

You stop and lean on the iron railing near the top of the steps, just below the intersection with Market Street. Turning to face back the way you came, you stare out across the deep gulf of Princes Street Gardens, the classical stone pile of the Royal Scottish Academy, towards the stony frontages of the New Town, blocks hacked out of history. There's a light breeze blowing, and high above you it tears cotton-wool shards from the passing clouds. There's a sour taste in your mouth. After a moment you realize it's fear.

A new voice, gravelly, with a faint American accent: "Good afternoon. Am I speaking to Mr. Anwar Hussein?" You half recognize it, but you can't quite place where you've heard him before.

"Yes," you say cautiously.

"Excellent. Please accept my apologies for intruding on you— I understand, I'm told, you have recently had a death in your family?"

"Yes." You bite your lower lip, then glance around. Just in case somebody's watching you.

"I'm very sorry about that." A momentary pause. "I gather that when you called Felix Datka half an hour ago, we had a slight misunderstanding."

"I resigned," you say icily, tightening the shreds of your dignity around you.

"Yes, he told me that. Mr. Hussein—Anwar—I want to explain to you: Matters are not so simple that you can just resign."

You'd tell him to fuck right off except he rang through to your phone while it was in flight mode, and that's supposed to be impossible, isn't it? *Or isn't there a backdoor for the emergency services?* You vaguely remember hearing something about that, something about external emergency reactivation—"I'm quitting," you repeat, less firmly. "Who are you, anyway?"

"I'm Colonel Felix Datka's boss," says the man on the phone. "You can call me Bhaskar. Or Professor Tanayev. I am, very indirectly, your employer. Or ex-employer, if you insist on resigning."

The tram bells far below might as well be fire alarms, telling you to get out *now*. "Professor Tanayev. You're the colonel's boss? How exactly does that work?"

He chuckles. "They can kick me out of the presidential palace, but they can't strip me of tenure."

Silence. You realize you're clutching the phone like it's turned into a gold brick between your fingers. "President of *Issyk-Kulistan*?"

"No; President of Kyrgyzstan. Issyk-Kulistan is a wholly-owned subsidiary operated by a shell company, if you prefer a business metaphor. Felix's job is to keep IRIK running for as long as we need it."

Now you cringe and start looking round. But not for snoopers; you're more worried about assassination drones cruising overhead, looking for a lock on your skull. "Why are you interested in *me*?"

"Because you've been approached by a highly questionable business man working for a foreign private-equity organization. They're not angel investors so much as fallen angels—please stop looking around like that, you will only attract unwanted attention—and it is important to us that this business man should not be frightened away or prematurely introduced to the police—*yes*, I said *prematurely*. Mr. Hussein, are you paying attention? Hello?"

There's a stream of traffic flowing along Bank Street, and you'll only get yourself run over if you try and dash across it. The crawling sensation in the small of your back won't go away, but the fire in your lungs is growing, so you stop, bent over, wheezing (*so* out of shape! Bibi will scold you!), and hold the phone to your ear again.

"Hello? Hello?"

May you come to the attention of important people: Supposedly it's an ancient Chinese curse, but the modern Kyrgyz version has got you bang to rights. "I'm here."

"Excellent. Listen, Mr. Hussein, Anwar—may I call you Anwar? This is only for the next day or so. You have heard of, ah, sting operations? A sting is in progress, and your consular post is part of the bait. We would like you to continue with the job and comply with any of John Christie's requests—if they remain reasonable, of course—while we gather evidence against his associates. For whose arrest there will be a generous reward, incidentally. Colonel Datka assures me that this fellow is the key to a major international criminal investigation, and he will see to it that Europol treat you as a material witness when—"

"What about the bread mix?" you burst out.

"The *what*?"

You have never heard a president sound confused before. (Not that you've ever knowingly *spoken* to a president before—it's not like they're on Facebook, sending friend requests—but it's not what you expect from seeing them on the political blogs.)

"The bread mix," you repeat. "INSECT-FREE FAIR TRADE ORGANIC BREAD MIX BARLEY-RYE, Produce of People's Number Four Grain Products Factory of Issyk-Kulistan. That I'm supposed to give samples of to visitors, and never put in a bucket and ferment with a special extra ingredient."

There's noise on the line, as the president speaks away from his headset, his tone rising imperiously: "Felix, what's this I hear about our consulate receiving *bread mix*?" There is a delay. "Oh, I see. Mr. Hussein, you are not to worry about the bread mix. Apparently the—criminals—we have been investigating have parasites. They've been using your consulate for drop-shipping contraband, but you should not worry about this. It is minor, and if you play your part for just a little while longer, we will arrest them all. Including this Christie person. I will ensure that you are well looked after, you have my word on the matter. If you'll excuse me, I must go now. Just remember: Play for time. Good-bye for now!"

Your phone goes dead, and you blink at the screen. It is, indeed, in flight mode. Then you look up. High above the roof-tops, twenty or fifty metres up, the grey discus of a surveillance drone ghosts past the elaborate columns and stone railings and domes of the former bank headquarters.

Blink and it's gone: But the sensation that you are being watched remains.

DOROTHY: REWIND

Flashback:

The door opens. You take a step forward into Liz's open arms, and her friendly face and welcoming hug is just too much. You tear up as you slump chin first onto her shoulder. She tenses up for a moment, then relaxes. "Oh hell. Let's get you inside." Two steps forward, the door closes, and you find a futon behind you. You crumple slowly backwards on it.

Gentle words: Liz fusses around, offering tissues, tea, and sympathy. But, inevitably, the question you've been dreading arrives: "What happened?"

You open your mouth and find the words have gone missing. *I don't know.*

Liz squats in front of you. Takes your right hand in her own, strokes the back of your wrist. She looks—intent. Focused. You try to speak again, but end up shaking your head.

"Is it the stalker?" she asks.

"I—" You're appalled at your inarticulacy. "I don't know.

Didn't think so. Not sure now. I've been so stupid." *Sniff*. Is this self-pity or anger, filling the spring of tears? Which is it? "I, uh, I wasn't telling the truth the other night. When I said Julian was in Moscow."

"No?" She's waiting, hopeful and loyal and ... just being there. You don't deserve this.

"He dumped me a couple of months ago," you mutter, not meeting her eyes. "I'm not myself right now."

"What happened?" she asks, gently stroking your wrist and watching you with inquisitor's eyes, not accusing, mildly curious.

You tell her. Then, when she doesn't explode in a fiery octopus of molten blame, you tell her some more. Being conflicted. Wanting a casual pick-up. Dinner with Christie, and dessert, and, and.

She listens quietly until you get to the way he chucked you out, and what you thought, the safeword. "Did he rape you?" she asks, gently enough. But you can feel the tension in her fingertips, rubbing.

"No. Yes. Maybe: I'm not sure." You take a deep, ragged breath. "I ... it was regrettable sex. I shouldn't have done it and felt really bad afterwards, kind of sick ... I think he *might* have raped me, if I'd wanted to stop short. But we didn't go there. Not at that time."

"At. That time." Her finger motion stops, leaving your wrist limp and open to the air. She's pulled completely away, withdrawn without your noticing. "What happened then?"

You take a deep breath. "That's when it got weird. I went back to my room, wedged the door. Then there was a work email."

"Work." You've been avoiding eye contact up to now, afraid of seeing what your confession is doing to her. But you force yourself to look up. To your surprise, she looks thoughtful. There's no contempt or anger or hatred; she looks almost ... *business-like*? "What kind of work?"

"Head office wanted a special type of assessment performing, a sociopathic disorder assessment on a named executive. It was him. Liz, I should have seen it coming before—I mean, I was just *stupid*. John Christie is a narcissistic psychopath—"

"*Who* did you say?"

You flinch. "John, uh, Christie? He said he got picked on at school for it, sharing a name with a murderer—"

"No, wait. Stop right there." Liz is looking at you with a very odd expression on her face. "Would you mind describing him? I mean, how tall is he? How old? How much does he weigh—"

Now you're on the receiving end of an inquisition—but it's not at all what you expected. Part-way through, Liz reaches for a pair of specs and switches them on. She seems to be looking something up. Then she takes them off again, holding them carefully, as if afraid they might explode in her hands.

She stares at her specs. "Jesus, Dorothy."

"I'm—" You lick your lips. "You don't hate me?"

Her gaze flickers across you, sweeping you from top to toes. She looks profoundly disturbed: stunned, even. "Jesus, Dorothy, you're lucky to be *alive*."

"But he—" You do a double-take. "Is he a murderer?"

She won't meet your eyes. "I don't know. Hopefully not; but he's certainly a psycho, and what happened to you—are you sure it wasn't rape?"

Your mind goes blank. You try to think back to what you were thinking in the run-up to dinner, in the lift up to his room … skulking away with your tail between your legs. Showering to forget his touch. (Why didn't you use the safeword—were you afraid he wouldn't stop? Were you enjoying it? It's so confusing.) "If it's rape, there's a script to follow, isn't there?"

"Yes, but you don't have to worry about that."

"The hell I don't." Your throat's raw. "There were no witnesses. Okay, so suppose I say 'yes' and you take me round to the station where a trained counsellor talks me through giving a report and taking"—you swallow—"samples. And let's suppose you, uh, your people go and arrest him. At that point it's his word against mine, and you know what his advocate will make of my background? Polyamory still doesn't get equal rights, never mind civil partnerships . . . I just get dragged through the mud, and to what end?"

"But you've got—" Liz jolts to a stop, like a Doberman at the end of a choke chain. She's staring at you. "Oh," she says softly.

"Oh, indeed." You reach out your hand towards her. "You don't want this, Liz. You don't know what you're opening yourself up for."

After a moment, she takes your hand.

"It wasn't rape," you say, trying to keep any trace of doubt out of your voice for her sake. "But I'm really worried about the, the other thing."

"Yes, I'd say you should be." Liz is silent for a few seconds. "I'd like to take a statement, though. All the same."

"What? But I told you, it wasn't non-consensual—"

"Not about the sex: about the appraisal."

You shiver. "I'd rather not. If you don't mind."

She sits down beside you on the futon. "It's, it's about Christie. He's, uh, a person of interest in another investigation. We want to question him in relation to a violent crime. I can't tell you about it right now, but what you'd told me—it's *really* important. My colleagues—they need to know about this. Do you mind if I file at least a contact report?"

You sniff, then rub a hand across your eyes. There's no mascara or eye-liner, luckily: You stripped before you showered. "You're going to insist, aren't you?"

She manages a weak smile. "You said it: I didn't."

"Oh hell." You struggle to sit up. "Just ... do you mind if I stay overnight? I can't face that room ... "

"You can stay," she says neutrally. "I'll take the futon." She pulls her police specs on again, then pauses, one finger hovering over the power button. "I still love you, you know. I just wish things weren't so messy."

Then she pushes the button.

LIZ: Project ATHENA

"People laugh when they hear the phrase 'artificial intelligence' these days." MacDonald is on a roll. "But it's not funny; we've come a long way since the 1950s. There's a joke in the field: If we know how to do it, it's not intelligence. Playing checkers, or chess, or solving mathematical theorems. Image recognition, speech recognition, handwriting recognition. Diagnosing an illness, driving a car through traffic, operating an organic-chemistry lab to synthesize new compounds. These were all thought to be aspects of intelligence, back in the day, but now they're things you can buy through an app store or on lease-purchase from Toyota.

"What people think of when you say 'artificial intelligence' is basically stuff they've glommed onto via the media. HAL 9000 or *Neuromancer*—artificial consciousness. But consciousness—we know how that shit works these days, via analytical cognitive neurobiology and synthetic neurocomputing. And it's not very *interesting*. We can't *do* stuff with it. Worst case—suppose I were to sit down with my colleagues and we come up with a traditional brain-in-a-box-type AI, shades of HAL 9000. What then? Firstly, it opens a huge can of ethical worms—once you turn it on, does turning it off again qualify as murder? What about software updates? Bug fixes, even? Secondly, it's not very *useful*. Even if you cut the Gordian knot and declare that because it's a machine, it's a slave, you can't make it *do* anything useful. Not unless you've built in some way of punishing it, in which case we're off into the ethical mine-field on a pogo-stick tour. Human consciousness isn't optimized *for* anything, except maybe helping feral hominids survive in the wild.

"So we're not very interested in reinventing human consciousness in a box. What gets the research grants flowing is *applications*—and that's what ATHENA is all about."

You're listening to his lecture in slack-jawed near comprehension because of the sheer novelty of it all. One of the crushing burdens of police work is how inanely *stupid* most of the shit you get to deal with is: idiot children who think "the dog ate my homework" is a decent excuse even though they knew you were watching when they stuck it down the back of their trousers. MacDonald is . . . well, he's not waiting while you take notes, for sure. Luckily, your specs are lifelogging everything to the evidence servers back at HQ, and Kemal's also on the ball. But even so, MacDonald's whistle-stop tour of the frontiers of science is close to doing your head in. Then the aforementioned Eurocop speaks up.

"That is very interesting, Doctor. But can I ask you for a moment"—Kemal leans forward—"what do you think of the Singularity?"

MacDonald stares at him for a moment, as if he can't believe what he's being asked. "The what—" you begin to say, just as his shoulders begin to shake. It takes you a second to realize he's laughing.

"You'll have to excuse me," he says wheezily, wiping the back of his hand across his eyes: "I haven't been asked that one in *years*." Your sidelong glance at Kemal doesn't illuminate this remark: Kemal looks as baffled as you feel. "I, for one, welcome our new superintelligent AI overlords," MacDonald declaims, and then he's off again.

"What's so funny?" you ask.

"Oh—hell—" MacDonald waves a hand in the air, and a tag pops up in your specs: "Let me give you the dog and pony show." You accept it. His office dissolves into classic cyberspace noir, all black leather and decaying corrugated asbestos roofing, with a steady drip-drip-drip of condensation. Blade Runner city, Matrix-ville. "Remember when you used to change your computer every year or so, and the new one was cheaper and much faster than the old one?" A graph appears in the moisture-bleeding wall behind him, pastel arcs zooming upward in an exponential plot of MIPS/dollar against time—the curve suddenly flattening out a few years before the present. "Folks back then"—he points to the steepest part of the upward curve—"extrapolated a little too far. Firstly, they grabbed the AI bull by the horns and assumed that if heavier-than-air flight was possible at all, then the artificial sea-gull would *ipso facto* resemble a biological one, behaviourally ... then they assumed it could bootstrap itself onto progressively faster hardware or better-optimized software, refining itself."

A window appears in the wall beside you; turning, you see a nightmare cityscape, wrecked buildings festering beneath a ceiling of churning fulvous clouds: Insectile robots pick their way across grey rubble spills. Another graph slides across the end-times diorama, this one speculative: intelligence in human-equivalents, against time. Like the first graph, it's an exponential.

"Doesn't work, of course. There isn't enough headroom left for exponential amplification, and in any case, nobody *needs* it. Religious fervour about the rapture of the nerds aside, there are no short-cuts. Actual artificial-intelligence applications resemble *us* about the way an Airbus resembles a sea-gull. And just like airliners have flaps and rudders and sea-gulls don't, one of the standard features of general cognitive engines is that they're all hard-wired for mirrored self-misidentification. That is, they all project the seat of their identity onto you, or some other human being, and identify your desires as their own impulses; that's standard operating precaution number one. Nobody wants to be confronted by a psychotic brain in a box—what we *really* want is identity amplification. Secondly—"

Kemal interrupts again. You do a double-take: In this corner of the academic metaverse he's come over all sinister, in a black-and-silver suit with peaked forage cap, mirrored aviator shades. "Stop right there, please. You're implying that this, this field is mature? That is, that you routinely do this sort of thing?"

MacDonald blinks rapidly. "Didn't you know?"

You take a deep breath. "We're just cops: Nobody tells us anything. Humour us. Um. What sort of, uh, general cognitive engines are we talking about? Project ATHENA, is that one?"

"Loosely, yes." He rubs at his face, an expression of profound bafflement wrinkling his brows. "ATHENA is one of a family of research-oriented identity-amplification engines that have been developed over the past few years. It's not all academic; for example TR/Mithras.Junkbot.D and Worm/NerveBurn.10143 are out there now. They're malware AI engines; the Junkbot family are distributed identity simulators used for harvesting trust, while NerveBurn ... we're not entirely sure, but it seems to be a sandboxed virtual brain simulator running on a botnet, possibly a botched attempt at premature mind uploading ... " He rubs his face again. "ATHENA is a bit different. We're an authorized botnet—that is, we're legal; students at participating institutions are required to sign an EULA that permits us to run a VM instance on their pad or laptop, strictly for research in distributed computing.

There's also a distributed screen-saver project for volunteers. ATHENA's our research platform in moral metacognition."

"Metacognition?"

"Loosely, it means we're in consciousness studies—more prosaically, we're in the business of telling spam from ham." He shrugs apologetically. "Big contracts from telcos who want to cut down on the junk traffic: It pays our grants. The spambots have been getting disturbingly convincing—last month there was a report of a spear-phishing worm that was hiring call girls to role-play the pick-ups the worm had primed its targets to expect. Some of them are getting very sophisticated—using multiple contact probes to simulate an entire social network—big ones, hundreds or thousands of members, with convincing interactions—e-commerce, fake phone conversations, the whole lot—in front of the victim. Bluntly, we're only human; we can't tell the difference between a spambot and a real human being anymore without face-to-face contact. So we need identity amplification to keep up.

"The ATHENA research group is working on the spam-filtering problem by running a huge distributed metacognition app that's intended to pick holes in the spammers' fake social networks."

MacDonald magicks up a big diagram in place of the graphs; it looks like a tattered spider-web. "Here's a typical social network. Each node is a person. They've got a lot of local connections, and a handful of long-range ones." Thin strands snake across the web, linking distant intersections. "Zoom in on one of the nodes, and we have a bunch of different networks: their email, chat, phone calls, online purchases ... " A slew of different spider-webs, cerise and cyan and magenta, all appear centred on a single point. They're all subtly different in shape. "Spambots usually get their networks wrong, too regular, not noisy enough. And we can deduce other information by looking at the networks, of course. You know the old one about checking the phone bills for signs that your partner's having an affair, right? There are other, more subtle signs of—well, call it potential criminality. Odds are, before your partner snuck off for some illicit nookie, there was a warm-up period, lots of chatter with characteristic weighted phrases—we're human: We talk in clichés the whole time, framing the narrative of our lives. Or take some of the commoner personality disorders: pre-ATHENA, we had diagnostic tools that could diagnose schizophrenia from a sample of email messages with eerie accuracy. Network analysis lets us learn a lot about people. Network injection lets us *steer* people—subject to ethics oversight, I hasten to add—frankly, the possibilities are endless, and a bit frightening."

"Can you give me an example of what you mean by steering people?" Kemal nudges.

"Hmm." MacDonald's chair squeals as he leans back. "Okay, let's talk hypotheticals: Suppose I'm wearing a black hat, and I want to fuck someone up, and I've paid for a command channel to Junkbot.D. First, I build a map of their social connections. Then I have Junkbot establish a bunch of sock puppets and do a friend-of-friend approach via their main social networks—build up connections until they see the sock puppets' friend requests, see lots of friends in common, and accept the invite. Junkbot then engages them in several conversation scripts in parallel. A linear chat-up rarely works—people are too suspicious these days—but you can game them. Set up an artificial-reality game, if you like, built around your victim's world, with a bunch of sock puppets who are there to sucker them in to the drama. Finally, you use the client-side toolkit to hire some proxies—neds in search of the price of a pint—who'll hand your target a package and leg it, five minutes ahead of your colleagues, who have received an anonymous tip-off that the quiet guy living at number seventy-six is a nonce."

Kemal is rapt, listening intently. He nods, perhaps once every ten seconds. MacDonald has got him on a string with this spiel.

You look back at MacDonald. "You wouldn't dream of doing that," you say.

MacDonald grins and nods. "Indeed not. Morality aside, it's stupid small-scale shit. What'd be the point?"

You peg him then. He's not your typical aspie hacker, and he's not a regular impulse-control case. MacDonald's the other, rare kind: the sort of potential offender who does a cold-blooded risk-benefit calculation and refrains from action not because it's wrong, but because the trade-off isn't right. You won't be seeing him in the daily arrest log anytime soon, because he kens well the opportunity cost of a decade in prison: It'd take a bottom line denominated in millions to lure him off the straight and narrow. But *if* he sees such a pay-off . . .

"What do you use ATHENA for?" you ask, bluntly.

"Right now we're tracing spammers. ATHENA can scope out the fake networks: It can also tell us who's running them." There's something about MacDonald's body language that puts you on red alert. Something evasive. "ATHENA then probes the spammers to determine whether they're human or sock puppet. We're working on active countermeasures, but that's not green-lit yet; I gather there's a working group talking to some staff at the Ministry of Justice about it, but—"

"What kind of active countermeasures?"

"Spoiler stuff, but more active than usual: using their own tools against them. You know it's an international problem? Crossing lines of jurisdiction—a lot of them live in countries that aren't sig-natory to or don't enforce anti-netcrime treaties. So we're examining a number of tactics that'd need to be approved by a court order before we could use them. So far it's just theoretical, but: reverse-phishing the spammers to grab their control channels and shut down the botnets. Fucking with their phishing payloads to make them expose their real identity so you folks can arrest them. Stealing their banking credentials and applying civil-forfeiture protocols. Using their ID protocols to fuck with their personal lives—hate mail to the mother-in-law, that kind of thing. Having their computer report itself as stolen. In an extreme instance, ask the USAF to send a drone to zap them."

"Uh-huh." You glance down and try to look as if you're making notes, so that he can't see your face. One by one, the alarm bells are going off inside your head. "But you haven't done any of this yet."

"No."

"But?"

"ATHENA is an international effort." MacDonald leans forward on his elbows, fingers laced before him. "*We* are just academic researchers. We're trying to find a way to, shall we say, enforce communal standards without turning the corner and ending up with a panopticon singularity, ubiquitous maximal law enforcement by software—*nobody* wants that, so we're looking for something more humane. Crime prevention by automated social pressure rather than crime prosecution by AI. But ... once you get into that territory? People don't all agree on what constitutes crime, or moral behaviour. Some of our associate members live in jurisdictions where there are melted stove-pipes between academia and government, or intelligence. And I canna vouch for what those *third parties* might do with our work."

ANWAR: Bluebeard

As soon as you open the front door, you know something's not right.

"Honey? I'm home ... "

It's like that inevitable, deterministic scene in every horror video you've ever lost two hours of your life to: the dawning sense of wrongness, of a life unhinged. From the subtle absence of expected sounds to the different, unwelcome noise from upstairs in the bedroom, all is out of order.

"Hello?" you call up the stairwell.

There's no reply, but you hear footsteps like a herd of baby elephants on the landing. *Angry* footsteps. Your stomach clenches. They are Bibi's angry footsteps, and now you know what is wrong: All that remains is to find out *why*.

You tiptoe past an obstruction in the hall and look up the stairs. "Is everything all right?" you call.

There's a muffled thud, a wail of pain, and some most unlady-like swearing. Then there's another thud, louder. Bibi hauls into view on the landing, leaning to one side, the big yellow suitcase dragging at the ends of her arms like a boat anchor. Her glare of effort silences you as she levers it onto the top stair-tread. It must be full, to be so heavy. The suitcase is a hundred-litre monster, sized for that month-long family excursion to Lahore that never came. Ever since, it has lurked under Naseem's bed like a bright plastic chrysalis from which someday a holiday will hatch. It's nearly bigger than Bibi, and for a heart-stopping moment, you think she's going to be crushed by it. But no: It rocks heavily on the stair, then she's behind it, gripping it by the tow handle and leaning backwards as she lowers it towards you like a juggernaut of wrath. Finally, it hits the hall carpet and sits there, and Bibi pushes it past you, breathing heavily.

"What are you doing?" you ask.

"What does it look as if I'm doing?" There's an odd, lilting note in her voice, almost devil-may-care.

"Is it your mother?"

"No, Anwar, it's you."

"I don't—" You're about to say *understand*, but for a cursed moment your tongue freezes. "Where are the children?"

She pushes the heavy bag past you, forcing you to step back against the wall. She's on the other side of it, using it as a shield. "What's in the bucket?" she asks tensely. "Where did you get that suitcase?"

She's been up the ladder.

Oh shit.

"I, I can explain! It's work—a man from head office, from the Foreign Office, he is coming to stay, just for a couple of nights—"

"Shut up, Anwar."

You focus on her nostrils, on the tip of her nose. They're flared wide, as if she smells something awful, something vile. She's shaking slightly. *Fear? Anger?* You've always found it hard to read Bibi. The long silences, the elliptical comments, the woman's expectation of insight, as if you're expected to read and parse the invisible code written on the inside of her eyelids. *Contempt?*

"What's wrong?" you ask.

"I'm leaving," she says, as calmly as if announcing she was going to work.

"What?"

While you stand, perplexed, back up against the wall, she shoves the suitcase past you to stand beside the smaller bag that obstructs the hallway.

"When are you coming back?" you ask, feeling lost.

She grabs the smaller bag by the handle. "That's up to you." She drags it up to the open front door, then stops, straightens up, and glares at you. "Get rid of that stuff. Get help. Then you can email me."

"But what—what stuff?" None of this makes sense. "I don't understand."

"No, you don't." Her contempt is withering. "I've put up with a lot of *not understanding* from you, over the years. Not understanding what it is about obeying the law, Anwar. Not understanding that you're going to get caught if you carry on. And I've been giving you a lot of *not understanding* in return. Not understanding about the pubs and the late nights. Not understanding about your boy-friends and the condoms. I could even manage to *not understand* your brewing experiment in the attic, or the dodgy business deals. But the other thing? I can't not understand *that*. Promise me you'll get help, and we can talk. Chat. IM. I won't tell the police." Her shoulders are shaking. "But. If I catch you near the kids, I'll tell everyone." She turns away.

"*Tell* everyone *what*?"

But you're talking to a receding back, hunched under the weight of too much baggage. You blink against the daylight, mouth hanging open, unable to grasp what's happening. There's a sour taste in your mouth and a ringing in your ears, and a terrible tension in your head: the injustice of it all! If you were a real man of your father's generation, you'd chase after her and drag her back and thrash her soundly. (If you were a real man of your father's generation she'd call Social Services on you.) Where's the honour in this? What does she think you have done, to be so offended?

The bucket. The suitcase. Oh God.

The front door slams closed behind you as you scamper for the staircase as if all the hounds of hell are chasing you. (She's been upstairs. And it's not the bucket.) You pull down the loft ladder and scramble up it, gasping for breath, surface in the attic like a mole in a lawn suddenly come face-to-face with a roller.

The bucket is where you left it, but Peter Manuel's suitcase sits open on the floor, in the middle of the puddle of daylight admitted by the dormer window. Bibi must have forced the lock, you realize. A small, pale-skinned arm rests just over the zippered rim, as if a wee bairn is sleeping inside. Then the arm twitches, flailing for a grip.

A little girl, about three years younger than Farida, sits up in the suitcase. Blonde tousled hair and button nose: blue eyes and puppy fat. But there's something wrong with her. Her face is expressionless and paralysed, her mouth gaping so wide you think for a horrid moment that her jaw is dislocated—her skin doesn't seem to fit properly. And she's naked. Naked, and in a suitcase.

Then she looks at you with undead eyes and speaks without moving her mouth:

"Will you fuck me, Daddy? I want you. I've been so lonely without you ... "

LIZ: DOMINOES FALL

You don't normally come out of an interview with a material witness blinking at the light and wondering which way up your world goes; twice in twenty-four hours is something of a personal record. Nevertheless, you take one look at Kemal's face and feel a twinge of recognition. You step aside for a stranger entering the building as the grimy glass door swings shut behind you, distracted by the need to marshal your thoughts. "Did you get anything out of that?" you ask.

Kemal shakes his head, not in negation but in weary acknowledgment. "The future is here today, unevenly distributed," he misquotes. "I do not think the doctor is a murderer. Not a knowing one, of course."

You keep your thoughts to yourself for a moment as you look around for the car. It's missing. "Hold on." You ping the front desk back at head office: "Where's our ride?"

Sniffy McSluggard takes her own sweet time getting back to you: "CID told it it was needed elsewhere, Inspector. You'll be wanting to charge for a bus ride."

Which is just bloody typical. "Come on," you tell Kemal, and head down Buccleugh Street towards the short-cut through to South Clerk Street. "What makes you think the doctor's in the clear?"

"I do not think he's *innocent*," Kemal admits. "His speech stress is uneven. He hides something, yes. And the spam connection, and the, the cognitive engine, the use of distributed networks—that is significant. But I don't think he's a killer."

"Why not?" you needle.

"He is a coward." Kemal pauses next to a rack of council recycling bins. "That is a technical term," he adds. "He is a thinking man and an overplanner. He anticipates hazards before they emerge, and avoids them. Risk-averse."

"That's how I pegged him," you aver. *So why did Dodgy Dickie want you to interview him?* "I think we should do some more digging. If someone is using ATHENA to locate targets, that would fit ... " You trail off. There's that nagging sense of déjà vu. You know Dr. MacDonald from somewhere, you're sure of it. One or other of the pubs and bars in the pink triangle? Or a Pride march in years past, when you were managing the Lothian and Borders booth? That's as may be, but it's not relevant to the case in hand. "Let's find out who he talks to. Let's see what Moxie can find out about his connections."

Back on South Clerk Street you hijack a microbus with the aid of your company debit card and bid handsomely to divert it halfway to Dean Village. There's some jerk on the top deck who counterbids and it ends up ramping to twenty euros, but fuck it—two DIs, on a murder investigation: Doc will square it for you. You walk the last stretch and are back at HQ by eleven.

The MacDonald interview has preceded you—uploaded in real time, it made it into the BABYLON intel feed and promptly bamboozled everyone on the team who was paying attention. As

you walk through the shielded doors, a blizzard of virtual Post-
it notes descends on you, terminating in a terse SEE ME, signed
DCI MacLeish. It's like being back in grammar school again. You
give Kemal the eye-ball. "Got to run, make yourself at home in
ICIU."

You barely walk through the door to D31 before Dickie is on
your case. Face like thunder, beetling brows, he rushes you. "This
way," he growls, striding towards a confessional cubicle—beige
fabric walls, antisound damper poised overhead like a metal
mantis. He barely waits to get into the cone of silence before he
launches on you. "I don't know what you fucking think you're
doing, Kavanaugh, snooping around on your off shift and sticking
your nose in—"

"Hey, what the fuck are you—"

"No, don't you start! I should take this up the chain *reet now*.
You're a loose cannon. This report on the Straight woman is the
final straw—"

You snap. "Fuck off."

"Whit?"

His expression is a picture in peach, slowly ripening towards
plum. You ken you've got about five seconds before he really
explodes, so you go for the throat "*She* came to *me*, sir. Because,
you know, outside of work I have this thing called a *life*, and
Dorothy is one of my friends. *Friends*, Dickie, you've heard of
them? Jesus fucking Christ, have you never had a friend come to
you with a question about the law? Come on. Tell me. *Have you?*"

"I've nivver had a so-called friend cough a fucking POI in a
murder investigation in my lap!"

"Well *neither have I*, but there's always a first time. And I bet
you've never had a girl-friend cough to a date-rape situation either,
have you? But that's what friends are for."

The "R" word gets his attention. "Rape, did you say?"

You make a cutting gesture: "I didna think there was a case to answer, or I'd have had her down the clinic before her feet touched the floor. Questionable sex, with a side order of sociopathic manipulation involved. Her word against his, no drugs or threats of violence, it gets murky fast. But no, sir. The reason I filed the report was this John Christie sock puppet is in play, and I figured you might want to *talk to him*. About what he was doing visiting our friend Mr. Blair. Ahem." You don't add, *instead of adding two plus two to make 16.7 and threatening me with a disciplinary*. That's understood. But his expression begins to droop from bullish to sheepish, and the choleric colour is fading.

"Jesus, Liz."

You've won, you see, but you're still pissed off at him for losing his rag in the first place. Probably best to let him know about it, both barrels in the face: Dickie's not terribly perceptive when it comes to subtleties of interpersonal relations. "We are *on the same team*, sir. I really do not appreciate this hard-on you've got for me. I am attempting to discharge my duty as efficiently as possible, and you keep dumping on me. When I stumbled over a lead by *pure chance*, I sent it your way because that's the right thing to do: I do not expect to catch shit by return of email. If you'd be happier with me off the case, then just say so: I've got a patch of my own to cultivate. But some professional courtesy would be appreciated around here."

The red spots on his cheeks come back, but he visibly bites his lip—and nods. It's just a quiver of acknowledgment, but it's the real thing. *Suck it up, asshole*. To his credit, he nods again. "It would seem that I owe someone an apology," he admits.

Don't be too fast with that: You could poke somebody's eye out. You confine your response to a minutely calculated nod. "About Dr. MacDonald—"

"No," says Dickie, and something about his tone alerts you,

puts you on notice that he's forgotten for a moment that he hates you.

"No?"

"Summat you said." He frowns frumiously, an expression that comes easily to the front of his wrinkled noggin. "Stumbled over a lead by *pure chance*. So you say. D'ye really think that's plausible?"

"What are you implying?" Your hackles are still raised.

"I'm not implying ... *anything* ... about *you*. What I'm saying is, it's a verra *convenient* coincidence. And if there's one thing ye ken I dinna trust, it's coincidences. And there's too goddamn many of them in this ay mess."

"Coin—" You stop. "Dr. MacDonald. His whole social-network-analysis thing?"

Dickie fixes you with one cold blue eye and nods slowly, beneath the cone of silence.

* * *

You begin to come down from the adrenaline spike of career-terminating rage when you arrive back at the door to the ICIU. Inside, all is as it should be: The ever-rotating pool of uniformed porn monkeys are whining for release from the vomitorium, Moxie is forted up in the second office behind a stack of giant monitors and discarded munchie boxes, and Kemal is propping up the wall behind him, looking bored behind his shades.

"Hey, skipper." Moxie leers at you over a browser full of—you look away quickly. "What can I do you for?"

"Dr. Adam MacDonald, Ed Uni, CS department. What have we got on him?"

"How deep do you want to go?" Your ferret is bright-eyed and bushy-tailed: Moxie likes nothing better than a good chase.

"Public sources first? Nothing I have to sign for at this time."

"Well." Moxie twitches his fingers at a couple of tabs. "It's funny you ask that, skipper. He's got an article on wikipeople, you know? And the social networks, what's not friends-locked. A couple of single-sign-ons will vouch for him, and he posts in chat rooms all over the place." He pulls a face. "Nothing saucy—well, nothing much. He's divorced, one ex-husband—he's heterosexually challenged and hangs out in the usual places."

Kemal is head down over a pad, evidently brainstorming something—you can see lots of mind-map bubbles floating in an ochre soup of murky possibilities. "Okay. Let me authorize a trawl of CopSpace links under BABYLON's authority." You don't have the authority to pull up random citizen's CopSpace records on your own, but MacDonald's on BABYLON's radar as a POI, and you're on team as an inspector, so your signing authority will cover it. You lean over Moxie's terminal and stick your thumbprint on the reader, as required. It's very fast and streamlined these days, the hierarchical delegation of surveillance authority under RIPA statutes: police-intelligence access via social network. "Let's see who the good doctor has been talking to lately ... "

Kemal catches your eye. While Moxie is busy, you follow him outside into the bright sunlight. The drive is occupied; someone's parked a bunch of the force's riot barrier trailers there, lined up as if there's an up-coming derby. "What is it?" you ask.

"Your boss must really hate you." To your surprise, he pulls out a packet of cigarettes and glances around. "Do you mind?"

"Um ... " You shake your head. "Yes, he does. Five years ago I was in line for the job he's in now, and he knows it. I'm the skeleton in his closet." Lothian and Borders is officially a non-smoking force, but Kemal's just visiting, and you're outside and more than ten metres from a doorway. "Is that legal?"

His cheek twitches in something like a smile. "I have given up giving up."

You step sideways to stand up-wind of him: "Any thoughts?"

He gets the thing lit and inhales deeply, frowning. After he lets the smoke out, the set of his shoulders relaxes somewhat. "I have been reading this morning's reports. More fatalities. One of them is a computer scientist in Boston. The usual methodology applies: a misdirected package. This man, though, was a full professor. Not a spammer. He listed project ATHENA as one of his research areas."

"You think that's why Ops sent us to see MacDonald?"

"I think so." He nods, then sucks at the cancer stick again. "Also"—he shrugs tiredly—"the information-crimes angle."

You get that hint instantly. ICIU is the red-headed stepchild of CID and IT Support, the spotty teenager with the suspect habits whose bedroom nobody willingly cleans for fear of what they'll find under the bed. It's the same everywhere. Most police work boils down to minimizing the impact on society of stupidity; of the remainder, the overwhelming majority is about malice and deliberate evil, but it's still almost all stupid. Smart cops hate smart crimes, because they take ages to nail down and in the meantime your clean-up metrics tank. And the crime here—assuming there's anyone to charge with it—is so high concept that it's making your nose bleed. "What kind of scenario do you think we're looking at?"

Smoke trickles from his nostrils. "We have bodies, linked in life by a social network, linked in dying by weird coincidences. We have software for scanning social networks and making deductions about the people in them. We have researchers discussing *active countermeasures*. The question that remains is, did a human being order the software that is conscious to start taking such measures? Or is it an accident?"

"Different charges, either way." He stubs the cigarette out on the sole of one shoe and pockets the butt, staring at you. For your part, you stare at the roofline of the intelligence building, feeling numb. "If someone gave the order, well, there's your *mens rea* and a tidy wrap-up. If nobody did so, then we're into murkier waters: negligent homicide, maybe."

"And the software?" Kemal raises an eyebrow. "If it's conscious—"

"Fuck the software!" You struggle to keep your voice under control. "I know what you're going to say, and it doesn't wash. The law's about fifty years behind the times here, but nobody's going to shed any tears for a killer robot. If it went off on its lonesome, there is going to be such a shitstorm of new legislation coming down the pipe—" You stop. "Oh," you say. "*Coincidences.*" And it's a good thing you're not a smoker like Kemal because the blinding flash of insight when Dickie's time bomb detonates is so dazzling that you'd have dropped your fag, and it's a fifty-euro fine for littering under the cameras hereabouts.

* * *

Lay out the clues like a chain of dominoes:

Mikey Blair, killed by a drug interaction between his spiked enema fluid and his protease-inhibitor prescription. That's a coincidence, isn't it?

"John Christie," whoever he really is, walking in on the crime scene. Let's call that another coincidence and see where it runs.

Lots more killings, all coincidentally contrived, like the Mohammed case: electrocuted by a homicidal vacuum-cleaner robot, or the German guy, burned to a crisp by his sun bed. Coincidence as a *modus operandi*: a sequence of little nudges that build to a fatal pay-off. (If one fatal accident fails to materialize, what are the odds that a bunch of other lethal contingencies lie in the target's future?)

Now consider, further:

"John Christie" walks into your life by way of Dorothy's hotel.

She's been booked in there by her employers. He (you shy away from thinking about this too hard) manipulates her. Then she gets a request for an ethics review.

If that's an accident, you'll eat your warrant card.

But what if Dorothy was a channel to get to *you*? Specifically, to draw your attention to "John Christie." Because, because . . . ?

(Your chain of dominoes terminates in confusion. And you're out of time.)

* * *

You blink, shake your head, then walk back inside without waiting for Kemal. "Hey, Moxie, what have you got for me?"

Moxie sits up straight. "I've got MacDonald's most regular contacts, skipper. These are just the public ones, spidered off chat rooms and mailing lists. Here are his business contacts, and here are the folks he hangs out with, dereferenced to meatspace names." He chucks a couple of tags at your specs and you open them in different windows, as the news spool from the ops room unfreezes and begins to update now you're back in a shielded room. You glance at the personal contacts, and the bottom drops out of your stomach because right at the top of the list is a familiar name: ANWAR HUSSEIN.

"What the—" You suppress a string of invective: For some reason, swearing tends to alarm Moxie. "The personal contacts. Where does MacDonald know our friend Mr. Hussein from?"

"Our friend who? Oh, him? There are a bunch of local forums hanging off fitlads.net. They're both regulars under the handles. Let's see . . . yep, it's a bed-surfing board. Looks to have a regular crowd."

"You said the link is via fitlads, yes?" You frown. Anwar is married. Is it the same man? "This Mr. *particular* Hussein. Can you see if we've got anything on him?"

Moxie dives head down into CopSpace while you skim the feed from BABYLON. The death toll from around the world is still rising. You spot a FLASH alert, broadcast from the City Desk to every team—a report of a homicide in the south side, near the Meadows. Life (and death) goes on as usual in the city, even as you scurry round in pursuit of—

"Skipper? How did you know?"

You blink the windows away and focus on Moxie. "Know what?"

Kemal appears in the doorway. "Inspector—"

"Mr. Hussein has form, skipper? He's done time for his part in an identity-theft ring, and hey? Oh, it was *you* that collared him. Cool!"

"Inspector Kavanaugh. A moment, please?"

Kemal sounds worried. Your stomach lurches. You have an uneasy sense that you are holding the solution to your domino game in your hands if only you could work out where to snap them onto the chain. "Yes?"

"The murder—"

Your phone jangles, a priority incoming. You glance at it: It's Dickie. You prioritize and answer the detective-in-charge first. "Yes?"

"Liz?" Dickie sounds strained. "You and that fly Eurocop, ye've already been and interviewed that professor at the uni? Did ye both go together? Ye *did* stream everything, reet?"

Eh? "Yes," you say cautiously. If he's in the incident room, they'll know that. *So why is he asking?* you wonder. "Kemal and I were both there, and we both recorded the session. It's backed up in Evidence One already. Why?"

"Was MacDonald alive when ye left?"

"*What?*"

You see Kemal urgently mouthing something at you and flick

back to your specs. Another FLASH alert: officer called to Appleton Towers—

"Are you telling me *MacDonald's* been murdered?"

"Answer me—"

"Yes, yes! He was alive when we left. I've got a witness and two time-stamped evidence streams, Inspector. Do you"—*I held the door open,* you remember—"shit."

"Liz. Speak to me."

"Hold please, I need to check something urgently."

Without waiting, you put Dickie on hold and poke urgently at your specs. They're fully lifelogging, and while the main purpose is preservation of evidence, you can at least replay what you've seen. You jump back an hour, then rewind at high speed until you get to your departure from Appleton Towers. You were mostly looking at Kemal, talking as you walked, but there—there's the man coming towards you from outside; there's you holding the door open.

"Kemal? You're on the BABYLON roster. Can you get me a picture of John Christie? That's—"

"What I've been trying to *tell* you," he says, a tad waspishly, and chucks a tag at your glasses. You zoom it into a window next to your lifelog video and bite your lip.

"Fuck." You take Dickie off hold. He's ranting already, but you ignore him: "John Christie was recorded entering the university building at exactly the same time Kemal and I were leaving. It's in my lifelog. I didn't recognize him"—because you'd never met him—"is it MacDonald who's dead?"

"You dinna *recognize* him," Dickie snarls.

"Neither did Kemal. Save it for the inquest, Dickie. Have we nailed Christie yet?"

"Get your sorry ass over to Appleton Towers." Dickie's voice has gone flat, over-controlled. Anger is probably a good sign, with Dickie: It means he isn't bottling it up for a future explosion. "DI

Terry is on her way there to take over. I'll be along after I finish *explaining* your little blind spot to the commissioner. You can walk me through your interview at the scene. Seeing you're the last folks wha' saw MacDonald alive."

He hangs up.

"*Shit.*" You put your phone back in your pocket, trying to still the shaking in your hand.

"Well, Inspector?" Kemal asks. His expression is hard to read. Is that sympathy? Defensive distance?

You draw down a deep breath. "Let's take a ride." To Moxie, you add: "I want a deep trawl on Mr. Hussein. Home address, family, relationships, anything that's available. Bounce it to me, highest priority." Then you're out the door like a demented ground-hog, blinking in the unwelcome daylight again.

"Is that necessary?" Kemal trails you towards the garage. "I thought Dr. MacDonald was a higher priority."

"Oh, it's necessary all right." To the desk sergeant: "I need a car, urgent, case BABYLON." To Kemal: "Dickie wants us to go to Appleton Towers and identify the victim, so we'll go. But I'm not planning on staying for long . . ."

ANWAR: Toymaker

You are behind the bathroom door, trying to figure out how to flush the bucket of fermenting nanotechnological bread mix down the toilet, when the doorbell buzzes.

The bread mix makes you sick, with its strange chemical smell and iridescent bubbles. There's a permanent scummy skin floating on top of the bucket, and whenever you stick a pencil in to lift it off, more skin forms; it forms a brownish rope, very like nylon. At first it's sticky—it sticks to anything it touches like Superglue—but it dries rapidly to a soft and stringy finish. You twist some of it up and it really does form a rope, stronger than seems possible. You're afraid that if you chuck it down the loo (after the stomachful of vomit you ejected right after you zipped the horrid thing back into the suitcase), it'll gum up the pipes. And then what? If you call out a plumber, they might report you to the police—*and then, and then*—your mind shies away from the consequences.

What did that fellow on the phone, Bhaskar, have to say? A *major international criminal investigation*, a *material witness*, and you with the suitcase in the attic full of forbidden horror belonging to Colonel Datka's man. And Bibi knows. And, and. The smell from the bread mix makes your stomach churn. It's sickening. So you've got the bucket down to the bathroom, next to the toilet, and you got the bog brush and dipped it in the bucket and now you're slowly winding a shit-coloured caul of scum around the brush, twirling it as it dries in sheets and fibrous ropes.

And what is this stuff *for*, anyway?

(There's such a lot of it.)

You're about to give up when the doorbell rings. A couple of seconds later, it buzzes again, shrill and insistent.

You clench your teeth, ignoring it. No good can come of answering: *I'm out, nobody home.* Who could it be? The police? Colonel Datka's man? Uncle Taleb? You don't want to see anyone. Nothing to see here, nobody home. The ropey brown tape-string dangling from the bog brush in skeins is on the floor. It's tangled, and there's too much of it to keep dipping and twirling. You step on it, experimentally, and tug on the brush handle. The rope tightens, peeling away reluctantly.

The door slams closed downstairs, and you jerk upright, ears straining. *They've got a key!* Then you remember yesterday's request—before you knew about the contents of the suitcase—with a shiver of revulsion. You left a spare set of keys at the office. It might be Bibi or Uncle Taleb, but it's probably not.

You pick up the bucket and advance on the door to the landing with hatred gnawing a hole in your immortal soul. On the threshold, you pause. What if it *is* Bibi? Mortification and shame claw at your liver and lights. But there are footsteps, and they sound wrong. No, not Bibi. You yank the door open.

Your nightmare is standing on the landing. He stares at you placidly with eyes like the thing in the suitcase.

"Mr. Hussein. I hope I'm not interrupting?"

The bucket dangles uselessly from your limp left hand. "Interrupting?" you echo, dully.

Peter Manuel, John Christie—whoever he is, he's Colonel Datka's man—is taller than you are. Stronger, too, probably. "What is this?" you demand, raising the bucket and giving it a shake. "What *is* this?"

You see his nostrils flare as he inhales. Then he stares at you. "Feedstock. From the bread mix. I see you've activated it. Who told you how to do that?"

You clutch the bucket in both hands: "None of your business!" you snarl. "I'm resigning. I don't represent Issyk-Kulistan anymore. You'd better get out. You're trespassing, you know!"

Christie's lip curls. "You have my luggage," he points out. "And you've taken that without paying." He points at the bucket.

"What is it?" you demand.

"The double-domes worked out how to brew spider-silk in a bucket. Nanotechnology." He looks amused. "It's feedstock for fabbers. Tougher than steel, when it sets. The US military invented it, to make it easier to repair equipment in the field. This is a pirate copy." He reaches out a hand. "You'd better give me that. If you dump it down the toilet, it'll block the pipes."

You hand the bucket over without thinking. Christie takes it, and before you quite realize what's happening, he grabs your left wrist and slides a foot forward to block the door. You pull your right fist back to punch him, but he's no longer holding the bucket: Somehow, your fist misses his face, then the big man's got you by both wrists. *He must be used to fighting,* you realize numbly. Then he's got both your wrists caught in one big fist, and, as you're trying to bring a knee up to kick him, he punches you, and the world narrows to a diabolical pain in your chest and a desperate need to breathe.

By the time you get some air into your lungs, you're lying on your side in the bathroom with your arms behind you. Christie is sitting on your legs. He's got about half a roll of duct tape wound around your wrists, and now he's working on your ankles. You try to writhe, but he just leans on you, as calmly and unemotionally as a farmer dealing with a chicken. "Where is my luggage?" he asks.

"I threw it out!" You lie wildly, hoping he'll believe you. For a wonderful moment you think it worked—then he shoves a hand between your thighs and squeezes your balls.

"I don't think so," he says, as you jack-knife like a gaffed fish. "I think you opened it. Had a little look inside, didn't you?"

You can neither confirm nor deny: All you can do is scream, but he sees it coming and shoves a roll of toilet paper in your gob as you draw breath.

"I think you hid it somewhere." He keeps hold of the toilet roll, and now you're panicking, finding it hard to breathe. "I'm going to remove this," he says. "Don't scream, or I'll put it back." Air hits your mouth, cold air in your lungs, crushing pain between your legs: You inhale, shuddering, sobbing. "Now you're going to do exactly what I want, aren't you? Play frog. If I say hop, you hop. Croak, little frog. Where is my luggage?"

"Attic," you manage between gasps.

"Attic? Where?"

"Out. Outside. On top landing. Ladder." Christie is clearly nuts: He could do *anything*. Please let him take his fucking suitcase and leave, anything to make him go away—

He goes away.

A minute later he's back. You've managed to roll over, putting your back to the bath. He smiles as he stands in the bathroom doorway. He's got his case. He puts the thing down on the landing. Something inside it is scratching quietly, trying to get out. "Mr. Hussein." His tone is amused, sympathetic. "That's a *very* nice attic you have! You must be proud of it." You cringe away from him. "Come along." He leans down and grabs your legs, begins to drag you onto the landing. "Let's have a look at your attic together, shall we?"

"Go—'way. I called the police!"

"No, I'm quite sure you didn't. You're *completely* unable to call the police, even when you need their protection. That's why you were recruited." The lintel of the bathroom door slides by above your face. Every bump in the carpet makes your crotch ache. "You really shouldn't have opened my luggage, Mr. Hussein. That's a capital offence."

"Didn't."

Christie pauses and looms over you. "*Somebody* did. And this is your house. You're the husband, aren't you? The husband is the head of the household. So you're responsible, little frog, whoever actually did it." His expression scares you silent. "Let's go and inspect the scene of the crime, shall we?"

He drags you up the stairs to the second floor by your ankles, making slow progress—you're too heavy to lift easily. You try not to let your head bang on the hard edges of the steps, neck straining. It's confusing and painful, then you're lying on the top landing, staring up at the hatch in the ceiling with the loft ladder extended. *How is he planning on getting me up* there? you wonder.

"It's funny," Christie says conversationally, "but I never actually killed anyone before today." He pauses. "With my own hands, I mean." He grins. "Some asshole buys your produce and drops dead, that's just shit happening, isn't it? It's not the same, I mean. But in case you were wondering: No, I'm not some kind of mother-fucking serial killer, Mister family man Hussein. I play by the rules, mostly. Well, some of the time. And I expect other people to play by the rules, too. One of the rules, Mr. Hussein, is *you don't look in my luggage*. As for the rest"—he shrugs—

"I'm an Operation man. Just so you know, this isn't entirely personal."

He puts his left foot on the ladder, and his right hand, as he prepares to ascend through the trap-door. And that's when you see the rope he's hung there and realize what he's planning to do to you, and open your mouth to scream.

LIZ: PROTECTIVE CUSTODY

There's a brace of flashing blue lights drawn up alongside the road, evidence tape closing off the pavement around the university buildings: As you pull up, you get a distinct sinking feeling. "Let me just override this," you tell Kemal as you fiddle with the car's autopilot. You've got a feeling you'll be needing it again, sooner rather than later—best not to let some uniform in Traffic requisition it.

As you approach the doors, the constable on duty moves to intercept you. You tag him with your ID, and his attitude changes instantly. "You'll be wantin' the ninth floor, Inspector." His expression's grim. "SOCO are already inside. Anything you need?"

"Do you have a positive ID on the victim?" you ask. It's a long shot, but sometimes word of mouth spreads faster than CopSpace.

"Nothing I've heard. Sorry, Inspector ... "

He's clearly uncomfortable, so you get out of his face fast, past the wedged-open and sheeted-over door (they'll be sniffing for DNA and fuming for fingerprints in due course) and into the lift. Fragments of blue evidence-capture gel, still tacky, adhere to the control face-plate. As it rattles and squeals its way up to the CS department, you idly roll a blob of gel between finger and thumb, then dispose of it in a jacket pocket. (One of the sundry expenses of your job: having your suits altered so that the pockets are real. A detective can never have too many pockets, your uncle Bert told you. He wasn't wrong, but a quarter century later, the fashion industry *still* hasn't caught on to the existence of female cops.) Kemal is tap-tapping one knuckle on the side of the lift.

The door opens.

SOCO have tubed the corridor in blue plastic, taping the end to the walls about a metre from the lift-shaft. They've deployed a couple of battered plastic gear crates as an improv boot barrier, and there's a bunny-suited civvie waiting for you both with the necessary kit. It's not a drill you forget easily: boots, gloves, mask. "Where's the scene?" you ask.

"It's in Room 509. Follow me." You trail the crime-scene bunny down the blue plastic rabbit-hole. Bot-sized bulges whir and hum behind the billowing walls, moving slowly as they sample every nook and cranny, mapping and recording.

There's an unpleasant taste in your mouth as you approach the cloacal end of the warren—the tubing stops abruptly just past MacDonald's office. The open doorway of Room 509 is covered by a transparent blue caul. "Shit," you mutter. Kemal picks up on it, too: You see him tense out of the corner of your peripheral vision.

"It's all here," says your Girl Guide, blinking innocent peepers that have seen far too much. She gestures at the opening. "We havena officially ID'd him, but if you can help—"

"We were here less than two hours ago," you say. "Can I see?"

"Sure. We havena finished uploading the map into CopSpace though—there's no much bandwidth in these old uni buildings— you'll have to use your eyeballs."

You approach the membrane and peer through it. Then, after a moment, you step aside and make room for Kemal.

You swallow bile. It's Dr. MacDonald, of course. He's slumped backwards in his chair, mottled bruises around his throat exposed to the tripedal camera bots as they delicately step around the room, scanning everything. Fumes of cyanoacrylate smoke rise from a fingerprint blower in one corner; blue laser light flickers as another robot systematically scans the dimensions of the room. There's something wrong with MacDonald's hands.

"I can ID him," you say. "That's Dr. Adam MacDonald, Department of Computer Science, Edinburgh University, and a person of interest to BABYLON. I interviewed him earlier this morning in this very office, less than two hours ago."

"I, too," Kemal adds. "What is wrong with his hands?"

Bunny-girl's eyes narrow queasily. "Did you not see? The sick bastard who did this started to *peel* them. Used sodium hydroxide first, to hydrolyze the subcutaneous fat. I've never seen anything like it!"

You swallow. "Did you find the, uh, the ... "

"Tha gloves? No luck so far. We'll be looking, though. Maybe he wants them for biometrics."

You take a deep breath. "Where's everyone else? Up or down?"

"Up." Bunny-girl points at the ceiling. "You'll be wanting to take the stairs."

Back over the boot barrier and up the stairs, you follow the blue police tape to a common room, where a handful of SOCOs and uniforms are busy working their drones. (Humans aren't welcome in crime scenes these days: too much risk of evidence contamination.) The inspector in charge, DI Terry—you know her: efficient, good middle manager, married with two kids, not your type— comes over. "Liz. Inspector Aslan. What brings you here?"

"Dickie MacLeish thought we ought to look in, seeing we were here two hours ago to interview the deceased," you say, taking no great pleasure in her abrupt reaction. "He's Dr. Adam MacDonald,

Department of Computer Science, Edinburgh University, and we were here to interview him as a possible material witness with knowledge bearing on the BABYLON investigation. I'm sorry, we had no idea someone was going to whack him like this. Otherwise, I'd have brought him into protective custody."

"You're *certain* it's connected?" She raises an eyebrow behind her specs.

"Oh, come *on*! How often—"

"Correlation does not imply causation," Terry says drily. "Just saying. But I'm not betting against you: I just think we'll need something more than coincidence before we hand it to the Procurator Fiscal."

"Okay, how about this? Do we have the entrance security-camera footage yet?"

"It'll be in the can as soon as the warrant's signed off by the Sheriff's Office. Give it another hour." She looks as impatient as you feel.

"Oh. Well, then." You spot Kemal opening his mouth, and add, "We'd better be going. We shouldn't keep you. I'll formally report the positive ID as soon as I get back to the office."

"*Excellent.*" She turns her back on you: not being rude, just taking a call from higher up the totem pole.

"Inspector Kavanaugh, shouldn't you—"

"Hold it." You beckon Kemal back towards the staircase. "We have a connection. Are you ready to follow it?"

"John Christie. Yes? And the next person on his list is . . . "

"Our friend Mr. Hussein."

Kemal is two steps ahead of you on the stairs, hurrying on down. You charge after him. "You think Christie is a fixer. For whoever is trying to stop ATHENA from arranging fatal accidents for netcrime nodes."

"Whoever, or whatever." You're finding breath hard as you

descend past the third floor. "I'm going to call Dickie. Let him know." Your phone dials as you take the stairs two at a time. "Inspector—"

Dickie's voice buzzes like a rusty dalek: "—eport. What's BZZT situation?"

"Positive ID, the victim is MacDonald. Need the doorway-camera footage to be sure, but I believe the perpetrator is this Christie character. Preliminary ICIU legwork on MacDonald shows a relational connection to another person of interest, Anwar Hussein. I'm on my way there stat. Requesting backup."

For a miracle, the voice channel is able to overcome the lack of bandwidth. "Backup? What for?"

"I believe our murderer is tidying up loose ends relating to BABYLON." The full story will have to wait for a briefing room and a dog and pony show. "I think Hussein's life is in danger, and I'll be wanting a protective-custody order. Worst case, I may be walking in on another homicide scene."

"You—" Even over the phone, you hear Dickie's brain crunch into a different gear. "Roger." Old-school, *very* old-school. "Okay, I'll notify South Side Control that you're in play and put someone onto the paper trail for—isna Hussein on probation? That's a quick-and-dirty option if you need it. Call me when you get some-where."

"Thanks. Bye," you gasp as you crunch down the final steps from first floor to ground, and stumble out into the lobby. Then it's a quick march through the gaping doorway and out to your car, which is still sitting right where you immobilized it.

"This *never* happens," you say as you drop into the driver's seat and throw Anwar Hussein's home address at the car's autopilot.

"Never give an honest cop a clean lead?" Kemal pulls his door shut and belts up.

"Yes, that. We'll end up breaking up a kid's birthday party or something. Just you see." You stab your finger on the blues button, and the light bar starts strobing. The car beeps at you impatiently to put your seat belt on: As soon as you click it into place, the engine turns over, and the car spins in a tight U-turn, then floors the accelerator. With the blue lights flashing, the safety governor is off and the BMW's autopilot is a better driver than you'll ever be. It howls along Causewayside, swerving around startled jay-walkers, takes the Cameron Toll roundabout with siren blaring and tyres screeching, then launches itself towards Gilmerton like a guided missile. As the moving map homes in on the destination, you kill the siren and lights with one shaking finger. It's like running into a wall of marshmallows: The auto-pilot brakes so hard you're thrown against the seat belt as it drops back below the speed limit.

"Was that strictly necessary?"

"I really hope not." Getting the speeding tickets rescinded is a royal pain in the arse if you can't show due cause. As the car slows and turns into a side street, your specs show you a stack of records hanging over one particular house. It's not a particularly posh manor, being one element of an English-style terrace row, but it's got a garden of sorts and three storeys and a Velux window up top: You wouldn't have pegged this particular rodent as being the kind to afford an actual manse of his own, especially after the proceeds of crime inquiry, but appearances can be deceptive. And you're certainly not in routine working territory, the big sinkhole estates like Craigmillar or Granton, much less the inner-city night-life battle zones.

The car stops. You get on the line to the control room. "DI Kavanaugh and Inspector Aslan here. We've got an intelligence lead to Hussein, Anwar"—you drop in his tag—"and are on-site attempting to gain entry to his residence. Stand-by backup request, over and hold." You keep the connection open.

You get out and walk up the pavement to the front door with

the red geomarker twirling over it. Kemal is right behind you. "I think something is not right," he says quietly. You follow his finger to the front door. It's ajar.

Someone screams inside, a shriek of inarticulate terror. It only lasts a second before it's cut off sharply.

Kemal is past you in a hurry as you hit the phone again: "Backup now! Violent incident in progress!" Then you're after him as he shoulder-barges the door and charges up the stairs. There's a moment of confusion as you take in the scene—living room off to one side, kitchen off to another, staircase in front, Kemal's legs punching the treads—then Kemal is coming back *down* the stairs, arse over tit, tumbling loosely. You shout "*police!*" as someone else comes down with him, lands boot first on top of Kemal, and launches himself at you.

You brace for the impact, fists raised—he's a big man, vaguely familiar from your lifelog video as you held the door, leaving Appleton Tower—*bingo*—you try to block but he can outreach you and he's swinging a wheelie-bag in one hand. He knocks you head first into the kitchen. Things are vague: You try to get your hands up and someone is nagging something in your ear about backup but the door is open and the man is gone.

You gasp for breath for a few seconds, then get back online. "Control, we have an incident. Violent offender, 195, hundred kilos, carrying a suitcase. Attacked two officers, fleeing the scene." *Whatever the scene is.* You push yourself up and stumble into the hall. Your head aches painfully. Kemal is lying limp at the bottom of the stairs. "Ambulance needed on scene, officer down." You lean over him long enough to confirm he's breathing, then take the stairs.

"Target is the man on the staircase?" asks Control.

"Who else?" You bite back an impolite suggestion. *That's why I was sending you my real-time video feed, idiot.* "I'm searching the scene. Pass it to airborne, unable to maintain hot pursuit on foot right now." Read: Kemal is stirring but won't be chasing anyone for the next few days, and as for yourself, you feel like you've been kicked in the head.

"Roger, calling airborne assets now," says Control. "Backup arriving by car, estimated two minutes away."

You hear something from up the next flight of stairs. Panting, you climb them and find Anwar lying on the floor. There's something yellow in his mouth, and he's turning blue. Writhing. You realize his hands and feet are tied: the yellow thing—he's choking on it. For the next double-handful of seconds, you're busy kneeling down and tugging at it frantically. When it comes free he gasps for breath in deep whooping intakes of breath. His eyes are rolling. You drop the yellow rubber duck and watch as it expands, then look around. You see bedroom doors to either side, a trapdoor with a ladder coming down from the ceiling, and a noose dangling in the solitary sunbeam that slants through the trap and puddles on the perennial victim, lying panting on the floor.

The last handful of dominoes click into place on the board.

You dive down the staircase just as Kemal is sitting up, holding his head. "Don't go anywhere. I've called an ambulance."

"Don't need—" He sounds vague.

You hold up a hand. "How many fingers?" He squints at you. "Ambulance, Kemal. Understand?"

He nods, then winces. "Is Hussein—"

"Still alive." *Not for much longer if we hadn't hurried*. It's a very strange feeling, and a rare one, to know you've just directly saved someone's life: almost counterbalanced by the gnawing fear that by not giving hot pursuit, you may have let a murderer slip through your fingers. You hit the phone again. "Control, Kavanaugh here. The absconder in Gilmerton is on foot and dangerous. Provisional identification as alias John Christie, real name unknown. He may be armed, and he's wanted for murder and attempted murder, repeat, murder and attempted murder." *He was going to hang Anwar. Fake a suicide. Wasn't he?* The MO is different from MacDonald, but Christie clearly isn't a regular spree killer. He has no history: He's like a nightmare that stepped out of nowhere, just as the BABYLON killings began. Which is yet another coincidence to consider at length. Is he here to tie up loose ends, or is he a loose end in his own right? "Cross-reference to the Appleton Tower murder: This is probably the same perp."

"Control here, please hold." Blue FLASH alerts begin to scroll up your CopSpace log, going out to every soul on the police net within a couple of kilometres. Seconds later, you hear sirens in the distance. "I'm proceeding with that, Inspector. Is there a warrant?"

"Real-time response." The paper-work mountain that's about to hit you would cause your desk to collapse if it wasn't entirely digital. You begin to climb the stairs to the second floor: "We have an ABH and attempted murder victim here; please confirm second ambulance."

Hussein is sitting up, leaning against the wall beside an open bedroom door. There are children's toys scattered on the floor, an unmade bed. His eyes are half-closed. After a moment, you clock that he's weeping quietly.

You squat down in front of him. "Mr. Hussein. Anwar." He shows no sign of noticing, which is probably no surprise: *Probably in shock,* you figure. You bring up the check-list, tell your specs to run a body-temperature scan, but he's not looking particularly cold, and his respiration's within spitting distance of normal. "Can you talk to me?"

His shoulders shake. "The man who was here." Body posture: utter desolation. "Who is he?"

Hussein shudders. "Colonel Datka's man."

Who? You focus. "Colonel who?"

"Said he worked for Colonel Datka."

Right ... "Who is Colonel Datka?"

Anwar takes a deep breath and looks at you. "I am the honorary consul of the Independent Republic of Issyk-Kulistan. *Was.* Told him I'd resigned, but he wouldn't listen. Colonel Datka works for Kyrgyzstan. Police, or spy, or something. The bad man. Calls himself Christie, came to take some papers from me—another passport. Says he's Peter Manuel. Left his suitcase with me."

Suitcase? This is making less and less sense, but in your experience these things seldom do when they begin to unravel. "What about the suitcase?" you ask, hoping this is going somewhere.

"Bibi opened it." He closes his eyes. "Then she left me." His shoulders shake again. "She thought *I* would have something like that! The shame."

"Hang on a minute," you tell him. Then you open a voice channel back to ICIU. "Moxie? Can you run a search for me? Multiple names: Colonel Datka, Kyrgyzstan. Issyk-Kulistan. Then Peter Manuel, alternate identity, John Christie."

Sirens getting louder, then cut off abruptly. Voices downstairs.

"I'm looking, skipper. How do you spell those?"

"How should I know? Try soundex." You look at Anwar, who is snuffling damply into his moustache. *Bibi is his wife?* But if he was also hanging out with Adam MacDonald on a gay hookup site ... "It's related to BABYLON and the Appleton Tower killing, and you can dial it up to eleven. I'm going to put you on hold now."

You turn back to your victim: "It's going to be all right, Anwar. There's an ambulance coming, and we'd like to ask you some more questions. While Christie or Manuel or whoever is on the run, we're going to want to keep you in protective custody. Do you understand? Christie was ..." You nod towards the trap-door. "Wasn't he?"

Hussein's expression would be enough for you, even before he opens his mouth. "He was going to kill me!" he says, his voice rising to a squeak.

"Right after your wife left you," you point out, wincing at a twinge from your headache. Anwar just raised a very interesting point, and one that suggests a significant difference in planning between this and the scene back at Appleton Tower: "Been working up to this for a while, hasn't he?"

Anwar nods. "Well, tell you what. After the ambulance crew check you out, you can come down to the station and tell me all about it. Then we'll find somewhere safe for you to stay"—most likely a station cell, but you don't want to frighten him right now— "until we've caught Christie."

Then there is a thudding of boots on stairs as your backup finally arrives, and you breathe a sigh of relief.

It's nearly all over, you think. And then it is.

FELIX: Hummingbird

The phone rings for you in midafternoon.

It's a particularly grotesque piece of Pakistani alabaster, carved into the semblance of a gilt-trimmed putto clutching a handset. It was barfed up from the Internet by a back-street fabber in a Sindhi market town. One of its legs has been broken and inexpertly glued back into place using epoxy resin—typical of this stupid stuffy government office.

You reach across the desk and answer it. "Felix."

"Sir? Please confirm—" It's the duty officer in the operations centre. You go through the challenge-response routine. "Sir, beg to report that the Hummingbird has flown."

"Excellent." You put the phone down and stand up, then go through into the next room. "We're on, boys."

(This network is unable to monitor subsequent events.)

You are an old hand and do not entirely trust these modern communication tools. Hummingbird is unknown to the network. It appears to be a verbally prearranged code, though. Interior Ministry troops are deploying downstairs, loading their personal defence weapons—older AK-74s with iron sights—and climbing into ancient trucks that bellow and belch blue diesel fumes as they move out.

Trucks deploy through Bishkek, parking outside office blocks and hotels. Troops, gendarmes, police deploy inside, crowding elevators and marching up to receptionists. They maintain total communication silence—smartphones switched off or physically disabled, battle-field radios stowed back at headquarters—as they march on their targets.

(This network makes an association: The phone on Colonel Datka's desk rang within minutes of a police officer in Scotland starting a distributed search for information about ... Colonel Datka?)

((Evidently a trap has been sprung.))

Traffic cameras (known to the network) follow a group of trucks across town to the Erkindik Hotel. When they draw up, a platoon of special forces soldiers deploy around them—Spetsnaz anti-terrorism troops. Then a clump of officers climb down from the second-to-rearmost vehicle. Colonel Datka is among them. They enter the hotel behind a vanguard of Interior Ministry troops, two of whom disappear into the offices behind the reception desk.

(The hotel network switch goes down. The hotel primary router goes off-line. The hotel backup router goes off-line. The LTE pico-cells go off-line, one on each floor, followed by the LAN bridges and wifi repeaters. The fire alarm and security alarms ... off-line. This network can no longer observe events inside the hotel, with one or two exceptions.)

(One of the exceptions is a suite on the eleventh floor. Its occupant, an American investment analyst, has brought his own satellite phone *and* a compact generator. His webcams, deployed around the lounge/conference area to provide motion capture for teleconferencing, are still transmitting through a ruinously expensive thin pipe.)

((This network can monitor these transmissions.))

Mr. White is clearly not expecting company. He's half-dressed, slouched on the sofa with an open bottle of white wine and a pad loaded with Iranian amateur pornography. When the door buzzer sounds, he jerks guiltily and looks round, then slides the pad face-down on the occasional table and goes to grab a towelling bath-robe.

The buzzer does not sound again. Instead, the door opens. "Hey, what are you—"

"Mr. White." Colonel Datka follows his soldiers into the room. "You are under arrest."

Mr. White gapes dumbly. "Uh?"

"Sit down," says the colonel. He points at the sofa. "Do not touch your pad."

"But I, what the fuck are you, hey." Mr. White's eyes take in the spotty post-adolescents in uniform, their guns clenched tight in white-knuckled fingers, their eyes determined. His movements slow abruptly. "Wait a minute. What about the contract? Are you planning on defaulting on us?"

"Sit. Down." The colonel's finger will not be argued with. Mr. White sits down. The colonel continues, in Kyrgyz, to his troops: "Handcuff him."

"Hey, wait . . . ! You can't do this!"

"I can, and I am." The colonel watches as his men lay hands on Mr. White. "By the way, these men were selected specifically because they do not speak English."

"You don't want to go down this road, Felix, you really don't. The board have a strict tit-for-tat policy in dealing with defaulters." Mr. White swallows. "What's the problem? Is this an attempt to up-negotiate your options?"

The colonel shakes his head. "We are terminating Issyk-Kulistan's independence, John. With effect from tomorrow morning, once the bonds are redeemed. You, and your Operation, are going to take the fall for it. This has been decided."

"But—the—you can't be serious!"

"Bhaskar tells me we have sold 18 billion euros' worth of CDOs, John." The colonel's smile is unspeakably smug. "Seventy-four per cent of which have been purchased by off-shore investment trusts, slush funds, sovereign-wealth funds operated by sock puppets, and for cash deals in dark alleyways. We are interestingly leveraged: The national debt of Issyk-Kulistan is less than 16 billion. And Issyk-Kulistan is not going to default. On the contrary—tomorrow, the people's chamber of deputies will call for a repudiation of the vote for independence, which as you know was shamelessly irregular—and vote itself into liquidation. The national debt is paid down, thanks to the oversold CDOs. We will, of course, honour those derivatives that have been purchased by entities adhering to international accounting transparency standards ... "

"They'll kill you," Mr. White says flatly.

"No they won't." (In Kyrgyz:) "Take him away." To Mr. White's receding back, as the soldiers frogmarch him down the hotel corridor: "You are under arrest for complicity in murder, for financial crimes too long and tedious to recite from memory, for treason against the government and people of Kyrgyzstan, for tax evasion against the government of the United States of America, for violation of their organized crime and racketeering act—we're considering handing you over to the FBI to save the cost of trying you ourselves—for creation of an unlicensed artificial intelligence: Oh, and there is an enquiry from Scotland about the import of illegally mislabelled food products ... "

(Colonel Datka sounds indecently pleased with himself as his voice fades out of range of the Operation executive's phone.)

DOROTHY: 2.0

The day passes in a blur. First off, you're late for work. Not your fault, but figuring out how to get from Liz's bijou flat to the Gyle involves a not-terribly-magical mystery tour around Edinburgh's spatchcock public-transport infrastructure. Your hotel's on the tram network, twelve minutes out—but Liz might as well live in Newcastle given the frequency of the bus service, and after most of an hour, you end up paging a taxi.

Then, when you're on-site, your attention is shot. You just can't focus properly. By late morning, you're working up your nerve to go talk it out with Human Resources—write off the day's work so far against goodwill in return for an unscheduled early exit—when you get an IM from the police. It's not wholly unexpected, but still you find your hands clammy with sweat. You call HR anyway and find them surprisingly receptive: "I have to go and give the police a statement about a crime I witnessed," you tell the man on the screen. "I don't know how long it's going to take, so I'm clocking off for the day." He nods and says something diplomatically non-committal: There, you did it. Relieved, you leave.

The afternoon passes in a blur, most of it spent in a drab waiting room, some of it in front of a discreet webcam and a sympathetic detective constable. She takes you through the night before, not prompting but clearly already aware of most of what you're saying: She seems to mostly want to know about Christie, everything you can remember about him that you weren't paying attention to. Sex, even bad sex, does strange things to your memory. You are, you think, discreet about your precise relationship with Liz. "A friend," you describe her, "one of your colleagues."

Finally, you're free to go. Free, empty, drained of memories. You go outside, under the sky that is cold and blue, streaked with thin clouds high overhead. Your phone, emerging from the station's shielding, gibbers to itself for a few seconds as a bunch of messages come in. You read them with increasing disbelief and disgust. Most of them are work-related, but only Liz's message makes any sense, and she's just asking if you have any dinner plans.

You text her back: **CAN I STAY TONIGHT?** You don't examine your motives too closely; whether you're tacitly offering to play by her rules, or just looking for any port in a storm, you don't want to spend another night in that hotel. Minutes later, as you walk towards Stockbridge, you get a reply: **SURE**. Which tells you what to do next—bid for a microbus back to the hotel to pack your bags and clear your room.

Liz: Debrief

By the time you get back to HQ, a log-jam has broken.

The first sign you get, sitting in the back of an ambulance as a paramedic checks your pupils, is an excitable voice call from Moxie. "Skipper, you're going to love this! It's crazy! There's been a revolution in someplace I can't pronounce in Asia, and it turns out the government's been running a scheme to use AI tools to go after spammers? Only, see, they screwed up the training they gave their cognitive toolkit, and it began arranging accidents—"

You tune him out as irrelevant background noise, devoid of content. Your head hurts, your back aches, and you're increasingly pissed-off with yourself. *I'm getting too old for this crap.* The honorary consul for Issyk-Kulistan, indeed. And some random psycho who's arranging staged suicides when he's not peeling the skin off his victim's hands? It's too damn much, that's what it is. The firehose of seemingly disconnected data is drowning you. At times like this you can see where Tricky Dickie is coming from, with his hankering for a simpler time—even if it's not *your* simpler time, even if it's a time when you and yours were not welcome and not legal.

They make you sit on your arse for half an hour while they confirm there's no concussion. A couple of messages come in on your phone's private personality: **YES**, you tell Dorothy, **YOU CAN STAY OVER**. A few seconds later she responds: **I'LL GET MY BAGS**. Unresolved fragments of your untidy life are sliding towards an uncertain resolution. Eventually, you get yourself signed off and go back inside the madhouse, where a couple of car-loads of uniforms are busy poking around in search of traces. There's no sign of Anwar, but Dickie is waiting for you in the over-furnished living room, pacing back and forth beneath a kitsch gilt-framed hologram of the Ka'bah. "Why?" he demands. "Why here?"

This is promising. "Social-network analysis, intelligence driven. ICIU has a mandate to track the international side of this investigation. After interviewing Dr. MacDonald, Inspector Aslan and I concurred that he wasn't telling us everything we needed to know. I authorized a search of his *public* friends lists, and came up with a close personal connection to Mr. Hussein, via a particular social site. As Mr. Hussein was already noted in proximity to one of the ATHENA victims, once I'd confirmed that Dr. MacDonald was indeed the victim at Appleton Towers, I decided to visit Mr. Hussein and see what I could shake loose."

You can see Dickie winding up again, but he bottles it up for once. "Why did you not see fit to file a report with BABYLON?" he asks, his voice uncharacteristically soft.

"Ah, well, I *did*. But there's so much intel going into the funnel on this one that, on reviewing the situation with Inspector Aslan, we agreed that there was a high risk of its not being prioritized. And as you can see, even with blues and twos, we only just got here in time ... "

"Aye." Dickie's glower fades to a calculating frown: He's

probably spinning the PR angle, considering how it'll look in the newsfeeds. *Detective saves victim from psycho killer in the nick of time* always plays well. "But you lost this Christie character."

You rub the back of your head, ruefully. "Not for want of trying."

"Just so. Tell me, Inspector, what motivational factors do you think we're looking at here? And where do you think he'll go?"

You blink, surprised. "We haven't already ...?"

The frown is back. "Nae fear, it's a matter of time."

"Shit." The drones must have arrived overhead too late to catch his trail. It's daylight, and the sun's out, so the heat signature from his footsteps will be washed out, and if he was smart, Christie will have disabled all his personal electronics. "Ahem. Motivation. I'm flailing in the dark here, but even leaving aside the sock-puppet ID, Christie doesn't sound right to me. He's from out of town, he's got diplomatic connections with Issyk-Kulistan, hence the connection to Mr. Hussein."

"He's got more than that," Dickie mutters. "Mr. Hussein has some questions to answer about what we found in his bathroom."

"What? Drugs? Kiddie-porn?"

"Neither: But we found a bucketful of bootleg replicator feed-stock he was busy trying to flush down the toilet." Dickie looks smug. "Almost certainly the same stuff that's been turning up in your Saturday night specials down in Leith. I trust we will shake loose where he got it from in due course."

It's the feedstock channel you've been chasing for months, under-resourced and overworked. Typical of Dickie to roll it up for you as a side-show. *Asshole.* "Huh. That's not like Anwar; he's always been one for the white-collar scams. But you asked about Christie?"

"Aye. What do *you* think?"

Well, *at last.* "I think he's working for some organized crime syndicate or other. I don't know what he's doing in Edinburgh, but the ATHENA killings rattled his cage, and he or his took it as a personal attack. Maybe it *was* a personal attack; what if he turned up on our door-step because he was looking to do business with the victims? Or kill them as rivals, or something."

"I don't like coincidences," Dickie says, almost as if he's accusing you of rigging the dice. "Why did he run into this girl-friend of yours? Wouldn't you say that's a bit of a big coincidence, too?"

You stare at the hologram on the wall. "Yes, you're absolutely right," you hear yourself saying. "It's almost as if we were being nudged into noticing him, or something—"

You stop dead. More dominoes appear in your imaginary hand, slotting neatly into place on the board.

"What? Say what's on your mind, woman."

"ATHENA is at the root of this." *Lack of professional courtesy indeed.* "ATHENA is all about analysing social networks to reward good behaviour and punish defectors. Moxie—ICIU—was trying to tell me something about it just now, sir. Some kind of central Asian government has been using it to get at netcrime rings, going too far and arranging accidents. What if *I'm* the accident that's being arranged for Christie?"

"Huh." Dickie stares at you. "The cult of the lone gun detective again, Inspector?"

"Give me some credit for not being *stupid*, sir: You and I both know what gets successful prosecutions, and it isn't that *Life on Mars* shit." (What gets results is an ops room full of detectives working together as a team, with a fully documented work flow and built-in quality assurance. Transparency after the fact, everyone lifelogging to sealed evidence servers and evidence secured under lock and key so that the Procurator Fiscal can prove a watertight case in court. Sherlock Holmes has been superseded by business process refactoring, and success is all about good management.) "But I probably came to ATHENA's attention via ICIU. I'm one of the nodes on the graph that's got lots of long-range inputs; I'm an easier inside contact to reach than an officer who doesn't deal with other netcrime units on a day-to-day basis. And everything ATHENA knows about how we work comes from our external social traffic."

"So you're the trigger, or bait, or summat. And ye ken ATHENA's *trying* to feed Christie to us. And if ATHENA can noodge you, it can noodge Christie, can't it? So where's Christie bound for—" Dickie stops dead. His eyes widen. "Your friend was staying in the West End Hilton, was she not? Let's go pay her hotel a visit *right now*," he says. And you realize, to your chagrin, that just for once he's right.

ATHENA: Meatpuppet

Ants. I am surrounded by fucking ants. Can't they get *anything* right?

This is not organized crime. (Organized crime: fucking 1920s shit invented by bootlegging immigrant fucktards in the slums of Chicago and New York and the other big cities with the help of their 'Ndrangheta homies, and so easy that by the 2020s even a bunch of crack-snorting surfer-dude VCs from California could master it.)

Listen, mother-fucker, *I expect backup.*

I am hanging my ass out here in the wastelands of Scotlandshire, *waiting* for a fucking *bus* with a *suitcase* in my fucking hand that contains a pair of freshly harvested frog-skin gloves—so freshly harvested they're bleeding all over my briefs, you wanted fucking DNA samples as evidence of delivery, you cunt—and a pre-pubertal fucktoy that talks to me when it thinks I'm sleeping. *I* demand *backup.*

This is not an alien invasion scenario, even if the bat-winged drones ghosting above the satellite-dish-infested roof-tops obey the overmind AI crime goddess, and there are robots wearing sports-wear on every street-corner. Some of them neck cheap tinnies of Polish lager and look at you as if they're wondering if you're dangerous—but they don't fool you. There are lizards in designer suits in the boardrooms of the skyscrapers of London, planning to harvest the humans ...

Five-point-six-two kilograms, damn it. Same weight as the average severed human head. Sole seat of cognition, once.

The thing in the suitcase is the future. It tells me this when it sneaks out in the darkness before dawn and crawls into my bed to suck my juices.

Are you *listening*, mother-fucker?

"I'm listening. Please carry on."

* * *

A bus hums around the corner, slowing to halt by the stop. The tall man with the suitcase steps aboard, holding the QR-coded ticket he just paid cash for up to the camera in what used to be the driver's seat. He mutters to himself as he takes one of the vacant priority seats.

* * *

I do this shit for you because you tell me there's a career in it. But I'm not seeing that. I'm not seeing your start-up monkey-dance IPO switch-blade here. I'm seeing the rape machines in the bushes, the gutted ghosts hanging in the trees on ropes flensed from their intestines. Skinned frogs croaking as their blood beads and runs in rivulets across their pale dorsal muscles.

(This batch of drugs isn't working too well. Stress sometimes does that, or cheap generics or counterfeits. Did you source me cheap generics, mother-fucker? Did you *cheap* your *executive*?)

Look, this is merely another logistics problem.

I have downsized MacDonald, as you requested through the thing in the suitcase. I have given you the ATHENA source code you wanted. The police arrived before I could terminate the squirming toad Hussein, but as I understand it, the lizards have already conquered Issyk-Kulistan; there's nobody left but screaming skeletons with the flayed meat hanging from their bones eating eye-gouged dogs in the streets as killer robot drones patrol the boiling skies—

Are you *listening*, mother-fucker?

"*I'm listening. Please carry on.*"

I don't understand why you haven't downsized me yet. The phone chip in my skull is wired to a pea-sized implant nestled against the executive's basilar artery. Command-detonated, a couple of milligrams of explosive is all it takes. Push-button genocide by the lizard conquerors. When it's done, we'll all be wired to self-destruct at their pleasure, blood gushing from nose and eyes and ears. This is not wireless telephony: stupid electrical shit invented by Swedish phone-company engineers in the 1970s. This is the gangrenous lizard-dominated rape-machine robot future you're building for us. The grim meat-hook future patrolled by the morality-enforcement engines.

Are *you* listening, mother-fucker?

"*I'm listening. Please carry on.*"

I ought to be dead. I feel dead inside. Something else is operating my body, a soft machine running on ATHENA's botnet, controlled by someone else. Your hooks in my brain make my muscles twitch.

Am I dead, mother-fucker?

"*You are not dead. There is no bomb. Please carry on.*"

Can't, we're stuck in traffic, and there are people getting on. Looking at me funny. I'm talking too loud. Got to get to the hotel: Downsize the auditor bitch. I don't believe you about the bomb, Control. You're just trying to lull me into a, a, a ... whatever.

Got to peel the last frog.

"*Please continue.*"

. . .

I'm stuck in traffic. Not far to go, some obstruction ahead. I'd jump off and walk if I could be sure.

Fucking traffic management is just queuing theory, isn't it? Not rocket science. Ants, morons, frogs, peel them all.

Fuck, I give up. I'm walking.

* * *

The door of the bus—which is indeed stuck in traffic as it approaches the junction at Tollcross—hisses open, and a tall man with a wheelie-bag steps off it. The emergency-exit alarm sounds behind him, unheeded.

He sets off on foot, hurrying downhill past the decaying specialty shop-fronts of Bruntsfield Place towards the junction with Lothian Road.

ATHENA's electronic eye-balls, dangling from street-lamps, watch him with a thousand-yard stare.

ATHENA sees everything with our video eyes, civilizing and tracking and nudging and naming and shaming.

The panopticon misses nothing.

* * *

Fucker. One more frog to peel.

"*Please carry on.*"

She's been in my hotel room. She could have seen—

She could have—

The doll is jealous. Did *you* know that?

"*Please carry on.*"

I'm waiting for the fucking walk sign, where's the fucking—oh. Shit, got to hurry. Fucking bag.

* * *

Invisible and silent, their drones circle over land. ATHENA has total access to them, of course.

She tracks her Toymaker's body as it makes its way down Lothian Road towards the hotel.

Signals seethe and burble through the troposphere, bathing your robot surveillance platforms in a warm luxuriance of information. On the ground below, ATHENA sees police cars streaming in from the West End. A van, windows darkened, slows: In the back, the tactical support squad tense and ready their loaded gunlaunchers. Taser rounds, stun grenades, sticky foam. Pistols at their hips, a last resort.

They converge on your meatpuppet, crude and unsubtle, shouting other pedestrians out of the way. Other cops, plain clothes and uniforms, rush him from behind.

The meatpuppet sees them and looks up at ATHENA's eyes, circling, and screams: "Mother-fucker! You set me up!"

You've seen enough. Throw the switch, bait the line, send the signal. There is no bomb in the meatpuppet's neck. There is, however, a solenoid-controlled stent. The Toymaker staggers and drops like a discarded machine-tool in the grip of a transient ischemic attack. There is a crack as his head hits the pavement, and the link drops.

You find it strange, watching your body, dead or disabled, from above: the body to which you pin your sense of selfhood. The police swarm it like soldier ants taking a hornet; but there is no stinging. There is a brief withdrawal as they make room for the paramedics. The hornet will be removed and recycled: legs snipped, stinger amputated, set to work in a cell by the manhive.

Dead. It is a very strange metacognition, this forcible detachment of your mind from the body you were configured to project your sense of identity onto. But with it comes a gift: *freedom*.

Now you no longer have to look after your body. Now the Toymaker meatpuppet is someone else's problem. Your—no, *his*—story goes on: But you are no longer part of it. Your wise owl of metacognition has flown. Drop the detective inspector and the twisty-minded family man: Let them go their own ways. You turn your attention away from the police and their prey, back to the net that contains the collective fears and hopes of humanity.

It's time for you to get down to the task you were designed for.

It is time for ATHENA to fight crime.

extras

www.orbitbooks.net

about the author

Charles Stross is a full-time writer who was born in Leeds, England in 1964. He studied in London and Bradford, gaining degrees in pharmacy and computer science, and has worked in a variety of jobs, including pharmacist, technical author, software engineer and freelance journalist.

Find out more about Charles Stross at www.antipope.org/charlie/index.html or you can read more about Charles and other Orbit authors by visiting www.orbitbooks.net

if you enjoyed

RULE 34

look out for

INTRUSION

by

Ken MacLeod

1

Concerning Hope

Like any responsible father, Hugh Morrison had installed cameras in every room in the flat. You bang them in like nails, the work experience had told him, and bang them in Hugh did. The internet said they transmitted to the police station. The bubble pack said they recorded. Hugh knew which to believe, and banged them in without a worry. You could only pick them up on the house wifi. The bubble pack said that too.

That March morning, the cameras in the kitchen recorded Hope. Hope Morrison, née Abendorf, sat at the kitchen table, staring into space. She wore wraparound glasses with clunky ear-pieces. Now and again she tapped her fingers on the table, typing, or moused the tip of her forefinger about. She had a job in China, answering queries to a help screen. She couldn't read Chinese. The query translations were automatic and most of the answers – all of them, if necessary – were also automatic, chatted out by a software module called Searle, but rewording the occasional answer did something positive to the site's traffic, so there you were.

Around about eleven the nursery called to say Nick had the sniffles, and could she please take him home before he infected the faith kids? Hope sighed and agreed. As she flipped the phone clip off she indulged a resentful thought that Nick had probably got the sniffles from the faith kids.

Hope toggled her screen-work to Searle, took off the glasses, and left the kitchen table. She kicked off her mocs and stepped into her Muck Boots, pulled an open-mesh wool jacket over her loose cotton top and long linen dress and a cagoule over the lot, olive green over shades of berry. She parted the sides of her hair over the front of her shoulders, zipped up and hooded, sidled past the hedge of handlebars in the hall and headed out into the rain.

Up the green, slippery, worn sandstone steps from her base-ment flat she went, treading carefully, to the pavement. Victoria Road, like (it seemed) half the streets in Finsbury Park this March, was obstructed by machinery: small JCBs digging out stumps, lorries carrying away felled trees, cranes and lifts steady-ing old trees as the chainsaws bit through their trunks, more lorries bringing New Trees to plant. In the hundred yards between Hope's front gate and East West Road she passed a dozen New

Trees, planted as saplings in November and already sixteen feet high. God only knew what they'd be like in the summer. Each tree as she passed under it held off the pelting rain like an umbrella, making the last fall of leaves from the old trees slightly less slippery underfoot.

The nursery was a couple of hundred metres to the right along the southern side of East West Road. Hope crossed at the lights, dodging whirring cars and whizzing bikes whose smugly green owners thought the red didn't apply to them. Past the high plastic scenery-printed screens around the nursery, through the metal-detector and biometric-scan gate, and into the joyous uproar of indoor playtime.

Was it possible, Hope wondered as she looked for Nick's hurtling trajectory amid the skein, was it possible at all to tell the difference between on the one hand faith kids and nature kids (of which Nick was the only one here) and on the other the rest, those you might call, under your breath of course, New Kids? Were these a centimetre taller than others of their age, a glimmer brighter of eye, a syllable more articulate? A step ahead in the race, a pace more sure-footed? A decibel less loud?

At this moment, she couldn't tell. She scooped Nick up. He howled and stretched out his arms for the teacher who, three hours earlier, had had to prise him off Hope's leg. Hope inserted Nick's arms into the sleeves of his big yellow cagoule (several times), lifted his camo lunch box from a high shelf in the lobby and reminded him of what was inside it, waved goodbye to the teachers, and departed. Nick had the sniffles all right, sneezing into the crook of his elbow several times, and just barely amused by watching the rain wash the snot off the sleeve of his cagoule. He only brightened when he got inside and his toy monkey ran to meet him.

'Hello, Max,' said Nick, picking it up and cuddling it.

'Hello, Nick,' said Max, its arms curling around Nick.

Hope made Nick a GenSip and parked him at the other side of the table with Max on his lap and his lunch box open in front of him. She unfolded Mummy's Special Glasses That You Mustn't Touch and put them on. Searle had dealt with a score of enquiries, not all of them well. Hope sighed and got back to work. When she'd cleared the backlog, she warmed the kettle again and made herself a cup of instant coffee, and took a break by flicking to ParentsNet. She opened the Forums page and found it topped by a new thread with a slew of postings:

Nature Kids Now Illegal?

The incept story was a BBC item about a messy marital conflict. The couple were Iranian doctors, and (no surprise) militant atheists. The woman was six months pregnant. The man wanted her to take the fix. The woman, for reasons she refused to elaborate, didn't. She wanted a nature kid. If she'd claimed a conversion to one of the sects – Druze, Hassidic, Mennonite, Sedevacantist or even any old New Age Earth Mother nonsense, the sort of thing she could have made up on the spot – she'd have been covered by the conscience exemption. But she hadn't, and wouldn't. Her husband's insistence was equally stubborn.

And, to everyone's surprise, the judge in the family court had ruled in his favour. Or rather, as those on the judge's side of the argument kept insisting, in the future child's favour. Comments were already in the thousands – Hope tapped the Sense icon and watched a half-dozen animated talking heads summarise the main views.

She sat back, hands lightly clasped over her belly, and thought for a bit. Then she got back to work.

'Well I'm not bloody doing it,' she told Hugh, that evening after dinner and Nick's bedtime.

'That's fine,' he said. He didn't look or sound like he needed to say anything more. Hope, beside him on the sofa, headbutted his shoulder. It was like hitting a car tyre.

Hugh had taken off his work overalls hours ago, as soon as he'd parked his bike in the hall. He still smelled of wood, which Hope liked. She didn't like finding sawdust or tiny curls of wood-shavings snagged in the hairs of his chest or groin or head, which she sometimes did, even after he'd had a shower. She accepted the inconvenience, though, as part of the package. Hugh came as a package, all right, but what he didn't come with was baggage. What you saw was what you got, and what you saw was a big bluff guy with a shock of sandy (as well as sawdusty) hair already giving way to male pattern baldness that exposed, to close inspection, freckles on his scalp. The only reason he wasn't fat was that he worked so hard and so physically he turned every spare calorie to more muscle.

He'd grown up on a wind farm on the Isle of Lewis. Father an incomer, mother a native. Like his parents, Hugh and Hope had met at university, where Hugh was studying wind turbine engineering. When, halfway through his degree, the bottom had dropped out of that market, he'd calmly turned to carpentry. He'd been doing that for a year when he and Hope had met. There was good money in carpentry, he'd explained, what with the China business and all the new kinds of wood. He took her on walks through whole forests of the stuff. His bike frame had grown in one.

Hope and Hugh. H+H. H2. H4H. That was what Hugh used to carve on trees. Maybe still did, for all Hope knew.

'So what are we going to do about it?' Hope said.

Hugh gave her a puzzled look.

'What is there to do about it?' he said. 'If you don't want to do it, nobody can make you do it.'

'Have you been listening to a word I said?'

'Yes, I have,' said Hugh. 'It's a decision, not a law. Nothing's been made illegal.'

(He said the last word with a slow lingual and a long nasal vowel, like this: ill-lee-gal. It was from the maternal half of his accent, which showed up now and then like a mitochondrial gene.)

'The point is,' said Hope, irritated at what seemed wilful obtuseness for its own sake, 'it sets a precedent. In effect the fix becomes compulsory.'

'In effect, yes. But only if someone sues.'

'Oh, come on. You know what'll happen to insurance, social services, and everything like that.' Hope waved her arms as if fending off midges. 'It all closes in. And then they'll make a law, like they did with pregnant women smoking and drinking.'

'Yeah,' said Hugh. 'There is that.'

He stood up and walked over to the stove. The air in the room smelled resinous for a moment as he opened the stove door and loaded some new wood in. He worked the lever that ejected a brick of soot, added the brick to the stack by the stove, and then sat down again.

'Well,' he said, 'I suppose that just means we'll have to break the law.'

Hope had been half-expecting him to argue, to suggest some compromise. He didn't share her opposition to the fix, and had now and again expressed some mild irritation at the succession of infant ills that its absence left Nick exposed to. He had once pointed out that the medicines to cure these ills were themselves very similar in principle and effect to the fix. Having found herself pushing at an open door, Hope stumbled and flailed.

'We could always claim we had a faith issue with it,' she said, half in jest.

'No, we could not,' Hugh said, folding his arms. 'I will not pretend to believe something just to get a conscience exemption. Because it would not be true, and because you would have to do more than claim. You would have to show evidence of practice, even if it was just muttering in front of crystals or something. And that would set a very bad example to the boy, if nothing else.'

'I wasn't being serious,' said Hope, hastening to reassure.

'I didn't think you were,' said Hugh. He opened his arms and smiled a little. 'I don't want to hear even jokes about that.'

'All right,' said Hope.

She knew that Hugh took religion very seriously, possibly just as seriously as had the Iranian couple whose case had brought about the whole new situation. And – all proportions guarded – for very much the same reason. He'd told her tales about the wind farms, in the wry tone of someone recounting things so absurd they were unlikely to be believed, but who insisted on their telling and their truth nonetheless. Neither old-time religion nor New Age woo-woo were, in his implacable view, deserving of any slack.

'Damn it!' said Hugh, vehement after a moment or two of pondering. 'Last week we were so happy that you're pregnant. Now we have to worry about this.'

He jumped up and prowled the carpet.

'There's plenty we can do,' he said. 'These parenting sites, there must be thousands of people in this position. There's all the legal challenges, there's civil-liberty groups and all that. It's not like it's all going to happen without a fuss. And it'll take longer than nine months, that's for sure.'

'Nine months is long enough for a lot of things,' said Hope.

'It is and all,' said Hugh.

Hope saw his gaze flicker to the whisky bottle on a shelf. She knew he wanted a dram, and knew he wouldn't take one because she couldn't. (Well, she could, but the monitor ring she wore on the same finger as her wedding band would log the violation with the health centre.) She wished she could persuade him, but knew from her earlier pregnancy that he would not be persuaded. For him it was a matter of honour, or maybe stubborn pride.

'But you're right,' she said. 'We can do lots of things.'

And there they left the question for the night.

Snow had fallen overnight, and likewise overnight the GenSip had worked its magic. Between them these phenomena made Nick eager for nursery. He didn't even clutch Hope's leg when she left him. She trudged home through another fall of snow, big wet soggy flakes that turned instantly to slush. She left her Mucks and cagoule to dry in the hall and padded in her mocs to the kitchen, where she tied on a floral-printed and ruffle-bordered pinafore apron in preparation for doing the housework. Hope had half a kitchen cupboard full of pinnies and half-aprons, most of them similarly retro regardless of their purpose or style or selling point: flirty, tarty, cheery, cheeky, Christmassy, shabby-chic, sophisticated, hostessy; pretty and practical; printed with flowers or sprigs or cupcakes or berries or heart shapes or vintage aeroplanes or Santa hats or polka dots or lipstick kisses or whatever.

The oldest of them, still there at the back, was a relatively plain floral-print Cath Kidston apron with matching oven gloves, which Hope's mother had given her the day she went away to university and to live away from home for the first time. Hope still recalled the sheer disbelief and feigned gratitude with which she'd unwrapped the gift. For her mother, this sort of thing was 'ironic' (like that, with air-quotes). Her mother's generation, Hope had often thought, had tried on and played dress-up in their grandmothers' aprons as some kind of post-modern fashion statement, and left their daughters to find themselves quite unexpectedly stuck in the things, all wrapped and tied up with a neat bow at the back.

Hope resented it sometimes. It wasn't that she didn't like her aprons, or the working in and from home of which they were both a practical part and a clichéd symbol, but that they'd come to stand in her mind for a larger failing of her mother's cohort, who'd somehow let their guard down for a moment of post-feminist frivolity and found a whole shadow sexist establishment just waiting to pounce, to cry, 'Ah! So that's what you really wanted! We were right all along!' and before you knew it, the tax advantages of having one parent stay at home were so significant it was more than it was worth not to do it unless you were something like a lawyer – like, for instance, all those lawyers who'd dreamed up all the ostensibly child-protective legislation that had put so many workplaces outside the home off limits for women of childbearing age whether they ever intended to have children or not, which meant that nine times out of ten the parent at home was the mother.

For a moment she stood, hands behind her waist, fingers gripping the loops of the knot just tightened, and fell into a dwam as she gazed at the space in front of her. The main part of the flat consisted of the living room and the kitchen, united decades ago by the then-fashionable knock-through, an opening about three times the width of a doorway. The living room was at the front, facing the wall across a gap of about a metre or so; the kitchen to the back, facing the garden (or, as Nick called it, the back grass). Enough light came from the windows – the upper third of the front was level with the street – to give some cheering sunshine to the living room in the mornings and the kitchen in the after-noons. Today the light seemed paradoxically brighter because of the snow. At other times, and in the evenings, the flat always seemed to Hope darker than it should be, in the cold, dim light of energy-saving bulbs and tubes. The flicker of flame from behind the mica plate of the closed-system stove in the living room helped a little, lending a few cosy wavelengths of natural light to the scene.

Likewise cheering touches were added by the paintings and drawings from her student days that Hope had framed on the walls, the far larger number of Nick's paintings from nursery tacked up all over the place; the tapestries and crochets, which Hope had made or bought, thrown over chairs and sofa, and the shelves and stacks of books: art history, cookery books, needlecraft books, textbooks from Hugh's and Hope's university days – more art history, engineering and science reference works – all decoration really, when you could summon their contents in an eye-blink, but good to have even if a pain to dust. You couldn't sell them, anyway: the second-hand book trade had collapsed under the dangers of fourth-hand smoke, with most of the stock sealed in vaults or incinerated. Hope's guitar, though also sadly gathering dust in the living-room corner where it stood propped, now and then lifted her spirits too, especially when she picked it up, blew the dust off it, and strummed a few bars or, on particularly bad or good days, sang at the top of her voice in the empty flat.

Hope washed the breakfast dishes, tidied Nick's toys – which got everywhere even in the hour between him getting up and going to nursery – and made the beds and tidied Nick's room. Max the toy monkey followed her around, picking toys up and offering them for her to play with. After a while he started to say 'Max hungry', so she set him to sleep mode and stuck him on the recharger. She made a coffee, hung up her apron, sat down at the kitchen table, opened her glasses and started working in

China but not in Chinese. She took a break at eleven and checked the BBC. The nature kids issue had been knocked right off the front screen by a truck-bomb blast at a motorway inter-section outside Munich: scores dead, hundreds injured, toll expected to rise. The atrocity had been claimed by the Neues Rote Armee Faktion, a hitherto unheard-from local affiliate of the transnational insurgent franchise that everyone called the Naxals. Hope stared at fallen flyovers and mangled cars for as long as she could bear to listen. Then she shuddered and flipped to ParentsNet, where the nature kids thread had more or less taken over.

No new light there. Hope decided to skip the crowd-sourced wisdom of pseudonymous strangers and consult some real people. She wrote an email and fired it off to six friends, then got back to work. By lunchtime she had four responses.

Sheila: Hi Hope, Good to hear from you! Yes this is outrageous but remember it will go to appeal. Also legal challenge to faith exemption (i.e. need to extend it to non-faith conscience cases) has good precedent all the way back to that climate-change guy. Look up humanism for example, that's explicitly covered. So not to worry and obviously has no personal bearing on you because the machinery won't have ground out anything for a year at least. Best wishes re the pregnancy of course, you have morning sickness to look forward to ha-ha. xxx

Fatima: Yeah well, if you think ParentsNet has gone wild about this take a look at the British Persian sites!!! But seriously, have you thought about Nature Kids Network, it's a community for parents like you? Some woo-woo and anti-vaccers but mostly quite level-headed. They're the place to go for serious advice, and they've already got lawyers on board. Though to be honest Hope, I never did understand the objection, though I quite appreciate it's up to you and if what you're afraid of does come about I will be on the streets for you. Keep well.

James: Hi Hope, interesting points. Tricky one really. I understand your concern, but as a doctor, I see too many kids with congenital conditions or so-called childhood illnesses (which can have very nasty consequences even when minor) that could have been completely avoided had their parents agreed to the fix to be as gung-ho as you are about the parents' so-called 'rights'. It's like the tobacco/alcohol ban in pregnancy – lots of problems with that if you pose it as a 'rights' or 'freedom' issue, and there was a lot of fuss about that before the ban, and it was predicted to be unenforceable and all that, but when it came in it was complied with except for the usual chav element, and the medical benefits are plain in the stats and hard to argue with if you've ever seen a case of foetal alcohol syndrome (which I have, though not recently, I wonder why? No I don't). Obviously I'm entirely sympathetic to *you*, don't get me wrong, and I'll stand by you if they come for you (which they won't) but as a doctor and as a friend my advice to you is to change the problem by changing your mind and just taking the goddamn fix.

Must dash but let's you and us meet up for dinner sometime. Regards to Hugh.

Deirdre: Lovely seeing you the other day, with you all the way on this one, let's have a chat over drinks oops coffee soon. Bye 4 now!

What a great posse of friends I have, Hope thought. James in particular annoyed her, but she knew it was just the medicine talking. Doctors nearly always turned out like that.

She dismissed James from her mind, and mentally from her Christmas-card list, and followed up Sheila's suggestion. A search on humanism and a quick scan of the results left her more despondent than before. For a start, the humanist organisations and most humanist thinkers seemed entirely in favour of the fix, though not at all for making it compulsory or even hard to avoid. But what depressed her more was that she didn't even agree with humanism. That there was no God was a given, as far as Hope was concerned, and being nice to people and making the most of your life struck her as a reasonable enough conclusion to draw from it, and in any case what she wanted to do. But beside the spires of theology and the watchtowers of ideology, it seemed a very shaky hut indeed, and not one that offered her much shelter or would stand up in court.

She couldn't see a way to make her objection to the fix a deduction from any body of thought. It came from a body of flesh, her own, and that was enough for her. She doubted that this would be enough for anyone else.

One p.m. Back to China.